Authority

The Tracker Sequence
Book 2

Jamie Krakover

Authority
Copyright © 2024 Jamie Krakover
Cover Artist/Illustrations: Jennifer Stolzer
Interior Format: Dorothy Dreyer

Published by Snowy Wings Publishing
PO Box 1035, Turner, OR 97392

ISBN Hardcover: 978-1-958051-52-8
ISBN Paperback: 978-1-958051-53-5
ISBN eBook: 978-1-958051-51-1

Dedication

For Karin Krakover, who fostered my love of science fiction and taught me the importance of friends.

Dear Journal,

It's been six months. Six months since the world (and my life) was turned upside down.

Six months since I ran from everything I knew and joined the Ghosts' underground movement to take down the tracker network.

Six months since Rufus Scurry nearly exploited an unknown loophole in people's trackers to mind-control them.

Six months of waiting for Dad to explain all his secrets. Why he hid the plans on my tracker and didn't tell me my whole life.

Six months since Harlow and I broke up.

Six months since Bailen became the best thing that ever happened to me.

And six months since Jake...

Died.

I *STILL* struggle with that word.

Losing my brother is the hardest thing I've been through. I find myself blinking and trying to open a tracker message to tell him something funny, share a picture, share something about my day, or just check and see how he's doing. Then I remember the network is gone and that he's not here.

While Bailen and Peyton have been there for me, they knew Jake in different ways than I did. Jake was a friend to Bailen and something more to Peyton. But their love was different. Sometimes, they don't understand what I'm going through.

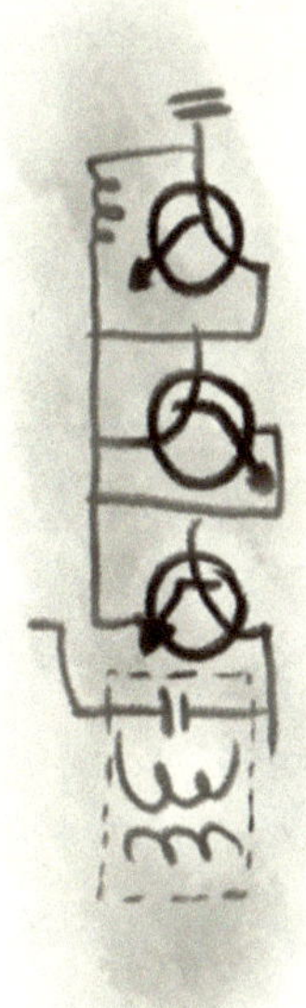

words were Jake's go-to, so maybe they will help me too. Admittedly, it's weird to write with a pencil and paper. The only time I had paper before was to draw, and even then, it was scarce. It's a little less so now.

These are the kinds of thoughts I would have stored on my tracker. Unfortunately, private recorded thoughts weren't as private as we all thought. Everything on the network was closely monitored and recorded by the authorities to read if they wanted. This feels more private, more intimate, even if the authorities have disbanded and there's no network or conversations left to monitor.

These thoughts I wouldn't even share with Lydia. As my best friend, she has privilege to a lot, but the pain I feel, the regret that strangles me—it's for me alone.

I've been in a dark place, grieving the loss of Jake and struggling to adjust to life without a tracker. Without access to information in the blink of an eye, and without him, I've forced myself to  move forward. I've been learning to type, working with sat phones, laptops, even old desktop computers, and doing everything by hand. I've managed to find some light through all the darkness and chaos.

I'm closer than ever with my friends and Bailen too. I find myself just getting lost in the moment. Forgetting where we came from. Just living.

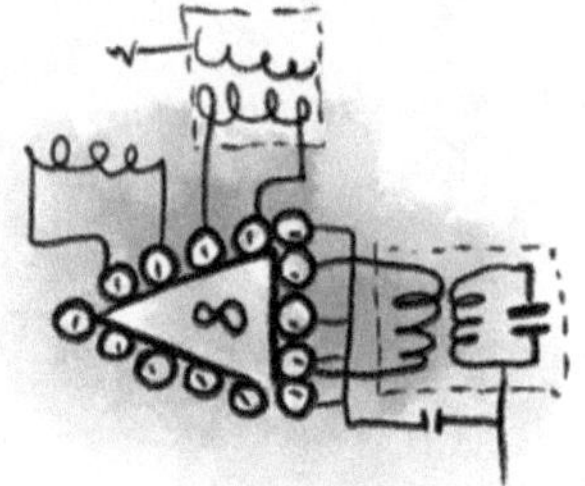

I need those times.

Even though the memories pop up when I least expect them. Even when they catch me off guard.

But it's in the quiet moments that the pain creeps back in. That the nightmares envelope me. When the feeling that something else is coming invades my mind. It's these thoughts that grab hold and won't let go...

-Kaya

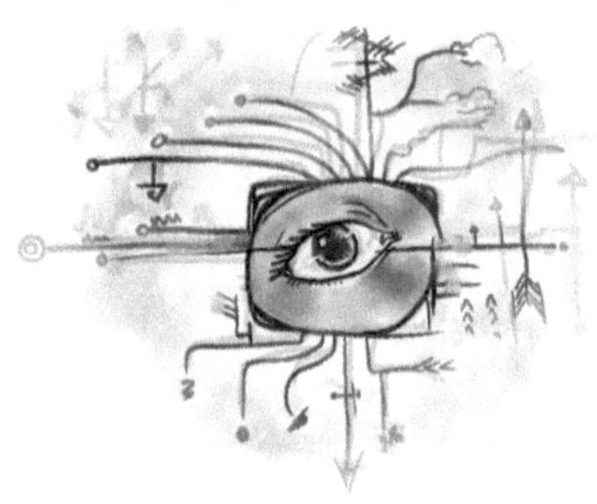

One

ailen Overland was going down—as soon as I could recall the right coding command. My fingers tapped the keyboard, willing my brain to remember. Why did I always forget this one? I should have created an alias, then I wouldn't have to remember the command I was searching for. As much as I didn't miss the iron grip of my tracker, instant access to every coding command ever created would have been really helpful right now.

If I pulled up the help documentation, would it be cheating?

"Done!" Bailen slammed his hands on the desk, rattling the row of computers on the long table, and jumped up from his chair in triumph. "I win again." But his giant grin faded the minute he saw the newest member of the Ghosts, Ava Hunt, relaxing on the opposite side of the table in her oversized argyle sweater. She had her chair reclined backward with her combat boots propped up on the makeshift desk.

She tucked her chin-length brown hair behind her ear and laughed in a carefree way, clearly enjoying herself. "Actually, I beat the pants off you both. I programmed my submission not to notify anyone so I could see how long it would take you to notice."

Ava tapped a button, and the challenge abruptly ended. Her time and score popped up on everyone's screens, with Bailen's score several minutes behind hers.

Bailen's face turned red. I stifled a laugh, but not well enough, because he whipped around to face me. "Kaya! You think this is funny?"

"Oh, it's definitely funny." I reached to push a wild lock of brown hair out of his eyes, but he knocked my hand away.

Ava had arrived three months ago at the Coderie, the respectable computer and equipment rental business that hid the Ghosts' underground tech. Shortly after joining, she'd given Bailen more than a run for his money in coding speed. As much as it bothered me that I had yet to beat Bailen in a challenge, it got under his skin infinitely more every time he wasn't the top dog. Even he couldn't deny having another excellent coder around was helpful in setting up resources for people who were learning to live without trackers and the instant access to knowledge and communication they provided. On the day of her interview, Ava helped wrap up crucial code that supported a government project to restore communications satellites before she was formally offered the job. But her skill wasn't always enough to stop Bailen's frustration from bubbling up.

"It's not fair. Emily was distracting me with questions. I couldn't focus." Bailen scowled. He didn't believe his excuse for a second.

"Did not!" Emily laughed like she was in on the joke even though it wasn't planned. Emily had been glued to Bailen's and my side ever since we unplugged her from the tracker network.

"Sure, blame your inadequate coding skills on a second grader. Real mature." Ava crossed her arms with a serious expression that had to be an act to rile Bailen up even more. She loved to get under his skin almost as much as Peyton. She had discovered Ava using her coding skills to give stolen money to people who had been victimized by the authorities and could no longer pay their bills. While Ava's mission had resonated with Petyon, it was Ava's sass and ability to ruffle Bailen's feathers that ultimately won Peyton over. She'd encouraged Ava to apply at the Coderie and asked if Ava would help play a trick on her twin, acting like they'd never met. When Bailen found out, he became salty, and their rivalry was born. He could hold his own against one of them, but when they paired up, it often was too much for him to compete with.

Bailen turned to leave, but I grabbed his arm. "Come on, you're still one of the best coders I know. Plus, I wouldn't have learned half the stuff I know without you. Why do you take it so personally?"

"One of?" He scoffed. "Not the best. I've always been the best."

"And now you're not." Ava reached for the keyboard and brought it to her lap, then typed in a few commands. Even though I'd learned to type fairly well, I still envied her and Bailen's speed and proficiency on the keyboard.

Ava's avatar donning a crown and a first-place ribbon appeared on all thirty computers in long rows, including on Bailen's laptop screen. Luckily, no one else was around to get mad that their pay by the hour computer sessions had been interrupted.

"I see he lost again," Peyton said, emerging from the hallway behind the payment counter.

"Ugh, don't start, Pey." Bailen sank back into his chair and cleared his screen.

"Touchy, touchy." Ava winked at Peyton, who sent a devious grin back.

"She's like your clone. One of you was bad enough." Bailen groaned.

"Up for another round, or are you finally going to admit that women are the stronger sex?" Ava wiggled her eyebrows, goading Bailen into the trap.

"Girls rule and boys drool." Emily stuck her tongue out at Bailen but couldn't keep the smile from exploding on her face.

He gave her a fake surprised face, then turned to Ava and pointed a finger at her. "Not a chance. It's on." Bailen typed some commands into his computer and a new challenge popped up on all our screens.

With Bailen randomly selecting the challenge from one of his favorite repositories, maybe I had a chance. He'd taught me a few of his tricks but made me promise I'd never share his secrets with Ava. He needed every advantage he could get. If only I could get Ava to share some of her favorite shortcuts, then I might be able to take them both.

"Emily, you can come help me this round." I patted the empty chair next to me. She skipped over and hopped into the chair. I'd started training her on little coding tricks I'd mastered. It was a good way to prove I understood what I was learning. Emily had a knack for coding and picked it up faster than I could teach her—hence all the questions she'd asked Bailen.

Peyton weaved her way between the narrow row of chairs set on two sides of a long card table with computer terminals set up every couple of feet. She pulled up a chair to an empty computer station next to Ava. "I want in on this one."

"Hey, with Pey joining, you might have a shot, Kaya." Bailen's smile didn't hide the fact that he loved to provoke us both.

Peyton feigned a hurt expression. "I don't know whether to be insulted or relieved I won't come in last place."

"Oh, it's on!" I dragged my chair up to the desk and twisted my monitor so the sun streaming in the storefront windows of the Coderie didn't interfere with my ability to read the screen. I could beat Peyton no problem, but if there was ever a time to beat Bailen, this was it. I glanced at Emily. "You ready for this?"

"Do you think we can win?" Emily asked.

"We can do anything we put our minds to," I said.

She nodded with an excited gleam in her eyes. Maybe next time I'd set up another terminal for her. She'd be running circles around me in no time.

Out of the corner of my eye, I glimpsed a look between Ava and Peyton. They were up to something. I glanced at Bailen, but he didn't seem to notice. Maybe I should've pulled out the popcorn and watched the show instead. It was bound to be good, but Emily wouldn't let me sit back and watch.

"Ready?" Bailen asked with a hint of competition in his eyes.

"I was born ready." Ava cracked her knuckles and laid her hands on the keyboard.

Bailen didn't wait for anyone else to respond and hit the enter key, starting the competition.

The challenge popped up on each of our screens. I skimmed it to get a general feel for the prompt and what skills I might need to leverage. It wasn't anything overly complex, something Bailen taught me to do a couple weeks ago, but I hadn't had a chance to teach Emily yet, so she wouldn't be much help. I'd have to pull it out of my memory. As I let everything sink in, I peered between the monitors at Peyton and Ava across the table, waiting for a hint at what was to come, but there was nothing except the clicking of fingers across keys.

I returned to my screen and started setting up some variables and quick commands, glancing sideways occasionally to see that Emily was following what I was doing. I was halfway through when a message window popped up on the screen with Ava's initials.

A.H.: I need your help.

Ava could win with only one hand on the keyboard. Was this some kind of trick?

K.W.: When have you ever needed my help?

A.H.: Do you want to beat Bailen or not?

I wanted to beat Bailen more than anything, but I wanted it on my own talent. Cheating wasn't my style.

Emily sucked in a breath, but I shot her a look, telling her to stay quiet. She held a finger to her lips. I nodded, then returned to my keyboard.

K.W.: Yes, but…

A.H.: Well, there's nothing in the rules that says teamwork isn't allowed.

She had a point there. But I wasn't sure Bailen could handle another defeat, even at the expense of a joke. He was starting to take these challenges a little too seriously. While teaching others old tech kept him busy, it didn't have the same stakes and sense of excitement that taking down the tracker network had. He didn't have to work on his obsolete program, TROGS, that tricked the authority's location scans. Without some difficult problem to solve, he'd lost a bit of his purpose.

Sure, we'd spent plenty of time in the Coderie, setting up outdated computers for people and enabling communication through old satellite internet services and phones. When we weren't doing that, we were assisting the government with transitioning decommissioned satellites into a working communications system for computers and phones. Even though we had plenty to keep us busy, many people were skeptical that the obsolete tech would continue to function, especially after the collapse of the tracker network. It was one more thing Bailen couldn't fix.

K.W.: That's true but...

A blinking P.O. with three dots appeared at the bottom of the chat window. Peyton had joined the fun.

P.O.: Oh, come on, you know my
brother could stand to be knocked down a
few pegs.

A little ego check was good every now and again, but Bailen had been knocked down a lot lately. Maybe he needed a break or a small win. Unless I could make it worth it for both of us.

K.W.: I'm in, under one condition.

A.H.: Name your price, Weiss.

K.W.: I want 5 solid training sessions
with you where you teach me your tricks.

Three dots appeared on the screen, then disappeared. She was considering my offer, but it was likely to come back with conditions. Ava always held some things close to her chest. While she was a great addition to the Ghosts and typically wanted to help, I couldn't help but wonder if she was hiding something and that's why she only shared things under the right circumstances.

K.W.: What'll it be, Hunt?

A.H: 2 sessions, and you better not
share what I tell you with Bailen.

P.O.: Ava drives a hard bargain. She's
not going to back down.

She said not to share it with Bailen but never said anything about Emily. If I taught her, then she could tell Bailen. This was playing out better than I anticipated.

K.W.: 3 sessions and it's a deal.

A.H.: Sold.

Now that the deal was done, I could sit back and watch. But the blinking three dots appeared again. This wasn't over. They needed me for something.

> A.H.: I'm going to send you some code.
> Need you to run it.

Well, that seemed suspicious. What was she up really up to?

> K.W.: Right, so you can mess up my
> machine?

> A.H.: I need the code to come from you,
> so it looks like an authentic win. If I beat
> him, he'll think I cheated.

> K.W.: We kind of are cheating. Besides,
> he'll be able to trace these conversations
> and the code you sent me. Or did you
> forget who you're dealing with?

There were so many things that could go wrong with this. Emily was reading over my shoulder, and her poker face was worse than mine. Luckily, Bailen was glued to his monitor, but he was bound to figure it all out. Maybe I should back out. Although those coding sessions could definitely come in handy.

> P.O.: Stop acting like you're going to get
> caught and enjoy the glory about to
> descend on you.

Before I could respond or change my mind, Ava stood with her keyboard in hand and looked over the monitors at Bailen.

"Only one winner. The rest are losers. Right, Bailen?" From the expression on Ava's face, it was clear she had him right where she wanted him.

"Hey, we're all on the same side. No need for winners or losers. Right, Emily?" I asked.

She nodded, but it wouldn't matter. Nothing I said would soften the blow for Bailen. Despite that, I had to try to take some of the suspicion off myself.

Ava winked at me, then typed in a few commands and hit the enter key extra hard for effect.

A huge block of code appeared on my screen. When did she have time to write all this?

A.H.: Run it.

Before I could respond, all traces of the conversation evaporated from my screen, taking the encrypted message remnants with it. The only thing that remained was the code. I skimmed it, looking for any obvious sabotage. When I was sure this wouldn't backfire on me, I submitted the job and waited for it to execute.

When it did, the coding challenge screens went black. I waited for the game to end and the summary screen of who won to pop up, but my screen remained black.

Bailen slammed his mouse down on the table. "Oh, come on! How is that even possible?"

I glanced at Ava, waiting for her gloating reaction, but her face was as blank as an unused canvas. Peyton's expression mirrored Ava's.

Now I was more confused than ever. Maybe I'd missed

something and the joke really was on me. Before I could investigate, Bailen grabbed my shoulders.

"How did you beat me?"

"Me? I…" But I didn't have the words, because I had no idea what Ava had done. I glanced at Bailen's screen where it displayed the summary screen with my name and time on it. Then it popped up on my screen as well.

"You did it!" Emily hugged me in congrats but then let out a laugh, giving it all away.

"Traitor," I whispered into her ear and nudged her with my elbow, which only made her laugh even more. I tickled her to try to cover it up. But Bailen's brain was already processing the scene before him. He had spent enough time around the two of us to know that Emily not only looked up to me like a big sister but also thought I was one of the funniest people she knew. Even though Jake had always been the funny one in the family.

Picking up on the suspicious activity, Bailen turned to his screen and examined the winning code, searching for answers that explained what had transpired. "Wait a sec. You stole my code and didn't even have the foresight to change the variables I used? I taught you better than that."

My shoulders slumped as if I had been scolded for wasting art supplies. My mind struggled to catch up, but I glanced over the table at Peyton and Ava, who were struggling to contain themselves now too. Bailen hadn't been scolding me, he was making an exclamation. He knew exactly what had happened.

"Ava! This has you written all over it." Bailen looked like he was about to pole vault over the table and tackle her. "And the fact that you tried to pit Kaya against me? If it wasn't for Emily…"

I wrapped my arms around Bailen's waist not only to hold him closer but also to keep him from strangling her. "It was just a joke."

"You were in on this?" Bailen wiggled from my grasp.

"Wait." I grabbed for his hand and gave him a knowing smile, the one that said there was more. "She promised to teach me her tricks."

"Oh, so you sold your soul to the devil?" But any trace of hurt behind his voice had disappeared. It was all teasing.

I laughed and leaned in so our foreheads touched. Then I whispered, "And while she told me I couldn't tell you, she never said Emily couldn't."

"Did I ever tell you I love the way your mind works?" He smiled, then closed the gap between our lips and kissed me.

I pulled him closer and allowed the kiss to deepen, filling my insides with warmth.

"Ugh, get a room. I'm going to vomit." Peyton loved to remind us how much she was disgusted by watching her twin make out with someone.

I drew back from the kiss. "We have one. If you don't like it, you can leave." I smiled at my quick wit, then I returned to kissing Bailen.

"That wasn't supposed to backfire," Peyton said, but her tone was off, almost as if we'd fallen into a trap.

Bailen must have heard it too, because he withdrew from the kiss and pointed a finger at Ava. "This isn't over."

"Far from it." Ava's face remained even, but her eyes glistened with more secrets yet to be revealed.

Emily wrapped her arms around me and Bailen, releasing the tension that had built up in the room. I'd felt a deep connection with her since the night we met. I'd grown particularly protective of Emily ever since Scurry mind-controlled Harlow and made him kidnap her. While we thwarted his attempt to use Emily to get me to comply with his plans, I still worried about the impact of that experience on her. Despite all the chaos that had unfolded, it was good to finally see her happy.

All of us, really. There was no better way to spend a day off school, joking around with some of my favorite people and learning a little code along the way.

I pulled Emily into a giant hug, then collapsed into a chair away from the commotion that had only temporarily defused. Emily hopped into my lap and laid her head against my shoulder like she often did.

Bailen leaned across the table so he was closer to Ava. "I know where you sleep. When you least expect it…" He paused for dramatic effect. "BAM." He clapped his hands together, making Emily jump in my arms.

Ava didn't flinch and stared him straight in the eyes for a few moments longer, then left without another word.

"I've got her right where I want her." Despite his words, a glimmer of uncertainty crossed Bailen's expression.

"Yep, you're right behind Ava, in second place." Peyton laughed, ducking out of Bailen's path as he positioned to tackle her in the small space between the rows of computers and the front information desk where people paid for support and made appointments. She sidestepped his oncoming attack and readied herself for the next wave.

"All right, you two are as bad as…" My words failed me as the last person I expected to see wandered slowly past the front window of the Coderie with a dazed expression. "Harlow!"

TWO

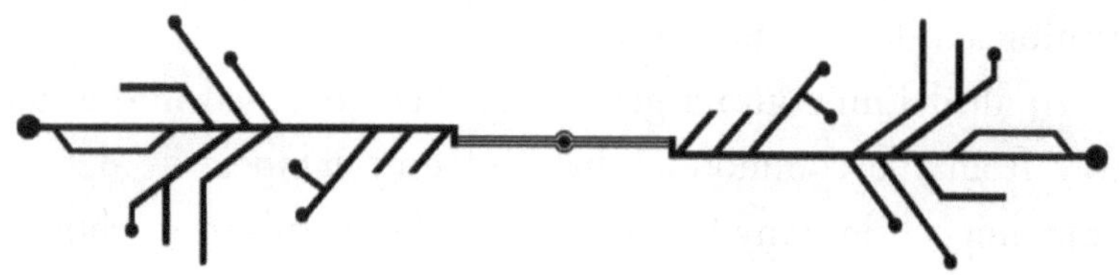

The name flew out of my mouth before I could stop it. Bailen recoiled, then looked at me with confusion. "You're comparing me to your ex?"

I shook my head. "No." I scrambled to explain. "He's outside." I pointed out the window to where he was passing the storefront much more slowly than the other people walking by.

"Oh!"

I expected Bailen to say more, but nothing else came. I kept staring at Harlow as he scuffed his feet across the pavement. His head hung low, shoulders slumped, mouth moving like he was having a conversation with someone, but no one was with him.

It never stopped feeling weird to see people unexpectedly. With trackers, it had been much easier to contact friends and avoid exes. But now, I didn't know how I felt about randomly seeing him when I least expected it.

"Emily, stay with Bailen. I'll be right back." I rounded the tables and rushed out the front door of the Coderie, leaving the coding challenges inside with all the old tech we'd restored. "Harlow?"

He either didn't hear me or didn't acknowledge. "Harlow!" I shouted his name, but he still didn't respond. I wished I could send him a tracker message to get his attention. Instead, I darted around a couple people on the sidewalk who were now watching me and tapped his shoulder. "Harlow."

He whipped around and snatched my wrist, twisting my arm a little.

"Ow!", I tried to yank my arm free, shocked by his reaction, but he didn't release me. "It's me, Kaya." I added my name when he didn't fully acknowledge.

He blinked, and slowly his gaze trained upward, but he said nothing. Even though he was staring me in the face, his glazed over eyes didn't register that I was standing in front of him. We hadn't seen each other much. Not since we'd broken up six months ago. But it didn't make sense that he didn't recognize me.

My stomach clenched. "Are you okay?"

His usually well-kept hair was shaggy and tousled, and he smelled like he'd just come from soccer practice, but he wasn't wearing his uniform.

I waved my hand in his face. "Earth to Harlow."

I snapped a couple times and finally he jumped. He blinked, and then his vision seemed to come into focus. "Kaya? What are you doing here?"

"You wandered past the Coderie. I was about to ask you the same thing."

"Oh… I'm … I'm not sure." He knitted his eyebrows in confusion.

"Can I…" I lifted my arm still in his grasp.

He looked down at his hand, only then realizing he had a vice grip on me and hadn't let go. "Sorry." The quiet word slipped between his lips as he released my wrist.

Bailen poked his head outside. "Is everything okay?"

"I'm not sure." I made eye contact with Harlow, but it was like he was staring through me, not at me. "Can you take Emily home? I'll meet you there in a bit."

Something had shaken Harlow. While we weren't dating anymore, seeing him like this worried me.

Bailen nodded but gave me a questioning look. One that asked more than just what he verbalized.

I waved him off. "I'll meet you at Emily's." I nodded to let him know it was no big deal, but it didn't change the concerned look on Bailen's face.

He retreated back inside.

I dragged Harlow down the street, a little farther out of the line of sight from the storefront window. "What's going on with you?"

"I'm… not sure." He rubbed his face. "What time is it?"

I checked the wristwatch I'd started wearing ever since the tracker network went down. "Twelve-thirty." It was the little things, like not having a clock in my line of sight when I needed it, that made me miss my tracker. I wished I didn't need an extra accessory to tell time.

"Shit!"

There was the old Harlow I knew. "What's wrong?"

"I was supposed to meet the guys at my apartment. Spring soccer meetup. They're probably tearing the place apart." Harlow dropped his gaze and scuffed down the sidewalk.

Even though he was more alert now, he still seemed off. I couldn't quite figure out what it was. "Harlow, wait!" I called after him, but he either didn't hear me again or was ignoring me.

I caught up to him and fell into step beside him. "At least let me walk you home. I have to go that direction, anyway."

He shrugged but said nothing.

"Is your family okay?" I asked, trying to grasp at threads that didn't seem to exist. Anything to try to uncover what might be bugging him.

"Yeah. Fine."

"That's it? Just fine?" He was never a big conversationalist, but this was extreme.

He shrugged again and stared at the concrete.

We stepped up to the corner and waited for the pedestrian crossing. Without an active tracker connection to signal we were ready to cross, we would have to wait for the light to change on its own. Which was perfect. It gave me a minute to understand what was bugging him. I moved in front of Harlow and bent toward his gaze so I could stare him in the eyes. "You can still talk to me, you know." I made a silly face, trying to get a rise out of him.

He nodded, but there was no hint of a smile or other reaction. Normally he'd either laugh or tell me off because I'd ditched him for Bailen, even though he was equally guilty on the cheating front. But he wasn't giving me a thing.

I turned to face the crosswalk. The signal changed. I followed him across the street like a duckling following its mom with a sense of helplessness. At least I could make sure he got home safe.

We walked another block in silence. When we reached the entrance to his building, he stood in front of it with his forehead resting on the glass door. I put my hand on his back to try to comfort him, but he shrugged it off.

"Whatever it is, I'm here if you want to talk."

He nodded, then opened the door. We crossed the pristine tile floor and stopped in front of the elevators. He stared straight ahead, deep in thought, but didn't budge, as if he'd forgotten that he couldn't request the elevator without his tracker. I reached out and hit the call button that had always been there as a failsafe but was rarely used until six months ago.

When the doors opened, he stepped inside and didn't turn around to face the doors. I hit the button for the right floor, then grabbed Harlow's shoulders and twisted him to face me. "Snap out of it. What is going on with you?"

"I haven't really been sleeping, okay?"

That much was obvious, but it seemed like there was something else causing the lack of sleep. I opened my mouth to press him further but paused. His exhausted expression told me I shouldn't pry, so I snapped my lips shut without a word.

The elevator doors squealed open. Harlow pushed past me and trudged down the hall toward his apartment. He checked his pockets for his keys but soon realized he didn't have them.

"Shit."

"Yeah, you've been saying that a lot."

He ignored me, trying the door. It opened. "Guess I forgot to lock it." The confused look on his face said there was more to that story than just innocently forgetting to lock his door because he was used to doing it with his tracker.

I opted not to pry, but did peer inside the apartment to make sure everything looked okay. The living room was as pristine as it always was, not a single piece of furniture out of place.

"Where are your parents?"

"On another cruise. Not sure when they get back." He let out a long, disappointed breath.

"Should I hang out for a while?" It felt weird to say that to my ex. I wasn't sure if I should leave him in this state or try to dig into what was going on with him.

"Nope, I'm going to the roof to find the guys. They're probably waiting for me." He swiped his keys out of the bowl on the table by the door, then closed it, locking it this time.

"Well, you know how to find me if you need anything."

He nodded again. Part of me wanted to knock his head from his shoulders. Normally I'd preprogram messages to send every hour to check in, but I'd have to wait until I got home to call and check on him. Hopefully, he would answer my sat phone calls on the ancient landline his parents had refused to give up. In hindsight, maybe they knew something the rest of us didn't.

The elevator dinged. Bailen and Emily got off.

"Kaya!" Emily bounded toward me and wrapped her arms around my waist.

Harlow dragged his feet down the hall and didn't look back. I wanted to rush after him, but with Emily holding tight, I couldn't. Instead, I watched him until he reached the door to the stairs. When he let it slam shut behind him, I continued to stare at the door, waiting for it to open again.

"What's his deal?" Bailen asked.

"I'm not sure. He seemed really out of it. Maybe he's just stressed. But he didn't want anyone checking in on him." I faced Emily. "Not that I could if I wanted to. I seem to have grown an extra appendage."

She giggled and squeezed me hard.

"Maybe we should surgically remove it." Bailen laughed and poked Emily.

"It seems serious. Can you help me with this, doctor?" I lifted her up by her arms.

Emily laughed louder. I couldn't help but join her. Hearing her laugh always put me in a good mood. Bailen grabbed her ankles, and we swung her a few times, then put her down before she lost her breath from laughing so hard.

"All right. Time to get you home. Your uncle said to be home by one," I said.

"Five more minutes?"

I shook my head, knowing she'd come live with me if I invited her, but her uncle, despite all his faults, had custody.

"I'll race you to the door." Bailen said, then took off.

"No fair, you're cheating!" Somehow, she was able to overtake him soon enough. They both stopped outside her uncle's door.

Bailen knocked as I made my way down the hall. He knocked again.

"Is he not home?" I asked.

Bailen shook his head to avoid cluing Emily in to yet another disappointment from her uncle. She didn't seem to notice as she fumbled under the doormat for the secret compartment with the spare key we'd left for her. She handed the key to Bailen. He unlocked the door. I pushed past them and checked the living room, which was a disaster of dirty dishes, piles of unwashed clothes, and crumbs. I headed down the hall toward the bedrooms. The lights were off. It was possible he was asleep. When I checked the master bedroom, though, I only found more piles of clothes on the bed.

By the time I returned to the front room, Bailen and Emily had cleared a space on the couch like it was no big deal the place was a mess. The front door opened. Emily's uncle wandered in without noticing us. He headed right for the fridge and grabbed a beer, then plopped into his armchair, not caring that he'd landed on a mountain of clothes.

He popped open his beer and propped his feet on the table. "Say goodbye to your friends, Emily."

"But…" She stopped when he shot her an expression that seemed to say don't argue with me.

Emily bounded up from the couch and threw her arms around me. "See you when I see you."

"When I see you." It was our subtle way of saying we'd always see each other again without leaving an endcap on the goodbye.

I shot Bailen a hesitant glance. He shook his head, answering my silent question of whether we should hang around longer. We both knew it would be worse if we did.

I was itching to press him on the issue, but without a tracker to send silent messages, it was a moot point.

"Call me if you need anything," I whispered to Emily. We'd given her a sat phone she hid in her room in case she needed to get a hold of me. Too bad I'd left mine at the Coderie. At least someone would answer it if she called.

She hugged me again, then headed back to the couch where she flipped on the news screen and found her favorite channel.

Bailen grabbed my hand and laced his fingers between mine before leading me to the hall.

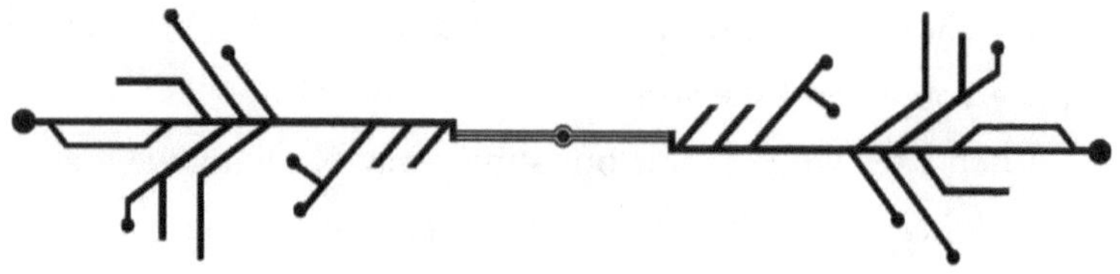

"I hate leaving her with him," I said once the door closed.

Bailen squeezed my hand. "I know, but he's the only family she has."

"We're more her family than he is," I muttered under my breath, knowing Emily would be better anywhere than with her deadbeat uncle.

Bailen must have heard me because he nodded once in agreement. We walked, hands intertwined, in silence all the way to the elevator and rode to the lobby.

As we crossed to the entrance, Bailen turned to me.

"We still on for our date?"

"Of course."

He leaned in and gave me a quick peck on the cheek. I turned to face him as he pulled away, letting him know I wanted more. He smiled and leaned back in for a more passionate kiss that made me want to live in that moment forever.

When the kiss ended, we stepped onto the sidewalk to enjoy

the sunshine.

"Ice cream?" he asked.

"Yes, then we can eat it in the park."

We walked the few blocks to the ice cream parlor, just enjoying each other in quiet. It was these moments I liked best. Spending time with Bailen and not having to fill the silence with responding to tracker messages and jokes. I often wondered if that's why Bailen and I continued to have such a strong connection. We'd been through a lot, but even when nothing was going on, we enjoyed each other's company.

When I pulled open the door to the shop, the cool air hit me. The sweet smell of sugar filled my nose as we walked past several tables of customers enjoying their treats.

"What are you going to sample today?" Bailen asked with a sly grin on his face.

I always tried something new, but in the end ordered my favorite standby: tuxedo swirl. Bailen loved to tease me about it. I peered into the freezer as I approached the counter. "Can I try some of the rainbow sherbet?"

"Sure," said the girl behind the counter.

After scooping a tiny bit out, she handed me the sample. I lifted the small spoon to taste it, and Bailen knocked my hand so the ice cream hit the tip of my nose. I laughed, then shoved the spoon toward him, asking, "Do you want to try?"

When he leaned forward, I angled the spoon upward so I could get him on the nose as well. "You have a little something right…" I giggled as I reached to wipe his nose, but he grabbed my wrist to stop me.

With my guard down, he stole the spoon from my other hand and smeared some of the ice cream on my cheek. I opened my mouth in feigned shock, but I couldn't hide the smile brimming.

I reached for the spoon, hoping for a surprise counterattack, but Bailen anticipated my move and shoved the remainder of the sample into his mouth. "Truce?"

"I guess," I said through additional laughter. Then I reached for the tip of his nose. "But you really do have some on your face."

This time he let me wipe it off, then he ran his thumb across my cheek to remove the trail of ice cream he left there. Heat rose in my cheeks along the line he drew with his thumb. His touch set butterflies off in my stomach.

Once we were both clean again, I stepped up to the counter and ordered my usual. I reached into my pocket to pull out my wallet, but it wasn't there.

"Shoot." I muttered under my breath.

"Is something wrong?"

"In all the chaos with Harlow, I must have left my wallet at the Coderie." I still wasn't used to carrying payment forms with me everywhere I went. It was so much easier to pay for things when all I had to do was think about it and it was taken care of. While most people had used that method, some had never given up using physical forms of payment, like credit cards and even paper money. It had taken a little while to get new payment cards out to people after the network went down. Paper money took a few months to start circulating, but now everything was relatively seamless.

"I got you." Bailen stepped to the counter and grabbed some money from his wallet.

"You sure? This one was supposed to be on me." I felt guilty because this was the third time I'd forgotten my wallet.

"Yeah, don't sweat it. You'll get the next one."

"Thanks." I gave him a quick peck on the cheek. But without

a tracker, I couldn't even gift him the money.

We stepped aside to wait for our cones and make way for the next customer. A man in a brown jacket with his hands in his pockets stepped up to the counter. With the girl distracted making our cones, he leaned over the counter and snagged the money from the open drawer.

Bailen flashed me a look, but I shook my head to tell him not to get involved. As the guy turned to run, Bailen stuck his foot out, and the guy tripped over it. As he righted himself, the girl behind the counter grabbed a decommissioned authority weapon from behind the counter and pointed it at the guy's head.

"Not today, Satan," the girl said as the weapon whined, letting everyone know it had reached full power. "Raise your hands slowly."

The guy raised his hands without a word.

"Drop the money."

He dropped the bills and rushed from the store.

"Shouldn't someone go after him?" one of the customers asked.

"Like who? The authorities are gone," another customer replied like the conversation had been rehearsed.

I swallowed hard. The complex realities of the world I'd help create bubbled to surface. Crime was at an all-time high without trackers to locate people. Many of the authorities who had been found innocent of crimes now worked for the government as law enforcement, but there weren't enough of them to support the increased criminal activity. Most crimes went unaddressed, and the people committing them knew it. Shop owners and even the general population bought weapons on the black market to protect themselves in lieu of increased response times.

I should have been more bothered by the attempted robbery,

but this was the third time in a little over a week I'd witnessed something like that. All I could do was shake my head at the new normal. Bailen squeezed my shoulder, but the scenario had numbed me.

The girl behind the counter, who also seemed completely unfazed, placed the old authority weapon back under the counter and finished scooping our cones. When she was done, we collected them and headed out of the shop like it was a normal afternoon.

When the cars stopped landing from the skyway exit, we crossed the street into the park. It was like we'd passed through a barrier into another world. While the skyway ran the edge of the park, once inside, it was very serene—the complexities of the world left on the other side of the street. We followed one of the walking paths to our favorite bench and sat down to enjoy our treats.

While we ate, the sounds of the park serenaded us—the chirping birds, the laughter of children playing on the playground, and dogs barking in the distance. I watched the trees sway in the breeze and leaned my head on Bailen's shoulder. He put his arm around me. The moment was perfect. Sitting with each other without having to say a word was quickly becoming one of my favorite things to do with Bailen.

On this bench, it was Bailen and me. Peaceful. No worries or justification about why we didn't need trackers anymore. No random crime spree unfolding right before our eyes. No weekly check-ins to make sure Rufus Scurry and the other worst offenders of Global Tracking Systems were still imprisoned. No work to acclimate people to the new state of the world. While it was a fun challenge helping others, it was exhausting at times. These calm moments where no one needed anything from us were everything. We could be near each other without having to do something for anyone else.

But it was also in these quiet moments I was able to see how quickly most people had adapted to life without trackers. It was almost normal to not have one, like everyone had forgotten a world with trackers. What I saw around me was the truth. No private conversations happening in the background while meeting someone else in person. No looming threat of an authority scan hanging above. Life was more convenient with trackers, but after them, everything was a lot simpler. The daily minutia carried a lot less weight.

Bailen kissed the top of my head. I laced my fingers through his, and he rubbed his thumb over my knuckles. The rhythmic motion soothed me.

I closed my eyes to take in the cool breeze on my face. When I opened my eyes, I relished the beauty of the flowers and trees in full bloom. It was gorgeous. I could appreciate the scenery without seeing apps and messages dotting my vison—the way it was always intended to be experienced. It was like looking at a painting, only in real life.

Bailen leaned down and kissed me. Long and slow. When he pulled away, I smiled at him. He returned an even bigger one.

"When do I get to learn these coding tricks?"

"Oh, so that's why you paid? Using me for my in with Ava?" I asked in a teasing tone.

"It is one of your best qualities." He tried to say it with a straight face but burst out laughing partway through.

"Maybe I won't be telling you any of those secrets." But I couldn't keep a neutral face either.

I sat up and met Bailen's gaze. "You know she can't win every time, right?"

"I know, but it doesn't make it any less annoying when she does." His expression was serious now.

"Why does it bother you so much?" I asked. Ava had a similar competitive spirit to Peyton, but she seemed to bother him more than his twin. I couldn't understand why.

"Because it feels like Peyton ganging up on me twice." There was a subtext in his words.

Normally, the playful banter with Peyton wasn't a big deal, but I think the stress of all the work he'd taken on at the Coderie was getting to him: the day in and day out of setting up computers, showing people how to access information on them, and repeating himself over and over again until people got it. While he loved tech, this wasn't what he loved about it.

I knew Bailen struggled to transition from rebel Ghost taking down the tracker network to helpful coder supporting everyday citizens, but I hadn't realized until now how much it really bothered him.

"You could just ask her for help," I said, half teasing him. Unfortunately, he didn't find any humor in my joke.

"She doesn't really share much… about who she is or her skills. Besides, we have different areas of expertise. Hers feels more relevant now." While Bailen was well versed in old tech and spent his time working around the tracker network, Ava knew more about satellites and how technology interfaced with them.

"Your skills aren't any less important. You just need to rethink how you use them. Plus, with your creative coding to repurpose tech, you'll be running circles around Ava in no time."

"Yeah, you're probably right." But based on his tone, he didn't seem convinced.

"Or maybe change is harder than we all thought. It's going to take some time to find our new normal." There were moments that felt normal, like sitting on this bench, but the tasks that were easier with my tracker still snuck up on me from time to time.

Bailen nodded but didn't say anything.

I opened my mouth to say more but paused, because something in my words sparked a thought. Maybe Harlow's lack of sleep was due to dealing with the loss of his tracker. We'd seen some folks with pretty severe reactions to the post-tracker world. The few conversations we'd had after we'd broken up, had all been superficial. It wasn't enough to determine what was really bothering him. Maybe he was just having a bad day.

"Shall we?"

Bailen's words broke me out of my thoughts. I looked up. He stood next to the bench and inclined his head toward the park exit. I nodded. We still had to shut down all the computers at the Coderie for the evening before I could go home to help set up for Shabbat dinner.

We walked the few blocks back to the Coderie with our fingers laced together. Despite the soundtrack of the city around us, I was consumed by what could be bothering Harlow.

When we finally reached the Coderie, Ava and Peyton had already reset several of the computers to the starting settings and were working on shutting them down for the night.

"Nice of you two to finally grace us with your presence!"

"Nice to see you too, Pey," Bailen quipped back without giving it a second thought.

Unfazed by their usual banter, I crossed the room and got to work shutting down the laptops we'd abandoned after the coding challenges. I packed them into our bags while Bailen worked on some of the community computers. Shutting down computers was the worst part of the job, something we never had to do with our trackers. They were always on.

When I finished our personal machines, I joined Bailen on the open machines. As I waited for the computers to power down, Wes, one of Harlow's soccer buddies, came barreling into the room and nearly steamrolled Peyton.

"Watch it!" Peyton growled at him.

He shook his head and grabbed her shoulders. "Where's Kaya?"

"Do I look like her keeper?" She knocked his arms away and stalked out of the room in typical Peyton fashion.

I rose from my chair and peered over the computer screens. "Wes? What are you doing here?" He should have been at Harlow's team gathering.

His head turned in my direction, but he didn't recognize me at first. Eyes wide and bloodshot, he stumbled toward me and steadied himself on a chair as if he had too much adrenaline coursing through his veins. "You have to help him."

"Help who?" I patted his arm in an attempt to calm him, but Wes jumped away from me.

"Somebody has to stop him." Wes grabbed his hair and pulled tufts of it between his fingers. His gaze darted around the room. He appeared desperate, a guy who had run out of options, which was odd for someone who was usually calmer than a shade of blue.

"Stop who? Wes, you aren't making any sense."

He slowly lifted his head. His eyes met mine with focused intensity for the first time since he'd bulldozed into the room. "Harlow… He… He tried to kill me."

Four

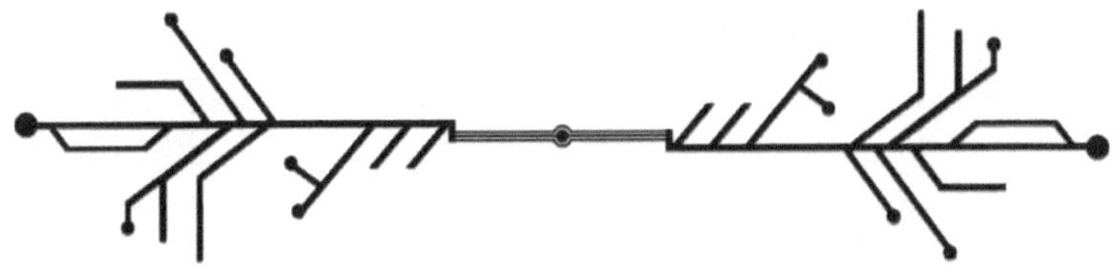

"What do you mean Harlow tried to kill you?" Harlow had been a mess when I left him, but he wasn't an axe murderer or anything. "I was with him a couple of hours ago."

Wes's eyes glazed over like he was lost in a bad dream. I grabbed his upper arms and shook him to bring him back to reality.

"Wes, focus! What happened?"

"I… I don't even know how to explain it." Confusion was plastered all over Wes's face.

It didn't make any sense. Sure, Wes was part of the soccer team, which meant he was probably at the party. The whole team hung out all the time. But teammates didn't try to kill each other. Compete, yes. Attack? Usually not.

I ushered Wes to a nearby chair. He sank into it.

"Start at the beginning. Did something happen at the party?" I dragged a second chair next to Wes and sat in it. Bailen raised an eyebrow, a silent question. After a single nod from me, he joined us with a third chair.

Wes rubbed his face, then stared straight ahead with a dazed expression. "I just…" He shook his head and stared at the floor.

I squeezed his shoulder. "Where were you guys? Still on Harlow's roof?"

"Yeah. We were having a barbeque. We always meet to talk strategy for the upcoming season."

"Was the rest of the team there when it happened?" Maybe if I kept asking him questions, he'd keep talking.

Wes shook his head. "Most of the guys had left. Troy, Harlow, and I were launching water balloons off the roof. Well, they were; I was asking them about their dates."

I scrunched my nose. Harlow hadn't mentioned anything about a date. Not that he'd offer that information to me freely. I had to admit it was a little weird to hear about his latest romantic exploits. "Okay, so then what happened?"

"Troy and Harlow started a competition about who could launch the water balloons the farthest and who could hit the most people without getting yelled at. You know how they get."

I nodded. They would compete over the stupidest stuff, including tracker disruptions that would get them hauled in for tracker diagnostics.

"So, they were competing, then what happened?" It was worse than pulling details from Lydia when she had a crush on a guy.

"Harlow started yelling and punched Troy. I stepped in to pull them apart like I usually do when they get in each other's faces. Troy stopped, but it was like Harlow couldn't hear a word I said. He turned on me. Tried to deck me, which he's never done before, so I backed away. He got really quiet, then without warning, started throwing glass bottles at us. When he didn't stop, I ran down the stairs and didn't look back." He sucked in several deep breaths as if he was still running.

"That definitely doesn't sound like Harlow."

Wes nodded but said nothing.

The story didn't add up. Harlow was never violent. Even after the tracker network downfall, he refused to carry a weapon of any kind. Sure, Troy and Harlow always took competitions a little too far, but they rarely escalated beyond words or a single punch. Wes was always able to stop them though. Harlow's behavior before had seemed odd, but this was a whole new level of concern. Despite that, I wondered how I fit into all this. "Why come here, of all places?"

"Harlow mentioned he saw you earlier. I didn't know where else to go. He wasn't acting like himself, and if I couldn't calm him, you always could."

"I don't think he'll listen to me anymore."

Wes nodded. "It's more than just calming him down. It was like he wasn't himself. He wasn't present in the moment. It sounds impossible, but I thought it might be tech related in some way. I knew you dated that tech guy, so I came straight here."

"That tech guy?" Bailen scoffed.

I shot him a look telling him to knock it off. This was serious. "Where's Harlow now?"

"Hell if I know. I wasn't going to stick around after that uncontrolled outburst."

"How do you know it wasn't a joke?" But as soon as the words left my mouth, I knew that's not what this was. Harlow liked competition and the occasional practical joke, but the Harlow I'd seen earlier in the day didn't seem equipped for either of those things.

"This was no joke. Even Troy looked scared and took off after I intervened. I've never seen Harlow not be able to snap out of anything. It was like someone else inhabited his body."

"What do you mean by that?" Bailen sat forward in his chair, suddenly reengaged in what had happened.

Wes jumped up from the chair. "What do you mean, what do I mean? Whatever that was, wasn't Harlow. The dude full-on wigged out on me, went silent and stared into space like he was comatose or something. When he snapped back to it, he screamed, started throwing things, and chased me. The guy's lost his damn mind."

As the words sank in, I studied Bailen. None of this made sense. Maybe Wes was right about it being a tech thing. Especially since Bailen perked up with the hint of a new challenge to solve. Something in what Wes said sparked an idea. Bailen's puzzle-solving expression returned, the one I hadn't seen since before we took down the tracker network.

"How long did he go silent for?" Bailen asked.

"I don't know. I didn't time it. Maybe a few seconds, but it felt like an eternity." Wes pulled tufts of his hair again and sank back to his chair, putting his head between his knees as if reliving the scene was too much for him.

Bailen tapped his fingers on a nearby keyboard but didn't actually type anything, like the clicking was helping him think. "If I didn't know better, I'd say someone hacked his tracker." Now Bailen was typing something into his computer, but I couldn't see what he was up to.

"Isn't that impossible?" The words spilled out of my mouth before I could stop them, only because I knew I had single-handedly destroyed the satellite link between our trackers and the communication servers, taking down the entire network. While Rufus Scurry had engineered a loophole in people's tracking chips that allowed them to be mind-controlled, once we shut down the network, there was no way to access it anymore.

"Most likely, but let's say hypothetically there was a backup." Bailen was grasping at straws, wanting there to be a mystery to solve, so he could have a bigger purpose again.

"I doubt there's a backup. Besides, we watched that server go dead." There was no way I'd let Bailen drag me down his rabbit hole.

"Think about it though, computers have backup batteries. You think Global Tracking Systems would invent a device that widespread and not have a failsafe in case the original malfunctioned?"

"Sure, there are usually backup plans, and I wouldn't doubt Rufus Scurry had one, but they arrested him and put him in a place no one will ever find him. If you're so sure, ask for an unscheduled check-in on Scurry."

"I already did." Bailen spun his computer around to show the image sent in reply.

I barely recognized the man in the black-and-white image. Scurry's hair was longer than I remembered, curly and scragglier, and his facial hair was overgrown like he hadn't been allowed to use a razor. His face looked older, as though many more than six months had passed. He sat on a cot with a single book on the small table beside him. His eyebrows had a murderous arch to them like he knew he was having his picture taken and who was requesting it.

A shiver ran up my spine. I looked away from the image. I didn't want to see him ever again. "See, right where we left him.

What makes you think there's someone else out there capable of this?"

Plenty of people were angry about losing their trackers, but the rioting stopped months ago. I couldn't believe there was someone else out there that knew about the loophole and wanted control of people.

"I saw Harlow before. There was something about how he looked. I was willing to write it off the first time, but this I can't ignore." Bailen's expression was as serious as stone.

"He looked tired and stressed." I glanced at Wes, but he still had his head between his legs, unable to process anything around him. "I doubt it's anything more."

"Think about it for a minute. There's always someone out there pushing boundaries. Who wouldn't jump at the opportunity to restart the tracker network? We should have planned for this." Bailen shook his head as though disappointed the thought hadn't crossed his mind before.

"Even if that's what happened, we have no proof." We had severed the connection between trackers and the satellites that allowed for instant access and connection. But I wondered if that was something easy to fix or restart.

"There's only one way to find out what's going on." Bailen had already retrieved his old go kit from the top shelf at the edge of the room and was filling it with equipment. "We've got to run some diagnostics on Harlow's tracker."

"Good luck finding him. He followed me for a little while, but I'm not sure at what point I lost him." Wes's muffled voice interrupted Bailen's scurrying around the room.

He had a point. Without active trackers, finding someone wasn't as easy as pulling up a computer and hunting down their tracker coordinates. We'd have to retrace his steps from his last known location.

Bailen seemed a bit flustered, but I couldn't tell if it was Wes's words that had shaken him or if it was because he was trying to remember all the things he needed to bring in his kit.

"We'll start at Harlow's roof and see if there are any clues. Hopefully, there's something to lead us to him," Bailen said.

It seemed like an obvious first step, but with Wes so shaken and Bailen in mission mode, I didn't think either of them was fully processing what needed to happen.

"Can we bring Jeremy?" Even though Jeremey hadn't been around as much the last few weeks, he still came to the Coderie on Fridays to help out and share his coding skills from his time with the Ghosts. If we were going to make any progress, I needed another clear mind—and some muscle in case we found Harlow in the state Wes had described.

"Already ahead of you. I pinged him a little bit ago."

As if on cue, Jeremy rounded the corner with a black box identical to Bailen's.

"All packed up?" Bailen asked.

Jeremy nodded and held up his kit like it was lighter than air. Those kits contained a ton of equipment, but Jeremy had enough strength to lift a truck, so to him it probably was an easy load. "Yep, I've kept it on standby ever since the riots."

"Then let's hit the road." Bailen headed for the door with a purposeful stride.

Jeremy wasn't far behind, leaving me to deal with Wes.

"Are you okay to come back with us?" I asked.

Wes lifted his head and met my gaze, looking through me rather than at me.

"WES!" I shook his shoulders. "Snap out of it." I didn't think I could handle any more zoned out guys today.

Wes slumped in a way that made his almost six feet of height appear insignificant.

I rubbed his back. "Come on, we need your help. I'll be there the whole time. We won't let Harlow hurt you."

He nodded and shuffled his feet toward the door. That was the best I could ask for. We met Jeremy and Bailen on the street corner outside the Coderie.

They chatted about what they might find and their approach to investigating Harlow's possibly defunct tracker. I only caught every few words because I couldn't help staring at Wes and the distant, confused look on his face. He was so shaken by what happened. As out of it as Harlow had been, maybe Bailen was on to something—but I wouldn't join that train of thought until I saw Harlow again.

The shadows of the high-rise buildings felt like they were about to swallow me whole. While the world was changing, nothing was simple. Some people were thankful to have their privacy back, but many more hated that the tracker network was gone. Even if they didn't know the Ghosts were directly responsible, it seemed like half the world indirectly blamed me for what had happened. And it wasn't a total lie.

A loud scream tore me from my thoughts.

"Somebody, help my husband! Help! Help me, please!"

Bailen and Jeremy tore off down the block toward the screams. I bolted after them, glancing to check for Wes, who had no sense of urgency. At least he was still moving in the right direction, even if it was at a snail's pace.

I skidded to a stop next to Bailen, who was inspecting an

elderly man lying on the sidewalk. Bailen put his ear to the man's chest, listening for breathing and a heartbeat.

I stepped around Jeremy and approached the elderly woman standing over the man. "Ma'am, what happened?"

"He clutched his chest and collapsed. He has a heart condition." Tears streamed down her face. "Can you call 911?"

"What's 911?" I asked, confused by the question. I silently cursed myself for leaving the sat phone at the Coderie yet again.

"It's how we used to call for help. I thought they said they were going to reinstate it." The woman let a long wail.

I hadn't remembered hearing anything about it, but it seemed like one more broken thing in our world, post trackers.

"He's still breathing, but I think he needs a hospital," Bailen said. Without waiting for any of us to respond, Bailen scooped up the man and ran in the direction of the hospital several blocks east of where we were.

The old lady's tears turned to loud sobs. "His tracker used to alert us of irregular heart rhythms. But ever since…" She wailed and clutched her pearl necklace. She sniffed and snatched a Kleenex from her purse. "His health has been declining. With the tracker readings, we knew when to go to the hospital."

She shook her head and slowly shuffled along the sidewalk in the direction Bailen had run off, mumbling about being married over sixty years.

I stood where the woman left me, unable to move. Stunned that despite all the bad we'd eliminated, we'd still left voids in the world. Trackers weren't all bad, of course, but ever since I'd joined the Ghosts, I thought the bad far outweighed the good. A small part of me wondered if I'd been wrong. Wrong to give up on the technology. Wrong to shut down the tracker network. Wrong to make that decision for everyone. Who was I to decide this?

Jeremy snagged his and Bailen's kits and nudged me as he stepped up to the next street corner. "Come on. I'm sure Bailen will meet us there."

I nodded and checked to make sure Wes was still headed in the right direction. He scuffed his feet, approaching the corner as if nothing had just happened. His hands slid into his jeans pockets and his shoulders slumped. His head was down, gaze fixed on the cracks in the sidewalk. Despite his state of shock, I almost envied his inability to register what had just happened.

When the signal changed, Jeremy, Wes, and I crossed the street and headed down the block to Harlow's apartment complex. While the path to Harlow's was clear, the destruction of the tracker network and the benefits we'd lost left more and more questions in my mind.

Five

Ten minutes later, we stepped onto the roof of Harlow's apartment complex. The party had long been abandoned. Several picnic tables had plastic cups and paper plates strewn across them, many with half eaten food and discarded drinks. There was no sign of anyone. The light breeze picked up some of the empty plates and cups, scattering them around the rooftop.

Jeremy inspected the leftovers from the party, starting with the table, while I walked the edge of the roof looking for clues. I tiptoed around two small piles of broken glass. At least that part supported Wes's story. Passing the empty cooler with broken remnants from the water balloon excursion, I ducked behind some of the chimneys in search of Harlow. We used to hide between them and make out. It was the only place we could get some privacy. But not even the blankets or candles we usually left behind were anywhere to be found. Our entire relationship had been erased. Maybe Harlow had been too.

I circled back to the main part of the roof, inspecting the plates and cups as I looked for signs of poison or other foul play, not that I knew what any of that looked like.

"Find anything?" I asked.

"Only an abandoned party, but I feel like we're missing something," Jeremy said with a sense of determination I hadn't seen since we'd thwarted the authorities.

I nodded in agreement. My brain was scrambling for other explanations for Harlow's weird outburst. The ironic thing was, if the tracker network was still active, Bailen or Jeremy could hack it to see if the food or drinks had any chemical imbalances or other anomalies to explain what had happened. But alas, everything came up empty.

I sat next to Wes at the end of the picnic table, where he stared off into the distance at the other high rises. I placed my hand on his shoulder, careful not to spook him. He didn't flinch but also didn't acknowledge my presence. "Anything else you can remember?"

He shook his head ever so slightly, then continued to stare into the distance as though searching for answers to his unspoken questions.

I crossed the roof to where Jeremy squatted over some empty alcohol bottles. "Do you think they were drunk?"

Jeremy lifted one of the bottles and sniffed it. "Probably, but based on what Bailen said, this didn't seem alcohol related."

He was likely right, but I couldn't find another explanation. The tracker scenario was looking more and more plausible. I didn't have the strength to admit that maybe this wasn't over like we had thought.

"We should go down to Harlow's apartment and see if we can find any clues there," I said.

"Sounds like a plan. Lead the way."

I glanced back at Wes, who was still staring into space. He wasn't going anywhere, and I wasn't sure I wanted to drag him through any more potential trauma. I knelt next to him. "Maybe you should go home and get some rest."

He nodded and slowly rose from the bench, making his way to the stairs.

I followed behind, with Jeremy on my heels. A couple of flights down, Wes opened the door and disappeared behind it, likely headed for the elevator. Jeremy and I continued on, stopping once we reached the fifty-second floor. I paused before opening the door. The last time I stepped through this exact door, I'd caught Harlow cheating. Despite being on Harlow's floor earlier, there was something about the door that stirred a visceral reaction within me. Something I wished I could forget. However, it was also the night I met Emily, and I wouldn't change that for anything. There was always some good with the bad.

I mustered up the courage and yanked the door open, walking to the right, toward his apartment. When we reached his door, I knocked. The door creaked open as if the place had been the scene of a robbery. The living room appeared identical to how it was a few hours earlier.

I stepped over the threshold. "Harlow? Are you home?"

The silence that met my call was deafening. Blood pulsed in my ears. I motioned for Jeremy to follow me. He did without a word.

"Harlow?" I tried again from the living room. "It's Kaya." I paused, unsure if I was talking to thin air or not. "Wes told me what happened. We want to see if you're okay."

Nothing. I rounded the corner and crept down the hallway

toward his room, the first door on the left. The door was open, so I peered in. Here was the disaster I had expected to find in the entrance. He was normally pretty organized other than his desk, which always had books and clothes from soccer practice draped off the chair.

But this was quite a different scene. His closet looked like it had thrown up all over the room. Dirty dishes were on almost every surface. His soccer trophies were everywhere, with broken pieces by the wall, lying forgotten. Even his posters of soccer legends and favorite actresses had been ripped from the walls, some hanging in pieces and others fallen to the floor.

This was not the Harlow I knew. There was something going on with him, something I didn't have an explanation for. Where was he? I continued down the hall to his sister's room. The door was wide open and looked unlived in. She was about to graduate college, so I wasn't the least bit surprised by the cleanliness there.

I crept further down the hallway and peered into the bathroom on the right. Nothing out of the ordinary there unless you counted the giant soccer ball shower curtain that was probably more enticing to an eight-year-old. Harlow had played for as long as I could remember.

"Harlow? It's Kaya." I tried again even though it wasn't likely to make him manifest in a deserted apartment.

Pivoting away from the bathroom, I stepped back down the hall toward the living room, since the only thing left at the end of the hall was Mr. and Mrs. Green's room. I motioned to Jeremy to do the same when a quiet creak sent shivers down my spine. I froze and listened, expecting another noise, but none came. I rocked on my foot, testing the floorboards, and was met with silence. Someone was in the apartment.

I waved to Jeremy and pushed a finger to my lips. I tiptoed toward the last door at the end of the hall, hoping I didn't find any squeaky floorboards. When I reached the door, I tapped it twice with one knuckle. I'm not sure why I knocked, maybe fear of what I might find inside. The door shifted with a creak, so I pushed it the rest of the way open.

The dark room had shadows from the bed and nightstands, as well as a chair from the corner, but no people shadows.

"Harlow? Are you in here?"

I stepped inside the bedroom, feeling out of place. The hair on my arms stood on edge, like something might jump out at any moment. The closet door was cracked. I reached for the knob to pull it open. It was pitch black. I fumbled for the light.

When I flicked it on, I screamed and leapt backward into Jeremy, who I'd completely forgotten was behind me. I grabbed the Jewish star hanging from my necklace and twisted the chain between my fingers while I waited for my breathing to calm.

Harlow sat in the middle of the closet floor, wide eyes staring down at his torn up, bloody knuckles.

"Harlow?" My voice was shaky so I tried again. "Harlow, are you okay?"

He didn't move or say a word, still frozen in shock.

"Can you get a closer look at his injuries?" Jeremy whispered so softly I almost missed what he said. He was much better under pressure than I was.

I gave him a single nod, then took a few deep breaths to calm my racing heart. But I didn't have time to waste. I stepped toward Harlow. He lunged forward. I jumped away from him, my breathing heavy, and landed on Jeremy's toe. "Sorry," I muttered.

"Stay back. I can't trust myself." Harlow's voice was raspy and slow, unlike his usual tone. I couldn't tell if it was pain, sadness, or something else.

"What's going on?" I whispered, afraid to spook him further. Before, an episode like this would have triggered the authorities, or someone would have alerted them with a tracker. If we called someone now, it would probably be hours before anyone showed up. We didn't have that kind of time. It was up to me and Jeremy to keep him calm while my insides were screaming at me. "What happened?" I asked again, trying to get Harlow to say more.

"I don't know. And that's exactly the problem. Just stay away. Before I hurt you, too." The words came out so quickly they blurred together.

Too? How badly had he hurt Troy? Wes looked relatively unscathed, but Harlow's knuckles were pretty raw. What had Harlow done? "Wes is fine; he went home. He told us what happened, or at least some of the story. Maybe you can fill in the rest?"

Harlow clenched his fists and rubbed his eyes with the back of his hand, smearing a light trail of blood across his face. "I wish I knew."

"How about we talk through it?"

He nodded.

I was pretty sure that was all I was going to get from him, so I continued. "Can you come out of there so we start at the beginning?" I didn't really want him to lunge at me again, but it seemed like he was calmer and more aware of his surroundings. Plus, I needed him to move so Jeremy and I could help him.

Harlow's gaze snapped to his hands. His eyes widened as he saw his torn-up knuckles for the first time. He turned his hands over and revealed more tiny cuts and scratches with dried blood across his palms. Pushing past me and Jeremy, he darted for his parents' bathroom on the other side of the room. He rushed to the sink, flipped it on, and started scrubbing his injuries, wincing as water seeped into the open wounds.

Then I remembered what Wes said about him throwing bottles and the broken glass piles. He possibly had some glass still in those cuts. I searched the drawers and grabbed the tweezers just in case.

"Harlow?" I said softly, but he wasn't registering I was there. I looked back and caught Jeremy searching the area. When he came up empty, he shrugged his shoulders, then nodded toward Harlow, silently encouraging him to talk to me.

I inched toward Harlow with my hand outstretched. Arm shaking, I gently touched his shoulder with two fingers. "Harlow?"

He whipped around, startled like he had been on the street a few hours ago. His gaze shifted toward me, finally realizing I'd said his name, but not seeming to understand. His shoulders slumped. He sank to the floor, leaving the sink still running. He dragged his knees to his chest and buried his face in his hands, not caring that they were soaking wet.

I stepped closer and reached slowly for the faucet. When I was certain he was done being startled, I turned the handle on the sink and shut off the water, then sank to the floor next to him. I rubbed my finger over an uninjured patch of skin on the back of his hand. When he didn't fight me, I gently pulled his hands down from his face.

"May I?" I held up the tweezers and pointed to his hand.

"Sure." He winced as I grazed a tender spot on his palm.

"You know you can tell me anything," I whispered, staring at my work so I didn't have to make eye contact with him.

He nodded. "But not this."

I blew out a long, slow breath in an attempt to stay calm. "Why not?"

"You already hate me. After this, you'll never speak to me again."

"Hate you?" I squeezed his shoulder. When he didn't flinch, I grabbed his cheeks and tilted his head upward, forcing him to make eye contact. "I could never hate you. I want to help. Because I care about you." Despite growing in different directions, we had come to a mutual understanding that we weren't right for each other. While things had been rocky since, I didn't wish this pain on anyone.

"You could never understand." He peeled my hands off his cheeks. His head slumped down.

"I'm listening. Help me understand." I had no idea what this was really about, but if he was struggling to explain it to me, it had to be something serious. He'd always been easygoing, even when we'd broken up. He'd been upset, but it didn't seem to affect him like this. If I couldn't get him talking, then I wouldn't be able to help him.

"Your tracker is dead. You could never understand."

"Try me," I said through gritted teeth. I'd been through hell because of my tracker—thinking I'd done something to cause my tracker to glitch, then running from everyone I cared about to protect them. The authorities had wanted to lobotomize me, and the Ghosts had wanted to study me. While I wouldn't have Bailen and the rest of the Ghosts as friends without the whole mess, I'd still lost a lot, including my brother. Harlow's words stung, but this was bigger than a one up competition on how much pain trackers had caused.

Dread circled me as the meaning of his words sank in. He'd

said my tracker was dead. Not his. I was afraid of what came next, but I needed to hear him say it.

"I went through things no one else experienced or understood, so while your situation may be a bit different, I bet I can sympathize."

He nodded once, as if he was trying to tell himself that it was okay to talk to me about this. Hopefully, the secret he'd buried was ready to come out.

"I'm losing time again." He rubbed his face and groaned in pain. "Larger chunks than before. It scared me, but now I'm starting to get flashes. I'm not sure if it's memories or nightmares. But if I'm doing something and not remembering, then I need to stop it."

I sucked in a deep breath. As much as I wanted there to be an explanation for all this, what I dreaded most was looking more and more like reality. Harlow was clearly under a lot of stress, which can do strange things to people. I hoped it wasn't what we all feared it might be. Either way, I was worried. "Harlow, I'm so sorry. Why didn't you say anything?"

"I don't know if it's real. And I didn't know if anyone would believe me."

"I would. The Ghosts would."

"Right, I'm supposed to talk to my ex and her new boyfriend about my issues. Sure."

Fair point. I could see the hesitation. "But you're talking to me now."

He shrugged.

Before he could refute anything, I added, "I appreciate you letting me try to help." I opened my arms to invite him for a hug. He side-armed me. It stung a bit, but when we broke up, we must have given up hugging privileges. At least this was forward progress. "If you really think it's your tracker, maybe we can look at it?"

"I guess." The soft words slipped through his lips without recognition that he'd said them.

I turned to Jeremy and waved him over. He stepped up with his kit and took out the sensors. "May I?" He held the sensors in front of Harlow's face.

"Sure. What have I got to lose?"

I grabbed his hand and rubbed my thumb over the back of it, careful to avoid his roughed-up knuckles. It was more in an effort to comfort him, but when he squeezed my hand in return, I felt relieved. Maybe we were okay. Maybe.

Jeremy attached the sensors to Harlow's temples and the base of his neck, then ran the wires to his laptop, one I hadn't seen in over six months. One I thought we would never need again.

Jeremy booted up the program. The sensors buzzed to life. Harlow sat still, unaffected by the vibration.

I glanced at the screen, eyebrows furrowed. I'd gotten used to reading some of the tracker diagnostics, but this one was a mystery. I turned to Jeremy, hoping he had some answers, but he shook his head. "After your anomaly signal, I'd thought I'd seen it all."

"But?" I asked.

"I've never seen anything like this. The reading is showing the tracker is offline and online at the same time, which doesn't make any sense."

"Do you think it's similar to when my tracker shut down, but it was still putting out a low-level signal?"

"Not exactly. It's like it's saying the reading is true and false at the same time. We're going to have to get him back to headquarters and get Bailen to help examine this further."

Harlow shot to his feet and ripped the sensors from his temples with a single tug. "I'm not going anywhere."

Jeremy winced. "Careful with the equipment."

"Sorry." Harlow shrugged, handing the leads back to Jeremy.

I rose from the floor and reached to peel the third sensor off the back of Harlow's neck before he damaged it further, but he dodged like a prize-winning fighter. I dropped my hands in frustration.

"Harlow, you can't keep going on like this."

His head fell, but he said nothing.

Maybe another angle would work better. "When are your parents coming home?"

"Monday. I think?" He rubbed his face again. "I'm not even sure what day it is anymore."

"Friday," I answered automatically more out of sympathy than anything else. "Since no one is around, why don't you come by for Shabbat dinner tonight." I nudged him playfully with my elbow. "Lydia will be there. It'll be like old times." Despite my calm tone, I silently hoped he'd take the bait. I couldn't leave him alone like this all night.

Harlow let out a laugh but quickly clamped his mouth shut, like he couldn't allow himself to be happy.

Friday night dinners with Harlow and Lydia had grown to be a tradition—well, at least before my tracker glitched. And before Jake… I couldn't let myself finish the thought. While I didn't cry every day anymore, Jake's death still hit me at the strangest times. Mostly when I was thinking about things he would have loved but would never get to see.

This weekend was supposed to be the first reemergence of those dinners. I'd been missing those connections with the people I cared about. Maybe it was fate that Harlow might be there after all. Lydia could help bring him back from whatever this was, and Dad could provide some insight into what was happening. Either way, Harlow needed a break from reality.

"Come on. I won't take no for an answer. Besides, my parents will be glad to see you."

Harlow lifted his head until he finally made voluntary eye contact for the first time. "They don't hate me?"

"Why would they hate you?" Harlow and I were friends long before we'd dated. Even though things didn't last, they never blamed Harlow for our breakup. My parents still respected him and said hi to his family at temple.

"After everything that happened."

I threw my arm around Harlow and hugged him even though he didn't reciprocate. "Just because we grew apart doesn't mean they don't want to see you. You're family."

He shrugged, not completely convinced.

"Besides, who else is going to finish off an entire plate of kugel?"

He laughed, then let himself fully smile and embrace it. The Harlow I'd known before was coming back a little.

"I need to shower," Harlow said, returning to a serious tone.

I glanced back to Jeremy, who had packed up his equipment.

"I can hang here for a bit if you want," Jeremy said.

"I don't need a babysitter," Harlow groaned.

"It's just in case something else happens. I can monitor it." Jeremy held up his kit.

"Whatever dude. TV's in the living room." Harlow disappeared down the hall, leaving my earlier invitation unanswered.

I nodded a silent thank you to Jeremy, feeling a little better about having to leave to set up for Shabbat dinner.

Jeremy angled his head toward the door and I nodded. Nothing else I could do here. If I loosened Harlow up a bit, there was a chance he'd let the Ghosts take a closer look at his tracker. The more I distracted him, the better. If I could get Harlow to show up to dinner, then we could start to understand what happened before anyone else got hurt, or worse, he hurt himself.

SIX

I rounded our dining room table one last time, checking every place setting for silverware, plates, and water cups. Then I laid out the candlesticks, Challah, and wine for Shabbat dinner. A knock at the door distracted me from my final count of the wineglasses. I gave up and made my way through the living room to the front door. No need to check the peephole to see who was here. It was mishpuchah, so I pulled open the door.

Bailen stood in the entryway in khakis and a teal button-up shirt that accentuated his green eyes. His wild brown hair was the only thing untamable.

"You look nice." I leaned in and kissed him. "Hope everything went okay at the hospital."

"Got there just in time. They're monitoring him overnight, but I stayed until his wife got there."

I stepped aside to let Bailen move into the entryway as I closed the door behind him. "It's a good thing you're fast." I nudged him playfully with my hip.

He grabbed my waist and pulled me in close for another kiss, this one deeper and more passionate, like he hadn't seen me in a week—which was ironic because we'd practically spent the whole day together, and over the last six months, we'd seen each other almost every day.

I stepped back from the hug and intertwined my fingers with his, leading him toward the couch. He plopped down in the center, and I nuzzled in next to him, allowing him to put his arm around me.

"How'd it go with Harlow?" he asked casually, but his tone dripped with concern.

"It's complicated. I'm not sure he's going to let us help him."

"I know you can be *very* convincing." He lightly tickled my side, and I giggled.

"Apparently not convincing enough." My gaze dropped to the floor, letting the laughter fade. I wondered if my Shabbat dinner invitation would go unanswered.

Bailen put his fingers under my chin and lifted my head. "What's wrong?"

"I didn't want to admit it, but I think you were right."

He smirked, enjoying the admission. "I'm always right, but what about specifically?"

"Harlow's tracker. Jeremy picked up a weird signal." I paused to collect my thoughts. "He thinks the network, or part of it, is active again. Someone might be exploiting the loophole to mind-control Harlow through his tracker again." I sighed as my shoulders drooped. "I don't know if I can handle another tracker catastrophe." My words couldn't convey the ominous cloud building inside me, the one that told me I knew the truth but didn't want to accept it.

Bailen ran his fingers through my hair, sending a shiver down my back. "Why do I always have to be right about the things I don't want to be right about?" He bent down and gave me a quick, reassuring peck on the lips. "Whatever this is, we'll tackle it together."

I squeezed his hand. "Together."

The front door swung open and Lydia strolled in. She plopped onto the loveseat next to the couch. She'd spent so much time here, my parents had given her tracker unlock access. When the tracker network came down, they'd given her the code to the door. "Sorry, did I interrupt something?"

"Nope. How's your day off been?"

Teacher development days were the best, but Lydia's parents always insisted she do something educational with single days off from school. I'd offered to let her join the coding sessions with the Ghosts, but she passed to work on her robotics build for the upcoming competition.

"Productive. We adjusted the arm so it's about ninety percent effective. We're going to crush this competition."

"That's awesome. I can't wait to watch the bot in action." Robotics competitions were more exciting than soccer games. Like soccer, they required strategy, but there was also problem solving on the fly and teamwork—without all the chest bumping. And the competitions were infinitely harder now without the direct tracker connection to the bots.

Bailen stared at me. "How come no one told me there were robots?"

I elbowed him and laughed. "Don't you think you have enough going on right now?"

"But robots!" He laughed as he tried to fake pout.

"Yeah, sure." He trudged back toward the dining room, passing Bailen without so much as an acknowledgement.

Bailen reached for my hand and led me back to the table. I sat in my seat between Bailen and Harlow, with Lydia sending me questioning glances across the table. I shook my head once to let her know to drop it.

"Harlow, it's nice to see you." Dad reached out his hand to pat Harlow on the back as he passed by, but Harlow didn't acknowledge him.

"How's school going?" my mom asked, oblivious to the tension but a welcome distraction, nonetheless.

"Fine," Harlow said. He collapsed into the chair next to me.

I poured Bailen a quarter glass of wine, then did the same for my glass. Since my Bat Mitzvah, Mom and Dad had let me and my friends have wine for Shabbat, but never a full glass. I mostly took a sip or two. I passed it toward Harlow, who made no effort to take the bottle from me. Normally, he would take a generous pour for himself, but he continued to stare as if he wasn't really here.

"How's the team looking for next year?" Lydia asked, trying to break the tension. As usual, she had stellar perception.

"Fine." Harlow continued to stare at his plate.

That's how this was going to go?

"Wine?" I tipped the bottle toward his glass, but instead of responding, he put his hand over the top, preventing me from pouring.

"More for me." Lydia reached across the table and grabbed the bottle.

"Are you okay?" I said under my breath to Harlow.

"No, my head is messed up enough as it is. I don't need wine to screw it up any further."

Fair enough, but the person sitting next to me was a mere shell. This was more than we'd grown apart and weren't dating anymore. This was serious.

We raised our glasses as Dad said the blessing over the wine, then we drank, but Harlow continued to sit unmoving, not participating. Mom uncovered the Challah and we sang the Motzi, blessing the bread. After that, dishes appeared from the kitchen. Food passed around, but Harlow didn't add anything to his plate.

When the kugel passed by me, I dumped a heaping spoonful on his plate without even asking because it was always his favorite. It was a last-ditch effort to get the old Harlow back, but he didn't react. Dad looked at me with a question on his lips he didn't voice—the one time a tech-filled Shabbat might have been useful. I could have filled everyone in behind the scenes with private tracker messages. Instead, we were left with awkward silence.

The clanking of silverware against plates rang out as Harlow stared at his kugel.

"How are the coding challenges going?" Dad looked at Bailen and me.

"Great!" I said a little too excitedly, happy for the distraction. "I smoked Bailen today."

"Cheated is more like it." Bailen nudged me with his elbow.

"Cheating or not, I'm glad you're teaching Kaya some coding through the challenges and having fun in the process." Dad smiled at me. He was always proud of my accomplishments, but the coding skills really resonated with him.

"No one cheated! We never said teaming up was against the rules." I laughed and Bailen kissed me on the cheek.

Harlow shot up from his chair and bolted from the room. I

shot Lydia a look and rushed after him. He was at the door by the time I rounded the corner.

"Harlow, wait!"

He stopped but left his hand on the door handle. "I'm supposed to sit here and watch you two play house and act like nothing is wrong?"

"That's not fair."

"You know what's not fair?" Harlow sounded exhausted. "That I have to go through this alone." He opened the door and stepped into the hall.

I ran after him. "I want to help you. Just let me do it." I reached for his hand but stopped. "Come back inside. Let's finish dinner, then we can talk to my dad about what's going on." I waited to see his reaction, but he stood frozen with his back to me. "Let us fix this."

"I don't know if you can." He turned to face me.

"What have you got to lose?"

"Nothing. I've lost it all already."

My heart broke into a million pieces. "That's not true." But my words felt empty. I'd had similar feelings when my tracker glitched. I had nowhere to turn. If it hadn't been for Jake, I wouldn't be where I was today. I'd probably be dead.

"Why don't you come back to dinner?" I angled my head toward the dining room.

"I'll pass. I'm not hungry."

"I can't let you go." I blurted the words before I thought about what I was really saying. "I can't let you be alone," I corrected, realizing that probably wasn't much better.

"Fine, but I'm not going back in there."

I swallowed hard and wondered where he could go. If he sat in the living room, he could hear everything, which would probably make him uncomfortable. If I put him in my room, he might run out after dinner when we all retreated in there. "Why don't you hang out in Jake's room?"

The words tasted like a dirty paintbrush in my mouth. I'd been in there once since he'd left for what I thought was college, but instead he'd joined the Ghosts and disappeared. After he'd died, the door stayed closed. The room remained untouched, as though refusing to go in there would somehow preserve his memory better.

He nodded, then turned down the hall without another word. Shoulders slumped, he dragged his feet toward the closed door. I watched as he pushed it open, stepped inside, and shut it with a quiet click.

What a mess.

I darted back to the dining room to find everyone laughing about something. Rather than ask what, like I normally would, I sank into my chair, hoping no one noticed my return. Bailen shot me a quick smile and then returned to laughing.

When the laughter died down, Dad turned his attention to me directly. "Someone want to clue me in now?"

"Harlow's taking a break in Jake's room."

Dad shot me the signature parental I-know-you're-not-telling-me-everything look, and I slouched in my chair.

"Harlow attacked Wes." Bailen spat the words like a reflex.

"Traitor," I mumbled under my breath.

"He needs to know."

"I know, but not like this." I shook my head, trying to clear the jumble of thoughts and feelings, but it didn't help. I knew Dad always wanted to help, but I still struggled to let him after the discovery that he'd hidden the secret to taking down the tracker network on my chip and never told me, leaving me to figure it out on my own. I'd said I had forgiven him, but I still had complicated feelings about it.

Dad watched me without speaking, knowing I'd crack under the pressure. He'd get what he asked for eventually. True to form, I could feel the urge to blurt it all out bubbling inside me. Mom gave me an encouraging nod. Lydia shrugged her shoulders, but her expression said she would have my back no matter what.

"Wes came by the Coderie after Harlow attacked him. We went to find him." I took a deep breath, stalling so I could figure out the best way to explain the situation. "Jeremy and I found Harlow hiding in a dark closet with his palms and knuckles pretty roughed up. He said he's been losing time again. Jeremy found a weird signal on Harlow's tracker, but we haven't had time to get him anywhere with the right equipment to dig into it further. It took everything I had to get him to trust me enough to show up for dinner. And now…" I trailed off, the tension of the boy I was falling for now and the boy I once loved tugging me in two different directions. I thought telling the truth was supposed to take the weight off your shoulders. This just made things worse.

Dad sat very still for a while, then looked questioningly at Bailen.

"I think someone is exploiting the loophole," Bailen blurted, breaking the silence.

"We don't know for sure." Evidence or not, I couldn't face another tracker catastrophe. But as much as I wanted to deny it, it seemed pretty clear someone was in the network, mind-controlling Harlow.

"What do we need to confirm this?" Dad asked.

"I need to get my equipment back up and running. And I need

Harlow to cooperate."

"Easier said than done," I muttered under my breath.

"Mr. Weiss, I could use your expertise as well. I don't know what we're going to find, but other than Scurry, you know the most about the loophole."

"Is there anyone else who might know about the loophole?" I asked, afraid of the answer.

"Scurry held that close to his chest. When he confronted me about it, he seemed surprised someone else had found out." Dad paused, deep in thought. "He's still…"

I nodded.

"Still in SuperMax. I asked for confirmation again this afternoon and received photographic evidence."

After the network fell, Rufus Scurry, creator of Tracker220, was escorted to an undisclosed SuperMax prison. You needed special clearance just to get in the building and a paper trail a million miles long to get near the guy. The courts had talked about deeper punishments like removing his tracker, but they couldn't gain concurrence on whether or not it would risk his brain function, so they left it. But if it wasn't Dad, and it wasn't Rufus, who was doing all this?

"Let's get started on the equipment tomorrow."

"On Shabbat?" I asked, shocked Dad was willing to give up his day of rest. He'd relished each and every one since the tracker network came down.

"I don't think we can afford to wait for the next attack to happen. We need to get ahead of this."

"I agree. I should start getting stuff out of storage." Bailen pushed his chair back, set his napkin on the table, and stood. The zest for a tech mystery brimmed inside him.

Mom set her hands down on the table and stood. "Sit. Eat dinner. We can figure this out tomorrow."

Bailen dropped into his chair, his eyes wide with fear that said he was afraid to cross my mom. I knew we could wait, but I feared Harlow might not. Despite Mom's caring, doting personality, the Jewish mom guilt was real. There was no escaping it.

Seven

I stood in the entryway, locked in an embrace with Bailen, hoping I could freeze the moment in time. The minute I let him walk out the door, everything would change. We'd go back to tracker mysteries, possibly fighting for justice—and after everything, I didn't think I had anymore fight left in me. I let out a long breath, resigning myself to the fact that I'd have to dig deep to find the strength somewhere inside me. I stepped away from our embrace, awkward silence filling the space between us.

Muffled voices drifted into the room from the kitchen, where Lydia assisted Mom and Dad with the dishes. The noise was a welcome distraction from the many things left unsaid. The world we never wanted to see again knocked at the door, inviting us back to another fight for our lives and freedom beyond anything that we could have ever anticipated.

"I'll bring Harlow by the Coderie in the morning." I knew it would be a struggle, but I needed to make it happen.

"Are you going to be okay tonight? I can stay if you need me to." He wanted to be with me, but he was also itching to get to work, powered by a new sense of purpose. There was also a hint of something more, like he had to keep an eye on me, or maybe something else.

I shook my head, but I wasn't sure I didn't need him. "I'll figure something out. You do what you do best." I nudged him. He pulled me in for one last passionate kiss then retreated backward into the hall, his gaze on me as I shut the door.

I turned and the padded envelope caught my eye. Maybe I should leave it for my parents. It stared back at me, begging me to investigate. I snagged it off the entry table and chucked it onto my bed. Maybe I'd share it with Mom and Dad once I knew what was inside. I needed more time to consider. Continuing down the hall to Jake's room, I sucked in a deep breath before knocking lightly on the door. No answer. I knocked a little louder. Still nothing.

I cracked the door and poked my head inside. "Harlow?"

"Mom?" he groaned.

Great, I woke him up. "No, it's Kaya."

Harlow shot up on the bed as though everything suddenly flooded back to him. I cursed myself for disturbing his few moments of peace. He slumped his shoulders, resigned to reality.

"Can I come in?"

"It's your house." He slid his feet toward the head of the bed, then patted the spot next to him.

I flipped on the lights, illuminating the standing lamp in the corner of the room, then grabbed Jake's desk chair and sat in it backward, the way he always used to do.

"I'm not contagious. You're not going to catch whatever is happening to my tracker."

"I don't know about that." I smiled at him playfully.

"Oh, come on, cut me a little slack." The corners of his mouth twitched upward, a hint of his old self before the scowl returned.

"Fine." I stood and plopped on the edge of the bed, leaving a good foot between us. He may not be toxic, but there was something going on with him. At least I wasn't home alone if anything happened. "But now you owe me."

"How does sitting near me put me in debt to you?" This time he smiled, not a full one that reached his eyes but enough to say he was teasing a little bit. Maybe the old Harlow was still in there. I'd have to pull it out of him.

"I don't make the rules, I just follow them." I laughed, then leaned over to nudge him with my shoulder.

"Miss, I-dismantled-society-by-taking-down-the-biggest-piece -of-technology-in-the-world, going back to her rule-following days?"

"Have you met me?" Sure, I'd abandoned everyone to join the Ghosts and take down the tracker network, but that wasn't what I originally planned. In fact, I'd had no plan when I ran, other than getting away from the authorities who wanted to lobotomize me to get to my glitchy tracker. Before that, I hadn't broken a single rule in my life. The authorities had made me nervous even when I hadn't done anything wrong. After witnessing a third robbery in a week and seeing an old man nearly die, a world without authorities and trackers wasn't the answer, either. I wasn't sure which was better, and anything that even remotely felt like breaking a rule, even an unwritten one, still made my insides squirm.

I'd loosened up a little, but I didn't like to push my luck.

"Yeah. I thought I knew you. But then you ran, and you're a different person now."

Well, that stung. I didn't feel that different. "I'm still me. I've just experienced more things now that have shaped who I am." I wondered if I should push further, but before I lost my nerve, I blurted, "Just like how the hurdles you face will shape who you become."

Harlow shot up from the bed. "What's that supposed to mean?"

Whoops, too far. I reached for his arm, but he yanked it away. "Harlow, please. I'm trying to help."

"Then take this thing out of my head." He grabbed his hair in frustration, or maybe it was an attempt to rip out something because he couldn't get to his tracker.

I remembered that feeling of powerlessness. "If that's what is necessary, I'll do whatever I can to support you. Why don't we start with everything that's happened."

He nodded, but his muscles were still tensed.

"You can talk to me. I'm still me. The part you know is still here."

He lowered back onto the bed but stared straight ahead. "It's been going on for about a month."

I opened my mouth to speak but stopped. I didn't want to set him off again.

"I didn't notice at first, until I started looking back and trying to remember certain events and there were stretches of... blankness." He shook his head. "I don't know how else to explain it, but that doesn't feel like it does the experience justice."

It was weird hearing Harlow struggle to find words. He had never seemed to be short on them the entire time I'd known him. But here he was, silently fighting to tell his truth, and I didn't have the right mindset to help him.

"Was it painful?"

"No, more isolating. Details I should have known, should have remembered, didn't exist. The more I tried to remember, the bigger the void got."

"Like the blankness was pushing back?" I asked.

"Yeah, actually. Almost like someone or something didn't want me to remember."

"That's so strange. What would there be to hide?"

Harlow shrugged. His gaze dropped to the floor. "I'm not sure, but this is exactly how it felt when…."

He didn't finish the thought, but I knew he meant when Rufus Scurry mind-controlled him the night I took down the tracker network.

"A week ago, I started getting flashes: drops of blood, a knife, dark rooms, a high-pitched scream."

"Are you sure it wasn't a dream?"

"Positive. It was so real, like my mind wanted me to remember something that was buried and shouldn't come out." He rubbed his hands on his thighs. "I think I did something bad." His voice was so quiet I barely caught it.

I threw my arms around him in an awkward side hug. "I'm so sorry." I didn't know what else to say, but a side hug didn't seem like enough.

When he finally stopped shaking in my arms, I slid back. "Do you want to know what happened?"

He shook his head. "I want it to stop."

"I think the Ghosts can make that happen. We just need to understand what's going on with your tracker. Will you let them study it?"

"Be a lab rat? No thanks."

Ironic. I'd said the same thing about the authorities wanting to reset my tracker and carve it out of my skull. When the Ghosts wanted to study my tracker, it was no better. It was hard to know who to trust. He wasn't entirely wrong in this case, either. It would require some level of study, and no one knew what it might do to his tracker or his latent memories.

"I can't promise everything will work perfectly, but I can promise I won't let you do this alone."

He took a deep breath and held it. Then he blew it out slowly. "I don't think I have a choice, do I?"

"Bailen and Jeremy are relentless. They won't stop until they figure this out. My dad won't let anything bad happen to you. You'll always be mishpuchah." When Dad had worked for Global Tracking Systems, he stole knowledge and took it to the Ghosts. Their combined technical prowess was bound to get to the bottom of what was happening.

Harlow side-eyed me. I knew this was about Bailen without having to ask. He'd had it out for him ever since he knew Bailen existed, even if he'd never said it. Bailen hadn't stolen me from Harlow, exactly—I fell for Bailen as much as he fell for me—but it had been awkward, and the timing was all jumbled. We were both just as guilty; neither Harlow nor I waited for the other after I ran, because neither of us knew if I'd come back. After everything we'd been through, we'd grown apart. Regardless, I still cared about Harlow. Those feelings were a jumbled mess now. I didn't know how to tell him I was here for him no matter what, even if the romantic feelings had changed.

"I promise it won't be the torture you think it will be." I smirked at him, but he didn't seem to notice my spirited demeanor.

"Don't make promises you can't keep."

Ouch. His ability to stab me right where it hurt the most was so finely tuned. When did he get like this? "How about we take it one step at a time? First, we investigate that signal on your tracker and figure out why you're forgetting things."

He nodded, then stood from the bed, eyelids drooping from exhaustion and stress. "I should head home."

"No." I popped up from the bed and threw my arm in front of him, a lame attempt to stop him from leaving.

"Really? That gangly arm is supposed to be an obstacle?" Normally, this would have been said in jest, but his tone was more of annoyance.

"I just mean you shouldn't go home by yourself. You can stay here, and we'll go to the Coderie tomorrow with everyone." I couldn't let him leave. I'd never get him to go to the Ghosts otherwise. And if he wandered off, I wanted to make sure someone was there to witness it. "Stay in Jake's bed. You're already here."

Harlow warred with the idea for a minute, then collapsed onto the bed, eyelids drooping even further. I squeezed his shoulder. He grabbed my hand in a way that said he needed support more than he was willing to admit. I stood there for an extra moment before pulling loose from his grasp, allowing my fingertips to linger in his a little too long. Then I retreated through the open door, flipping the light off as I left.

I returned to my room, where Lydia was half-heartedly turning pages in a book but mostly staring at the package I left in my room.

She shot to a sitting position, crossed her legs, and shoved the book off the bed with a thud. "How'd it go with Harlow?"

I collapsed next to her and rubbed my face. "He's really messed up. I don't think he knows what he wants. Which is making it infinitely harder to convince him to have his tracker looked at. Not to mention Bailen."

"You mean Harlow not wanting Bailen there, or Bailen's jealous energy toward Harlow?"

I shot her a look and smacked her leg with the back of my hand. "Oh, come on. It's not that bad."

She made her *seriously* face. "You could cut that tension with a knife."

"UGH!" I buried my face in my hands. "Why do the guys always have to make something so simple, so complicated?"

"Because it's pretty complicated. Your ex needs your boyfriend's help to uncover some craziness with his tracker that shouldn't even work, and your boyfriend is freaking out over the time you're spending with your ex. The optics aren't good."

"There's no way Bailen is jealous. He knows I want to be with him."

Lydia cocked her eyebrow. Maybe she was right. Was I too close to Harlow still? Either way, I couldn't leave him to deal with this on his own.

"Hey"—she nodded at the foot of my bed—"what's with the package?"

I shot up and snatched it, thankful for the distraction. "I'm not sure. Why is Jake getting mail now?" I blinked away an impending tear to maintain my composure even though my insides were starting to quiver.

"That's a great question, but you won't know until you open it." Lydia nodded at the padded envelope, silently inviting me to answer the question hanging in the air.

"Maybe I should turn it over to my parents and let them deal with it," I said, second guessing my initial thought that the package was meant for me. Just because Jake died in my arms without my parents around didn't mean they should be left out of all the things related to him after his death.

"No." She snatched it out of my hand. "I think it's meant for you, see?" She pointed to some letters on the bottom of the label I hadn't noticed before. FFOB. "I think that message is for you."

She was right. FFOB: found family over blood. Mishpuchah. "Huh," was all I could manage to get out. We were family, so that didn't entirely make sense. Then I remembered the poem he'd painted on the wall at school for his senior project about how family wasn't always blood related. While I was family to Jake by blood, he'd also chosen me to be in his life, making me found family. But one thing nagged me. "What if it's for Peyton?"

Peyton was the one person of Jake's found family I hadn't known about until it was too late. Sure, she was around when I ran to the Ghosts, but she'd kept her relationship with Jake a secret until her walls came crumbling down and the admission of how much she missed him came spilling out. Her connection to Jake made it equally probable that she needed to know about the contents of a package with FFOB.

"Then why send it here?" Lydia asked. She always had a unique way of logically lining up all the facts into an undeniable truth.

"Good point." I tried to come up with a better reason, but more questions formed. "Why is it addressed to him and not me?"

"We won't know until you open it."

I paused to weigh the consequences of opening my brother's mail. The timing of it couldn't be a coincidence. The hole in my heart ached for a deeper connection to him. "I guess you're right." I tore the top of the padded envelope and dumped it onto my bed. A single USB drive tumbled out.

"That's it?" Lydia asked, sounding a bit disappointed there

wasn't more to the mystery.

I nodded, but several questions stirred inside me—the biggest being, what was on it? The only computers with USB drive access were at the Coderie. I'd have to sneak away and find some time to explore the contents when no one else was around. Easier said than done.

I shoved it in my pocket and turned back to Lydia. "I can't do anything with it here."

Her shoulders slumped. "So anticlimactic."

I nodded but knew deep down there was more to the story to uncover, like who sent it and why now?

But Lydia's disappointment differed from mine. She'd been a great sport after I'd run out on her mid-conversation to escape the authorities before going dark and not responding to her thousands of messages. She could have easily written me off, but when we finally reunited, it was like no time had passed at all. No hurt feelings or drama. She helped me through the emotions that came after Jake's death. That's one of the things I loved best about Lydia: she accepted me, flaws and all.

I made a silent vow to myself to keep her in the loop this time, no matter what secrets this drive held.

But so many questions swirled in my head, so many words left unsaid. "I'll have to find a computer to read this away from prying eyes."

"Oh, no you don't. You have to tell people about this."

"You just told me it was meant for me and not to turn it over to my parents. Which is it?" When had everything in my life become a moral dilemma?

She lowered her gaze. "I just meant you should see what it is. You can't go back to hiding everything from everyone. The secrets didn't turn out so well the last time."

I shuddered as she hit a touchy nerve. She was right. I didn't have to do this by myself, but this one felt personal.

"I promise to clue you in when I figure out what's on the drive." I held out my hand.

"Deal." Lydia accepted. We did our secret handshake to cement the agreement.

The tension in my shoulders released slightly. I had more allies than I did before. But after Rufus Scurry killed my brother and turned innocent people into his own personal mind-controlled zombies, it was hard to know who to trust.

It seemed likely there was something else going on that we'd missed. If it wasn't Scurry, someone else out there had the ability to exploit trackers against a person's will. We'd have to be careful who we trusted. I was sure Lydia wasn't an unknowing mole, but that could change at any moment depending on how all this worked. And there was a chance I had a potential rogue under my roof right now. We needed to uncover the mystery behind Harlow's blackouts. Hopefully, Bailen could get his equipment up and running before whoever was behind this struck again.

Eight

A scream ripped me out of a deep sleep. I bolted upright, eyes adjusting to the sparse light in my room. Slowing my breaths, I looked over to the spare bed in my room where Lydia's breathing was even and unaware of the noise. I blinked my eyes to get the time before remembering to glance at my watch. It was an hour that no human should have to witness. Maybe I'd dreamed it.

A second scream tore through the air. Lydia's quiet breathing continued, but that definitely wasn't a dream.

A third scream interrupted my scrambled thoughts.

"What in the world?" Lydia groaned and rolled over.

"Harlow," I said as I remembered he was still here.

I flew out of bed and slammed open my door. At the end of the hall, Dad flipped on the light, bleary-eyed and barefoot. He gave me a questioning look. I nodded at Jake's door as a fourth scream erupted. After a handful of steps, I swung open the door to Jake's room without knocking. Dad followed at my heels.

I rushed to the bed and shook Harlow. He jolted awake and pulled away until he was able to focus on me.

"It's Kaya. You're okay. You're safe." I squeezed Harlow and rocked him back and forth in an attempt to calm him, but he struggled underneath my hug and shoved my arms away, knocking me off the bed. Dad caught me before I toppled to the floor.

I stood in the middle of the room, unsure how to proceed. Unsure if he was in full control. I couldn't help but think of the nights I woke up screaming in pain after Jake died. But this pain sounded different. It had an element of guilt behind it. More than just sadness, it included a mixture of remorse.

Lydia knocked on the doorframe and peered inside. "Everything… Okay, never mind." She backed away slowly and shot me a what-can-I-do look.

I could barely focus on her. Harlow drew my attention back, but my body was powerless to act or know what to do. There was no rulebook for this kind of thing, no right answers. It hurt to see him in such pain. To struggle so much.

"Harlow?" Dad asked with a hint of more than one question in his single word.

"What?" Harlow snapped in a low tone.

The way he responded made me shudder, but at least it proved he was in control of himself.

My dad nodded at me, silently encouraging me to help get him talking.

"It's okay," I whispered and approached him with outstretched arms, like trying to get near a stray dog.

When I was able to get close enough, I wrapped my arms around Harlow, burying my head in his shoulder. I kept rocking him, shushing him softly so only he could hear. We needed to figure out what was happening to him for everyone's sake, especially before Harlow lost who he was and couldn't fight the pain anymore.

My dad cleared his throat. He wanted me to say something. Bad dreams don't always stick around, and without tracker access, it would be harder to rewind and figure out what happened. I rubbed Harlow's back, then took a deep breath and pulled my head back from his shoulder.

"Do you want to talk about it?"

Harlow nodded, but hesitation filled his face. Dad sat in Jake's chair. "I know this will be extremely difficult, but I need you to tell me everything you remember. Spare no detail. It might help me figure out what's happening to you and your tracker."

Harlow collapsed in my arms, but his ragged breaths slowed as he gathered the strength to do what he had to. He was always strong, but I didn't know how he handled this alone for so long. Even with people willing to help, this had to be impossible. But then I thought about everything I'd done alone six months ago: ran from everything I knew and everyone I loved, eventually ran to find answers, endangering the Ghosts and their whole operation. Getting captured by Rufus Scurry himself before figuring out the truths I had on my tracker all along that allowed me to destroy the network. Now it might have all been for nothing, because the world wasn't better. People were still hurting, their privacy still violated in new and different ways.

"There was so much blood."

Harlow's voice was so quiet, but the word *blood* jolted me from my thoughts. I'd heard it from him before, but if he was remembering more of what happened in the past, then maybe he was involved, a witness—or something worse.

"I know this is difficult, but whose blood?" Dad prodded.

"I… I don't know." Harlow pulled back and rubbed his face. "I don't think it was mine." He paused, face straining as he fought to remember what came next. "It was all over my hands." He closed his eyes for longer than usual, then opened them wide. "There was a girl there, but I don't know who she was. I tried to help her. She had tiny cuts up and down her arms and legs." He shook his head, then let out a long breath. "That's it. I can't remember anything else."

"Good. Is this the first time you've seen the girl?" Dad asked, nudging him down a path that would hopefully unlock some hidden secrets.

I continued to rub Harlow's back to keep him calm.

"This is the first time I've seen her, in a memory… dream… nightmare…" He let out another long breath that didn't calm his breathing. "This is so messed up. I don't have the right words to explain this."

"What about—"

"Wait." Harlow's face lit up, not in an excited, happy way, but in a way that said something was coming together. "I haven't seen her before in my visions. I still don't know the word, but it's not important because I've seen her before in real life."

"Where?" I asked.

"The night you took down the tracker network. Mr. Scurry made me put an authority weapon to her head."

"Emily!" I grabbed Harlow's shoulders and shook him as fear ripped through me. "Is she okay? What did you do to her?" I didn't know whether to be mad at him for potentially hurting a part of my family or sad for his unexplained pain from trying to help her.

Dad shot up from the chair and pulled me from the bed before

I could get any answers. "Sit here and take a deep breath." He stared me right in the eyes until I obeyed. He gave me a reassuring nod before turning back to Harlow.

I glanced at the doorway where Lydia still stood in the hall. "I'll have your mom reach out to Emily's uncle," she said as though reading my mind, then disappeared down the hall toward my parents' bedroom.

I knew Emily's uncle wouldn't be pleased to get a middle of the night wake up call, but I needed to know she was okay.

Dad sat on the edge of the bed, preventing me from moving back to support or possibly strangle Harlow. Maybe I needed a few more deep breaths.

Dad put a hopefully comforting hand on Harlow's knee. "I need you to think hard. Does this feel like it happened, like a memory, or does it feel like you were watching a movie?"

"More like a movie. I'd struggled to find those words before, but it's always felt like I was watching it happen through someone else's eyes."

"Thanks. That's very helpful." Dad shot up from the bed without another word and was out the door, nodding at me to follow him into the hall.

When I arrived, Dad looked at me with tired but serious eyes. "Watch him, but if Harlow stops responding to you, don't get too close or try to stop him. Get a hold of me immediately. Understand?"

I nodded. It was hard to argue when his tone was so serious.

"What does it mean?" I asked, afraid of the answer.

"Nothing good."

"Don't leave me in the dark again. Tell me what's going on." I stomped my foot like I used to when I was a frustrated little kid, but I didn't care. I wanted answers, not more secrets.

"I think someone is exploiting the loophole. They're mind-controlling Harlow, forcing him to do things against his will, then making him forget they ever happened. These things he's seeing like movies are actually flashbacks, residual memories buried deep down and resurfacing when his subconscious is most active. I'll need some tests to confirm, but I'm almost certain."

I didn't understand how he could know that from a few quick answers, but I nodded my head. Bailen had said the exact same thing. If two smart people said it, the likelihood that it was correct was growing.

I asked one of the million questions swirling around in my head. "Is he dangerous?"

"When he's awake, no. But when he's being exploited… it's hard to say. Keep an eye out for signs, and if they come up, keep your distance. If you get in the way, things could get ugly fast."

A lump formed in my throat. So, it was safe to be around Harlow until it wasn't. We couldn't let him go through this alone, but I also couldn't put myself or others in danger. We needed to know who was behind this to stop it. "How are they accessing the network?" I dared to ask.

Dad shook his head. "I don't know, but Harlow could be the key to unraveling that very mystery. I sure as hell intend to find out." He rushed into his room without another word.

I turned to Harlow, but he was already back to sleep, likely worn out from the nightmare and screaming.

I plodded back to my room and found a note on my pillow from Lydia. *Emily ok. Talk more in the morning.* I sighed in relief and collapsed into my bed, listening to Lydia's quiet breathing beside me. Sleep did not come for some time, though.

The next morning, Dad was gone by the time I woke up, probably already at the Coderie even though Saturdays were his day off. I crept out of my room and propped open Jake's door. Harlow's long, slow breaths caused his chest to rise and fall. Good. He hadn't run off somewhere, and he was still in control. I made my way to the kitchen to pour myself a bowl of cereal.

"Oh, no you don't."

I jumped and looked up to find Lydia in the doorway with her arms crossed. "Huh?" I said through a mouthful of food.

"What is going on?" Lydia glared at me like she was about to tear me to shreds.

I chewed the rest of my food slowly, then swallowed hard, trying to find the words. It didn't matter how I said them, it wasn't good. But Lydia hadn't been involved the last time, so I wasn't sure where to start. It wouldn't matter. She'd be there for me.

"We're not sure yet, but it sounds like someone is exploiting the tracker loophole. We won't know for certain until we can study Harlow's tracker."

"How?"

"I wish I knew, but the Ghosts will get to the bottom of it."

Mom stepped into the kitchen and grabbed a yogurt from the fridge. "Your father left in the middle of the night for the Coderie."

I nodded. "And Emily?" The rest of the night came flooding back to me. Fear settled in my gut.

"I called over to check on her again first thing this morning."

"And?" Mom really was going to make me pull this out of her, but the expression on her face said it all. Despite Lydia's note, this wasn't good.

Mom grabbed my shoulder, then sat in the chair next to me. "Emily is okay now, but she was attacked. They don't know by who, but it was minor cuts and bruises and a few stitches. She's back with her uncle and doing fine."

I sucked in a breath as my mind swirled. Lydia shot me a look filled with the same question I was slowly asking in my head. Did Harlow do this? And if so, when?

But then I remembered his night terror flashback, and how I found him in the closet. The timeline was coming together. If Harlow did this, first he was mind-controlled, then he attacked Wes, then Emily, and then I found him in his parents' closet with blood on his hands. He didn't remember he'd attacked Emily until late last night.

My mind spun. Despite all the evidence, I didn't want it to be true.

The question was, why would whoever mind-controlled him go after Emily? Maybe she was at the wrong place at the wrong time. She did live down the hall from Harlow.

But it all seemed a little too convenient. Why harm a little girl? Especially one that didn't have a lot of people in her life. The only possible connection seemed to be me. But if that was the case, why not just come after me? As plausible as the timeline seemed, the motivations didn't line up.

And as much as I wanted to check on Emily, I wondered if that would put her in more danger. I'd call her later, just to be sure.

"I guess we'd better wake Harlow and go to the Coderie. It's the only way we might get some answers." I spooned several large bites into my mouth, then dumped my bowl into the sink and headed back to my room with Lydia on my heels. Lydia and I dressed in record speed. I swiped the USB drive off my desk and shoved it into the back pocket of my jeans before braving my way across the hall.

I tapped lightly on the door and was met with a groan. I glanced back to Lydia with my best *I need backup* look. She nodded. I flipped on the lights and stepped into the room.

"Hey, sleeping beauty," I said, trying to lighten the mood.

Harlow snorted but said nothing. At least he hadn't completely lost his sense of humor.

"You ready for this?" I stepped into the room to show him I was serious about getting going.

He grabbed a spare pillow and slammed it over his head with a loud huff.

Only one way to solve this problem.

I raced across the room and jumped on the bed, yelling "EARTHQUAKE!" like he used to do to me. He, of course, learned it from Jake and knew it annoyed me, but I figured a little lighthearted payback might soften the mood.

Harlow didn't move, but the next thing I knew, he swept my foot out from underneath me and I landed flat on my back on the bed. "Oh, no you don't!" He pinned me to the bed by my arms, and our eyes met. He looked at me with an intensity that I hadn't seen since before we broke up. I froze, trying to catch my breath.

Lydia cleared her throat loudly. "I thought we had somewhere to be this morning."

"Right." I shook my head to clear my thoughts.

Harlow released my arms. I slid off the bed. Our eyes locked for longer than usual. The real Harlow was still in there, still worth saving. I just didn't know how we were connected anymore.

I stepped toward Lydia but didn't take my eyes off Harlow.

"I'll let you freshen up, but we're leaving in five minutes."

"Got it," he said, barely audible, as if everything had finally flooded back and he'd buried the real version of himself again.

I pulled the door shut behind me.

Lydia elbowed me. "Cut that tension with a knife."

I turned my back so she couldn't see my extremely conflicted face.

Less than twenty minutes later, we rounded the corner toward the Coderie and stepped inside the windowed storefront that sat street level. The room was just as we'd left it after our coding competition—long card tables with computer stations set up—but no one was around. It wasn't completely unusual for a Saturday morning, but the quiet hum of the machines left an eerie sense that something bad was about to happen.

I motioned for Lydia and Harlow to follow me behind the counter to the long hallway, where there were a few offices and the back stairs to the basement.

"Hello?" I called out, hoping someone might be hiding in the back.

Bailen appeared at the top of the stairs like he'd been waiting for us. "We're all set. Come on down."

Next to me, Harlow's muscles tensed, but Lydia grabbed his hand. "Come on, Harlow. Let's go see what this is all about."

I let them pass. Bailen made his way up the narrow hallway, past Lydia and Harlow. When they disappeared down the stairs, he threw his arms around me and lifted me up so we could kiss, then held me there for a few moments to stare into each other's eyes before placing me back on my feet.

His eyelids drooped more than usual, but he otherwise seemed his usual self.

"You've been up all night." It wasn't a question. I knew he hadn't slept.

"I took a power nap, but we've been up since your dad arrived." He looked down, alluding to the fact that there was more he wasn't saying. It was bad.

"Just spit it out."

"Your dad thinks there might be a backup network or some sort of redundancy we missed, and someone is using that as a back door to access the loophole in Harlow's tracker."

"How? I communicated with every single one of those satellite links. That box was dead when we left." But something I thought was an illusion the night we brought the network down pricked my memory. A blue light I thought was my eyes adjusting to the darkness. Maybe it was something more, something we never could have anticipated. I should have mentioned it, even though it seemed like a fluke. Could I have avoided some of this pain for Harlow?

"What are you thinking?" Bailen asked.

"I thought I saw something in the cabinet that night, a flash of light after the server initially died. But I was tired and injured so I thought I was seeing things. Do you think this could be related to what I saw?"

Bailen shook his head. "Let's not jump to conclusions until we have more answers."

His calmness and unwillingness to make rash decisions was reassuring. Now that we knew there was a problem, we could collect the right data to back everything up.

Bailen held out his hand. I laced my fingers through his, following him toward the basement steps. At the top of the stairs, I pulled him back to me.

He smiled at first but then saw the worry on my face. "Now it's my turn to ask you: what's up?"

"Have you talked to Emily this morning?" I swallowed hard, the guilt washing over me for not calling immediately after Mom told me.

"No, why do you ask?"

I opened my mouth to tell him but then thought better of it. If he had to help Harlow, he wouldn't take kindly to knowing Harlow had done something to her, even if he may not have been in control when he did it. "It's nothing, just wondering how she's doing since we left her yesterday."

"All this craziness has you worried about those you care about, huh?"

"Yeah, something like that," I mumbled as Bailen started down the basement steps with me right behind. I couldn't help but worry, even if Mom said her injuries were minor. Emily must have been so scared. But I had to focus on what was happening with Harlow if we were going to stop this.

When I rounded the corner into the equipment room, the padded lounger was in the middle of the floor. Harlow was already seated in it, with his legs dangling over the side while Jeremy hooked up the discs to his temples and the base of his neck.

The setup resembled the Hive, the original Ghost hideout, only the space was a lot tighter. Fewer computers, but more people all staring at Harlow, packed in tight because the Ghosts never anticipated needing this equipment again. I shuddered as memories of my time in that chair flooded back. Everyone thought

I was either going to save them or self-combust.

Bailen withdrew his hand from mine and headed toward the computer terminal with three large monitors. I stepped beside Peyton, who was whispering with Ava. Was that a laugh that just escaped her lips?

Across the room, Peyton and Bailen's dad, Mr. Overland, chatted with my dad. He'd told me to call him Myles, but calling him by his first name was almost as weird as seeing him with my dad. They were two people cut from opposite sides of the same technology. Mr. Overland wrapped up his conversation with Dad, then rounded the outside of the room, stopping beside me and reading my expression. "Brings back memories, huh?"

I nodded, afraid that if I said anything, the words would come out shaky.

Mr. Overland squeezed my arm. "Don't worry, we'll figure this out just like we figured out your mess. He's in good hands."

I nodded again, knowing that was true, but kept my eyes on Harlow as he leaned back in the chair and Jeremy draped the wires over him so they wouldn't tangle. Lydia stood by Harlow's side, periodically squeezing his hand. Almost how Jake and I had intertwined our pinkies when they'd examined my tracker. I should have been over there with him, but instead I rocked on my heels, feeling powerless. Was this really what it had been like before?

Jeremy moved behind the bank of monitors with Bailen at his side. They both got to work typing commands and checking the settings.

"We're all set. Let's get started," Bailen said over the monitors.

"You'll feel a little tingle, but you shouldn't feel any pain," Jeremy added to smooth out Bailen's abrupt bedside manner.

Harlow closed his eyes and laid still. His breathing slowed like he was drifting off to sleep. He had to be worn out from reliving those horrors over and over again.

Before I knew it, data started appearing on the screens. Jeremy and Bailen typed in commands periodically. Dad stepped up and pointed to a few peaks on the graphs that were plotting. Jeremy and Bailen nodded along. I watched their faces for clues of what they were seeing, but they all had blank expressions, like they were the world's greatest poker players. Based on the things they'd seen, nothing fazed them anymore.

They all nodded again as if coming to some sort of an agreement. Bailen entered one last command. The hum of the machine slowed to a quiet lull. Just as anticlimactic as the last few times I'd sat in the chair.

It took everything in my power not to rush to Bailen's side and bombard him with a million questions. Especially since Jeremy left a vacant place while he helped Harlow remove the wiring.

I shoved my hands in my back pocket to stop myself from doing something stupid, and my right hand brushed against the USB drive. With everyone distracted, now was the perfect time to go investigate. As much as I wanted to hear the preliminary findings of Harlow's tracker signal, I needed to explore this drive more.

I bolted up the wooden steps, skipping over the creaky one, and raced down the hall and around the counter to plop in front of the first terminal. The main room was still empty. Perfect. No one to bother me.

I shoved the drive into the slot and booted up the computer. My heart pounded louder than the processor. I entered in a couple of commands to pull up the contents of the drive. A single file stared back at me, daring me to open it. I sucked in a breath and input the command to access the file. To my surprise, a lot of white space appeared surrounding three dark words.

Beware the loophole.

Nine

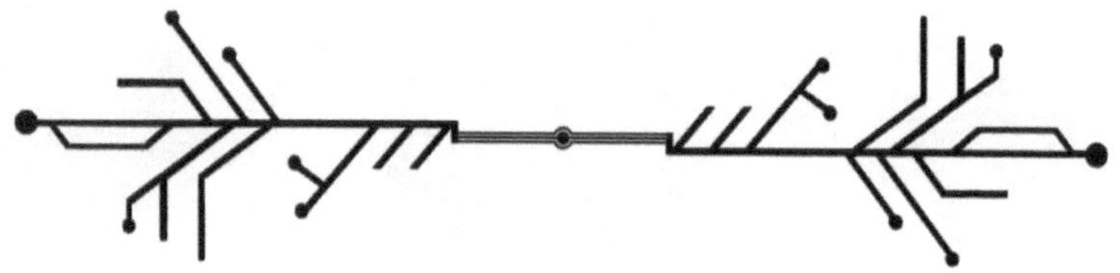

This had to be some kind of sick joke. What did that even mean? The package had come for Jake, but that didn't answer the question of who'd sent it. The cryptic message didn't really tell me anything I didn't already know, or at least what we already suspected. The question was, how? How was this all possible? Why had someone sent a drive that only had three words on it? It didn't make sense.

I disconnected the drive and shoved it back in my pocket, then rounded the desk toward the back hallway and nearly ran into Bailen.

"Where'd you go?" he asked.

"Bathroom." I stared over his shoulder, hoping he couldn't tell I was hiding something. "What did you find on Harlow's tracker?" I asked, trying to change the subject.

Bailen pulled me into one of the small offices cluttered with boxes and a broken-down loveseat. He plopped onto the cushion, sending dust into the air, then patted the seat next to him.

After closing the door, I flopped next to him, laid my head in his lap, and hung my legs over the arm of the couch. Bailen ran his fingers through my hair.

"There's definitely something active on Harlow's tracker. And it's talking to something."

"What though?"

"That's the question of the hour. There's no network active that it should be able to talk to."

Chills raced up my spine. First the message on the drive, now the confirmation that there was some sort of active network. "What does my dad think?"

"He suspects the same thing. Someone made a backup plan. My dad confirmed that suspicion as well. But none of us are sure where they're hiding it. The signal has numerous layers of encryption, so it might be impossible to trace."

"And Scurry?"

"Still in the same hole we left him."

Bailen stopped twirling my hair. I looked up at him. "How are we going to figure out who's doing this?"

He leaned down and kissed me. I ran my fingers through his wild hair and down his neck. His breath caught in his throat before the kiss deepened. I pulled Bailen closer. I couldn't get enough of the kiss. I needed to forget the world around me. He lifted my head from his lap and stretched out next to me. It was nice to have these few moments of peace.

I rolled to face him, and he pressed his forehead to mine. I closed my eyes and breathed deeply as we wrapped our arms around each other. Our breaths fell into sync. When he finally sat back from the embrace, leaving too much space between us, a sense of emptiness flooded me. Hopefully, there would be answers to fill that void.

Bailen's eyes searched mine, or maybe he was trying to commit me to memory, but something in his expression said things were about to change yet again. Everything was shifting so quickly. In a time where I was ready to move on, something had grabbed hold and dragged me back. I wasn't sure how this would affect me, affect Bailen, or affect us. While our relationship had been born in chaos, could it survive another round?

I opened my mouth to express my concerns, but Bailen put his finger to my lips. "Let's just enjoy one more quiet moment before we blow everything up again."

I winced at his choice of words. We'd lost so many people we'd cared about to explosions, both real and metaphorical. But he was right, so I gazed at him, soaking in his brilliant eyes. The swirls of green reminded me of the grassy area at a park Jake and I used to visit as kids.

Jake.

I shot up to a sitting position on the couch. There were too many questions nagging me to let them go unanswered any longer. We needed to know for sure how someone was leveraging the loophole to control Harlow.

Bailen sighed, then sat up. He put his arm around me and rubbed my shoulder in an attempt to calm me without breaking the silence between us. I didn't want to kill the mood either, but this whole thing was slowly eating away at me.

"What's the plan? How are we going to trace this signal?" The words spilled out before I could form more coherent thoughts.

"We aren't." Bailen shrugged as though not worried in the least.

"What do you mean we aren't? You're kidding, right?" My

voice rose an octave. The biggest scandal since the network collapsed six months ago, and he was just going to sit on his butt and do nothing. That didn't sound like the Ghosts at all.

Bailen's smile grew as he saw the realization hitting my face.

"Wait a minute."

He was definitely up to something. "I have a plan," he said with a growing smirk.

"Of course, you do." I poked him in the ribs, but when he didn't respond, I added, "And that plan is what, exactly?" A sad realization washed over me. If he could hold the plan in this long, he was hiding something.

"We're going to leave Harlow remotely connected to our tech and track the signal when it's in use. It's harder to mask when it's active. We'll have more time to trace the origins."

I slid away from Bailen. "Are you sure it's wise to let Harlow go through one of those nightmare-inducing control sessions again?" After everything I'd seen, I knew the answer was no, but I wasn't sure how to convince Bailen. Harlow was already traumatized in irreversible ways. One more nightmare could send him over the edge, especially if he hurt anyone else.

"He'll be closely monitored."

"Did he agree to this?"

Bailen's gaze shot to the floor. "Not exactly."

"Someone has to tell him. You have to let him decide if this is the right thing to do." How could Bailen be so reckless with Harlow's life? But Lydia was right all along about the tension. I should have known.

"If he knows, it could risk the whole operation. If this person who has access to him can control him, they not only have access to what happens around him, but they could possibly gain access to his thoughts and memories if they hooked him up to the right equipment. We have no idea what these people are capable of."

"But he's been here. Wouldn't whoever has access to his tracker know he's getting help?"

"They'd know he came to a tech center, but no centers have the technology to do what the Ghosts do. That's the only advantage we have right now. If we tell Harlow, it could compromise the whole mission."

He might have had a point, but it still felt reckless and unfair to do to Harlow what had been done to all of us. It betrayed his trust. I didn't know how long I could keep this secret. I owed that much to Harlow.

"What if he hurts someone?" I swallowed hard as I thought about Emily. Not a question of *if* but *when* Harlow did it again. He would be powerless to fight it. "What if we can't stop him? I don't think I can let him go through that again." The words tumbled out of my mouth.

"You can't let him?" Now it was Bailen's turn to jerk away from me.

"That's not what I meant. It's just, I watched him last night. He's in pain. This is changing who he is."

His face scrunched into a seemingly unnatural look. "It's too risky. You, of all people, should understand that."

"Please? He's still my friend." The word tasted metallic in my mouth. "I don't want anything bad to happen to him."

Bailen scowled. I felt the need to defend myself even though I shouldn't have to. "He doesn't have anywhere else to go for help."

Bailen's scowl grew. I sucked in a deep breath, choosing my next words carefully.

"Watching what he went through, I wouldn't wish that on my

worst enemy."

Bailen stood from the couch but said nothing.

Time for another tactic. This was exactly what Lydia warned me about… tension that could be cut with a carving knife. I'd been so blind to it. "Remember the nightmares I had when Jake died? Harlow's looked a million times more terrifying."

"You were sleeping with him?"

"No, let me explain."

But it was too late. Bailen's face changed again. His eyes turned hard, sharp, almost mean. "You cheated on him with me. Who's to say you wouldn't do it again?"

The words stung like an arrow to a bullseye. The truth hurt. But I'd only cheated because Harlow had done it first, and we'd grown apart. Things felt right with Bailen, or they had until now. My nerves fizzled and cracked inside me. We'd never fought like this before. My mind spun as I tried to explain why what he'd said was false. None of the words seemed good enough.

"He stayed the night." The words came out faster than I could control them, and each phrase sounded worse than the last. "In Jake's room, not with me."

Bailen stormed toward the door, but I grabbed his arm to stop him. "Would you just hear me out?"

He froze in place, breathing heavily. Possibly contemplating his next move. Instead of turning to face me, or asking me to go on, he pulled his arm through my fingers, opened the door, and left without another word.

My brain screamed to go after him, but every bone and muscle refused to respond as if the authorities had grabbed control of my tracker and rooted me in place.

Why did Bailen have to make everything harder? I thought he

trusted me. Nothing had happened with Harlow. Bailen was under a ton of pressure, but that didn't explain his behavior. He was pulling away from me because… he was jealous. And jealousy was a powerful weapon when wielded in the wrong hands.

I slumped onto the couch, the weight of the situation too much to bear. I needed to reassure Bailen that the only person for me was him. I needed to help Harlow, but no matter what I did, that wouldn't change my relationship with Bailen. He was the one who grounded me. Led me through the most difficult time in my life. Helped me be a better version of myself.

My breaths echoed in my ears. My heart pounded harder as it tried to pump the anxious energy coursing through my veins. I couldn't lose him. We had defied the tracker network together. We needed each other, and there was no doubt I'd need him again before all this was over. I'd have to find a way to get him to see it was nothing more than a friend helping a friend. Let Bailen see how important he was to me.

I rose from the couch, but my head spun from standing up too quickly. I squeezed my eyes shut and rubbed my temples. After a few deep breaths, I opened my eyes again.

A light blinked in the corner of my vision. My heart raced as a chat bubble appeared in the lower right-hand corner of my field of view with S.I.R.E. where two initials normally would have been.

My legs buckled. My knees slammed to the floor. I cried out in pain, but it came out more like a gasp as I tried to catch my breath. Questions flooded my mind.

None of them would have answers until I opened the message.

My breaths quickened as I blinked twice, quickly falling into a life I thought I'd left far behind.

S.I.R.E.: THIS ISN'T OVER. IT'S ONLY JUST BEGUN.

I blinked twice to minimize it. Fear wrapped its nimble fingers around me and squeezed my stomach. I gagged, choking down bile and coughing as I tried to get to my feet.

I needed help. I tried to scream, but my throat was too dry to allow much sound to come out.

I rushed toward the door. Before reaching the threshold, the chat bubble flashed again. Pausing mid-step, I opened the next message.

S.I.R.E.: TELL ANYONE AND I'LL HURT EVERYONE YOU LOVE. S.I.R.E.: YOU KNOW WHAT I'M CAPABLE OF. S.I.R.E.: I'M WATCHING YOU.

The messages disappeared the minute I finished reading it.

My heart pounded in my chest as the realization washed over me. Things were unfolding faster than we could unravel them, and someone was targeting me now.

I had to get to Bailen. Despite our fight, he would believe me. But with my tacker active, whoever S.I.R.E. was could easily track my movements and messages. They'd know if I didn't keep their secrets. If they could reactivate my dead tracker, they could listen to my conversations or control me the way they had Harlow.

I had to tell someone, but I didn't know how without S.I.R.E. finding out. On cue, another message appeared. I wasted no time opening it. The adrenaline coursing through me guided my reactions.

S.I.R.E.: It was so easy to control
Harlow. Weak minded. While it took far
longer to get to you, I always get what I
want. It's only a matter of time before I have
control over you, too.

I sucked in a deep breath in an attempt to stave off the terror building inside me. Before I could reply, another message popped up.

S.I.R.E.: Unless you do everything I tell
you…

This wasn't just about me. This was blackmail. Rage boiled inside me as I tried to formulate a plan.

The answer was clear. If Bailen could use Harlow as bait and get mad at me for helping him, then I could do some investigating on my own. I only had to decide if I could live with the consequences. I'd already lost my brother, so I knew the answer. Until I could figure out a way around the threat, this secret was mine to keep.

K.W.: Ok, let's play.
S.I.R.E.: Excellent. Stay tuned, more to
come.
K.W.: I look forward to it.

In a way, I did. I would nail whoever this was to the floor and make them suffer for every pain they caused me and those I cared about. I may not be able to talk about this mysterious message, but I could tell Lydia about the file on the USB drive.

I bolted from the office with renewed purpose and smacked right into someone else. I pushed past but halted when met with harsh words.

"Watch out! You don't need to barrel through here like a wrecking ball," Peyton snarled.

I didn't have time to deal with her attitude. Her moods swung more than a pendulum. Sometimes we were best buds, and other days she avoided me or attacked me as some sort of punishment for Jake's death, even though it hadn't been either of our faults. It had taken me far too long to realize she was dealing with the grief in her own way.

I whirled around to give her a disgusted look, but when my eyes met hers, her face softened.

"What's going on? You look like you've seen a ghost."

"It's nothing," I mumbled, then headed down the hall toward the steps to the basement, hoping she wouldn't follow me. I didn't have the energy to explain it was something much, much worse.

Ten

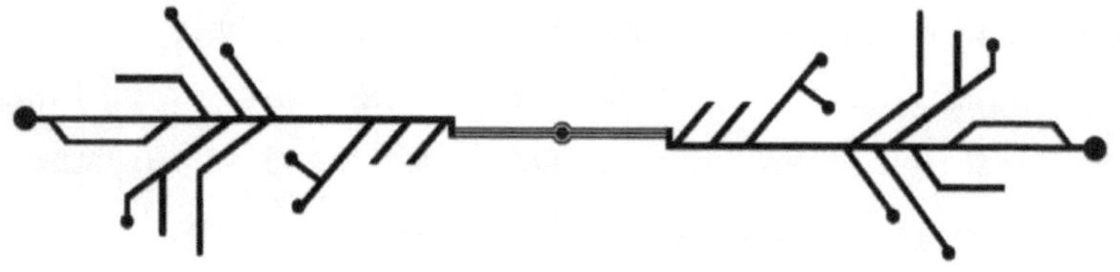

"Lyd..." I bent over and put my hands on my knees, huffing from running through the secret storage cellars underneath the Coderie. "Lydia," I gasped again, finally getting the word out loud enough for it to carry.

A few paces down the darkened, narrow hallway, a door creaked opened and Lydia's smiling face popped out. But her smile faded as she saw me. "What's up?" She stepped out of the room and eased the door closed behind her. "Did you look at that drive?"

I grabbed her hand and dragged her further down the damp hallway to the final door. "Not here." I opened it and pulled her through, letting the momentum carry her toward a round table with several chairs around it. I pushed her into one and plopped into the next one over. I'd occasionally used this room to draw when I got a sudden burst of inspiration between coding sessions. No one really knew to look for me here other than Bailen, who frequently spent time watching me as I drew, but he wouldn't come looking for me now. Not after our last conversation.

I slumped over, chest heaving, afraid to say anything.

"Kaya, what's going on? You know you can tell me anything."

I nodded, thinking carefully about how to tell her without S.I.R.E. catching on. Trackers used to allow for communication, access to knowledge, location tracking, and health monitoring. They also allowed for recall of dreams, conversation recording, memory recall, and the sharing of those saved files. When the network came down, all that changed—people gained privacy, but all capability was lost. However, if the loophole changed that, I'd have to be careful. Someone could be watching my every move, see who I was with, mind-control me, or something worse, making this trickier than ever. "The answer to your questions is yes."

Maybe if I didn't connect the dots, it wouldn't be clear if someone happened to be listening in. Lydia was quick to pick up subtle hints, so I didn't have to worry about her keeping up.

"And? What did you find?" Her eyes widened expectantly.

"One file."

"That's it?" Did you—"

I waved my hand under my neck, cutting her off.

She nodded.

I snagged one of my drawing pads on the edge of the table and grabbed a pencil from the case. I held up three fingers.

She nodded again, clearly understanding the three, but shrugged her shoulders and mouthed, *What?*

I twirled the pencil to find the edge I liked best, then wrote in our shorthand, *Words.*

"That's it?" she asked.

"SHHHHH."

Why? she mouthed. She pointed to me, then her eyes, a silent question asking if I was being watched.

"I'm not sure."

"Got it." She stared at the paper as if expecting the words to magically appear there. I scribbled the first word on the page in our secret shorthand, making sure not to look down at the paper. When she acknowledged, I flipped the paper sideways and found a new spot on the page for the last two words. As soon as she nodded, I ripped the page from the notepad and tore it up into pieces that were too small to be put back together. I opened my mouth to swallow some of the paper, but Lydia grabbed my arm.

"What? We can't be too careful."

She blew out a breath and shook her head. "That's overkill, don't you think?"

"I guess you're right." But I palmed a bit of the paper confetti and shoved it in my jeans pocket with the USB drive, then threw the rest in the trash can by the door.

"What do you think it means?"

"Better question: why risk sending it for just that?"

She rubbed her temples like she did when she worked a tough math problem. "Keep that thing close. I think there's more to it than meets the eye."

I nodded. She was right.

She stared straight ahead, not making any sounds, but I could tell the thoughts were swirling in her mind. Finally, she snapped her attention back to me. "What if it's like your tracker?"

"What do you mean?"

She nodded at the pad, but I scrunched my face in confusion. Lydia snatched the pencil from my hand and started drawing a series of lines and squiggles that looked familiar. Then the realization hit me like paint splattering on a canvas. I grabbed her hand, and she stopped drawing. When she looked at me, she finally saw my realization.

I took the pencil and wrote 220, to signify the 220 drawings that had been secretly loaded onto my tracker over time and ultimately led the Ghosts to the tracker schematics and the loophole. While we thought we'd snuffed out any possible chance the loophole could be utilized again, someone had found a way into the system.

More importantly, she wasn't pointing to the schematics from the 220 files, but to the files themselves. She was telling me that maybe the USB, like my tracker, had hidden files. Someone wouldn't have risked sending me this unless it was important. It was a lot more than three words. But finding those files wouldn't be an easy task.

"I think you're right." We were in perfect sync, per our usual fashion. "But how do we find the rest?" I asked, trying to be as cryptic as possible.

"I think you know the answer to that." She winked as if to say I should ask the smart techy nerd I was dating.

"We just had a massive fight." I buried my head in my hands, remembering his painful reaction. Our spat wouldn't be over quickly. Bailen's ability to ice someone out was worse than spending an hour in a walk-in freezer.

"Harlow." It was a statement, not a question. She'd warned me about the tension. I'd been too blind to see it, or maybe I wanted to be naïve for a little while longer. Too bad it had blown up in my face.

"How'd you guess?" I nudged her with my arm.

"I hate to say I told you so, but…"

"Yeah, you were right. Do you want a cookie or something?" I laughed even though everything was hitting the fan again. I was so glad I didn't have to abandon Lydia again to keep her safe. It was good to have her on my side this time. If recent events were any indication, we were going to need everyone possible to help solve this mystery.

"So…" She paused. I wasn't going to like what came next. "When do we tell Bailen?"

"I don't know if I can. He's stressed and jealous." The word tasted off in my mouth even though I knew it to be true. If I told him about the USB, then I might have to tell him about the mysterious message from my tracker, and that could make everything a lot worse. He'd want to accelerate the timeline and would push harder to use Harlow as bait. "He's got a lot on his plate. Do you think it's wise to add one more thing? This could just make things worse."

"I don't think you have a choice. You've come a long way on your skills, but I think this is above your head." She paused, and I could tell she was thinking something she was afraid to say. "Unless you want to ask your dad."

"Absolutely not. He'll take it away and never let me help." Even though I knew I should tell him too, there had to be a reason the package was addressed to Jake instead of Dad or me—unless whoever sent it didn't know Jake was dead and expected him to be around. Maybe they were trying to warn him Scurry was using him as a pawn. I couldn't quite put my finger on it, but something in my gut told me, in his absence, this message was meant for me.

"Then you know what you have to do," Lydia said, as if her words would help make the situation better between Bailen and me.

I nodded. I had one option left. The answer was staring me in the face all along, and it wasn't the one she was expecting. If it wasn't Bailen, I knew exactly who it had to be. Too bad she'd just steamrolled me in the hallway.

"Now that's a face I haven't seen before." Lydia half laughed, but there was a hint of fear behind it. She didn't like where this was headed. "No, you can't be serious."

"If it's not Bailen, then it has to be."

"But can we trust *her*?"

She didn't mean Peyton—she meant Ava. If I enlisted Peyton's help, she would ask Ava to crack the code, which was the kind of help we needed. She was the only person who could code circles around Bailen. While Peyton was improving her skills too, she'd found a friend in Ava, so there was no way she'd do this without Ava's help. Plus, they both owed me one after the stunt they'd pulled during the coding challenge. The only question was, did I want to trade in those coding lessons for help on this drive?

"This is the right move. Jake trusted Peyton. I do, too. And anyone Peyton trusts, I trust by proxy." I chewed my lip as all the possible things that could go wrong swam through my head. "Besides, Peyton deserves to know."

Lydia eyed me with an unasked question that made me squirm.

"I know she's not my best bud, but it involves Jake. Maybe she knows something. Besides, she and Ava have grown close. It's my only alternative."

"I still think you should tell Bailen." She looked at me the way Mom did when she was trying to guilt me into something.

"I will!" I sucked in a long breath, and when I let it out, I muttered, "When the time is right."

Lydia shot up from the chair. "It's been a while. I should go check on Harlow."

"Do you want to come with when I talk to Peyton?"

"Yeah, just give me a sec." She crossed the room and slipped through the door, leaving it cracked.

I tiptoed after her and quietly peered into the room Lydia had emerged from previously. She sat on the edge of the bed and brushed the hair on Harlow's forehead. His quiet breathing said he was fast asleep.

Lydia looked toward the door, then back at Harlow once more before heading back to the hall. She closed the door with a quiet click.

"Seems like he's finally resting peacefully." I said, glad his nightmares weren't affecting him right now.

"Yeah. He needs some solid sleep."

"Should we get someone to keep an eye on him?" I asked, remembering what Bailen said about secretly monitoring Harlow but unsure that was the kind of watching he needed.

"Nah, we won't be gone long."

I nodded but couldn't bring myself to tell Lydia about the bait situation, even if she would likely side with me. I couldn't add to this disaster.

We continued down the narrow hallway and pushed the backside of the bookshelf that led into the small, makeshift cellar where all the computer equipment was kept for monitoring trackers. I was surprised to find the room empty. I would have thought Bailen or Jeremy would have been there analyzing code, or even Dad poring over his notes and trying to understand what was happening and who was causing it. Maybe they'd finally decided to get some sleep, or they were in the war room discussing what to do next.

Either way, the eerie quiet gave the sense that something bad was about to happen. I proceeded up the back stairs and rounded the corner, then stopped dead in my tracks. Peyton had Ava pushed against the wall, their arms entangled and roaming each other's backs and hips. The unending kiss they were locked in seemed to be their moment of bliss in this insanity. I guess we were back to stealing moments when we could get them. We all deserved better, even if I was a little surprised to find them in each other's arms.

I cleared my throat, then loudly said, "Get a room."

"Very funny," Peyton said against Ava's lips, then she went back to kissing her.

Peyton pulled back from the kiss. Ava's devious grin appeared. Peyton nodded as though indicating they had some kind of secret between them then proudly said, "We don't think we need one, but if you don't like it, you can go elsewhere." Peyton leaned in for another kiss and Ava met her halfway. They kissed with wild abandonment, not caring that we were watching.

I was going to need a new tactic. "So… when did your door start swinging in this direction?" I cringed immediately after I said it, knowing it was mean, but it would do the job.

Peyton threw her arms down and stepped away from Ava, who stood against the wall with a smug expression on her face, a look that said she knew Peyton was going to tear me to shreds and Ava was going to enjoy watching it. "Not that it's any of your business, but my door swings in all directions."

Ava pulled Peyton close to her, and the tension in Peyton's shoulders eased. Her lips parted slightly. They met with Ava's again. She seemed to be enjoying herself.

Time to pull out all the stops. "AHH, my eyes are burning!" There was a hint of sarcasm and a hint of truth in the statement. Despite our ups and downs, Peyton had become like a sister. Likely because of the revelation that she'd secretly dated Jake. While I was glad to finally see her happy again, I definitely had seen enough of the semi-public make out session. I needed something to get her to stop and focus on me.

Peyton slowly withdrew from Ava's embrace. "Sorry. This was hot, but the mood is gone now."

"Now that I've got your attention…" I trailed off to make sure she wasn't going to cross the hall and deck me.

"This better be important, Weiss." Her gaze trained on me, eyes burning with the heat of a kiln firing pottery.

Wow, my last name. She meant business.

Lydia snorted behind me. "Oh, it's important."

Peyton glared at her but said nothing.

Before the situation escalated further, I blurted, "But not here. We need some protection." I needed some lead lining or a limestone cave to ensure I wasn't being watched.

"Why so cagey?" Ava finally joined the conversation after she'd composed herself.

"Long story. But not here," I said, waving my head toward the back door where the alley housed our flying crotchrockets.

"Tell me one good reason I should go with you." Peyton crossed her arms as if this was the final straw before it came to blows.

"She got some important mail," Lydia jumped in, trying to ease the tension.

Peyton was clearly unamused. "So?" She reached for Ava's arm, signaling I was out of time to convince her.

"Do the letters FFOB mean anything to you?" I asked before she could get away.

Her face changed from pissed to sad in an instant. "Jay—"

"Yes, but shhhh." I pressed my finger to my lips and angled my head toward the back door now. "Seriously, not here."

Peyton gazed into Ava's eyes like they shared an unspoken language. "I have to go take care of this."

"Actually…" I trailed off, knowing I was pushing my luck.

"Spit it out!" Peyton was so over all of this. I wasn't sure if she was going to punch me or collapse into a ball of tears.

"We're going to need Ava." I paused, then quickly added, "If that's okay." It really wasn't a request, but there was no way around this without her.

I pulled open the back door. This time, everyone followed. I stopped in front of my bike, Jake's old bike, to acknowledge the flaming art I'd previously drawn in his memory. I hoped this wasn't all in vain. Securing my helmet, I climbed on the bike.

"This better be good." Peyton hopped on her flying crotchrocket and kick-started it.

Moments later, we were airborne. I turned southeast toward the Hive. Everyone rode in silence. The wind whipped past. I wished it would take all my worry with it, but the questions swirled in my stomach, making me want to hurl.

As we crossed the river into Illinois, I angled my motorbike down toward the woods. Once I hit the ground, I cut the engine, allowing the bike to roll into a broken-down shed. The others did the same behind me and came to a stop inches away.

The Ghosts had repaired some of the shed but decided that the more tattered it looked, the less likely anyone would mess with it. It still had my crazed art on the walls, the black paint that I thought had been scribbles but turned out to be parts of schematics buried deep on my tracker.

I climbed off my bike and dangled my helmet off the handlebars. Without a word, I moved toward the back of the shed and pushed the pitchfork hanging on the wall. The trap door in the floor slid open. I stepped onto the creaking stairs; squeaks behind me told me the others weren't far behind. We proceeded down the narrow hallway, but as we approached the main computer room, I froze. Hushed voices drifted into the hallway.

Eleven

I held up my hand. The others stopped in their tracks. But I was met with only silence. My heart pounded so loud I was surprised no one heard it. I sucked in a ragged breath. The murmuring commenced again. I sighed in relief as I recognized the quiet voices.

"Dad?" I asked.

"Jeremy? Bailen? Dad?" Peyton added, not missing a beat.

"Uh, yeah? Pey, is that you?" Bailed called, louder than before.

We rounded the corner. Bailen and Jeremy were in front of several terminals while Dad and Mr. Overland were poring over some old schematics I'd drawn.

"Well, it sure as shit isn't the tooth fairy," Peyton said with a hint of annoyance in her voice. "Care to explain?" She eyed me with an unsaid question on her lips.

"I had no idea they were here." I looked at Bailen, who suddenly was very busy staring at his laptop screen.

Peyton shot me a look that said she didn't believe me for a

second.

"I swear." Honestly, if I'd have known they were here, I probably wouldn't have come. I wasn't ready to face Bailen.

Lydia caught my attention, "Well, while we're here—"

"Nope, this is a girl's thing." I grabbed Lydia's arm and dragged her toward the back corridor in the direction of the room I had stayed in.

"Whatever." Bailen rolled his eyes and went back to muttering under his breath to Jeremy.

"Have fun, girls," Dad called after us, seemingly oblivious to all the unspoken drama. Mr. Overland didn't look up from the drawings to acknowledge the awkward situation.

"Thanks!" I yelled back and pulled Lydia toward my makeshift Hive bedroom. Peyton and Ava followed behind like attack dogs on patrol.

I stepped into the room and backed against the wall so the others could file in, then slammed the large metal door shut with a loud clang.

"All right, enough with the charade. Who is going to tell me what's going on?" Peyton stood against the far wall with her arms crossed, next to my mural of drawings that contained all the people I loved. The ones I'd drawn, all with Jake's eyes. In a way it was fitting.

"Kaya thinks she's being watched," Lydia explained before I could think of where to start.

"Lydia, geez." I slapped the bottom of her foot that dangled off the edge of the bed and plopped down next to her. Thank goodness for the signal blocking protection the Hive provided.

"What does that have to do with us?" Peyton asked.

"Nothing," I said, eager to change the subject. No one could know about the messages on my tracker. The fewer people who knew, the less likely S.I.R.E. would catch on. Who knows what they would do if they found out I'd told other people. With the shielding at the Hive, as long as I didn't save any memories of this while my tracker appeared inactive, I should be safe.

"Then remind me why we're here?"

"Because I need your help." I tried to swallow the lump forming in my throat but it only grew more painful. "You deserve to know, but I couldn't talk about it at the Coderie."

"We get it, cause you're being watched." Ava grabbed the only chair in the room and sat backward in it, reminding me of Jake.

"Right." I took a deep breath, then prepared my story.

Peyton's face hardened. "You've got three seconds to spill or I'm out of here."

"I got a package," I said before I could lose my nerve. "It was addressed to Jake."

"So, you're opening his mail now?" Peyton scoffed, but I could see a hint of intrigue in her eyes.

"He's dead. He's not exactly coming back to open it." The words came out harsher than I anticipated. They cut deeper than I imagined they would. "Honestly, I was so confused I didn't know what to do with it or what it meant."

"She wanted to turn it over to her parents until I showed her the letters on the side of the package," Lydia added, finally steering the conversation in the right direction.

"Okay, I'll bite. This better have something to do with FFOB." Peyton shot me a look that said if I didn't get to the point soon, she was going to bolt faster than the night she'd told me I wasn't the only one who'd loved Jake.

"That's exactly what it has to do with," I said.

Peyton's eyes grew wide, but her expression saddened like she'd seen a ghost. Maybe we all had. "So, he sent it to himself?"

"That's one theory," I said, knowing there was always more to puzzles like this. "The other is that someone else sent it to him. Someone who knew enough about him to know the importance of FFOB, but someone who maybe didn't know he'd died."

"Who the hell would that be?" A hint of desperation entered Peyton's voice, like she was grasping hold of any possible connection that remained to Jake, no matter how tiny.

"I'm not sure." She had a point. The people who knew him best all knew what had happened.

"But more important is what was inside." Lydia couldn't help herself, she loved to tell a good story. And once again, I appreciated her keeping us on track. It was only a matter of time before either of the dads or one of the guys came looking for us.

"Just tell us already." Peyton clearly didn't enjoy Lydia's flare for the dramatic.

"It was a USB. And before you ask, yes, I looked at what was on it," I added, eager to move this along.

"You plugged a mysterious jump drive into the Coderie computers?" Ava asked.

"What? We think it's from Jake. What could go wrong?" But suddenly I didn't feel so great about my decision to dig further without help.

"Only a million and one things. That's the trouble with our tracker generation and why the authorities almost won. We didn't know about all the embedded malware on old tech. The authorities scammed a lot of people who wouldn't get on board with the trackers." I'd never heard the cautious side of Ava before. I didn't think it existed beyond her wild ability to flaunt her coding skills and turn everything into a competition.

"How do you know all about this stuff?" I asked, genuinely curious because I hadn't ever heard Ava talk much about her past. Beyond witnessing her incredible coding knowledge, she'd never mentioned how she'd learned it all.

"I was trained in old tech. I know almost every trick to find hidden tech viruses and even how to make my own."

"Funny you should mention that." Lydia was really eager to see how this one unraveled.

"I take it you want me to look at the drive," Ava said, not missing a beat.

I knew I liked her. She didn't mince words and got right to the point.

"Yeah, exactly. When I plugged it into the computer, there was a single file with three words."

Peyton crossed the room and stood next to the bed as if being closer to me and what I had to say would bring her closer to Jake or bring a part of him back.

"'Beware the loophole' was all it said. I'm not sure what it means other than it's likely linked to what's happening to Harlow." I wished I had more computer skills so I could have dug deeper into the drive. My theory didn't have much evidence to stand on.

"Do you think it means Harlow's not the only one?" Lydia asked.

Ava let out a long breath. I caught a hint of fear in her eyes. "I hate to admit it, but I think that's exactly what it means."

While I was glad my instincts weren't off, the fear of what that meant crept up inside me. "Why control people in the first place?" I never understood why the authorities needed that capability. Sure, freezing people in place to arrest them seemed useful at first, but it was a gross invasion of free will, and they'd abused it. Used it against innocent people like Lydia's brother.

"While freezing people made it a lot easier to catch criminals, I'm not sure people need to be mind-controlled to comply. I've seen the effect on people able to control others beyond just freezing them. They get drunk with power," Ava said with a concerned look, implying maybe she knew more than she was saying.

"We have to find out what's on that drive. It could contain information to help fight this loophole." I had no doubt the USB drive was the key to this.

"I think this is a really bad idea." The fear on Peyton's face was hard to ignore.

It was odd to hear her try to be the voice of reason. Something about that drive must have scared her.

"Why?" I hoped the question wouldn't send her over the edge.

"Whatever is on that drive could be the reason Jake isn't here today."

I shook my head. It had taken me months to come to grips with the fact that his death wasn't my fault. "The explosion was an accident. You were there, you should know that." The angry words flew out of my mouth before I could stop them.

Peyton's face hardened. "All I know is the supply run was supposed to be clean. We tripled-checked it. But something changed." Her voice was shaking. I couldn't tell if it was from fear or anger.

"We'll never know for sure unless we check out that drive." Ava had already grabbed her laptop from her backpack while Peyton and I were debating.

I jumped up from the bed and crossed the room in two large strides. Yanking the USB drive from my back pocket, I placed it onto the table next to Ava. "Have at it. I hope you have better luck than I did." Deep down, I knew she'd find something but wasn't sure if it would destroy Peyton or me in the process.

Ava typed a whole bunch of commands into the prompt screen before even acknowledging the drive on the table. "Okay, let's see what kind of secrets we have in our hands." She slid the USB drive into the laptop on the first shot, making me wonder how she managed that.

I looked over Ava's shoulder. I tried to track what she was doing as she opened windows, checked information, and typed commands in the prompt window, but she moved too quickly for me to follow her path. After another long string of code and an error response, she sat back and chewed on her thumbnail to help her think better.

I glanced at Lydia, but she shrugged her shoulders. Peyton had finally sat down at the foot of the bed and pulled her knees up to her chest. She was afraid of what Ava might find on the drive. I'd never seen her shut down so quickly.

"What can I do to help?" There was likely nothing, but my nerves were too on edge to wait around and do nothing.

"Keep quiet. I'm trying to think," Ava shot back, then leaned forward and typed in some more commands. An error message popped up again, but when she clicked okay, dozens of windows popped up with hundreds of files.

"Whoa!" Ava pushed back from the computer with eyes wide as if it had a contagious virus.

"What the heck is all that?" I knew none of us had the answers, but I couldn't take the silence any longer.

"Let's find out." Ava moved her mouse over the file.

"WAIT!" Peyton flew from the bed and was across the tiny

room in moments. "We have no idea what this drive is or where it came from. What if it's a trap?"

But it was too late; Ava had already clicked one of the files. A password box popped up. "Doesn't matter. They're all encrypted. It's going to take a while to crack all this."

"Should we, though?" Peyton asked.

"Seriously? Now you get a conscience? What is going on?" I asked, a bit annoyed by her hesitancy.

She wasn't telling us a reason we should be wary.

Peyton twisted her long, dark hair into a knot. "I know exactly what's on this drive."

I froze. This was the last thing I expected from her. "How?"

"Because I've seen it before. Well, not everything, but…" She trailed off as she struggled to find the right words. "It was a short time before Jake sent me to bring you to the Hive. He had been acting really strange. He told me he'd been losing chunks of time. I didn't know why he was blacking out, but it's pretty clear now."

I drew in a heavy breath as Peyton's words confirmed what I'd always suspected. Someone had been exploiting Jake's loophole, controlling him. Making him the mole to the Ghosts.

"I went looking for him one night when he didn't come to hang out. He was typing furiously on his laptop like his life depended on getting all the information out. The minute he saw me, he closed the file and slammed the laptop shut, but not before I saw something similar to this: hundreds of encrypted files in multiple folders."

"And you're sure it's the same?" I wondered if all this Jake talk was triggering some false memories. If I was being honest with myself, it was pulling my emotions in a million different directions.

"Positive. How many people have hundreds of encrypted files?

And I remember the exact USB sticking out of his computer."

"Did you see anything else from the drive?" Lydia asked, trying to gently steer the conversation forward without spooking Peyton.

"No, that was the first and last time I saw that drive until today. But the state Jake was in when I found him tells me no good can come from the contents. He was obsessed with finishing what he started on the drive, but he refused to talk to me about it. Maybe there was a reason for that—the secret should have died with him." Peyton returned to the bed and drew her knees up to her chest again.

Peyton's words gave me pause, but if they were true, we wouldn't have the USB drive now. "If we're going to unravel this mystery, we need to know what Jake was tied up in, and we need to figure out if Harlow is linked to it in some way." I sat on the edge of the bed and squeezed Peyton's knee. "Are you going to be okay if Ava decrypts these files?"

This was such new ground for us. I'd never seen Peyton crumble before. Usually, her walls were up and it was impossible to know what was going on, what she was thinking, how she was feeling. Something about this drive terrified her. I needed to find out why.

She nodded ever so slightly.

"Are you sure? I don't have to do this." Ava caught Peyton's gaze from across the room. "I'll stop if you tell me to."

Peyton nodded again, then buried her face between her knees. "Do it. I need to know what happened to him. What had him so scared."

Ava returned to the files and entered some more commands, then sat back in the chair again. "This is going to be a beast to crack. Mind if I hold on to this drive?"

"Sure, but let me know the minute you find out anything new."

Lydia's eyes widened, and I sensed a hint of frustration bubbling inside her as if I was making a grave error.

"And make me a copy," I added. "Give it to Lydia if you can't find me."

Lydia's shoulders relaxed. "I'll keep it safe."

"Sure thing." Ava shut down her computer and removed the drive before shoving it in her front pocket.

A knock echoed off the metallic door. We all jumped like we'd been caught with the lights on after bedtime.

Twelve

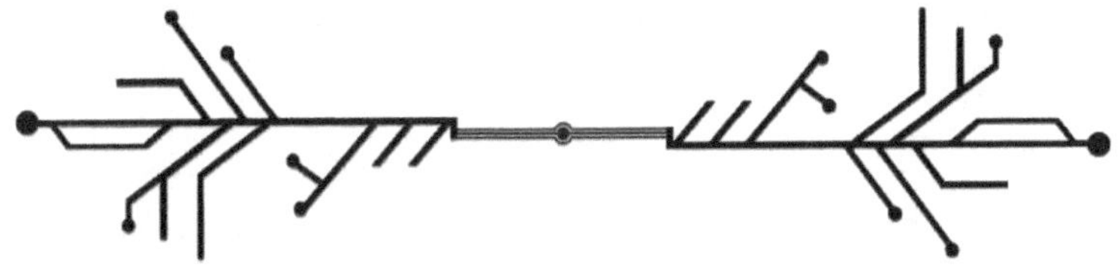

Once I caught my breath, I shuffled to the door and opened it with a loud screech. Bailen, Jeremy, and Dad stood outside.

"What are you girls up to?" Dad asked, clueless to Bailen standing behind him staring at everything but me.

"We've been talking over some things... You know, about the loophole." I figured if I gave a little detail, he wouldn't ask too many questions.

"About that..." Dad trailed off.

What he was about to say would probably upset me.

"Dad, you promised you wouldn't keep things from me anymore, so just spit it out." I froze in shock as the words that tumbled out sounded more Peyton-like than my own. Dad's secrets had left me alone, torn me away from everyone I cared about and sent me down a path that almost killed me—and ended Jake's life far too soon.

I looked at his eyes and found a hint of hurt surrounded by

concern.

"I'm sorry," I muttered under my breath. I hadn't meant to be so harsh, but if the worst was happening, I needed him to tell me everything. I couldn't let him keep any more massive secrets from me. It had damaged my trust in him and made it difficult to repair.

"I think my daughter and I need to have a chat."

"And that's our cue to leave." Peyton shot up from the bed, grabbed Ava's hand, and dragged her from the room.

Jeremy looked at Lydia, but she nodded him on. Then she stood from the bed, embraced me, and whispered in my ear, "This might be the perfect time to tell him."

I shook my head. Dad had been avoiding me since this whole thing started again. Well, before that, actually. He'd been putting up a wall ever since we'd "talked" about why he'd hidden those files on my tracker as a baby, why he'd never told me, why he'd dropped clues my whole life, and why he'd left me to figure it out on my own. While my brain understood why he'd done it, my heart hadn't fully forgiven him for everything he'd put me through. He owed me answers. Not just the surface level he'd been giving me for the last six months, but an honest explanation for everything he'd done. If what he had to say was good enough, then—and only then—could I maybe start trusting him with my secrets.

Jake taught me that found family was real. That I could trust the Ghosts and their mission even though I hardly knew them at the time. He'd built that trust with them since the day Dad dropped him off on their doorstep rather than letting him go to college. Jake had been in on part of the secret about my tracker, but he'd been a victim of Dad's lack of explanation, too. He'd made amends with me. Dad still had a lot to make up for. Through his actions, I learned that blood relation didn't mean as much as I thought it had. If Dad wanted to be family, then he needed to prove it to me, blood or not. He didn't get to be trusted just because we shared DNA.

Lydia nodded and whispered, "I get it." She knew how I felt about this, but her face still said I should reconsider. She withdrew from our hug and pulled the door shut behind her, leaving the air heavy with things unsaid.

I sat on the edge of the bed and Dad grabbed the chair, somehow knowing I didn't want him next to me. Scenes from when Jake came to see me after I first arrived at the Hive flashed through my mind. He had managed to explain his side to me well enough. Maybe Dad would too.

Dad took a deep breath, then began. "Bailen walked me through his plan for Harlow's loophole exploitation. It's well thought out and airtight."

"Great, so now Bailen is using you against me?" If Bailen wasn't icing me out already, it'd be me putting him in the freezer. Everyone in my life suddenly had some sort of explaining to do, some trust to repair to prove that maybe they could see beyond what they thought was best and understand the whole picture. Their plan didn't have Harlow's best interest at heart and didn't consider what he or I truly needed. He failed to recognize how important it was to me to help others and not lose anyone else.

I needed someone who would help me figure a way out of this mess on my own terms, not theirs.

"I'm not going to get in the middle of what's going on with you two. It's none of my business."

"Good, then stay out of it." I crossed my arms and stared at the fuzz balls on the blanket beneath me.

"Kai, what is this *really* about?" Dad remained in his chair and made no effort to comfort me, and I was glad. I didn't want his pity.

"It's about all the secrets. Everything I believed about my life was a lie." Tears welled. The pain I'd been through bubbled inside me. Even though Dad was proud of the outcome, I still felt like maybe shutting down the tracker network hadn't been the right answer. Maybe there'd been another way, but the events that led me here had shoved me on a path I couldn't get off of, a path Dad laid the foundation for. A path he gave me no choice but to walk.

"I thought we had moved past this, but clearly the reemergence of the tracker loophole is pressing on a sore spot."

"Sore is an understatement," I muttered. "It still doesn't change what you've done."

"I did what I had to do. Let me tell you the whole history and see if that changes your perspective a bit."

I nodded, but frustration and anger still churned inside me. His view felt very one sided. I wasn't sure his explanation would alter how I felt.

"Trackers revolutionized the world. It changed how we did everything—from communication to convenience. Some of it was good; life expectancy increased with the health monitoring capabilities, crime dropped with the location tracking, evolution of modern conveniences moved faster, and people communicated more. But things slowly changed."

"The world sounded much better at the start." And despite the implementation of tracker technology happening before I was born, I'd heard these stories before in school when they taught us the history of trackers.

"It was. People viewed trackers as a huge leap forward, but others didn't want anything to do with it. Then some decided the technology needed to be regulated. To some degree, they weren't wrong. People were abusing trackers, scamming others with apps and communications that allowed access to bank accounts and personal information. They found ways to hide in the system. But the regulations came, and they needed an entity to hold everyone accountable. Slowly, things shifted from freedom, accessibility, and a world where things were shared freely, to a place where people were commanded to do things and expected to comply. Every action was tracked, every conversation monitored in case it could be used to prove someone's guilt. The bad actions of the few led to overregulation for the general population."

My brain swirled. It seemed like a natural progression until it wasn't, but I didn't understand how so many people just accepted all the restrictions and loss of privacy as it unfolded. And it still didn't explain why I should forgive Dad for what he'd done then and what he was doing now. "Why didn't more people fight the changes? Fight the authorities?"

He shrugged, less from not knowing and more from recognizing the irony of the situation. "I don't think we will ever fully understand the transition. Looking back, there are a few things I do know. Things happened over time. People didn't seem to notice that they were being monitored at first. And if they never had issues or never had a run-in with the authorities, there was very little negative impact or change to their lives."

"Out of sight, out of mind, I guess." I knew the full truth of the statement. While I grew up knowing in my gut there was something off about the authorities, most of the time I didn't think about them because I didn't have to deal with them much, until that night in the woods.

Dad nodded. "The problem was, and still is really, that only a few of us see the bigger picture. See the bad things that are coming."

"But how do you know it will be as bad as you think?" I paused, because even I knew this wasn't good. "How do you know your actions are the right ones?"

"I don't for sure, but this seems like the best way to stop whatever this is."

I scowled. "Is it though? You, Bailen, and the others won't listen to what anyone else has to say about this."

Dad let out a long breath. "I can see this situation is bringing up some hurt feelings. Maybe you need some time—"

"This isn't about hurt feelings." I cut him off before he could finish. I had heard enough, and it still didn't add up for me. "It's about you running off with Bailen and treating him like a Jake replacement and ignoring me in the process." Those words weren't exactly what I'd meant to convey, but having said them, I realized they weren't a lie.

He winced, but I couldn't stop. It was all spilling out of me like a knocked over can of paint.

"You're siding with him on a plan that's probably going to get Harlow killed. You sided with him when you recruited his dad and whole family to run the Ghost operation, and you sided with him when it came to Jake, too. You sent Jake here and didn't tell me. You let me think he was ignoring me, instead of trusting me with the truth."

My words came out harsher than I intended, but I was struggling to get my true feelings out. Struggling with how to tell Dad that he'd left me out of every important decision and was doing it all over again. Nothing had changed.

My eyes welled with tears. Every time I'd needed Dad, he'd

lied to me. He was supposed to be my dad. Supposed to be my support system. While Mom never got in the middle of us fighting, at least she always heard both sides of the story and provided comfort. Dad couldn't sympathize or even attempt to see my side of the story.

Instead, he took the one person I'd needed during a time when I'd sought answers. He'd left me to deal with the weight of the world alone. I shouldn't have been surprised that he left me out of the loop again when it came to Harlow and his tracker issues. And heaven forbid he ask how I'm doing through all this.

Dad sat silently, as if he was contemplating how to smooth this all over. I let the silence persist. I couldn't tell him everything that was happening with S.I.R.E. He'd sideline me. He'd lock me in the Hive and never let me out. Then I couldn't stop them from getting Harlow killed. Harlow didn't deserve to be used as bait. His life was worth more than being some pawn for a greater cause, even if that cause carried a weight bigger than one person.

Dad's actions had sent Jake down a dangerous path that got him killed. If I was being honest, he'd put me at risk too, put me in a situation that could have gotten me killed as well. He made a tracker-free world more important than his children. More important than me.

In the beginning, I wasn't old enough to tell him not to hide those files on my chip. He'd used me to solve his problems. Put me in the path of the authorities with a wish and a prayer that something bad wouldn't happen to me. He's lucky nothing did. After everything, I couldn't let him do the same thing to anyone else.

Dad took a deep breath, then finally broke the silence. "You know you're always my first priority." He leaned forward in the chair, but I slid back against the wall so my legs lay across the bed.

"You probably said the same thing to Jake, and look where that got him," I spat back. I watched as his expression hardened, but his eyes saddened. I should have cared that I was hitting below the belt, but I didn't. He needed to know his actions had consequences.

He opened his mouth to speak, but a knock at the door stopped him. The metal clanged as the door swung open. Bailen poked his head in. He quickly found Dad, ignoring that I was even present.

"It's time. Harlow's loophole is activated."

"I'll be right there."

"You let him leave the protection of the Hive so you could use him as bait?" I grit my teeth to avoid yelling all the awful thoughts spiraling in my head.

Bailen's gaze briefly caught mine before shooting to the floor as he closed the door. I wished Bailen could put his jealousy aside.

"Don't do this." The chances of this ending badly for someone I cared about were incredibly high. "There's got to be another way. Something less risky." The desperate words flew out of my mouth faster than I could think them.

"I'm afraid we're out of time." Dad stood from the chair and crossed the room to the door. "If we don't track down whoever is responsible, this could have dire consequences for the whole world."

"What about dire consequences for the people we care about?" I spat back. "Someone else is going to die, and I'm going to blame you." The words had to have stung my dad, because even I felt how heavy they were dangling out there. I wasn't sorry I said them. He needed to hear the blunt, honest truth.

Dad paused and lowered his head. Maybe he was having

second thoughts about this conversation. He pulled open the door but didn't turn to face me. "After everything that happened to Jake, no matter what, I love you. Keeping you safe is all I care about." He closed the door behind him without another word.

And that was exactly what I was afraid of.

Thirteen

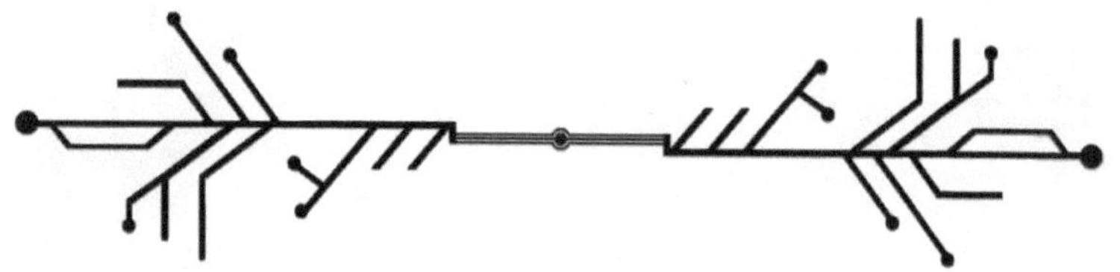

After taking a few minutes to let the shock drain out of me, I stomped down the hall into the Hive's main computer room. Bailen was at a terminal typing away. The big screen along the back wall was powered on. A large map of the city displayed a single red dot, which I assumed represented Harlow's current location. Jeremy and Dad sat on either side of Bailen, pointing at lines of code and monitoring data that was already being collected. Mr. Overland was inputting parameters on a few computers off to the side.

Ava was at the next set of computers, running some code of her own, and Peyton sat in the chair next to her, but her focus was glued to the projected map. The rest of the room was a complete mess. Boxes everywhere, half hooked up computers, wires draping over tables like they'd been abandoned mid-setup. The Hive had never been perfect, but this wasn't anywhere near its full operational capacity.

Lydia stood next to Peyton but looked up when I entered the

room. I shook my head to tell her not to ask, but she was already making her way across the room toward me. Probably to tell me how wrong I was to not tell my dad.

"Are you okay?" she asked.

I blinked in surprise, not expecting that question. "Why?"

"Because you look like you've seen a ghost, and I'm not talking about the coding geniuses in this room."

I half laughed but knew she was picking up on the unrest of the room. "I just don't think this is the right way to track down the source of the loophole. I think it's putting Harlow in unnecessary danger."

"I'm worried about him too, but we all know if anyone is going to figure this thing out, it's the people in this room."

I shrugged because, while she was right, I didn't like how they were going about things. But the time to argue with them had passed. The red dot on the map was on the move. "How do we know his tracker is being exploited right now?" I wanted to ensure this really was as airtight as Dad and Bailen said it was.

Bailen opened his mouth to speak but quickly closed it as though suddenly remembering he was still mad at me.

Jeremy came to my rescue instead. "We hacked into his tracker and are able to watch his brain waves using the tracker's health monitoring capability. Right now, it's like Harlow's sleepwalking. He's not fully conscious but not fully asleep either."

The answer surprised me. Maybe they really had thought through a lot of the details about how it all would work. But that didn't mean I wouldn't keep asking questions to ensure nothing had been overlooked.

"Let's see where he goes," Dad added.

"What are the likely candidates?" Jeremy asked.

"I'm sending over some data now." Mr. Overland didn't look up from his computer but kept typing.

Bailen flipped to a new window with a chat screen from his dad. "Based on our data, there are a couple of old authority hideouts: the authority station and Global Tracking Systems." Several blue dots appeared on the projected map ahead of where Harlow was headed.

Ava moved around the computers and picked up a laser pointer from the edge of the table. "There are a couple of other safe houses and off-grid authority buildings in these two quadrants." She circled a couple areas on the map with the laser.

"How do you know that?" I wondered how she had access to what appeared to be secret information. Only Lydia seemed to register my question. Everyone else was busy with their tasks.

"I used to work for the authorities." Ava said it so matter of fact, like it wasn't a big deal.

I opened my mouth to ask one of the many questions forming in my mind, but Bailen cut me off.

"We don't have time to debate her past."

His words stung more than I expected. I wasn't sure if it was because he didn't seem to care about her past, or if it was something he knew and had chosen to keep from me. Or because he was more focused on using Harlow as bait than looking for flaws in his hastily constructed plan. Regardless, the divide between us was now a chasm. I could no longer see him on the other side.

"Ava, bring me the coordinates. I'll get them added to our database," Bailen replied in his natural tone, demonstrating his ease in talking to anyone but me.

Ava handed him a scrap of paper with some coordinates on it. The new dots appeared on the screen one at a time as Bailen entered them into the computer.

"He's turning. That knocks out a couple of possible locations." Jeremy typed some commands into his computer.

Several dots on the map went gray. Lydia and I watched as Jeremy and Bailen adjusted the map to the changing conditions.

"His vitals are still strong." Dad input more commands into his computer. "Right in range with what we'd expect from someone under the tracker influence." He paused, realizing that wasn't a good enough explanation, and added, "There's no indication anything will change from this state."

"Let me know if you need me to look at the failsafe code," Mr. Overland said to Dad.

Dad gave a slight nod. His reluctance to share more made me think they were up to something, but they weren't ready to share with the rest of us. I swallowed hard and hoped it was something that would protect Harlow.

Lydia put her arm around my shoulder and pulled me toward her. I was glad she was by my side. There was no way I could do any of this without her. Especially if things took a turn for the worse.

When the map was down to about a dozen locations, the tension in my shoulders released. I sat in a nearby desk chair. Maybe nothing bad would happen to Harlow. Maybe it really was a routine plan.

Despite feeling a little better, my guard was still up, keeping an eye out for anything out of the ordinary. I made sure to check on Ava more frequently after the bomb she dropped, but nothing seemed out of the ordinary with her. That didn't make me worry any less, since I'd handed over the most important message from Jake less than an hour earlier. I hoped I wouldn't regret that decision or trusting Peyton's judgement.

As Harlow's red dot turned another corner and two more spots grayed out on the map, my breath caught in my throat. In the bottom right-hand corner of my vision was a blinking box with "S.I.R.E." inside. I backed away from Lydia, who was also watching the map, and moved into a desk chair on the edge of the room. I sat at the computer to make it look like I was checking on something, but if anyone looked close enough, they'd see the computer wasn't even plugged in.

Panic welled as dread washed over me. Not only was S.I.R.E. watching, but they'd reached me in the Hive. Sure, the Hive was still being reconstructed, but it was lined with material designed to block tracker signals. How was this message getting through? Maybe the Ghosts had missed a section when rebuilding and there was a hole in the coverage. Either that or S.I.R.E. was eight steps ahead of us and I'd have to be faster.

I closed my eyes, took a deep breath, then blinked twice while thinking about the message. It popped up instantly.

S.I.R.E.: Who is watching who?

My breathing quickened as terror gripped my insides. How could S.I.R.E. possibly know what we were up to? I whirled around in the chair so my back was to the map and all I could see was an empty wall. If S.I.R.E. was watching through my eyes or my tracker, I didn't want to give them any more information than I already had.

Before I could think of something witty to respond with, another message appeared like a stream of consciousness app.

S.I.R.E.: If any of your friends interfere
with my plans, I'll make sure they're next.

My mind spun like a pottery wheel. My brain felt like collapsed clay on the spinning table. How was I going to stop this from ending badly for everyone I cared about?

K.W.: What about me?

S.I.R.E.: Keep your friends out of my
way and everything will be fine.

I risked a glance back at the map. Only three dots were left, Global Tracking Systems and two underground authority prisons. I sucked in a long breath, knowing what I had to do if I was going to protect Harlow. I surveyed the room. Everyone was head down in a computer except Peyton, who was hyper-focused on the map.

I shot up from my chair, but Lydia blocked my path.

"Oh no, you don't." She held her hand in front of my face as if that would stop me. "You're up to something aren't you?" whispered close to my ear so no one else would hear.

My eyes widened. I should have known she could read me like a fortune. "Lydia, I have to do something."

"If you go, I'm telling them your secrets."

I examined her expression. There was no bluff there. She'd expose me if I left. My gaze darted, but everyone was oblivious to us, occupied by their current tasks. I weighed the options in my mind over and over again. Each time I came to the same conclusion.

"Tell them if you must, but I have to stop this." It was all clear to me now. This mysterious contact never said I couldn't stop them. They said to keep my friends out of the way. I intended to use that ambiguity against them. I looked once more at the map. Two dots left, but it didn't matter anymore. I knew exactly where Harlow was headed. "I'm sorry," I said to Lydia, making sure my tone conveyed the full message to her—that I couldn't let Harlow go through this again, the pain of losing control. I was going to put a stop to this, and I'd do it alone if I had to.

I bolted around Lydia and down the long, narrow hallway toward the trap door. I raced up the steps, letting the trap door slam shut behind me. Two long strides put me in front of the bike. I smashed on my helmet, mounted the flying crotchrocket, and kick-started it with one swift movement. Revving the engine, I peeled out from the barn, the wind whipping past me. Then I was in the air and headed right for Global Tracking Systems.

My mind buzzed with whatever S.I.R.E. could possibly want there. But the more questions that flooded my head, the more I could tell what they were after. There was only one thing in that building that might help with the loophole: the server I overloaded when I brought down the tracker network. While the network had remained dormant, a part of me always questioned if I really had seen a light in that server box. Everything in my gut told me that thing was allowing access to the network in some way. Allowing someone to access the switches in people's trackers and mind-control them just like they had with Harlow.

Maybe the connection was sleeping or playing dead, but someone was trying to use Harlow to wake it up. I couldn't let that happen.

I landed on the roof of the building but, unlike last time, the roof was dark and no authority guards were anywhere to be found.

The building had been abandoned shortly after that night we all snuck in and shut off the tracker connections to every living person on the planet.

It was on this roof I saw a side of Bailen I had never wanted to see, the warrior within. The guy who would stop at nothing to end the tracker network. As much as I'd hated that side of him, he'd done what was necessary to protect me. At the time, it had scared me, but now I'd give anything for that Bailen, just some small part of him. At least Bailen had done what he thought was best for me, even if it was when he'd been at his worst. I'd take the worst of Bailen now over being iced out completely. Then I wouldn't have to do the right thing by myself.

I cut the engine on the bike and sat unmoving for what felt like an eternity as I tried to slow my breathing. I could do this. Even though I knew where to find Harlow, in the back of my mind I had no idea how to stop him. No way to snap him out of the mind-controlled state. Whoever controlled him wouldn't stop until they had what they wanted. Maybe I'd just destroy the server and go from there. It wasn't a solid plan, but it was a start.

I climbed off the bike and hung my helmet from the handlebars. It was a few short strides to the stairwell door. I reached for the handle and held the cool metal in my hand, pausing to take a few deep breaths. When I'd mustered up all the courage I could, I yanked the door open, the electronic lock long since deactivated. I stepped into the dark stairwell.

None of the lights activated, long detached from the authority tracker network. The door banged shut behind me and I jumped. Total darkness enveloped me. My breaths were all I could hear. I should have brought a toolkit with me, but my impromptu actions had left little time for preparations. I reached for the button on my watch and activated the small light. It wasn't nearly enough to illuminate the whole way, but it let me see a few steps in front of me, enough to slowly creep down the stairs to the tenth floor.

When I finally reached the landing, I allowed myself a few moments to calm my pounding heart. The last time I was here, Bailen and I were nearly killed by an explosion that ripped through the air vent we'd used to avoid the authorities guarding Rufus Scurry's office. Afterward, I'd spent weeks in the hospital recovering from an abdominal wound. The scar still hurt when the weather got bad.

But there were no guards for me to avoid this time, and likely no booby traps left to spring. Just me and Harlow… and whoever had control of him. I opened the door and bolted down the hall, briefly pausing at the crossway to get my bearings, then turned right down another hallway. I instantly recognized the hall leading up to Scurry's office. Rounding the corner, I stopped in front of a wooden door. It had been left cracked open, a gold plaque with the initials R.S. etched into it still firmly affixed.

I pushed the door open, revealing the office inside in complete disarray. Papers were strewn across the floor like fall leaves in a yard. The floor to ceiling screen along the back wall was blank, the computer running the fake city view shut down or broken. The L-shaped desk had open books and additional papers scattered across the surface, and half the drawers lay open with the contents bulging out.

I faced the wall with the glass trophy cases, where most had been broken or knocked over. One case sat slightly ajar, as if it had been left that way for the last six months, untouched from the time Bailen cracked the code on it. We'd entered the brains of Global Tracking Systems and I'd helped him find the satellite server to shut down the tracker network. The case creaked as I pulled it all the way open and stepped into the server room. This time it was quiet and dark. No vibrating floor, no overhead lights, no hum of processing computers.

Dim red emergency lighting lit every fifth row or so, but otherwise the floor was abandoned, at least at first glance. I sucked in a deep breath as I prepared myself for what I would find. The quiet darkness had a somewhat calming peace to it. A prickle moved up my spine, reminding me to remain alert, to not let my guard down.

Many of the server casings were empty where rows of boxes once sat. The equipment had long since been seized by the government as part of a bigger investigation that led to the decommissioning of the authorities, but some of it remained. If I was a gambler, I'd bet money one important item probably still sat untouched.

I stepped down the aisle where the box had been located. I stopped before proceeding past the line of empty casings. A dark shadow of a person who resembled Harlow's form stood completely still, staring into the housing. The exact place where I had thought I'd seen a light blink back on for a brief moment so many months ago. Where I'd sighed in relief before the world came crashing down around me.

Had it been the right decision? Was it my right to decide the greater good for everyone else? Some people may have thought the conveniences and benefits outweighed the bad. Who was I to decide for them? I had less clarity on those questions than ever before.

"Harlow?" I called quietly, afraid I might spook him even though I knew he likely wasn't in full control of his actions.

The shadow stood still for a moment. But as I was about to inch toward the figure, he turned and stepped out of the shadows. The red light lit up his face, void of any expression. The shell of a person I knew so well. A ghost holding the machine I'd never forget.

Fourteen

"Harlow, hand me the box." I swallowed hard and held out my hand. "Please. Let me help you." Though I pleaded with him, I knew it was in vain. He'd told me when it happened, he was aware but unable to act. There was no way S.I.R.E. would let him hand that box over to me. It was too important.

"I thought I told you not to interfere." It was Harlow's voice, but it was robotic and emotionless. Hollow.

The hair on my arms rose. My insides squirmed as I realized I had no idea what S.I.R.E. was capable of when exploiting the loophole. Were they at the limit of what Harlow was able to do, or could they exceed his human abilities and leverage his untapped brain filled with endless possibilities? The thought sent a chill through me. But no matter what Harlow did, I couldn't hurt him. *Focus on the box. Break it and this is all over.*

I repeated the plan in my head. In the back of my mind, I wondered if it was true or if it was just a futile attempt to delay the inevitable.

"You told me not to let my friends interfere. You never said I couldn't." Though my words sounded confident, my insides were anything but. The threat came out shaky.

"Nice try, but this will all be over soon," Harlow's robotic voice said.

I tried to tell myself it wasn't him, but all I saw was the pain in his eyes. I wondered what was going through mind as he watched this unfold, unable to act. Was he rebelling against every evil thing forced upon him? Or had he given in to the pain and let whoever this was take over?

I had to believe Harlow had some fight left in him, but the image of Harlow bent over his bleeding hands in his parents' closet flashed through my mind. That wasn't the Harlow I knew. I'd give everything to have the old version of him back.

I closed my eyes and focused on the determined and cocky soccer player, the one that didn't take defeat lying down. The person who mocked a challenge and took it to the next level. That guy was still in there. I was sure of it.

"Harlow." I swallowed as the right words spun through my mind, hopefully weaving into a master plan. "I know you can hear me. Listen to my voice. You have to fight."

"Your petty pleading won't stop this. Nothing can." Harlow's mouth moved, but the voice coming through it sounded less and less like his.

I hoped I wasn't making it worse for him.

"Harlow, focus on my voice. I know you're hurting. I can't imagine the amount of pain you've been through. But you're strong. Stronger than any person I know. And the most stubborn person I've ever met. So stubborn, I know you'd never let some random asshole get the better of you. You always fight your way to the top, no matter the consequences. Remember that night in the woods. You won. Win again. I know you can."

I studied him, hoping the words would sink in, but he was still frozen. When I was about to give up, Harlow's biceps twitched. It could have been an involuntary reflex, but deep down, something told me he'd heard my words. What I'd said had sparked something inside him. He was signaling in the only way he knew how, the only way he could.

"Yes, that's it. You fight. Don't let them win."

Harlow stared blankly ahead. I scanned over his unmoving form, looking for another signal, but there was none. I opened my mouth to try again but closed it as he set the box down. I stepped toward the box, but before I could take another step, Harlow charged and closed the distance between us. I didn't have time to pivot and run. Harlow's hand closed around my neck and lifted me up.

I gasped for air, clawing at his hand around my neck. Despite feeling the pain of my nails digging into his skin, he was powerless to release me. I choked and tried to speak, but barely any air came out. My heart raced as my feet kicked Harlow without any reaction.

As my vision blurred, two shadows darted behind the servers in the next row over. Two more to my left. I squeezed my eyes shut as I gagged, trying to find the air that wasn't there. I opened my eyes again, wheezing, but everything around me was dimming. Narrowing to pinpricks.

CRACK.

I crumpled to the floor as air rushed into my lungs. I gasped over and over again. My chest heaved as my vision slowly unblurred. I pushed up to my knees. Harlow lay inches from me in a heap.

"WHA—" I sucked in a few more gulps of air. "What did you do?" I gasped again. "I was getting through to him."

"I didn't hit him that hard," Bailen said as he lifted the satellite server from the ground and tucked it underneath his arm as if he was protecting it from me. His expression was slightly smug, like he'd given Harlow what he deserved. The sadness inside me morphed to anger.

"He's unconscious!" I'd never been so unhappy to see Bailen. Near death or not, he'd ruined my one shot to get Harlow to fight, and now S.I.R.E. was going to retaliate. I didn't know who was next, but my gut twisted. This was far from over.

"He was going to kill you. I had to do something," Bailen spat back in a way that said he expected me to thank him for saving my life.

"You have no idea what you've done!" The words flew out of my mouth in a rage. Deep down, I knew my anger was misplaced. Yet it boiled inside me. Protecting one person close to me would certainly lead to pain for someone else. I was spiraling, unable to stop the chain of events about to unfold.

"What *I've* done? You made sure we'll never find out who is behind the loophole. What were you thinking, Kaya?" Bailen's chest heaved like yelling at me had taken more energy than he expected.

I opened my mouth to scream at him again, but Lydia emerged from the row of servers. "Oh no, you don't." She threw her arms around me in a huge hug. I squirmed beneath her, but the more I squirmed, the tighter she squeezed. I tried to shove her off, but she kept squeezing, making it impossible to maneuver. The pressure slowed my breathing and my racing heart. When I finally stopped fighting, she loosened her arms slightly. I let her hold me in a secure place as my mind cleared.

When I was finally calmer, I let my gaze meet Bailen's and found hurt in his eyes. I'd betrayed him. It was written all over his face. But worse, what I saw in the pain was sadness that someone else was comforting me instead of him. Even if it was Lydia, he looked at me as though some piece inside him was missing.

Peyton emerged with Ava on her heels and wrapped Bailen in a hug. He stared at me over her shoulder but didn't hug her back. The pain in his eyes said it all. The divide between us had continued to grow. I wondered if it was beyond repair.

"What did you tell them?" I whispered into Lydia's ear.

"Only that you'd come here to stop whoever was controlling Harlow." She released me from her hug and stepped back. "The rest they need to hear from you."

I nodded. I didn't want to tell them. I didn't want to put them in more danger. But at this point, if S.I.R.E. was going to make good on their threat, then it no longer mattered if I kept their secrets or not.

Jeremy, Dad, and Mr. Overland emerged from another row. Dad's gaze instantly fell to Harlow, who was still collapsed on the floor. He grabbed a small tablet from his back pocket and scanned through some files.

"Still breathing, vitals look good. Just unconscious." Dad said as if he was a doctor reading medical reports on some random patient.

My heart ached at the thought of them treating Harlow like a pawn, but there was something more pressing I had to address.

"I need to tell you all something," I blurted before I lost my nerve. "Harlow isn't the only one having tracker issues."

Dad pocketed the tablet and, with a few long strides, closed the space between us. He grabbed my arms and turned me to face him. His gaze locked on mine, but it quickly became uncomfortable, and my gaze fell to the floor. "I made sure your chip didn't have a loophole switch. How is that possible?"

I shook my head and backed away from Dad's grasp so I could address everyone at once. If I didn't have a loophole switch, then whoever was doing this couldn't mind-control me, but they could monitor my tracker and where I was going. It seemed less likely they could hear the things I said. But it wouldn't matter if they could hear me, because what would get me in trouble with S.I.R.E. was how everyone would react.

"It's not the loophole. Someone is watching me. Reaching out to me anonymously on my tracker. Threatening me."

I looked at each of my friends in turn, searching for signs that I'd betrayed them. Looking for expressions similar to the one I'd seen on Bailen's face moments earlier. Surprisingly, I didn't find anger, only concern. Even Bailen had a sad expression that said he might forgive me because he ached for the pain I'd been potentially been through.

"You came here to stop whoever was watching you?" Bailen asked with a glimmer of hope that I hadn't tried to thwart his plan.

"Not exactly." I stuffed my hands in my pockets, hoping to find something to squeeze but only found a small piece of fuzz.

Bailen's face hardened as though I'd betrayed him all over again.

"Then what?"

"Let me explain." I could tell everyone was losing patience quickly. "Whoever this person is threatened to make one of you next their next loophole experiment if any of you interfered. So I tried to stop them myself. Because I couldn't let you use Harlow as a pawn, put his life at risk."

"How could you have been so stupid? After everything?" Bailen balled his fists and paced. "You should know by now, not to do any of this alone!" he yelled, but it seemed more out of sadness and frustration than anger.

Dad grabbed my shoulder, but I shrugged it off. "You know we're here for you. You don't have to do this alone."

I stood silent because I couldn't find an answer. I didn't know who had my back anymore. They all cared, but they also wanted to do things their way. But the cost of doing that would be too high. I wasn't going to apologize for what I'd done, even if I was being equally stubborn. They were wrong to use Harlow as bait. Tracking down this person was important, but not as important as keeping everyone I cared about safe. I didn't know how to put all that into words, so I stared at Harlow's crumpled figure on the floor.

Right then, I swore to myself that whoever came after those I cared about would pay for what they'd done, even if it was someone I'd previously thought was family.

"Let's go back to the Hive and get you hooked up to the computers. Maybe we can track down whoever is sending those messages. Chances are high it's the same person behind Harlow's loophole hack." Jeremy leaned against an empty rack nearby. It was the first reasonable thought I'd heard in days.

"I have some thoughts on how to identify this person," Mr. Overland added.

I nodded but kept quiet. I no longer had any energy to fight this—I needed answers.

"Let's collect any remaining computers. I suspect the authorities took anything of value, but we might find something they didn't know to look for," Dad said as he opened the nearest server column and started searching.

"You won't find anything there." I stepped further down the aisle, and then I saw what I was looking for. Something I'd wanted to search but also never wanted to see again. The terminal where I'd seen Jake's face with a number underneath it.

I bolted down the aisle and touched the screen, hoping it would illuminate. But after quickly tapping it, I discovered it was dead. I kicked it in frustration.

"Easy on the goods." Peyton called down the aisle.

"It's just a server terminal, nothing important on there," Ava said. "It's why it's still here. It wouldn't have any kind of evidence on it."

I wanted to ask her more questions about her previous job, but instead I pressed forward. "This is what we want. Trust me." I couldn't let them walk out of here without the list on that terminal. Without the answers it held.

Dad stood behind me with a questioning expression. I crossed my arms and stared at him.

"If you say it's important, I believe you." He bent down to inspect the connections. "There's definitely something here that doesn't belong." He repositioned himself so he could stretch further. "Someone put an external drive on this terminal to use it as more than a monitoring station." He held up a small USB and righted himself.

"What's that noise?" I asked as a distinct clicking emanated from the terminal.

Bailen's eyes widened in terror. "BOMB!"

Fifteen

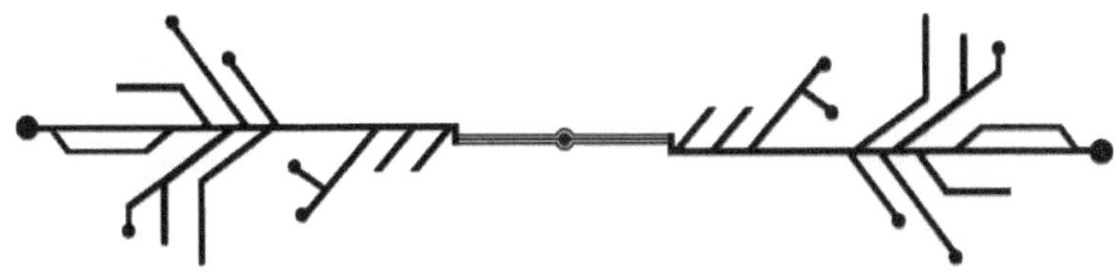

Everything slowed to a crawl. Everyone fanned out from the terminal. I hit the floor and felt the pressure of someone else on top of me. The force triggered a flash of memories. Memories I'd buried so deep. Memories I hoped to never see again. I was back in the storeroom during the supply run. The one that was supposed to be routine.

Bailen and Jake were on top of me.

My ears were ringing.

Destruction around me.

Gavin blown to bits.

Bailen's bloodied arm. Peyton ripping shrapnel from it.

Jake heaving. *JAKE.*

My mind cried out as I coughed and struggled to breathe. "Get off me!" I screamed. I didn't know who had dove over my back to protect me. If they didn't move now, I was going to lose it.

My body wracked with sobs. My head throbbed. My muscles twitched.

I pushed up from the ground, shoved whoever to the side, and crawled on my hands and knees. Dust clogged my throat and I heaved. I didn't make it far before the vomit burned up my throat and landed in a puddle right in front of my path.

I collapsed to my side and wailed, letting the tears stream down my face. Strong arms wrapped around me. I tried to fight them off. They squeezed tighter and tighter as more images flashed through my head.

Jake grabbing his stomach.

The grunt.

Him coughing up blood.

Jake collapsing in my arms.

His mouth moved, but I couldn't hear the words. It didn't matter. I remembered them like it was happening in real time.

The tears streamed down my face as I wailed and grabbed my head.

"Shhh," Bailen whispered over and over again in my ear, his breath hot against my neck.

I squirmed and fought. I didn't want to be comforted—I wanted this to end. I didn't want to have to shrug off any more collateral damage. No amount of comfort would talk me out of it. Too many people I cared about were gone or hurting. And it was all my fault.

When would it end? My body quivered. I heaved again, but there was nothing left in my stomach.

My mind swirled as voices around me called out, checking in on everyone. The sounds were muffled in my still ringing ears. I couldn't look up from the vomit on the floor. The stench made me sick again. The burn in my throat made it hard to swallow.

I screamed and coughed and cried. Bailen's hold tightened

around me as he rocked in an attempt to calm me, as if that would fix everything that had happened. As if it would remove the memories and the fear of what was happening again.

But nothing could replace the pain that laid dormant inside me.

I don't know how much time passed. At some point, Bailen lifted me from the ground and passed me off. Dad carried me out of the building. I couldn't look to see who was with us and who wasn't. I locked myself in the terrifying memories of the past. My body shook. My eyelids drooped.

I sucked in a deep breath and then gave in to the pain. The darkness fell over me.

I awoke in a bed, the concrete walls vaguely familiar. I rolled over toward the mural on the other side of the room. The drawing of all the people I thought I'd lost staring at me through the eyes of the one person I'd never see again. It was like losing Jake all over. A fresh wound had been ripped open, bringing all the pain that came with it.

And then, for the first time, I saw her. Sitting in the chair. Ripped jeans, black tank top, long brown hair drooped around her face. The last person I expected to be there.

Peyton.

She had her head between her knees and looked about as bad as I felt. I sat up quietly, watching her. She hadn't noticed me yet. I couldn't imagine her trauma from this either. Similar in so many ways, but different in the kind of love we had for the same person. Could we finally be there for each other and relate on common ground, or should I roll over and try to sleep it all off?

I positioned my legs to roll over again when Peyton sniffed. It was so quiet I almost missed it, but she was crying. I watched as her hunched back shook ever so slightly. It was a far cry from the girl who took down multiple unicopters to get me here in one piece all those months ago. If she was in that much pain, why was she sitting here? Why not let Ava comfort her, or Bailen? I'd shoved him away enough. While part of me regretted it, it meant he should have plenty of time for his twin without me around.

But I knew the answer. I couldn't explain why, but it felt right to have her in the room, like the world had stopped crumbling for a brief moment. Like I didn't have to navigate this alone. She didn't need to speak or make a noise for her presence to be felt—for Jake's presence to be felt through us both. That was why she was here. She was going through the exact same thing I was. The kind of love we had for my brother didn't matter, just that we had both loved him in our own ways.

"I saw him." I swallowed and tried again. "Flashes from when…" As the words hung in the air, tears welled in my eyes. One squeezed out and ran down the side of my cheek, leaving a warm streak ending in a salty tang on my lips.

She nodded but said nothing. I patted the bed. Her head slowly turned and lifted enough that I could see her red eyes and puffy cheeks. She slid the few steps from the chair toward the bed, then collapsed next to me. We both shook to the sound of our sniffles as the tears streamed down our faces.

Time had no meaning anymore. It was impossible to know the hour. But I could tell neither of us was sleeping—merely trying to make it from one moment to the next.

"I miss him," she whispered. It was so quiet I almost didn't hear it.

"Me too," I said softly. "All of this is bringing up so many memories. Making me rethink everything I did and everything I know."

She nodded. It was more than just an affirmation, it was a shared experience, shared pain. I watched her chest rise and fall, rise and fall. The rhythmic breathing soothed me while her occasional ragged breaths reminded me that this was all still real. It gave me something to focus on that wasn't the pain exhausting my entire body. Something to help me move forward as the seconds ticked on.

When I was finally numb to it all, I said, "I guess I should go let them plug me into the computers and study my tracker again, huh?"

Peyton snorted. It was almost a laugh. Nothing I said had been funny, but I couldn't help but laugh. She joined in.

"I'm surprised they didn't study you in your stress induced nap."

Now it was my turn to snort. She was right. "They only care about the tech, the means to an end." The words felt metallic in my mouth, like I'd come to the right conclusion but for the wrong reasons.

Peyton shot up as if something I said had finally sunk in, driving her to action like a much needed shot of adrenaline. "He cares about you. You must know that."

I stared at the wrinkled sheets. "Then why does he have to be so stubborn about it?"

"His actions aside, he has the best intentions."

I pulled my knees up so I could curl into a ball. "He certainly doesn't act like it."

"You haven't exactly made it easy on him." Peyton paused, catching my gaze. "For what it's worth, you two are good for each other. Fix this."

I nodded again, knowing she was right about it all, but I couldn't find the words to respond to her truth bomb. The reality was, I was trying to protect him too. If he wasn't using Harlow as bait, then he wouldn't have the chance to walk right into a trap. Why was he the only one allowed to protect anyone?

I owed him an apology for everything: for not telling him about going after Harlow, for keeping the messages from S.I.R.E a secret, and for not telling him about the drive. But I wasn't done doing what I had to.

A knock at the door jolted me from my thoughts. It slid open before Peyton or I got up. Bailen stood in the doorway, shoulders slumped, frown on his face and messy hair in his eyes.

"Your ears musta been burning." Peyton sprang up from the bed, pretending our commiseration hadn't happened.

Her hard, indifferent exterior returned. While many people wouldn't notice it, I knew she was falling apart from the inside out.

"Yeah, yeah, insert witty comeback here." Bailen's tired voice was almost monotone, like challenging Peyton had lost all the joy it once held. He looked at me through sad eyes. "If you're up for it, we should start running some tests on your tracker."

I shifted my gaze to Peyton, who winked at me. "I meant what I said."

Bailen raised a curious eyebrow at her, his twin intuition failing him. Peyton waved her fingers at Bailen and dashed from the room, leaving him with a hurt and confused look on his face.

A pang of regret flowed through me. This was my fault. Maybe not all of it, but we'd broken each other's trust. The last time that happened with someone I cared about, I'd been running from Harlow into Bailen's arms.

"We should talk," he whispered.

I nodded in agreement, trying to buy some time and hoping the right words would come to me, but with each grating second of silence, my mind became more and more blank.

Noting my struggle to speak, he added, "When you're ready."

While the words were simple, they showed me that he finally understood I wasn't shutting him out, just trying to process things in my own time.

He held out his hand and I accepted. Together, we walked in silence to the main computer room with our fingers intertwined. It was a simple gesture, but it had me wondering if there was a path to repairing us. All I needed was that single glimmer of hope.

sixteen

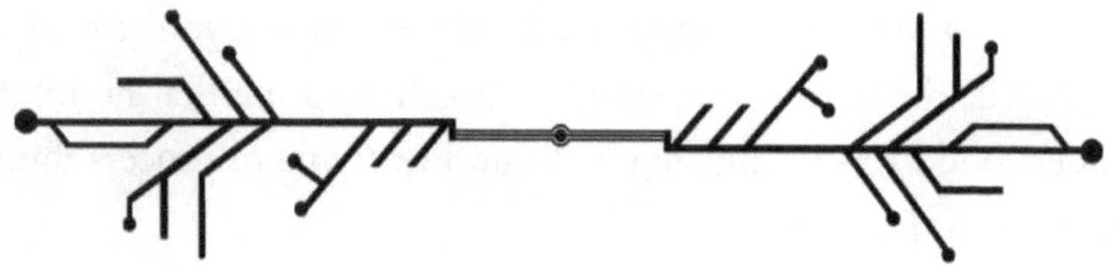

It didn't take long for Jeremy and Bailen to hook me up to the computers. The long, heavy wires draped over me weighed on my mind too, leaving questions about the fate of the tracker loophole. Dad and Mr. Overland were at the main computer, while Bailen and Jeremy flanked either side of them like some weaponized group of coders. As mad as I was at Bailen and Dad, I wouldn't have trusted anyone else with this.

"Ready?" Jeremy asked over the top of the large monitors.

"You're sure whoever this is won't be able to track what you're doing?"

Everyone ignored my question but Jeremy. "We're just looking for signals and trying to trace them, not using your tracker or sending any data to it. Should be undetectable."

"Then let's get this over with." The faster I was out of this chair, the faster we could stop whatever this was and I could get back to smoothing things over with everyone.

I didn't flinch as the sensors on my temples and the back of my neck began to hum with the familiar vibration. Despite the soothing buzz inside my head, tears streaked my face. The one person I really needed right now, to come squeeze my pinky and make a joke like everything was normal, wasn't here. Jake would never be able to comfort me again.

Sensing my discomfort, Peyton pulled up a rolling chair next to me and gave my forearm a quick squeeze. Lydia joined me on the other side and held my hand. It wasn't the same, but knowing there were so many people here for me helped ease the pain I had tried to numb for so long. I sucked in a deep breath and closed my eyes, letting the hum take me temporarily to another place.

"Looks like we got all the data we need," Bailen called through the monitors without standing to look up at me.

"And?" I expected some kind of resolution, though I knew it would take time to pick through.

"Everything appears normal on the surface," Dad said in a tone that implied he didn't fully trust the data.

After everything I had experienced, I knew there was always something bigger below the surface, lurking and waiting to rear its ugly head.

Peyton and Lydia backed away as Bailen came around to disconnect me. His breath beat on my cheek, prickling my skin as he gently peeled the sensors from my skin. His touch was so soft it drew attention to how close he was and how much I wanted to lean in and kiss him. Our eyes met. I found a mixture of confusion and longing in his gaze. He wanted the same thing but wasn't sure if he should act on it. If we had been alone, I might have seized the opportunity, but I looked to the side and the moment passed.

"I think I found something."

I froze at the intensity of Ava's tone. An anxious chill swirled inside me as Ava stood up from another set of computers across the room and brought a USB stick with her.

Not the one I'd given her, or even the one that triggered the bomb in the terminal at Global Tracking Systems, but a third.

"What is it?" Bailen asked.

"Some old encryption codes the authorities used to send secure messages." Ava shrugged like it was no big deal.

Bailen looked like he wanted to ask more questions but stayed silent. As much as I did too, I took my cue from the room.

"Here's a backup. I kept the main file on my computer off the network in case someone tried something." Ava handed the drive to Jeremy, and he plugged it into his terminal.

I stood from the chair and rounded the table to join everyone at the trio of computers that sat next to the padded lounger I'd been in. As I drew closer, I noticed that not everyone had come from the explosion as unscathed as I had originally thought. Ava had a large cut over her eyebrow that had been glued shut, and little cuts slashed the backs of Jeremy's hands. Dad had no visible cuts but winced as he stood from the chair to make room for Bailen. I hoped it was just some sore muscles and not something more serious. Despite not having been at Global Tracking Systems, Mr. Overland appeared stressed and more tired than usual. A camera on one of the screens showed Harlow resting peacefully in one of the nearby rooms.

"I've got the analysis running. It will take some time to find the anomalies." Dad's tired eyes passed over me with a stern expression that said we still needed to talk.

I nodded in understanding, but my nerves frayed. Everyone wanted to talk, share their thoughts and plans. But did they want to listen to what I had to say? They didn't seem to want to understand my point of view. I'd do whatever I could to fix it. If today proved anything, I needed all the allies I could get.

I turned from Dad to focus on Ava and her findings. She was pointing to files on the drive and instructing Jeremy what to open.

"See these traces here?" Ava pointed to a series of numbers on the screen.

Jeremy nodded and highlighted some text, then pasted it into another file. Bailen watched over his shoulder.

"I ran several searches on the data source, but it just led me in circles until I dissected the code. This section was the only piece that didn't seem to line up with what the code was doing. But I was afraid to run it." Ava bit her thumbnail, which I didn't see her do often.

"Someone was definitely being clever, but not clever enough," Jeremy said as he moved parts of the code into separate lines and began to reorganize the pieces.

"Is that what I think it is?" Bailen asked.

"If you think it's a standard issue authority IP address, then you'd be correct," Ava said.

"Who would be using an authority IP address embedded in a trace function?" Jeremy asked.

"Someone who wanted to be found, but only by people of a certain rank. In fact, it's not a tracer at all, it's a call to action to anyone who might be watching." Ava's normally tricky to read face displayed a horror I never expected to see. "I've only seen this kind of coding one time, and it was when Scurry put a bounty on Kaya's head."

"So, he's after me again?" I blurted without thinking.

"We can't know for sure. It could be one of his right-hand people. Either way, this proves the signal used to send you messages is tied to him somehow," Ava said.

"How do we find whoever this person is?" I asked.

"This data hidden IP could be the key to finding them. And if we play our cards right..." Ava looked at the guys with anticipation.

"We can set up a secure connection and create a digital search to map out the key locations," Bailen said as a glint of adventure rose in his expression.

"I'll get a secure server going." Jeremy started typing so fast his fingers were a blur.

"I'll pull up the list of safe house locations and cross reference it with the list Ava provided us," Mr. Overland said.

Dad rolled his chair over to another set of terminals. "I'll test for vulnerabilities. I have an idea what this person might be looking for."

Ava joined Dad at a nearby computer. "And I'll set up the profile, so it looks legit. It'll probably be an old look, but hopefully they'll buy that it's someone that was deep in hiding for a while."

"What can I do?" I asked, suddenly feeling completely useless. Peyton and Lydia nodded their heads. They were in, too.

"One of you should keep an eye on Harlow's location and make sure he doesn't take another adventure," Ava said without looking up from her screen.

I caught Lydia's gaze and she nodded. As much as I wanted to protect and help Harlow, the optics right now weren't good. She knew the only person I trusted outside myself was her.

"Pey and Kaya, that leaves you on tracker vitals. Keep an eye on Harlow's metrics. We don't need him crashing on us," Bailen said.

I searched his face for any lingering tension on the topic, but he had already immersed himself with loading the IP tracing protocol and was waiting for Jeremy to finish the server.

"On it." Peyton rounded the main bank of computers to approach another, smaller set.

I followed on her heels. "What exactly are we looking for?"

"Any spikes in his breathing or heart rate, signs of distress, or unknown signals. If there's even the slightest blip, I want to hear about it," Dad said, very serious.

Shivers crawled up my spine in a combination of anticipation and fear. If we could get whoever this was to respond, it could give us a serious advantage, or it could backfire spectacularly. On the plus side, I had an excuse for fixating on Harlow to ensure he was okay.

Peyton and I stared at the screen. The rhythmic rise and fall of the lines for his heartbeat and brain function were somewhat hypnotic. I had to squeeze my eyes shut and open them again to make sure I didn't fall into a daze.

"Secure server is done," Jeremy called out.

"Standing by with the tracer," Bailen said.

"I'm almost there with the profile." Ava typed in a few more commands, then sat back and reviewed her code. "I think that's it."

"This is some gorgeous code. I don't see any vulnerabilities. Not even the risk protocol that most coders miss," Dad said with an approving smile—one I wished he'd give me more often instead of the coding prodigies.

"Thanks. I learned from the best." A hint of sadness crept into Ava's voice. "Or I guess we'd call them the worst now, but the authorities had some seriously smart people working for them."

"They were good at charming people, that's for sure." Dad squeezed Ava's shoulder. "One day I will finish making amends for the things I've done on their behalf." Dad's gaze found me through a series of monitors. He winked at me before returning to his work.

While we hadn't finished our talk yet, that was the first time since finding out Dad's involvement in my tracker glitch that I knew he might actually mean what he'd said.

"Everything's in place then?" Bailen scanned the room for confirmation. The devious smile that erupted was one I hadn't seen from him in a long time. He was finally finding the excitement again.

When everyone nodded in agreement, Bailen started the trace. "We're going to hit whoever this is where it hurts."

"I don't want to get ahead of ourselves, but for once it feels like we might be a step ahead. I'll keep a cross reference of all the pings and surrounding areas with our list of known locations just in case, though." Bailen's dad didn't look up from his terminal, deep in thought.

The room lit up with a buzz of excitement. We might actually finish this thing once and for all.

"Tracer is working its way through the pathways. Singapore, London, now it's bouncing off, Moscow, Toronto… This is one of the most complex traces I've ever seen," Bailen said.

"They really don't want to be found, except by their greatest and most determined allies." Ava's face was more serious than I'd ever seen it. Working for the authorities, she must have seen and participated in horrors I couldn't even begin to imagine. The trace was likely bringing up some bad memories.

Peyton tapped my shoulder. "You got this for a minute?"

"Yeah." There was a silent agreement between us now. I knew what she needed to do, and I was more than happy to watch the steady beat of Harlow's heart as he slept not far away.

Peyton crossed the room and grabbed Ava's hand. They stood

next to each other, staring at the monitors in silence.

"The trace is slowing," Bailen said.

"Must be getting to the end result." Jeremy pointed to some lines on the map. "I'm betting in this area."

"How'd you know?" Ava asked.

"It's a pattern." He indicated the lines crisscrossing over the map. "They all converge here if you wrap it around the globe." Jeremy circled an area on the map.

"There." Ava pointed on the map to a precise location without even reviewing the list Mr. Overland had been working on.

Bailen looked at Ava with a curious eye. "How do you know that's the right location?"

"It's an old safe house and meeting place. I wasn't sure at first, but when the trace got going, I was almost certain," Ava said.

"They're nothing if not consistent," Dad said.

"You've been there before?" I asked.

"No. But I've heard stories." Dad's gaze shot to the floor as if there was much more that he wasn't saying.

"I think the trace is complete," Bailen said as the lines etched deeper into his forehead.

"What's wrong?" I asked.

"It's acting like it's finished, but it's still running something," Bailen said.

Ava stepped up to her terminal again. "It's checking our credentials. One sec." She typed in a series of commands. "Since it's an older profile and credentials, it will take some time for them to verify."

But before I had time to wonder if we might get caught, a red light blinked in the corner of my vision. I had another message from S.I.R.E..

Seventeen

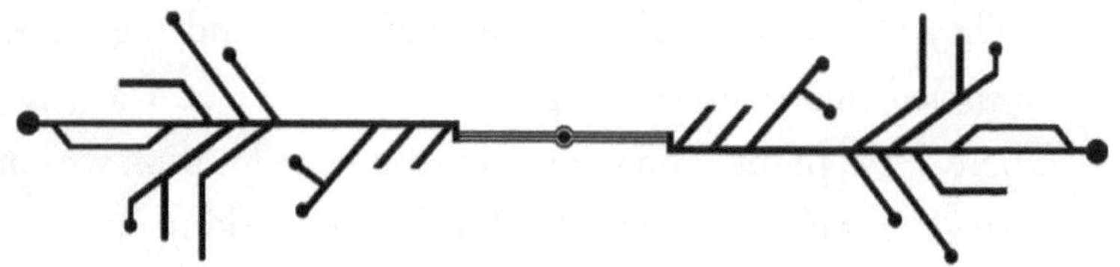

sucked in a huge breath and braced myself for what might come next. I exhaled, blinked twice, and thought about the message.

S.I.R.E.: Congrats, you found me.

My heart pounded as my breathing grew ragged. We weren't as inconspicuous and clever as we'd thought we had been. Of course S.I.R.E. was steps ahead of us. The advantage we thought we had crumbled in front of me. But if the information wasn't coming from my tracker and Harlow was close by but not within earshot, how did S.I.R.E. know what we were doing?

K.W.: Do I win a prize?

The best I could do was beat S.I.R.E. at their own game.

S.I.R.E.: No...

K.W.: Then what do you want?

S.I.R.E.: Come alone...

So, it was a trap. S.I.R.E. wanted me and me alone. That's what this had been about from the beginning. I should have known. But I also knew the lies I'd been telling and the secrets I'd kept were hurting everyone I cared about, including myself. I couldn't keep playing by these unfair rules. I had to fight back.

K.W.: I can't.

S.I.R.E.: Then you're not the girl I
thought you were.

Who did this person think they were? They didn't know me. Or at least if they did, they must not know me well, because just about everyone I cared about was either dead or in the Hive with me. And I'd stop at nothing to protect everyone around me.

S.I.R.E.: Do I need to demonstrate what
I'm capable of?
I don't think that little girl can handle
much more torture.

My hands balled into fists as the anger simmered inside me.
K.W.: Don't you dare touch her.

S.I.R.E.: I don't have to. I have someone
else who can do it for me.
Unless you play by the rules...

I gritted my teeth to avoid screaming. I couldn't believe he would make Harlow go after Emily again. She was innocent in all this, and Harlow didn't deserve to have flashbacks from something so horrific.

Trap or not, I had to stop S.I.R.E. I reread their messages to make sure I hadn't missed anything, but it only made me angrier. My vision focused on one line that left me questioning.

Whoever S.I.R.E. thought I was, they were wrong. The person I was before was gone. In a way, I was still figuring out who I was. Even if I didn't have all the answers, I was stronger than before. No one else would die again because of me. We'd all lost enough. I channeled my anger into my reply.

> K.W.: We're going to play by my rules.
> Or I'm not playing at all.

> S.I.R.E.: Tsk tsk…

Was that it? I held my breath, waiting for more. Calling S.I.R.E.'s bluff couldn't have been that easy. I had them right where I wanted them. I wasn't going to back down. Not this time.

> S.I.R.E.: There will be consequences if
> you don't obey me.

> K.W.: What consequences? You don't
> ACTUALLY have any power, do you?

I knew it was a bluff. Whoever this was clearly had power over Harlow. I needed to put them on the defensive for a change.

S.I.R.E.: Who shall be next?

K.W.: No one. This is over.

I closed out the chat bubble and crossed my arms, trying to hide my rapidly rising and falling chest. But as I glanced around the room, no one was paying any attention to me. They were hyper-focused on the data collected from my tracker and the trace to find whoever was behind this. They hadn't noticed my absence from the group.

An alarm on the computer next to me drew my attention. *SHIT!* Harlow's vitals were all over the place. "Dad, something's happening!"

A pit formed in my stomach as my body went numb. Whatever the alarm was, it was all my fault.

Dad turned to me slowly but stood frozen in place. When his head lifted, his eyes were glassy. Far away. The same thing I'd seen in Harlow when…

Fear gripped my insides and squeezed so tightly I had trouble catching my breath. My heart pounded in my chest. I collapsed to the floor, ready to let a stream of tears loose. S.I.R.E. had a lot more power than I'd thought, and I'd enabled him to exercise it.

How could this person keep punishing me? They knew so much about me. I knew so little about them. And now they had control over another person I cared about deeply. I was chasing dominos that were already falling one after another. No matter what I did, I was unable to catch up or alter the path we were on. I couldn't keep fighting when S.I.R.E. had all the advantages.

It wasn't fair. I'd make them pay. For all of it.

A rage boiled inside me.

No one else would fall victim to this. No one.

A new chat bubble appeared in the corner of my vision. I quickly opened it, afraid of what I might see.

S.I.R.E.: Looks like Daddy wants to
come out and play.

K.W.: I'm coming for you.

S.I.R.E.: Good girl.
Now make it fast and tell no one.
You know what's at stake.

I closed out the chat window and squeezed my eyes shut, allowing the tears to pool in the corners. I looked back at the group, the people I cared about the most. None of them had any idea the advantage they thought they had was all but evaporated. And as unfair as that might be, I intended to let them continue to think they had the leg up to give myself a head start. I snagged a pencil and scrap of paper and scribbled a quick note.

Going to stop this once and for
all. Don't come after me. -Kai

It was a futile attempt, but at least they wouldn't wonder where I went. I backed away from the terminal that was still beeping and gave one last glance to Dad, who was still frozen in place. No one else had realized what happened. I wasn't sure how long S.I.R.E. would hold Dad under his control or what S.I.R.E. might make him do. Regardless, I was out of time.

I said a silent goodbye to everyone and whispered a quick r'fu-ah sh'lei-mah for Dad, even though a healing prayer wasn't exactly the best fit.

Before I could second-guess myself, I turned for the tunnel. I snagged a go kit off the rack by the entrance and bolted down the hall for the trap door. The picture of the map with S.I.R.E.'s location was burned into my memory.

I would make S.I.R.E. pay for everything they had done. Hopefully, I wasn't too late to stop this.

The trap door banged shut behind me as I tore across the barn to my flying motorbike. I passed the bike with the green four-leaf clover on the front. Bailen's bike. He'd always said it was his good luck charm. I could use all the luck I could get right about now. I circled back, fixed the go kit to the back of Bailen's bike, then hopped on. A quick kick start and the engine roared to life. At least if I didn't come back, he'd have something of mine left behind—my bike. Jake's bike that Bailen had gifted me.

As I tore through the woods, I didn't bother to check if anyone was following. They'd be behind me as soon as they realized I was gone, angry at me for ruining things again, for not telling them what was happening. But it was this or let S.I.R.E. continue to manipulate those I cared about most. I engaged the flying mechanism and took to the skies.

Angling the bike away from the city, I found the skyway out of town. If I stuck to the main roadways at least for a bit, maybe I could blend in with traffic. As I flew toward my intended target, thoughts raced through my head. I had no idea how to find S.I.R.E. once I arrived. There was a high probability that this would be a trap, an excuse for S.I.R.E. to lock me up and lobotomize my tracker.

Maybe S.I.R.E. was going to end the one advantage Dad had created by putting secret tracker plans in my head and ensuring my tracker didn't have a loophole switch. If I was the only person he couldn't control, then I was a threat. If S.I.R.E. could control whoever he wanted, who was next?

I shook the thoughts out of my head. I needed to focus on how I would handle S.I.R.E. once I found them. Or even worse, I had to figure out what to do if S.I.R.E. wasn't really there and had just lured me away to do something even more sinister.

As I neared the abandoned back roads, I disengaged the flying mechanism and plummeted toward a large field in front of an old farmhouse. The bike bounced once, twice, three times before finally sticking to the ground. I steered toward the house and parked out front.

The pitch-black house had a large wraparound porch and two stories. It was in good shape other than needing a new coat of paint. Why lure me here if no one was home? Or maybe that was the point. I turned off the engine and removed my helmet.

A message blinked in the corner of my vision. So, S.I.R.E. was still watching. I blinked twice and let the message open.

**S.I.R.E.: Ditch the bike, come around
back to the barn.**

S.I.R.E. wasn't in the house, but I noticed several cameras affixed to the columns on the porch. Though probably nearby, they were hiding like the insect that they were.

I snagged the flashlight from the go kit, leaving the rest of the box on the back of the bike. Flipping on the light, I rounded the back of the house and quickly found the barn, which was in much worse shape than the house. Several of the windows were blown out, and the large door was off its hinges. I crept toward the dark barn, my boots thudding in the dirt with each step forward.

My nose tickled as the scent of rotting hay and manure overwhelmed me. I shined the light around the barn, finding old tools and equipment, as well as empty horse stalls. I checked them all just to be sure, but no one was there.

Just as I was about to give up and abandon the barn, another message appeared on my tracker.

S.I.R.E.: The hay loft.

I made my way to the ladder, but as I set my foot on the first rung, another message appeared.

S.I.R.E.: Ditch the flashlight.

I shined the light around the barn, noticing several cameras. No sense in fighting them. If I didn't obey these simple commands, it was only a matter of time before they found someone else to control. My mind wandered through a list of all the people I cared about. Would they stoop so low as to control both Mom and Dad, or was Dad the only person they dared involve? A twinge of regret rumbled through me at how I'd left Dad with his glassy stare and incoherent state.

I set the flashlight on the ground so it illuminated the ladder to the hay loft. As I climbed upward, my heavy breaths echoed in the large space. When I reached the top, I walked the edges, searching for some kind of clue that stood out in the dark, but I wasn't quite sure what I was looking for.

K.W.: Care to help me out? Why am I
here?

K.W.: Or even better, how about you
show yourself instead of being a coward.

S.I.R.E.: Testy, aren't we? Have
patience.

K.W.: You've used up my last ounce.

S.I.R.E.: Far corner. There's a trap door.

I moved to the other end of the hay loft. The moon shined through the large holes in the roof of the barn. I brushed aside the piles of wet and rotting hay. A metallic ting caught my attention as I continued to clear the area with my foot. A metal handle appeared. I bent down to clear away the rest of the hay from the edges of the trap door.

A loud creak rang out as I forced the heavy door open. I proceeded down the dark ladder, a single light glowing about twenty feet down the hole. One rung at a time, I continued until I'd passed what felt like two floors. Finally, I set foot on solid ground. As I stepped into the darkness beyond the ladder, a set of fluorescent overhead lights flicked on, illuminating a long tunnel dug out of the dirt.

As I crept down the tunnel, my footsteps echoed against the walls—or maybe that was just pounding in my head. My heart thumped faster with each step I took. I searched for doors or another tunnel, but there didn't seem to be one. When I reached the end of the long pathway, a left turn took me to a smaller passage that seemed to appear out of thin air. Another long hallway illuminated ahead of me as the lights behind me blinked out.

My skin crawled at the thought of someone watching me so closely. I hoped the lights had motion sensors. I scanned the ceiling and corners for cameras but found none. Either they were well hidden or S.I.R.E. didn't care about this tunnel.

When I finally reached the far wall, I took a right turn this time. The lights again flipped on ahead of me and darkness followed behind.

Another mud tunnel with no doors, just light. I raced down that tunnel to find another turn, this time back to the left. I continued running, ignoring the lights coming on as I did, and then turned to the right, again expecting to find another tunnel. This time there was a large door ahead. I bolted to the door.

Black letters were painted on the gray metal door that looked out of place in the mud tunnel. As I approached the door, the letters became clearer: *START HERE* with an arrow pointing to a panel inset in the mud wall. I opened the panel and found a number pad. The words "Select the right number" had been scrawled across the top of the device.

Select the right number? What kind of game was this? There was no way I could figure out the code. I waited for some kind of message from S.I.R.E. to clue me in to whatever sick joke they were playing, but nothing came. Maybe they wanted me to ask first.

K.W.: What am I supposed to do with this?

I waited in silence, listening to the blood pulse in my ears. But no answer came. Maybe S.I.R.E. had given up, or maybe they were just stalling me. If they didn't hurry, Bailen and the others would find me, and S.I.R.E. would never get me alone. Or maybe that's what they wanted all along.

I wished I had some way to contact Bailen. He'd know how to hack this keypad.

**K.W.: Enough games, you win. Tell me
what you want from me.**

But my message was again met with silence. I cursed myself for leaving the kit on the back of the bike. At least if I'd brought it, I could have unscrewed the back of the keypad and hooked it up to the Ghost decryption tech.

But S.I.R.E. couldn't have guaranteed I grabbed a kit or that I'd have the right tech to crack this keypad. It would have to be a number I knew. I wracked my brain for what the code could possibly be. S.I.R.E. had to be someone I knew at least a little bit. It had to be a number that meant something to both of us.

My body froze as my mind tried to puzzle through the questions speeding through my thoughts. There was only one time I'd seen numbers in relation to trackers: when Bailen and I broke into the server room inside Scurry's office. It seemed strange that this person would use the same code, but I closed my eyes and tried to picture the numbers lighting up as Bailen used his device to crack the code and open the secret door in Scurry's office.

When I was pretty sure I had the right digits, I entered them into the panel. The keypad flashed red, and the door didn't budge. I tried a second time to ensure I hadn't mistyped it. Still red. I tried several variations of that code in case I got something wrong, but I was again met with red on the panel. This wasn't Scurry then, or at least not linked to Global Tracking Systems.

Maybe it was a word and not a number sequence. Each number stood for a series of letters on the old phones and keypads I'd seen. I put in a couple words like "tracker," "authorities," and, "loophole," but the keypad flashed red each time.

What about the coordinates for this place or the IP address they masked? But neither of those worked either. I screamed and grabbed my hair. I slid down against the wall and pulled my knees to my chest. This was useless. There were an infinite number of possibilities. I'd never crack this.

I took a deep breath. If nothing else, Bailen and the others were probably on their way here already. How long would it take them to find the trap door? I doubt I would have looked for something in the hay loft. They probably wouldn't either. But I had to hold out hope they were coming.

As I stood and turned to head back down the tunnels to keep an eye out for the others, my tracker blinked with a new message. *FINALLY,* something.

S.I.R.E.: You're thinking too hard.

K.W.: If you want me to come to you,
you're going to need to do better than some
verbal taunts.

S.I.R.E.: No need to get testy like your
brother.

K.W.: YOU DON'T KNOW ANYTHING
ABOUT MY BROTHER.

S.I.R.E.: I knew him well actually…

S.I.R.E.: Probably better than you.

Anger boiled inside me and erupted in the form of a scream so primal I couldn't control its escape. I wanted to punch whoever this was. How dare they toy with me and bring Jake into this? I cursed S.I.R.E. for the reminder that Jake wasn't here anymore. This was the cruelest punishment of all, crueler than anything S.I.R.E. could ever do to me.

I'd get in that door if I had to break the keypad to do it. I turned from the door and bolted down the tunnel. I flew down the next corridor, racing toward the exit, ready to get the kit, not caring what S.I.R.E. thought or if they retaliated. They had made this beyond personal. They'd made it about Jake.

I skidded to a stop. A question filled my mind. Why make it about Jake now, when S.I.R.E. had previously mentioned hurting everyone I cared about? S.I.R.E. couldn't hurt Jake anymore. No one could. But S.I.R.E. could use Jake against me. Why mention him by name unless…

The thoughts swirled in my brain faster than I could keep up. I spun around and bolted back to the keypad, my heart thudding so forcefully I thought it might fly out of my chest. The passcode had something to do with Jake. I entered his birthday, the first logical number I could think of, but the lights blinked red. Maybe the day he died—S.I.R.E. liked to twist me into knots. But that didn't work either.

I paused, trying to think like S.I.R.E. What would they use that related to Jake? Suddenly, the answer hit me like a splash of paint flung at a canvas.

There was only one number I'd ever seen associated with Jake that was tracker related. The number underneath his picture when I'd seen it flash on the terminal in the server room, the night I took down the tracker network. This wasn't about Jake. This was about revenge.

It was about punishing me for taking down the network.

I entered the number 70285 into the keypad and the door clicked, confirming my worst fears. My body tingled as I pushed open the door, afraid of what I might find, but the room was dark. I reached my hand along the wall, searching for a light switch, but only found a rough surface. I took a tentative step into the room. The light flicked on.

Eighteen

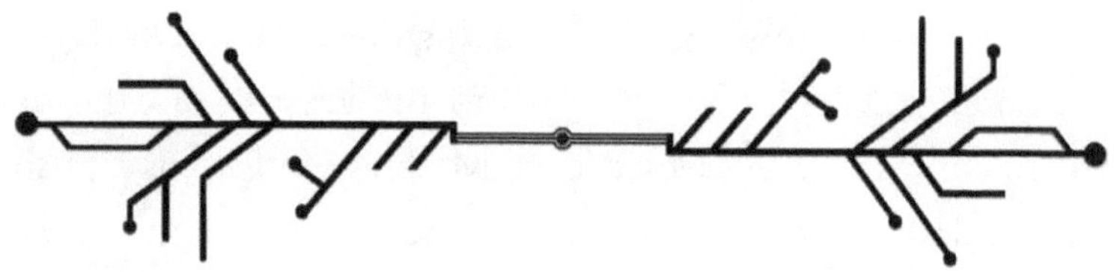

The room was empty. It was a mud box about ten square feet. Not a single chair or computer. A camera hung from a single set of fluorescent lights suspended from the ceiling. I ran my hands along the walls, looking for hidden bumps or dents. Nothing.

The door creaked behind me. I pivoted toward it, watching in horror as it swung shut. The electronic lock engaged with a quiet set of clicks and thuds. I ran to the door and pounded on it.

"Let me out!" I screamed, but there was no one to hear me.

Searching the door for secret levers or buttons, my heart raced. S.I.R.E. had played me like an authority guard engaging the tracker arrest protocol. While I wasn't frozen in place, I was paralyzed to do anything outside this room.

There had to be a reason for this. What was S.I.R.E.'s end game? Maybe they wanted to take me out of play or wear me down until I fully complied. But S.I.R.E. already had the tracker loophole to control those I cared about most hanging over my head. What else was S.I.R.E. up to?

While I expected some sort of trap, I'd misjudged whoever this was, completely underestimated them. They were downright vengeful.

I inched around the room a couple more times as I searched for something I might have missed in the first pass, but there were only mud walls and the light beating down from overhead. Checking the door once more for good measure, I resigned myself to the fact that I was here for the foreseeable future. At least until someone decided I needed food or water, or they wanted to elevate this game to the next level. In the meantime, S.I.R.E. was enjoying the show.

I leaned against the wall and slid to the floor, propping my back up. I stared at the camera, daring whoever this was to make a move. When I got bored, I examined my black utility boots and tried to piece together everything that had happened to figure out where I went from here.

Why this room? Why this place? None of this made any sense. I blinked to open a chat bubble to S.I.R.E., then paused. Maybe this was exactly the point. A distraction so I wouldn't keep chasing S.I.R.E. Or better yet, maybe the room was designed for me and me alone. I had to think like S.I.R.E. Bailen did this often when he was trying to get in the head of the competition. Think like the enemy, he'd always say.

Bailen... Maybe there was a chance of him finding me, assuming he wasn't so mad he didn't care where I'd disappeared to. Surely the others would. They'd miss me, as would Mom and Emily. As I retraced my steps, I realized S.I.R.E. had planned around that as well. Someone would probably find the bike, and maybe the flashlight. But with the cameras, S.I.R.E. would find a way to distract and drive them away on another wild chase, hurting someone I cared about in the process.

I rose from the floor and circled underneath the light, inspecting it and the camera slowly as I went. Maybe I could knock out the camera without damaging the light. I slipped off my boot and threw it at the light fixture, not so hard to shatter the bulbs or knock it from the ceiling but strong enough to hit the camera.

My aim was off. The light clanged and swayed a bit, but the camera stayed put. Afraid to miss again, I circled back to the door and examined the creases. It was a solid piece of metal, the wiring to the locking mechanism hidden somewhere inside the walls.

I dug my fingernails into the dirt. A little embedded itself under my nails, but there was no visible dent or crack in the mud wall. Using my nails would take too long to get to the wiring. I was out of viable options.

I slid back to the floor and lay on the ground, staring up at the light, hoping for a new perspective. I positioned my cheek on the cold, hard floor and blinked, waiting for inspiration, but nothing came. My body sagged in defeat; my muscles twitched from exhaustion. I hadn't slept much in the last few days, and now it was catching up to me. If S.I.R.E. had stopped playing the game, then I was done, too.

The light above flickered—or maybe in my tired state, I was seeing things that weren't there. But then a loud sizzle and a crack erupted. The bulbs in the fixture shattered, taking the light with it. I covered my face as tiny shards of glass rained down around me. I shook off my clothes and sat upright, feeling for the wall and the door. It was still closed, so I leaned against it. Now what?

A chat bubble with J.W. appeared in the corner of my blackened vision. J.W.? I only knew one J.W. and he was dead. I opened the profile and inspected it. Now S.I.R.E. had taken this too far. Impersonating Jake? This was no longer a game. It was beyond personal. I briefly thought about ignoring the message, but my curiosity got the better of me. I let the thought of the chat bubble fill my mind and blinked twice in quick succession.

A low breath escaped my lips as I began to read.

J.W.: We don't have much time.

I froze in place, afraid to spook the imaginary spirit in the room. This was not what I'd expected. Very different from S.I.R.E.'s tone and actually very Jake-like, which I knew was impossible. A million thoughts whirled through my head. I tried to pick through them and decide how to respond. I let the words fill my mind and blinked to send them.

K.W.: I've apparently got all the time in the world.

A subtle nod to my precarious situation, but the usual kind of humor I used with Jake. If this was tied to Jake somehow, they'd pick up on the tone.

But I shook my head and cursed myself for getting my own hopes up. I was there when he'd died. And while the Ghosts knew about his death, we hadn't told many other people, even after I'd reconnected with Mom and Dad. It didn't make sense.

Maybe someone had hacked his tracker. Or cloned his alias. The thought sent a jolt of anger through me. How could someone do such a thing? Maybe this was another elaborate trick. I dug deeper into the profile, opening different descriptions, favorite music, favorite book, his bio, reading each component line by line. It appeared identical to how I remembered it, right down to the jokes and puns in every section. This was either him or an incredibly accurate duplicate copy of his profile.

> **J.W.: Time is all relative to the individual.**

> **J.W.: A long nap for you, an infinitesimal series of calculations for me.**

What an odd thing to say. While the light teasing felt like a remnant of Jake, the words didn't align. They also weren't as condescending or cryptic as S.I.R.E. either. Maybe this was a third party.

> **K.W.: No time for naps. I need an escape plan.**

> **K.W.: Can you help me?**

I silently added, *whoever you are*. While I wasn't sure I could trust J.W., anything was better than waiting for S.I.R.E. to make their next move.

> **J.W.: By my calculations, there are two exits to the room.**

I started to ask how they knew that, but my tracker must have been traceable. While Jake knew things about tracking chips from his time with the Ghosts, he was never a coder. He had other skills that must have been useful to them.

That thought hit me like a ton of paint cans. I'd never really known what he did for the Ghosts. There was never time to ask. I'd had one conversation where I reconnected with him, when he explained why I should join the Ghosts. I should have asked him then, but I didn't. Instead, I wasted the time I'd had, and I cursed what was stolen from me. All things considered, whoever was on the other end of J.W. knew enough to hack a dead tracker, meaning they probably weren't Jake. But maybe they could still help me—if I could even trust a person impersonating my brother.

I refocused on J.W.'s reply. Two exits. If there really were two, where was the second one? I'd searched the room pretty thoroughly. What had I missed? But the more I thought about it, the more I realized I hadn't searched the whole room. I'd only searched the walls.

K.W.: Trap door?

J.W.: Yes, but it's a trap…

J.W.: Not in the traditional sense,
though.

More riddles.

J.W.: Find the door, find your answers.

Before I could ask any more questions, the alias and the profile disappeared, like it had never existed in the first place. What kind of person or tracker account could just disappear off the grid? I mean, I'd gone off grid, but my tracker was designed to glitch. It was an anomaly. But I had to think differently. This wasn't the tracker network I knew growing up. This was a loophole, and probably some kind of backdoor network. It was a possible failsafe designed to function when the tracker network went down, or something designed to be more than the tracker network but disrupted mid-development.

The second option felt more likely, based on the unpolished nature of the responses. I wasn't dealing with well-vetted tech. I was dealing with someone's last ditch effort to maintain control over people and whatever was hiding in the dark corners of the network.

J.W. and S.I.R.E. felt like opposing forces. While J.W. was probably from the shadows, S.I.R.E. was front and center. S.I.R.E. had made it very clear from the beginning that they had all the power and some ability to act on it. But how was S.I.R.E. unaware of J.W. and vice versa? The answer I was seeking felt just out of reach.

I slowly crawled in the dark, running my hands over the hard floor in search of some kind of latch or hole that might indicate a trap door. I methodically crawled from one wall to the other, then inched over and crawled back until I hit the far side of the room.

Nothing.

What had I missed? Was the mechanism in the ceiling? No, it couldn't be. There was no access to the ceiling unless... It seemed so obvious. I couldn't believe I'd overlooked the possibility. It had only been six months since I'd been opening doors by hand, but it had quickly become the new norm. This room required an active tracker. While the loophole had given S.I.R.E. access to mind-control others, my active tracker functioned differently. I didn't have a switch allowing for mind-control, but I did have access to some kind of network. My tracker was the key to solving this mystery.

I reached out for an unlocking app and thought about unlocking a door. When the app activated, it told me there was one door, but I didn't have permission to open it. That door must have been the main door to the room. Checking again, I found the second door. This one I did have access to. I thought about unlocking it. A loud hiss erupted from the ceiling. A metal clank made me jump, then a light from above flicked on, illuminating a metal staircase that descended from where the light fixture used to be.

I scrambled to my feet and climbed the stairs to find a small, circular room with floor to ceiling computer terminals and monitors. It was like some kind of secret control center. But it was impossible to know who had set all this up.

"Ah, Miss Weiss. You've finally solved my riddles," said a familiar voice.

Chills ran up my spine as I turned in the direction of the voice. On one of the monitors, a familiar but unwelcome face appeared—that of Rufus Scurry.

His hair was longer than I remembered, curlier and scragglier than his usual clean-shaven, polished business look. He wore a nondescript gray shirt, not a vibrant gray but a dull, faded one that highlighted the trials he'd been through. His face looked older, like many more than six months had passed, but the sneer that crossed his lips was unmistakable. He wasn't done toying with me, not by a long shot. He intended to make me pay for everything that I'd done.

"What do you want?" I blurted before I could fully process everything. If I could see him, he could likely see me. It wasn't clear from the video monitor where he was or why he'd chosen to lure me to this place rather than face me in person. My mind swirled more and more as the evil grin on Rufus's face grew. He knew he was about to win a chess match he'd masterfully plotted out. He could see the panic building inside me and was enjoying the show.

But when his creepy smile fully formed, he sat quietly watching, taking in his moment of triumph. I quickly realized how woefully unprepared I was for this situation. J.W.'s warning of a trap had given me no indication to expect something of this magnitude.

"Sit down. We need to have a chat." Rufus pointed to the single beat-up office chair behind me.

I sat, but not because he asked me to. I wasn't sure my knees wouldn't give out on me. "About what?" I spat.

"About how you're going to repay your debt to me." If he'd had a mustache, I was certain he'd be twirling it. It was quite clear he was enjoying every minute of watching me try to maintain my composure. He had me exactly where he wanted me—waiting for me to squirm and make a mistake.

"You've already taken everything from me! I have nothing left to give!" I screamed at him. I wanted to burst into tears because I knew I still had just about everything to lose, but I wouldn't give him the satisfaction.

"I want the only thing you have left." His grin disappeared, and somehow the blank look was more frightening than his previous expression. "Your freedom."

Nineteen

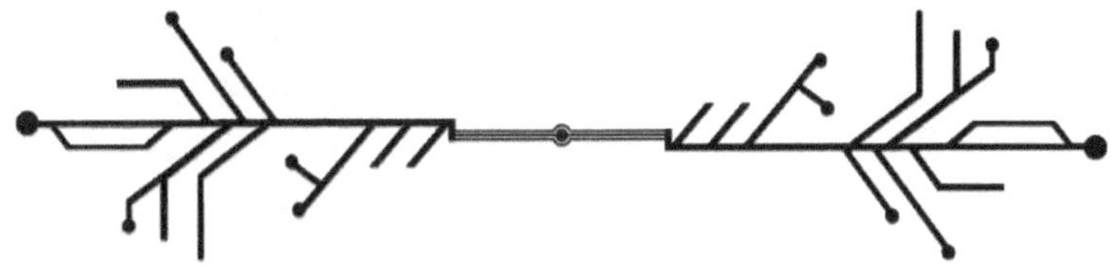

After spending years under the control of the authorities and the tracker network, I didn't have any freedom left. Even though I'd given the world a newfound sense of freedom, I'd quickly learned that I'd signed myself up for a lifetime of cleaning up the mess I'd made. My current situation was no exception.

"If this is freedom, then take it. I don't want it." Despite the recognition of truth, my words didn't change the glee Scurry experienced during our exchange. And to make it worse, I wasn't sure how he'd even managed to set up the conversation. He was supposed to be in a maximum-security prison without access to any technology. I hadn't heard any news about him escaping since we last checked on him. Either someone was allowing this, or he'd weaseled his way into a better situation.

"I need a favor from you." His words dripped with an air of authority that he shouldn't have in his current situation.

"You're going to answer my questions first," I shot back before he could sway the conversation further in his direction. The more I kept him on his toes, the better chance of him slipping up and telling me something that might help me out of this mess.

"Sure, I've got all the time in the world." He crossed his arms and leaned back in his chair.

My head swirled as the words I'd just shared with J.W. repeated almost verbatim from Scurry's mouth. Maybe J.W. was a ploy like the rest of this. I scrambled to come up with a good line of questioning, but my mind came up empty.

So I started with the basics. "You're S.I.R.E." It intentionally wasn't a question to let him know I was on to him.

He nodded but said nothing.

I waited, hoping he would expand, but he didn't. "So is a four-letter username a new protocol?"

"No, just simply a name—mine, to be more specific."

I gave him a confused look, which made his smile widen.

"My first name isn't Rufus. It's actually Elliot... Elliot Rufus Isaiah Surry." He leaned back against the bed, waiting for the light bulb to go off in my head.

E-R-I-S... or S-I-R-E backwards. I should have known it was another part of his game.

"What do you really want?" The words spilled out before I could stop them, but I knew deep down there was more he was withholding.

Scurry leaned forward, anticipating this question most of all. "Isn't that obvious?"

"Enlighten me."

"If you have to ask, you're not as smart as I thought you were."

The answer was simple, but with Scurry, it was never what it appeared to be on the surface. There were always a million things underneath the initial intent that had to be dug up like an ancient tomb. Even still, I needed to hear him confirm it. "You want your life back."

He winked at me, a small gesture that was goading me to go on. He wasn't going to indulge me with any concrete answers.

"The real question is, why? You mind-control the world, then what's left? Where's the fun in that?"

He laughed, not the mean, sadistic kind that usually erupted from him but a genuine laugh. "You and I aren't so different, you know."

Great. More half-answers. "We are nothing alike."

"No?" He uncrossed his arms and stood. Then shuffled to the far side of the room to pour some water. The camera panned out, showing more of the space, a bed and the single chair he'd been sitting on. Near the bed sat a small end table with a single pitcher of water. The walls and floor were rough unfinished concrete.

It didn't tell me anything other than he was still locked up some place without many resources beyond a camera that was likely meant to keep an eye on him. Of course, he'd figured out how to hack and manipulate it, just like he did everything else.

"You want to control everyone. I want to set them free. That's opposite ends of the spectrum."

"You exchanged one cage for another."

I scoffed but quickly composed myself, attempting to erase any sense of emotion from my expression. "Things are a lot better off now without the tracker network."

But I wasn't sure I believed those words. I'd seen both worlds, and neither seemed like a good solution. The right answer definitely wasn't a full-on mind-controlled and monitored world. On the flip side, taking away technology that had some positive influence wasn't exactly the answer either. My thoughts flicked back to the old couple on the street. Were they really better off without the health monitoring capabilities of their trackers?

The sneer returned. Scurry sensed my internal doubt. "The world devoured technology and proved they enjoyed being mindless zombies. I merely quenched their insatiable hunger for it."

"Technology sure, but they never asked to be your personal mind hacks." And in that moment, I knew the answer wasn't one or the other, but both. A little of each. With everything came a balance. We just had to find the right parts to include. "You know there are real people behind those trackers with lives, hopes, and dreams. They're not your pawns."

"No, they aren't. They used the technology with reckless abandon and let it control their lives. They needed someone to show them the way."

He was sick. He thought people needed him and his tech. In reality, he'd taken it all too far and was afraid to give up the power. Despite all the ramblings of a madman, one question remained in my mind. "Why me?" I asked.

"That, my dear, should be obvious."

I gritted my teeth to avoid showing him how angry I was at all these games and half-truths. Had he ever seen me as more than a chess piece in his game? I crossed my arms and stared right at the screen, hoping the camera caught my expression that plainly said I was done playing.

When he realized that I wasn't going to answer his manipulative questions, he said, "You were the one person standing in my way. Without you, I rule the world."

"Rule? When you finish, there will be no one left to think for themselves. You'll be nothing more than a glorified puppet master."

"After allowing trackers to run their lives, they deserve what they get. The world was headed to a uniform state of people wanting someone to show them the path to follow. I merely gave them strings and opened the curtains. When this is over, they'll open their arms and beg me to fix this mess—and fix it, I shall." He closed his eyes like he was contemplating his next move. When he opened them again, he blinked quickly in succession. He was activating something. "One thought and I have someone under my thumb. Who should be next?"

"Wait!" I cried. Something about him made me leap to reaction instead of waiting to see what else lay below the surface. Everything I'd said and done had already let him know he'd won.

When his smile returned, I knew he had me exactly where he wanted me. "If you do exactly what I say, I'll spare them."

Spare them. Not me. Tears welled in my eyes. As long as everyone I loved was safe, I didn't care what happened to me. I couldn't live with myself if I lost anyone else. They could learn to live without me, but I couldn't live without them, especially after all the pain and misdirection I'd put them through during this loophole and trying to protect Harlow. If my final act was protecting them, it'd be worth it.

"You're bluffing." It was a sorry last-ditch effort to see if I could wiggle out of this.

"Am I?" The expression on Scurry's face told me everything I needed to know.

I swallowed hard, then chose the only path left. "What do you need me to do?" The words were so quiet I almost didn't hear them myself.

Rufus didn't miss a beat. "That's my girl." The L curled on his tongue like he was enjoying this more than he thought he would. "When I set you free, you'll receive a set of coordinates and instructions. Follow those to the letter and no one gets hurt. Deviate, and I'll show you firsthand the consequences."

An image snapped into my vision without me opening any apps. It was dark at first, but a little bit of light seeped in, then disappeared. The third time it appeared, the small amount of light remained. The view panned upward toward a petite figure sitting in a chair across the room.

"You're awake!" said a voice I'd know anywhere.

It was Lydia. How was this possible? Before I could think of more questions, Lydia spoke again. "Harlow, are you sure you're okay?"

The camera moved up and down slightly, and then the realization washed over me. Scurry had hacked my tracker to allow me to witness what he saw when he controlled Harlow.

"This isn't funny. Say something." The thin shadow approached, and I got a better look at Lydia as she reached out her arms.

The scene shook me to my core. Harlow wasn't responding because he couldn't. Because Scurry had control of him.

"Wake up!" Lydia pleaded as the camera view bobbled. She was trying to shake Harlow back awake.

Harlow's arm snapped up, and his hand wrapped around her neck but didn't squeeze.

"Enough!" I screamed. "Let them go. I get your point."

"Tell anyone—"

"Yeah, I get it. You can mind-control someone and force them to kill, and no one will know it was you. Get on with it." I wasn't in a hurry to do Scurry's bidding, but the faster I moved this along, the faster I saw his endgame and some way around this. Maybe that would involve getting a message to the prison guards, or Bailen and the others. I'd have to be careful. If Scurry could mind-control anyone, then there was little limit to what he could do.

"Then we have an understanding?" Scurry asked with a sly smile.

"Send me the details. I'll do whatever you ask." I wasn't sure that was true, but for now, I could at least appease him.

"Very well. We have a deal. Follow my instructions, and Harlow and the others remain safe. But if you put one toe out of line, remember what power I have. I won't hesitate to flex it beyond him."

I nodded because I was shaking so badly, I wasn't sure my voice would come out clear enough. I had signed a deal with the puppet master, and now he was pulling my strings, too.

Twenty

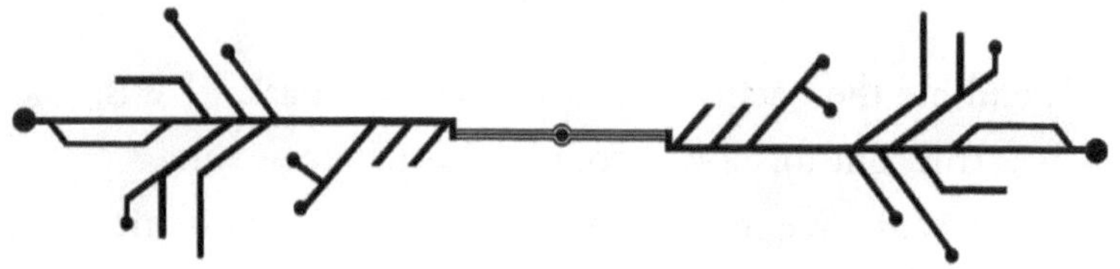

The video feed to Scurry went black. I collapsed to the floor and screamed until my throat went dry. Curling into a ball, I squeezed my knees into my chest, shut my eyes, and listened to the sound of my breathing. I knew I should get up and take inventory of all the computers and equipment in this makeshift command center, but I needed a minute. A minute to let my mind go in circles and grieve everything I was about to lose once again.

I'd done it before, but this time was different. When I ran from the authorities, I didn't know I'd be running straight to my brother and the best thing that ever happened to me. It had been a huge risk, but it had worked out. Now, my brother was dead, and I'd likely lost Bailen. There was no one to catch me after this leap. I was alone. If I asked for help, I'd lose everything. There'd be nothing left to live for, but right now, there was something left to protect.

I opened my eyes, expecting a message to be waiting on my

tracker, but there was none. Not from Scurry or the mysterious J.W. I stared at the floor and waited for inspiration to strike, but nothing came. I couldn't make myself move.

I told myself to get up, then said it out loud, hoping that hearing the words would spur me to action. "Get up, Kaya," I said again, more sternly. It was Mom-like enough to spur me into action. What I wouldn't do for a hug from her right now.

After another few deep breaths, I pushed off the floor and inspected the equipment: a couple of monitors, some keyboards and keypads, but no apparent power switches. Either they were hidden in the casings, or the equipment was activated remotely. While Bailen had taught me quite a few things about computers in the last six months, this was beyond my knowledge. It was painfully obvious that Scurry had thought through every inch of this place. He'd been planning and making contingencies for a long time. No amount of knowledge would have prepared me to go toe-to-toe with him.

It was the other side of the double-edged sword that was letting Scurry keep his tracker. If they had removed the earliest prototype from his head, it might have caused brain damage and lost tracker knowledge that only he possessed. But leaving it meant dealing with the world's most sophisticated and calculating mastermind. He knew he had the winning hand all along—he just had to let it play out.

Regardless, I was determined to use his confidence against him. I was halfway through crawling around the base of the equipment, looking for some way to stash a message on the off-chance Bailen or one of the others found their way here, when the grinding sound of a motor drew my attention.

I rushed down the steps in time for the metal door to click and swing open. It was a large, open room with a drain in the middle of the floor, not the mud hallway from before. It looked like an unfinished basement—rough gray walls, single light bulbs with chains in a few strategic places, and hookups for what looked like a washer and dryer that hadn't been there for a very long time. At the far side of the room, a set of wooden stairs led to a single door.

It didn't make sense. How had I gone through the same door and ended up somewhere completely different? Unless he'd somehow turned the room, like a revolving restaurant, so the door led somewhere else.

I stepped outside the door, and it instantly slammed shut behind me. The motorized sound ground a second time. The door disappeared, leaving a rough gray wall and no other exit but the stairs. So much for leaving a message behind.

I closed my eyes and searched my tracker for a chat app. It was grayed out. I checked my connections to the network, but there were none. It was like Scurry had never reached out.

The path forward was obvious, but the lack of instructions from the control freak bothered me. He clearly wanted ownership of the situation, but he had a funny way of showing it.

I scanned the room, looking for anything that would aid in my escape or tip the Ghosts off that I had been here. When I found nothing, I sighed and crossed the basement to the stairs. They creaked with each step. When I reached the door at the top, I pushed it, expecting to find someone's house. Instead, I found a single empty room with one window. Dust bunnies gathered in the corners and a cobweb hung from the sole light fixture. A single couch and a small end table were the only furniture, aside from a built-in bookcase filled with old books and knickknacks. Nothing out of the ordinary stood out.

My gaze panned from one end of the room to the other, looking for anything that might allow me a small advantage. But once I resigned myself to the fact that this was an abandoned room and there was nothing to write with in sight, I crossed to the bookshelf. I reached for one of the books, but it didn't budge. I checked them all, but they were just for show, not actual books. No way to even tear out letters from the pages to leave a message. He'd thought of everything.

I abandoned the room through the single exterior door. Outside the small cottage, I stepped onto the porch, which overlooked a large field. In the distance was the house I'd parked my crotchrocket in front of. So that was his game: cut me off from the outside world and everything I knew.

I stepped off the porch, intent on retrieving my bike. A notification light blinked on my tracker with the initials R.S. We were done with the S.I.R.E. thing, then. Closing my eyes, I thought about the message, then took a single calming breath before opening my eyes again.

R.S.: Don't even think about it.
Around the back of the house there's a
bike. Use that.

I screamed several choice words into the night air and then stomped around the back of the building. Sure enough, there was a motorcycle chained to a small tree, with a busted headlight and a spare for its front tire. This thing looked older than my parents, one of those original flying motorbike retrofit kits. He had to be joking.

As I got closer, I saw the chain was held on by an old-fashioned four-digit combo lock. But before I could even reach for it, another message notification popped up from R.S. I opened it.

R.S.: 1115

I spun the digits into place and the lock clicked open. Another message arrived on cue.

R.S.: Keys are in a false rock at the
base of the tree.

After walking to the base of the tree, I discovered the rock in question. I flipped it over to find the secret compartment with another combo. No message arrived on my tracker. I punched in the 1115, but it let out an awful buzz and a solid red light popped on. I tried 70285. The lock beeped with a solid green light. I was hardly surprised that Scurry was taunting me yet again with Jake's death. I opened the compartment, and the key fell into the palm of my hand.

"Here goes nothing," I muttered under my breath.

I circled back to the bike and unlocked the hidden compartment in the seat. No helmet. *What a cheap bastard.* Wouldn't he be sorry if I decided to ram this thing into a tree? I slammed the seat down and climbed aboard. After a few struggled groans from the engine, it kick-started with a rumble. Before I could open a chat bubble to say now what, a map popped up in my vision with a blinking dot that was me. A second blinking dot appeared in red.

"Message received loud and clear," I muttered under my breath.

I released the brake and whipped through the field before

taking to the sky. As I went airborne, I noticed headlights in the distance aimed right at my bike and the abandoned house. It had to be the Ghosts. I revved the engine as loud as I could, hoping one of them would notice. A message popped up in my field of vision.

R.S.: Do that again and there will be consequences.

K.W.: I'm not used to this ancient piece of crap. The gas is sensitive.

It was a total lie, but I had to play it off.

R.S.: Perhaps you need a reminder...

K.W.: All good, it's under control.

R.S.: It better be. We wouldn't want anyone to have any accidents now, would we?

I ignored the threat and angled the bike in the direction the map indicated. Based on my calculations, it would take about twenty minutes of flying time to arrive at the destination. As I leveled the bike off, I glanced over my shoulder to see if anyone was following, silently praying that they were. But the four bikes in the distance landed near where I had left my bike and cut their lights immediately. With a busted headlight, they likely wouldn't see me. I wished more than anything for Bailen's hacking skills so I could reach out to him in some way.

**R.S.: Keep it steady and not too high up.
You wouldn't want to draw any unwanted
attention.**

It was like he was reading my mind and twisting my thoughts. While unwanted attention might save me, the price Scurry was asking for wasn't worth it. With his endgame still a mystery, I wasn't sure I wanted to push my limits too far. I needed an exit strategy, something that would limit the collateral damage. My mind raced. Unfortunately, no ideas manifested.

I twisted the bike away from the farmhouse and silently said goodbye to my friends—who, if they were lucky, would find the control room but wouldn't find me.

As I flew through the darkness, I allowed myself a few moments of regret. Regret for trying to do this alone, regret for my friends, regret for my parents and Emily, regret for what might happen to all of them, and regret for what would happen to me. A single tear streaked down my cheek.

I sucked in a deep breath. When I exhaled, I sent all the regret with it. No amount of guilt would fix this situation. I'd made the only choice I could, the choice with the least amount of collateral damage.

The map flashed in the corner of my eye as my dot approached the red one in an abandoned part of town. It was an old industrial corridor. The warehouses had been abandoned, most of the businesses occupying them were fronts for funneling money, hacked tech, and other illegal activities. The only people who frequented these buildings now were the remnants of the authorities, who used them as hiding places.

That made it the perfect hiding place for Scurry. While the

Ghosts had finally surfaced and the majority of people like Ava, who'd supported trackers, had found other callings, the authorities who remained loyal to the cause had gone underground. It still wasn't clear if Scurry had broken free from SuperMax and he'd meet me there, or if he had something else planned for me.

I spotted the large warehouse indicated on the map and circled the building, looking for a place to land while scoping out the situation. It was completely abandoned. Some of the doors had chains holding them shut, but there was not a guard in sight.

I landed the bike by one of the side entrances. Going in the front door probably wasn't the most inconspicuous option. As soon as my wheels touched down, another message popped up.

**R.S.: Go inside. There's a box waiting.
Bring it with you.**

So, I was his errand monkey now? As much as I wanted to ask what kind of box I'd find, I didn't want to play further into Scurry's hands. I'd get the box quickly and then leave before anyone saw.

I cut the engine on the bike and stormed through the side door of the building. It clanged loudly behind me as it slammed into the metal frame rather than closing flush, evidence of the building's age.

Aside from some old machinery, run down forklifts, empty shelves, and broken palettes, there was nothing to see, just a warehouse darkened by the years of dust built up on its high windows.

While I was naïve enough to expect the box to be right inside the door, it was nowhere to be found. I stepped down to the first aisle of empty shelving but found nothing of interest.

I continued down the aisle and noticed a small office at the end of one of the rows. I turned the corner and headed toward it. The office door had a shattered window. Someone probably tried to break in at some point, but there was no scattered glass left behind. As I approached the office, I found it in complete disarray—file cabinets knocked over, papers everywhere, and desk chairs overturned. Someone was looking for something, but I couldn't tell whether it directly aligned with what Scurry was up to or it had something to do with the prior businesses at this location.

I stepped inside the office to search for the box, realizing I had no idea what size it was or if there was even a box to begin with. Maybe Scurry wanted me separated from the group, hence this demented scavenger hunt. And yet, no note from Scurry on where to find what he sent me here for.

K.W.: A little help? This place is huge.

I sent the note, but no reply followed. Maybe Scurry wasn't as closely tied to my activities as I thought. I backed out of the office and headed toward the bike, intent on making a run for it. Not even halfway to the door, another message appeared.

R.S.: Second floor.

What did that mean? I was in a warehouse. There wasn't exactly an elevator. I scanned the edges of the large space until I found a set of steps leading to what appeared to be a small, lofted area. From this distance, I couldn't tell what the area was intended for.

"This better be good, Scurry," I muttered under my breath.

Not because I believed it, but because this place was sending chills up my spine, and I needed to hear something familiar.

I tore down the aisle toward the stairs. My breathing was heavy as I approached my destination, but I didn't slow. Taking the steps two at a time, I stopped at the top to catch my breath. I looked over the railing at the abandoned warehouse below, checking to see if someone was coming up one of the aisles after me, but there was no one. The quiet was eerie instead of calming.

I pivoted away from the railing to find half a dozen desks with paper and old equipment strewn about them. No computers, but there were some old circuit boards and other small electronics. I swiped a couple of memory sticks and some USB drives. Bailen and the others might have a use for them—if I ever saw the Ghosts again. Swallowing hard, I made my way to the back corner of the loft where a desk sat away from the others. The surface was empty other than a thick layer of dust.

The old chair creaked as I sat in it and reclined, propping my feet on the desk. So much for that box, huh Scurry? If he wanted me out of the way, congratulations, consider me outsmarted. I slammed my heel down on the desk in frustration and it clanged, not just because the desk was metal, but because the center desk drawer was loose and possibly had something inside.

The drawer screeched as I pulled it open. Inside was a set of two keys with a number on them: K54. I inspected the lock on the side of the desk, but it didn't match. I stepped to the next desk and it didn't go there either. Scanning the room to see if any of the desks stood out, I found no clues. I worked my way up each aisle until I stopped at the last desk in the first row. The only thing I hadn't searched yet. But it, like the others, didn't match the keys. Maybe the keys were useless. I almost tossed them over the railing when I noticed a small lockbox on the other side of the desk.

I picked up the rusted metal box and read the number around the lock. K54. Finally. Unlocking the box left me with no additional answers. Only another set of keys, this time with the imprint T53.

"If I wanted a challenge, I would have gone back to Bailen and Ava for coding classes," I said, hoping the sound of my own voice would provide some comfort. But hearing Bailen's name in my voice only reminded me of how much I missed him, missed the old us. It left me wondering if we were beyond repair. If I'd made the right decision to keep him out of this.

T53. That number sounded familiar. I spun around and went back up the second row of desks, checking the locks again until I found the matching desk. I quickly unlocked it and yanked open the bottom drawer to find a box.

The cardboard box had no writing and was secured with clear packing tape. I lifted the box, which was surprisingly heavy for its size, and peered at the underside. A small bit of writing drew my attention: 70285. This had to be it.

Setting the box on the desk, I fell into an old desk chair and reclined as I stared at my find. Did I open it and risk Scurry taking my curiosity out on someone I cared about, or did I ignore the contents and bring him the box that would surely make things worse?

Neither seemed like a good option. I could leave the box and pretend I never found it, but that might escalate things beyond my ability to deal with Scurry. I leaned forward and whispered to the box, "You'd better be worth it." Then I ripped the tape off the top of the box and stared at the contents.

A large metal box similar to the one I'd fried in Scurry's secret server room lay in front of me. I didn't know enough about the equipment to know if it was exactly the same. If I was a betting person, I'd count on the fact that Scurry needed this to have more power over whatever he was using to mind-control people.

There was no way I could let him get his hands on this tech. But if I kept it from him, he'd make my life miserable by punishing those I cared about.

Before I had time to think through all the possible outcomes, a light blinked in the corner of my vision. I had an incoming message, and there was no indication of who it was from.

Twenty-One

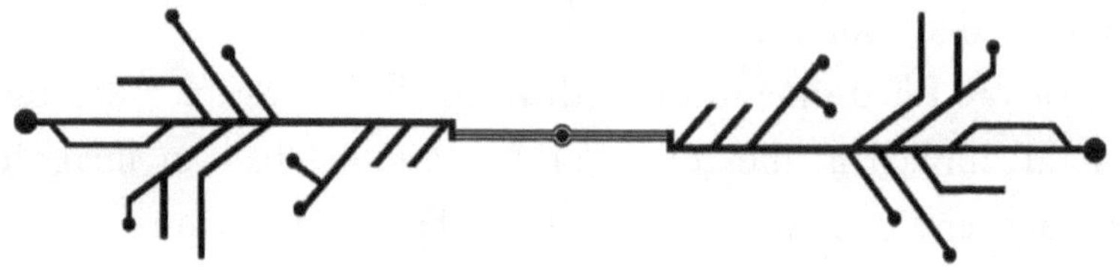

It had to be Scurry. He was going to demand his box. I closed my eyes for a long time, my mind swirling with all the ways this could go wrong. There were too many to track. When I opened my eyes, I thought about the message to read it.

: Open the box.

That was new. No letters indicating a handle of any kind. I thought about the message and accessing the profile, then blinked twice. The profile was empty too. Without that information, it wasn't a standard issue tracker profile, not even a hacked one. But it didn't feel like something Scurry would say either.

: Hurry. We don't have much time.

But that was almost exactly what J.W. had said the last time they reached out. I thought about my response and sent it on, exactly as before.

K.W.: I've apparently got all the time in the world.

: Time is all relative to the individual.

The reply cemented things. J.W. was reaching out again, but likely scrubbed the profile and initials to help mask their presence. Maybe they were hiding from Scurry or worried about someone else finding them. If J.W. was hiding, then I shouldn't ask to confirm the identity. They could remain a mystery—at least for now.

I inspected the box, saw the screws holding it together, then rummaged through the desks for a screwdriver. When I found one, I removed the six screws and lifted the metal top off the box. Circuit boards and connectors stared back at me. Definitely not my area of expertise.

K.W.: Now what?

: Cut the green wire. Think of it like a four-leaf clover. It's your good luck charm.

What an odd thing to say, even if J.W. was all about odd things. It had to be the same person. The fact that they mentioned a four-leaf clover was the most interesting part. My mind flicked back to Bailen's bike, now sitting outside the farmhouse. Had Bailen and the others found it? Were they still looking for me?

I'd first noticed the image the night Peyton stole his bike to rescue me. The loud crotchrocket engine had roared above me, drawing my attention to the four-leaf clover emblem. The bike landed between me and the authorities. They were moments from cuffing me and dragging me to Global Tracking Systems to cut into my skull and remove my tracker.

It was the night I met the Ghosts. The night I'd met Bailen. The night I found… I couldn't finish the thought. It was too painful to think about Jake.

I circled back to what I knew about Bailen's bike and the night I'd met him. He'd never talked about the symbol, nor what his connection was to it. Now I wished I had asked him, even if it was something seemingly insignificant. Maybe this was Bailen's obscure way of trying to get in contact, trying to protect me.

As much as I wished for that to be true, this didn't sound like Bailen. Just as the bike had been my out before, maybe this "four-leaf clover" J.W. had handed me was my out now.

Following the four-leaf clover before had ended well, but was it really the right decision now, when Scurry had my life and so many others in his hands, ready to crush us all? On the other hand, I'd been looking for a chance to take back control, and here it was staring me in the face. I grabbed a pair of wire cutters from the desk drawer and put the green wire in between the sharp nose of the tool.

There was no going back if I cut this wire. Despite being in over my head, if I gave Scurry this box, things would get a lot worse for a lot more people, including those I cared about most. If I sabotaged this box, Scurry would take it out on my family and friends. Best case, this would stop whatever loophole was at work. If nothing else, it would buy some time.

Without another thought, I clipped the wire. My heart sped as

I instantly regretted the decision. What had I done? Even though my gut was a swirling mess of nerves, my mind quietly whispered that it was the right decision, consequences or not.

: Good. Now make it look like an
accident.

K.W.: How?

: Fray the edges so it looks like it rubbed
against the metal divider.

I looked down at the wire and how the majority ran along a vertical metal plate dividing two of the circuit boards. How had J.W. known that? Either they had a schematic or they were seeing what I saw. Neither thought was very comforting, but J.W. was right. If I made it look like the wire had frayed over the divider, maybe I could play this all off as an accident. I stripped the wire coating back and unwound the wire fibers. Then rubbed each side against the rough edge of the divider wall. That should do the trick.

: Now see the box with the blue light.

I nodded even though J.W. couldn't see me. That blue light had taunted me ever since the night we took down the tracker network. I thought I'd seen one blink inside the box that was in the brains of the tracker network, but I convinced myself I'd imagined it. Now I was certain I hadn't.

K.W.: Let me guess, you want me to
destroy it and make it look like an accident

too.

: Clever girl. Make it happen.

I thought about how to make that happen, but honestly, I didn't need to pretend. I picked up the box and took it to the top of the stairs, then dropped it. A smile erupted on my face as I watched it clang down each step until it crashed to the first floor. Consider it destroyed, or so I hoped.

I grabbed the screws, the cover plate, and the screwdriver and bounded down the steps. After flipping the box, I inspected each component. Most were unharmed, but a few had cracked circuit boards. The component with the blue light was fractured. That should do the trick. The problem was making it look like an accident. Before I could think up a plan, I received another message.

: Nice work. Now hurry, he's waiting.

Well, at least someone was pleased with my actions, even if it would piss off Scurry. The only positive part would be watching the disappointment on Scurry's face when he saw his plan had been unraveled.

As I fastened the cover back onto the box, I realized I hadn't heard from Scurry in a while. Not that I cared, but if he wanted the box so badly, why all the silence? Something didn't feel right. Maybe the guards at SuperMax were watching him too closely, or maybe he'd already plotted and enacted his escape.

J.W. had popped up at the exact right time again—in Scurry's absence. The thought had the hairs standing up on my arms. I'd get to the bottom of whatever weird things were going on. Until then, I had a box to deliver.

I opened a message to Scurry.

> K.W.: Where am I taking this thing? It's
> heavy.

No response came for several minutes. I put the box under my arm and made a beeline for the door. If I didn't hear from Scurry by the time I was on the bike, I would head back to the Hive. When I reached the door, I yanked it open with my free hand and darted to the bike. I dumped the box into the compartment in the bike's seat, smiling to myself as it banged against the sides. Kick-starting the bike, I reoriented to point in the direction of the Ghost hideout. As I released the parking brake, a message with the initials R.S. appeared in the corner of my vision.

I swore under my breath and opened it.

> R.S.: Follow the map. You have 20
> minutes to get here.
> It should only take you 15.

How generous of him to give me five extra minutes to figure out what to do next.

> R.S.: Need I remind you what happens if
> you're late?

Pushy, pushy. Something had accelerated his timeline. I released the clutch, revved the engine, and aimed the bike skyward. My mind raced faster than the wind whipping past me as I tried to piece together not only what Scurry was up to, but what was forcing him to move quickly. If I could figure that out, I might be able to gain an advantage. In the back of my mind, I wished it was Bailen who had caught up to Scurry. Outside of my own sabotage, the Ghosts really were my only hope.

Distracted by my thoughts, I nearly missed an important turn headed farther out of town. Scurry was taking me to the middle of nowhere.

As I approached a large building surrounded by two sets of barbed wire fences and flanked by multiple abandoned guard towers, my tracker message indicator light blinked.

R.S.: Land in the back field. There's less security there.

Security. He was routing me to the back door with the hope I wouldn't get caught. I landed the bike and cut the engine. I sat motionless as I tried to process it all. Scurry was manipulating and calling the shots, but someone was still watching him too. As off as this whole scavenger hunt felt, the final steps to the end didn't feel nearly as satisfying as they should. Was I about to be sent on another chase, or was I missing an important piece of the puzzle?

I scanned the fence and looked for signs of movement but found none. I checked each guard tower, but they were all empty. In all the searching, I didn't find a way in either, which left more questions as to why Scurry wanted me to park around back.

The lack of security guards was only the beginning. He didn't want me to get caught because it would mean he'd get caught too. Which meant he wasn't here by choice. He was still where they'd left him to rot. And Scurry was manipulating me to get what he wanted, holding the people I cared about hostage until he could get his network back online. And he wouldn't stop there.

Once back in the network, he could control everything. He'd free himself and rebuild it all. That was his plan all along. It had nothing to do with revenge, although he probably enjoyed that piece, too. He wanted his life back, his throne atop Global Tracking Systems. He wanted to be in control again and for the world to bow before him willingly. If they refused, he had a tracker loophole waiting for them.

My gut twisted as the whole realization crashed down around me. I'd been his pawn and allowed this to happen. Why me? Why not control someone else to bring the box to him? I had to be missing something. If this task was for me, then he not only wanted his box, he wanted something from me. He was moments from turning the world back into the controlling, scary place it had been six months ago, and he wanted me out of the way while he did it.

But I was done playing his game. Done letting it happen.

I turned the key on the bike and revved the engine. Before I could get very far, a terrible pain shot through my head, and the scream that erupted from my mouth echoed inside my mind. It was an electric jolt unlike any feeling I'd experienced before, like someone was trying to break a wall in my mind. I grabbed the sides of my face and cried out in agony, but I quickly clamped my mouth shut as the volume of the noise amplified the pain. I pushed all the emotion back into my tracker the way I had when I'd fought the network in the past. It didn't appear to shut anything down, but the pain was gone, and my mind was clearer.

Spinning the back wheel out, I turned the bike away from the prison and gunned the engine, racing through the empty field. Empty until a shadow appeared in the distance. The dark outline of a human, someone tall and muscular, but I couldn't see who. I turned the bike, and the figure darted with superhuman speed so it once again blocked my path. I turned the bike the other way and again the figure dashed in front of me. As the distance closed between us, I engaged the flying mechanism.

I pulled back on the handlebars, angling the bike skyward just in time to sail right over the figure. At the last second, the figure raised its arm and grabbed the bike. The engine choked and sputtered as the bike stopped briefly midair. I jolted forward when the bike abruptly changed directions. Then I was falling, being yanked downward until…

CRASH.

I slammed into the ground. The air rushed from lungs. I coughed and gagged, trying to catch my breath. The weight of the bike was on top of me, and then it was gone, as if some superhuman had picked it off me like a feather and tossed it aside. Despite the lack of weight pressing on me, it still felt as though a large boot held me down. The pressure on my chest didn't ease. I coughed and gasped, trying to find air that wasn't reaching my lungs.

After what felt like several minutes of straining to breathe, I was finally able to inhale without wheezing. I tried to push up from my stomach using my arms. They buckled beneath me. On the second attempt, I was successful. I pulled up to my knees and turned to sit in the grass as I attempted to slow my labored breathing. I looked up at the bulky figure hovering above me.

A searchlight in the distance circled the field. As it passed by, I found the glassy eyes of Troy Ackerman staring back at me.

Twenty-Two

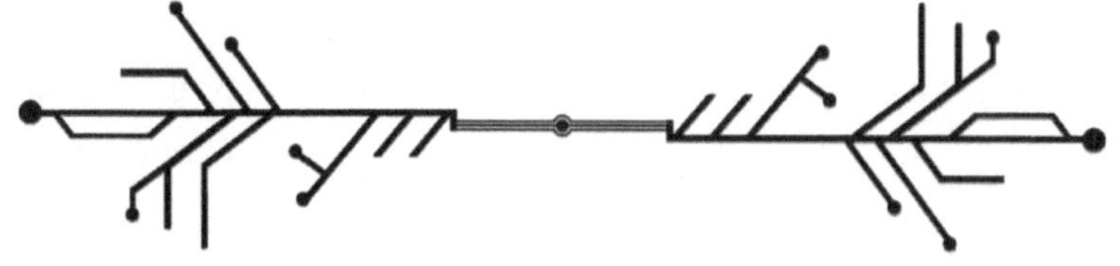

I opened my mouth and closed it several times, waiting for the right words. But no words would help me out of this situation. I'd seen that glassy look before. While there was a very slim chance I could have appealed to Troy Ackerman—the competitive soccer star who always wanted to win and the guy Lydia had crushed on—mind-controlled Troy Ackerman was another story completely. There was no reasoning with this shell of a person with superhuman abilities hovering over me. Was there anyone Rufus Scurry couldn't touch?

Everything in my mind screamed run, but my body shook, not from fear, but from the pain and shock of everything transpiring before me. Troy not only wasn't in control of his actions, but he'd hulked out over the last six months. He had never been a small guy, but this Troy looked like he'd bulked up and grown half a foot in the blink of an eye. Mind-controlled or not, I had very little chance of outrunning him or beating him in a feat of strength.

Scurry knew this. It's why he'd lured me to the back of the

building where he could strategically plant his backup plan in case I tried to run. I'd fallen for it just like he'd wanted.

I twisted into a crouching position and launched myself onto my feet. I bolted through the long grass in the field. While I had no idea where I was running, I knew I had to get away and hide from Troy and Scurry. Then maybe I could send for help somehow.

The grass rustled behind me. I didn't have time to glance back. Heavy panting echoed in my ears, growing louder with each step. Troy was there. I picked up my speed, but I was far from the athlete Troy was. He'd been training his whole life, building the stamina required to run a soccer ball up and down a field repeatedly for over an hour. I'd spent too much time painting pretty pictures of people running. Too bad sketching an athlete didn't grant me their abilities. The longer I ran, the more my muscles burned. I ignored the pain and kept going.

As my breaths grew closer and closer together, my throat dried out. It wasn't a fair race, but I ran anyway, scanning the field for a place to hide. If I didn't take the slim chance of escape, I'd regret it. I spotted some trees in the distance, but they seemed too far out of reach. Even if I could get there, Troy was on my heels. I'd never get enough distance to hide.

Arms wrapped around me and squeezed out my remaining breath. Our momentum carried us forward, somersaulting over each other. In all the tumbling, zombie Troy still managed to hold tight to my waist. I squirmed, but he was like a boa constrictor. The more I moved, the tighter he clung to me.

"Stop fighting or I will snap your neck." It was Troy's hot breath beating on the side of my face, but his voice was slower and gravelly with Scurry talking through him.

"Go ahead and kill me. I don't care anymore." At least if he killed me, I'd die knowing I didn't contribute to the downfall of millions of people's freedom.

"I can see how little we value ourselves. But maybe we care more about others around us," the gravelly voice continued. Through all the talking, Troy's face lacked any emotion—a puppet without any free will. Even without the emotion, I knew Scurry was enjoying this. "Perhaps I should take Emily instead."

I instantly stopped flailing.

"That's better."

The hot breath on the back of my neck made my skin crawl. I hated myself for cooperating, but Scurry knew every single soft spot and when to twist or squeeze them.

"I didn't do it for you." I couldn't have said any truer words. The man knew no boundaries and would take over the mind of a little girl, scar her for life, all to get me to do exactly what he wanted. No ends justified those means.

I regretted how busy I'd become. Sure, I'd recently spent an afternoon with Emily, but it never felt like enough. I couldn't withstand the tornado of guilt building inside me. After all she'd been through. Scurry mind-controlling Harlow to kidnap her, her mom gone, and her poor excuse for an uncle… She needed some stability. I'd been that when we'd unplugged her from the network. We had connected when she was alone, and that bond grew every time I saw her.

Lately, the time we spent together never felt like enough. Each time I had to leave her with her uncle wore me down.

My insides burned with frustration. I couldn't be everywhere at once. I couldn't protect and save everyone. Every decision I made came with a cost to someone I cared about. But of all those people, if something happened to Emily, I would never forgive myself for it. I owed her better than the shitty hand she'd been dealt.

For the first time, I understood why Bailen got so angry when I tried to take on the world alone. It meant losing the ability to do everything he possibly could to prevent bad things from happening. I understood his need to help. We may not have agreed on the approach to fixing things, but by keeping him out of the loop, I'd eliminated his best chance to try. Eliminated my best chance at preventing this whole mess.

This was all my fault.

I wouldn't be here now if I'd trusted those around me. Talked through options. Thought through things a bit more. Maybe we could have come to a compromise and maybe not, but at least I wouldn't be here alone trying to fight some evil mastermind who could manipulate someone twice my size.

My body went limp, refusing to go on, but my mind wouldn't let me quit. *Not yet*, it said, *there's still work to do.*

With one muscular arm, Troy yanked me onto my feet and pushed me back toward the mutilated bike. Scurry must have taken my collapse as me giving in. Best to let him continue to think that. I looked into Troy's dead, glassy eyes but found nothing there— no soul, no light, no person. He was so deeply controlled, I wasn't sure the person underneath existed anymore.

"Don't even think about it." His mouth moved, but it didn't seem like the words were coming from Troy.

Maybe through Troy's glassy eyes, he still saw the fire in mine.

"You have this all wrong," I spat. I wanted to say so much more, but Scurry wouldn't understand it anyway. The man lacked compassion, lacked understanding of others, lacked empathy, and lacked the ability to see that others may not want the same things he did. That it was okay to disagree, but not okay to force his will upon others. There was no reasoning with someone like that.

We approached the bike. Troy opened the seat and lifted the box out. He tucked it under his right arm and grabbed both my wrists with his left hand.

"Let's go."

He dragged me toward the fence topped with barbed wire.

This was about more than just the box. Scurry wasn't done with me yet. While I went willingly, my mind spun, trying to find any path of resistance. I couldn't connect Scurry's plan for me to his bigger picture. I wished Bailen or even the mysterious J.W. would come back. They always seemed to appear when I needed them most. My heart raced as we marched closer and closer to the chain-link fence. I was running out of time. The minute I was inside, it would be impossible to do anything—no running, no messages, only complying with the ravings of a madman.

I couldn't hack my tracker and get a message out. I didn't have the skills for that, but the thought of J.W. gave me an idea. I'd used his profile to try to unmask him. If I updated my profile, Bailen might see it. It was a long shot since he wasn't really on the network anymore, but maybe he'd look, considering the state of the loophole and my disappearance. I had to try something.

While there was a small risk Scurry might find it too, it was more likely he wouldn't look in plain sight. But I made a cryptic message just in case. Using a rail cipher, I carefully crafted a message to say *WITH RS* hidden in the profile updates. Since Bailen cracked the previous one, he'd likely know to look for it again. It wasn't much, but hopefully if he searched my profile, he'd know how to find me.

At the fence, Troy shoved me face first into the chain links. The metal dug into the skin on my cheek and arms. With his other arm, he ripped a hole in the fence without much effort. Hulk was an understatement. This was beyond mind-control. It was using the tracker's connection to the brain to push a body beyond its limits, which meant eventually Troy's body would give out. I didn't know exactly in what way, but it was something to keep an eye out for. While Troy was never my favorite person, he didn't deserve the pain it would cause, but it might be my only chance of escape.

Troy pushed me through the hole in the fence and marched me toward the long, dark building. The few windows along the hallways were unlit, devoid of sound or movement. As more of the building came into focus, Troy angled me away from the door and pointed me toward a small, open window with no screen or bars on it. I could fit through the space, but a glance back at Troy told me there was no way he would. Which left me with more questions than answers.

Before I could formulate a complete thought, Troy lifted me and shoved me through the window feet first. Once my head and torso cleared the glass, he dropped me. I crashed to the floor with a thud and lay still for a moment to catch my breath. I moved my arms and legs in an attempt to relieve some of the pain shooting like pins and needles through my body, but the act was useless. Using a folding chair, I heaved myself to my feet.

Troy reached inside the window and placed the box on a nearby counter. As I reached for the open window, he slammed it shut in my face. He bent the frame, which let out a sickening scraping noise in protest. I pulled on the window with all my strength. It didn't budge. Through all the grunting and tugging at the window, Troy stood still as a statue, staring through the glass, his gaze connected with mine. If only my eyes could shoot daggers or flames. Instead, I left him with my best pissed off look, hoping Scurry would get the message.

I turned from the window and examined what looked like an abandoned breakroom. There was a rusted sink and a vacant spot on the wall where a fridge used to be hooked up. A small, round table sat in the center of the room with four folding chairs. I reached for the chair, intent on breaking the glass window, but the blinking red light on my tracker stopped me.

I let out an exasperated scream, not caring who heard me, then opened the message.

R.S.: Grab the box. Take a right out of
that room and continue to the end of the
hall.
Be quiet.
Don't get caught.

Don't get caught? Was he kidding? I was already caught. Getting caught might get me out of this mess. Or I could make it worse. A million scenarios ran through my head. Continue to let Scurry manipulate me, or explain to the guards why a sixteen-year-old girl was in their super-secret prison, then scramble to explain what Scurry was up to before I got into even more trouble than I was already in. They'd think I was making up some kind of cover story or they'd call my mom or dad. Maybe that was exactly what I wanted. I snagged the box and tucked it under my arm.

I peeked into the hallway, but without any windows, it was darker than the breakroom. The walls were white and boring, and the tile floors were equally so. Shadows loomed, but none in the shape of a human form.

Where were all the guards? Surely someone knew what he was up to.

Scurry said go right, which looked like a really long hallway, but left looked like the direction of offices or maybe a guard station. I stepped into the hall and bolted in the opposite direction Scurry had instructed. Maybe this would be easier than I thought.

But I skidded to a stop as a large shadowy figure appeared at the end of the hall.

"Help me!" I screamed.

The figure blocked the way with his large arms crossed. Another one of Scurry's zombies. I took one step toward the figure, but it countered with two steps. After another step, the figure took four. I ran at the large man, hoping I could squeeze around him, but the figure took a defensive football stance and caught me midair around my waist as I tried to launch around his blockade.

"Nice try," the deep, gravelly voice said.

I punched the guy in the stomach with my free hand, but he didn't even grunt in reply.

The large man lifted me, box and all. He carried me under his arm like a large, rolled up canvas. I kicked and screamed to no avail. He proceeded down the long hall, past the breakroom and around the next corner. We approached what looked like a checkpoint, a large door with barred windows and a guard station. It was empty, but the man carrying me extended his badge on the elastic and scanned it next to the door. A loud buzz rang out as the door clicked.

He pulled open the door, shoved me on the other side, and closed it without stepping through. I pounded on the door and kicked it. I threw the box. It clanged against the metal. The noise echoed off the walls. I screamed, but the man stood with his back to the door, and no one seemed to be within earshot of the commotion.

I turned from the door, grabbed the box, and crept down the short hallway, which had two options. The one to my right ended in a single door. The one to my left was a long hallway that curved somewhere out of sight.

I didn't wait for instructions. It was clear Scurry wanted a face-to-face meeting. To get that, I'd have to go deep into the bowels of this prison. The single locked door wasn't going to get me there.

I ran down the hall, turned the corner, and paused to get my bearings. Floors and floors of prison cells loomed above me. The ones on the first level were open and empty. It didn't seem all that secure for a maximum-security prison, even an abandoned one. I needed to find solitary confinement, or better yet, the places they put people they hoped no one would ever find. The kind of holding cells they didn't tell the average person about. I knew they must exist because that was the only kind of place they would put someone like Scurry.

But it didn't add up. If he had control over so many people, why not improve his situation a bit, or leave altogether?

I walked the cells more slowly, looking for some kind of secret hallway or stairs to another area of the prison. But there was nothing aside from the ordinary cells. I had to be missing something.

As if on cue, the light on my tracker blinked.

R.S.: Enjoying the scenery?

**K.W.: Enough with the games. Let's get
this over with.**

R.S.: As you wish.

I shrieked as a loud metallic crash rang out behind me. I pivoted and headed back in the direction of the sound. I stopped in front of a cell where a bed was lying in the center of the floor. Knowing it hadn't been that way before, I stood in the doorway of the cell, wary that the bars might close if I stepped all the way in.

Outside of the bed being detached from the wall, nothing felt out of place. Maybe this was just a fluke. The moment the thought crossed my mind, the wall with the sink and toilet swung open with a creak, revealing a dark doorway.

Somewhere dank and hidden for sure. I scanned the cell block before stepping toward the secret passage. After three steps, I was across the cell. A bang behind me made me jump, sending my heartbeat into an erratic rhythm. I didn't have to look back to know the cell door had slammed shut, trapping me inside, forcing me into the dark passageway.

I pushed the doorway open, and it screeched in protest. Behind it was a stone stairwell lit by single bulbs every twenty feet or so. While I was tempted to throw the box down the stairs, I left it tucked safely under my arm as I started down. Cold air surrounded me, the temperature dropping the farther down I went.

I continued down the stairs quickly, losing count of how many I'd traveled. When I finally reached the bottom, I found a single wooden door. I twisted the knob and, to my surprise, it opened without any need for a key or electronic lock. I stepped into a long white hallway with flickering overhead lights. Toward the end of the hall was a large bank of windows. My footsteps echoed off the walls as I moved closer to them. They weren't really windows at all, but a two-way mirror that peeked into what appeared to be some sort of observation deck.

The glass overlooked a narrow room with rows of computers and dozens of monitors stacked in a grid. All the monitors were shut off except one—the very last monitor on the bottom row. A camera watched Rufus in a small cement cell with a single bed, nightstand, chair, and his pitcher of water. The same room he'd been in when we had our chat in the secret passageway at the abandoned farmhouse. Scurry sat on the bed staring up at the camera. His direct stare bored into me, sending a shiver of dark anticipation up my spine. I watched the monitor, staring back at him even though I knew he couldn't see me.

In front of the monitor bank sat a skinny man in a black authority uniform slumped over in the chair. At first glance he looked asleep. I banged my fists on the glass and screamed, but the man didn't move. I ran the rest of the way down the hall and rounded the corner to a set of doors. Most of them were locked, but a single one opened to a metal ladder attached to the concrete wall. A tunnel downward. I tucked the box under my arm, then climbed down the ladder. At the bottom, I stepped out of the alcove into the long room with the computers.

I rushed to the man but stopped short of reaching out to him. He had a glassy look in his eyes. He wasn't sleeping. He wasn't dead either. He was under Scurry's control. How many puppets could Scurry have at once? It had to be exhausting.

I backed away slowly, hoping the lack of sudden movements would keep the guard from waking up. But the man sprang from the chair and grabbed my free wrist before I was fully out of reach.

I yanked my arm and twisted, but his grip grew tighter with each maneuver I made. The man pulled me further into the computer bank toward another open doorway. This one led to another set of stone steps, but they only appeared to go down about half a floor.

I nearly tripped and dropped the box as he hauled me down the steps toward another guard station, which looked identical to the previous one. The only difference was this station had two gates. I knew what was coming. It was useless to try wriggling free, and yet I wanted Scurry to know every step of the way I would not give in so easily. I struggled and twisted until the man badged open the first checkpoint and shoved me through it. Once he slammed the door shut, the second buzzed loudly. I turned to the man, but he was already halfway back to the stone steps.

The door ahead of me continued to buzz. I grabbed the knob and threw it open. The buzzing stopped, but I could still hear the echo in my head along with my footsteps as I moved down the hallway with renewed purpose. I had to be getting close. I turned the corner. The hallway was filled with black numbered doors lining both sides.

I passed each set of doors, odds on the right and evens on the left. When I reached the final door, numbered twenty, I stared at it. I wasn't sure what I was expecting to happen. None of the doors had any knobs or handles, clearly set up so only one person could open these doors. I searched my tracker to see what might be in the area or if there was an unlocking app. Sure enough, I could access a single door.

How could Scurry give me access to the door but not use it himself or have one of his puppets do it for him? Was he choosing to stay here? I was in too deep now to make sense of the madness. I had to give Scurry the box before time ran out and he started taking this out on more people I cared about.

I opened the unlocking program. It had five white, empty boxes on a black screen: a five-digit pin. I used the same number from the secret passageway at the old barn. Sure enough, the door buzzed. I took a deep breath, opened the door, and stepped inside.

Twenty-Three

Scurry leaned back on the bed in a white jumpsuit, legs crossed, hands behind his head, staring at me with a smug look on his face.

I tossed the box to the floor with a loud thud. His arrogant grin turned to a grimace as the box slid and scraped across the rough concrete floor. I took the smallest hint of pleasure knowing something I'd done finally had gotten to him. "There's your dumb box. Now leave me and my friends alone."

I turned toward the door, intent on leaving, but the quiet clearing of his throat stopped me.

"What did you do to it?" he asked. His voice was stern but not above his normal volume.

I pivoted away from the door. "Nothing." I dared him to call my bluff. "You should talk to your goon who ripped the bike out of midair and crashed it to the ground with me and the box on it."

He threw his legs over the side of the bed and pushed his feet to the floor. He crouched next to the box and turned it over. As he examined it, small components scraped and clinked along the inside, likely coming loose in all its adventures.

"Well, then I guess I'll have Daddy come fix it. We were friends after all." The smug expression returned.

My face scrunched. With fists balled, I screamed, "You leave him out of this!" So much for a subtle approach. I hated that he got under my skin so easily.

"Why? He started it." Scurry paused, waiting for a reaction, but this time I refused to give him one.

Sure, Dad had planted the glitchy tracker inside my head. Even though I still hadn't fully forgiven him, I never wanted him to be part of Scurry's demented puppet show. My options were brain surgery, hide forever, or take down the tracker network. Not much of a choice. Taking down the tracker network had caused a lot of pain, but I wasn't sure there was a better path forward. We would have to forge ahead and make things better, going forward with what we'd learned from the past.

"I said, leave him alone." This time my voice was steady and stern, hoping Scurry would get the message.

Scurry shrugged. "Perhaps another way, then?"

He was toying with me, and while I wanted to scream at him, I remained calm. "Answer me one question before you do. You clearly have the world at your fingertips. Why stay here? Why not break out?"

He nodded. "If I leave here, the government will launch a manhunt for me. I needed a place to lay low and formulate my plan.

"Why not have the guards bring you what you need? You clearly have control over this place. Why use me?"

A sly grin erupted on his face. "I think you know the answer to that."

I nodded but said nothing.

"I had to keep an eye on you someway. Distracting you with a task that further set everything in motion was an added bonus. Alas, this setback will cost you." He nodded at the box.

"I owe you nothing." I crossed my arms and glared at him.

"Perhaps your boyfriend can come fix it, then. I hear he's quite the tech wiz." His grin deepened.

Dread swirled through me as the horrific realization washed over me. He had Bailen too. Not physically, but under his tracker chokehold.

I'd kept Bailen out of the loop for his own protection, and now he hated me for it. Despite that, I never thought it would come to this. If I wasn't alone before, now I truly was, without any options. There was no limit to the lengths Scurry would go to isolate and defeat me.

"You can do what you want with me, but I'm begging you, leave them out of this." I'd have gotten down on my knees and pleaded if I thought it might help, but I knew it wouldn't.

"Begging? Tsk. Tsk. I thought you were above that." His grin widened. He'd break me beyond repair before this was all finished.

"This is between you and me. Your quest for revenge is with me. Leave them alone."

Scurry's grin faded, quickly replaced with a venomous expression. "It's a little late for that."

"What, afraid of a fight, old man?"

My heart fluttered in my chest. I knew that sassy voice. I whirled to find Peyton standing in the doorway.

I'd never been so happy to see her. Words failed me.

"Oh, don't go all gooey eyed on me," she said, stepping into the room. Ava followed close behind.

Jeremy slid inside after and crossed the room to Scurry. He snatched the box out of Scurry's hands and tossed it to the doorway. I thought it was going to crash to the floor until Bailen appeared in the doorframe and caught it.

He grimaced at me and shrugged. But when his gaze locked on mine, I found relief in them, a glimmer of happiness to see me. The air rushed from my lungs. I don't know how I got across the room, but I quickly found myself in his arms. I had so many things to say as the tears streamed down my face. The only word I could get out was, "How?"

"Let's just say I got your message." He smiled, then leaned in.

Before I could respond, his lips were on mine. I'd forgotten how much I missed kissing him. Forgotten how much I needed him. Forgotten how mad we were at each other. It was just him and me. Every other worry fell away.

"AHEM!" Ava cleared her throat.

I jumped back from Bailen, remembering we still had a job to do, but he pulled back slower than I expected considering the immediacy of the situation.

"Prisoner is secure." Jeremy shoved Scurry toward the door.

Scurry's hands were bound with authority cuffs, but despite his situation, he still smirked, then closed his eyes as if in quiet meditation.

"That was easy." Peyton shrugged.

I shook my head. "He's up to something. We need to disable his tracker before we leave."

Jeremy set his go kit on the bed and opened it. He grabbed some wires and his laptop, organizing what he needed.

Bailen opened his mouth to speak, but I held up my hand to silence him. The glint in Scurry's eyes told me everything I needed to know.

"She's right, you know." The bands dropped from Scurry's wrists and clanged to the floor.

"What the…?" Jeremy bent down to retrieve them, but his eyes grew glassy. He turned toward Bailen and pulled a knife from his belt.

"Jeremy, you don't want to do this." Bailen held out his hands, readying himself to block.

"He can't hear you," I said.

"I think his subconscious can." Bailen backed away slowly as Jeremy walked toward him with the knife extended. "Jeremy, I know you're in there. SNAP OUT OF IT!"

Bailen shook his head and withdrew his knife as well, while Peyton maneuvered behind Jeremy. Ava reached for the laptop and started booting it up.

"I don't want to have to use this." Bailen whirled without warning toward Scurry and ran with the knife.

I gasped, but Bailen stopped dead in his tracks, then pivoted toward Peyton.

"BAILEN, NO!" I screamed, knowing he would never forgive himself if he harmed his twin.

Peyton dodged the attack right into Jeremy, who wrapped his muscular arms around her and held the knife near her throat. Peyton kicked and pushed off from the floor, but Jeremy's grip was tight. He held the knife firmly, inches from her face. Ava abandoned the laptop and launched herself at Jeremy. She tried to pry his arms off her, but Peyton's eyes went glassy and Jeremy released her.

Ava backed away and crouched, readying herself for an attack.

"How many of them do you think he can control at once?" she

asked, wondering if she would lose control next.

Then I'd be alone.

The only one Scurry couldn't control because my tracker was an anomaly. "I don't know, but can you keep them busy?" I launched at Scurry, who now had the damaged box.

"Uh sure, no problem. I'll just take on three of my friends at the same time." It was the first time I'd heard Ava sound uncertain. Almost scared. But she could handle it. At least I hoped she could.

Scurry dodged my attack, but it was merely a distraction. I blinked and searched my tracker for his connection. He had to be using something to access the other trackers. It wasn't obvious at first. Hidden behind a rogue program on his network, I found what I was looking for. I was proud I'd retained some of the programming tricks I'd picked up from Bailen.

I queried the sleeper program. It asked for a password. I pivoted and launched at Scurry again, aiming for the box. I put in several possible passwords as I punched and kicked at Scurry, but none worked. Scurry dodged my lame attempts to distract him and lifted the box out of my path.

"I could do this all day," he said with a grin.

I secretly hoped it wouldn't take all day to crack his password. I needed in. I needed a way to stop him.

"Watch out Kaya!" Ava screamed from behind me. I dodged Jeremy's right hook, but I couldn't warn her as Peyton swung her baton into the back of Ava's knees, sending her to the floor. Peyton swung the baton again, connecting with Ava's stomach. She crumpled over with a groan.

I ducked in time to avoid Bailen charging toward me. I was seconds from being pinned down, and not in a good way. My mind raced as I tried to think of how to crack into the program that controlled everyone. None of the passcodes and pins from my time chasing Scurry and his box worked. I'd have to brute force the access. I quickly opened a command prompt and thought about some password decryption code Bailen had taught me. The lines of code filled in as quickly as they entered my mind, but it could take up to an hour or more to run. I didn't have an hour. I barely had a couple of minutes.

I set the program in motion, hoping something would land. But the focus on my tracker had cost me. Bailen had backed me right into Jeremy and Peyton, who each grabbed one of my wrists and shoved me toward a wall, holding me there with firm grips. I squirmed and kicked, but it was no use. Nothing registered in their pain receptors while they were under his control.

Scurry set down the box and stalked toward me. "I'm going to enjoy this." Bailen stood behind him, glassy eyed, staring at me. My heart shattered into a million pieces. Not only was Scurry going to punish me, he would also make Bailen do it, make him watch as he tortured me. Slow and painful. Enough to take me out of his way but not so much to kill me. I closed my eyes. A single tear squeezed out and rolled down my cheek.

I quickly blinked additional impending tears away, using it as cover to check the brute force program. It hadn't unlocked the access to Scurry's tracker yet. I was doomed. Bailen stepped toward me and lifted his knife. He tilted it back and forth, the light reflecting off the blade.

"Bailen, I know you're in there. Listen to me. You don't want to do this. I know deep down you don't. You have to fight this. Fight with every ounce of passion you have." But my words weren't getting through. I screamed, not in terror but in uncontrollable rage, shoving all my emotions out on my tracker connection—all the pain, frustration, and anger I'd accumulated through this whole ordeal—hoping a small fraction of it would reach Scurry.

Scurry laughed, deep and sadistic. He had won. I was out of options. I squeezed my eyes shut, not wanting to see what came next, but the whine of an authority weapon hummed. The electric static of the gun firing buzzed in my ears. I opened my eyes in time to see Scurry crumple to the floor. Ava stood over him, frozen in shock.

"I've… I've…" She closed her eyes, trying to erase the scene before her. "I've never fired one of those before. Even on the stun setting."

"I find that really hard to believe," I said, motioning to Scurry's crumpled body.

Ava either didn't hear me or was still in too much shock to react.

Bailen, Peyton, and Jeremy all blinked and looked around. Once they had their bearings, Peyton and Jeremy released my arms. I rubbed my wrists, then blinked to check if the hacking program had ended with Scurry out cold.

As I opened the app, my tracker flooded with so much data it blocked my vision. My head exploded with pain. I stumbled, crashed to the floor, then slid across it. My knees scraped against the concrete. I took a couple seconds to catch my breath, then rolled over and inspected the files laid out before me.

There was a lot there, but it was apparent what Scurry had been up to, what he had come so close to executing. And while we'd suspected it all along, seeing his plans as concrete evidence didn't make the outcome any less shocking. He'd been building a network to control every human with a tracker, and he was going to use them to mold the world how he saw fit.

Twenty-Four

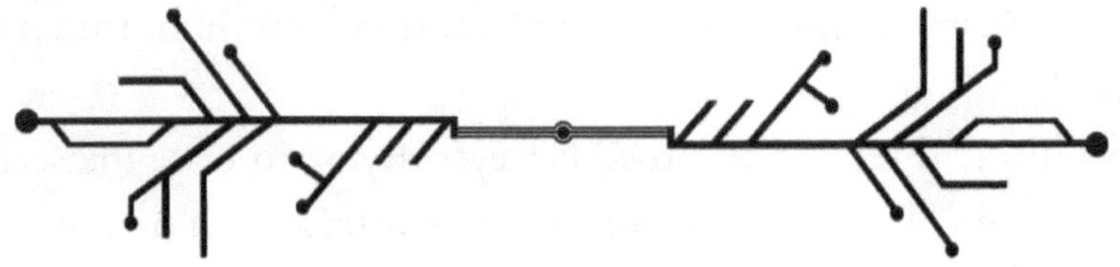

After tossing and turning most of the night, I woke alone in my bed at the Hive. While I'd wanted to get right to work, it was my father who put his foot down and insisted I sleep after my recent escapades with Scurry. As much as I wanted to argue, the exhaustion overcame me more easily than I'd expected. But nightmares plagued me at every turn, people I cared about turning into mindless zombies, then suffering from the vague memories of what they'd done.

In between that, I dreamt of losing Jake over and over again. I didn't know if it was better to sleep and not rest from the nightmares or stay awake worrying about what was to come. But with Scurry back in Ghost custody, and them investigating how he got access to a network, there was one less thing weighing on my mind. They had temporarily deactivated his tracker so they could understand everything he'd been up to. Once they had the necessary answers and data, they would remove Scurry's tracker permanently. It would soon be over.

A knock on the door echoed with a loud bang.

"Come in!" I called, swinging my legs over the bed.

"Good, you're awake." Bailen smiled, his carefree one that I'd missed so much during my solo adventures. It quickly faded, as if he remembered how mad he was at me. "We need to talk."

And there it was.

I could ask what about, but it would be a waste of words; I knew exactly where this was headed. I wanted to sit here and pretend for a little while longer that there wasn't this huge rift between us. That I hadn't disagreed with him on how he handled Harlow. That I didn't have to run off and keep him in the dark to protect everyone. That I hadn't withheld important information from the Ghosts. But I hadn't seen another path then.

I should have apologized and explained everything, but something held me back. It wasn't fear, but I couldn't explain it. Instead of going right to the heart of the matter I asked, "How's Harlow?"

Bailen jerked in shock like I'd broken some of his computer equipment. Clearly, that wasn't the right thing to start with. But I didn't know what to follow it with, so I sat silently watching as the anger boiled inside Bailen, about to explode.

He balled his fists and shot up from the bed. "You know what? I can't do this anymore. Watch you focus on him and cut me out over and over again."

"Focus on him? I did all this for you." My voice matched his tone and anger, but my insides burned with pain and emptiness. How could he not see it? This had all started with Harlow, but now, knowing Scurry could control anyone on a whim, we needed answers. "I did this to *help* Harlow. Not to spite you."

"Isn't that the same thing?"

I wanted to scream, *No, it isn't!* Those two things could exist at the same time. I could want to be with Bailen and protect him while still caring about what happened to Harlow as a friend. I had to call it out.

"You're jealous!"

His chest heaved as I watched the anger of the word fill him up. But he stayed put, unwavering without making eye contact. "When it comes to you, I always have been, and I always will be. You have to know how important you are to me. I can't lose you." His shoulders sank, giving in to the emotion. He'd lost the will to be angry, and the only thing left was pain.

My insides melted. For the first time, I truly comprehended how much I'd hurt him when I'd shut him out. He'd misread my running away from him as running back to Harlow when, in reality, I was clearing a path back to Bailen. I was trying to keep us both from getting killed. In the process, I'd still managed to hurt him, and myself.

"You won't lose me." I sucked in a deep breath. "And if you'll let me explain it all from the beginning, you'll see I did this because I care about you so much too. Because I can't lose you, either."

I held out my hand but didn't make any attempt to grab his. If this was going to work, he had to meet me halfway.

He looked down at my outstretched hand, then accepted, allowing me to lace my fingers between his and pull him down to the bed next to me. Part of the emptiness evaporated knowing I wasn't alone in this, that he'd accepted my olive branch.

I looked him in the eyes and said, "You're everything to me, which is why I ran. Why I didn't tell you." I paused to collect my thoughts. "Scurry manipulated me, held you all over my head, and forced my hand. Keeping secrets was the only way out. But in fairness, I did leave a note." I leaned into Bailen and nudged him with my shoulder.

His lips quirked upward ever so slightly. "A vague one," he muttered under his breath.

"I ran to protect all of you. I reached out when I could. And you managed to find me despite everything."

Bailen nodded but didn't say anything, waiting for me to tell the rest of the story. I took a deep breath, then let the words tumble out. I didn't leave out a single detail. From Scurry's demented maze, to the video call, to the help from J.W. The weight pushing down on me slowly lifted with each word I spoke, with each truth I revealed.

When I finished, Bailen squeezed my arm and pulled me into an embrace. I buried my face in his chest. He kissed the top of my head. I felt safe in his arms. The world had been peeled away. I could finally focus on us. He lifted my chin so he could gaze into my eyes, now glistening with tears.

I shook my head, and tears streamed down my cheek. He wiped them away with his thumb. I closed my eyes, committing this to memory. If I'd had enough time, I would have drawn the moment, but I was better off living it. He rubbed my back. As I gained my composure, my mind flashed back to what had happened in Scurry's cell. I hadn't checked on Bailen since the incident.

"Are you okay?" I asked, but the question was more about what he'd been through than how I'd treated him.

He nodded, but the glint in his eyes darkened as he picked up on what I'd implied.

"What was it like?" I asked.

"Like I was a passenger in my own body, watching things

happen but unable to stop them."

"That's what—" I wanted to say, *"Harlow said,"* but knew it would make the situation worse. "That's what I'd heard. I can't imagine what that would be like."

"It was only a few minutes, and it was enough for me to know that I wouldn't wish it on my worst enemy." Bailen's gaze dropped to the floor.

The irony of that statement wasn't lost on me. Not that Harlow was his worst enemy, but they had something in common now that wasn't just me.

"How long before we take the tracker out of Scurry's head?" I asked.

"Days at most to find a doctor willing to do this under the table. Plus, we need information from his chip but can't risk him having access to it much longer."

"What are you going to do if he mind-controls someone again?"

"We're trying to keep him sedated. I have some ideas to interrupt the process, maybe a program to block the connection or at least interrupt it, but I want to study your tracker again to understand if your lack of loophole switch is the only reason he can't manipulate your tracker or if there's something else we can leverage." He winked at me as if there was much more to studying my tracker.

I nodded in agreement. Neither of us was deluded enough to think this was over, even with Scurry in custody. He was playing the long game. I stared at the floor, the sudden rush of that reality hitting me hard.

Bailen squeezed my shoulder. "He won't win."

"I know, but you didn't see that other side of it," I said. "Feel how lonely it was fighting a losing battle."

"No, but I do know what it's like to be left in the cold."

My gaze met his in a silent apology. I couldn't say it again. The guilt overwhelmed me, but I was sure he caught my meaning. Bailen placed my legs over his lap. I leaned in until our lips met in a quiet but passionate kiss that swept away the whole ordeal for a few moments.

When he pulled away, he laughed. "You know, you're wrong about one thing."

"What's that?" I asked, wary that whatever he'd say might start another disagreement about how Harlow's situation should have been handled, or how I should have told him about Scurry's threats despite what he might do to everyone I cared about.

"You were wrong to think any of us could have gone on without you."

I opened my mouth to speak, but he pushed his index finger to my lips. My words caught in my throat before I closed my mouth to hear him out.

"If you were gone, I couldn't have gone on. My insides would have died right along with you. It wouldn't be living. It would be existing in emptiness and nothing else."

I took a deep breath. He held his finger up once again. "So don't ever do ANYTHING like this again, Kaya Weiss. Do you understand?"

I nodded and leaned toward him.

"I need to hear you say it." A hint of a smile snuck out through his manufactured scowl.

"I promise not to run off without informing you," I said with a small giggle, then grabbed his finger and pulled it down so I could kiss him again. Both of us smiled and laughed through it this time.

I didn't know how much time passed, but it didn't matter. It was time we'd both needed to repair the wounds that had formed. We kissed and cuddled next to each other, ignoring the chaos around us. I lay with my head on his chest, listening to his heartbeat thumping. It was as if the world wasn't falling apart around us. It was just normal—something I wasn't sure I knew the definition of anymore.

But the longer I stayed there, the more I knew there was more I needed to say about J.W. and the drive. There was also someone else I had to clear the air with. Someone else I owed an explanation to, just as Bailen had let me have mine. I didn't want to leave this moment. I wanted to clear the rest of the air with Bailen, but the guilt began to eat away at me.

I sat up.

"Is something wrong?" Bailen sat up as well.

"No, this is perfect. More than perfect. I needed this more than you know." I bit my lower lip, struggling with how to say I wanted to stay here forever, but I was also wrestling with what should come next. He would understand the complexities, but it didn't make it any easier for me to say it. I stared at my hands.

"It's okay. Go talk to him." Bailen's words said one thing, but his expression said another.

It took a second to realize we were thinking about different hims. He meant Harlow.

"No." I put my hand over his. "I need to hear my dad out. He deserves a chance to explain everything. I owe him that."

Bailen's expression softened. "Oh. That makes sense." He

paused, struggling with what he wanted to say next. "But if you need to talk to Harlow, I'm okay with that too. I get it."

I nodded, then kissed him again. "Thank you. It means a lot to me that you understand." I paused, weighing my next words carefully. "You should probably talk to him, though."

Bailen's expression changed but not to anger, more to a question.

"You two have more in common than you think." I rose from the bed and stepped toward the door, but Bailen grabbed my hand and dragged me back to the bed. "But before you do, I have to tell—"

"Shhh." He pulled me back to him and pushed his finger to my lips. "Five more minutes." Then he leaned in for another kiss. I laughed as my mind went blank, letting myself get lost in the moment all over again.

I found Dad poring over digital schematics and watching tracker footage in the main computer room at the Hive. His normally tousled hair was more out of place than usual around his kippah. He was so engrossed in his work he didn't hear me come up from behind.

I touched his shoulder lightly. "Dad, can you take a break?"

"Hmmm," he mumbled.

"Dad!" I shook him, fearing the worst, but he finally turned to face me.

"Kai," he said in a tired voice. Despite the exhausted tone, his pitch indicated he was happy to see me.

"Got a minute?"

"For you, I have all the minutes you need." He smiled, not his full smile, but enough to say he was glad to finally have the opportunity to chat about anything with me.

I pulled up a chair next to him. "I'm ready. I want to hear the full story. I want to understand." The words came out shaky, but despite the nerves building inside me, I needed to hear him out. After everything that had happened, now was the time I needed to hear the truth. Not only because it might provide insight into the current situation but also because I was finally ready for the answers he had for me.

Dad took off his reading glasses and turned in his chair to face me. "All right. I'll start at the beginning and if you have questions, stop me." He rubbed his hands in his lap, wiping the sweat from them, more of a subconscious gesture than nerves. I could tell he'd thought and rethought about what to say. I wondered if he had considered he might never get a chance to explain himself, especially after I'd shut him down the last time.

"I don't need the beginning; I've heard it a million times before." I swallowed hard, collecting my thoughts. "I need the truth. I need to know why. Why you did it, and why you never thought to trust me with your secret. The secret I had to bear alone."

"When the authorities started monitoring and taking away freedoms, I saw the path we were walking, and it wasn't a good one. But when I discovered trackers contained a loophole switch under the guise of controlling the vilest of criminals, I knew something was off. I confronted Scurry and asked why he'd never disclosed it to the public. He waved me off with some excuse about it being for everyone's protection and if we told people, it would lose its usefulness. I disagreed but kept silent to take the suspicion off myself. I had a very small window to make sure this loophole didn't impact the entire public—didn't impact you and millions of others. Scurry and the authorities had already proven he could take free will away in the sneakiest of manners, but there was nothing to stop him from making it more permanent."

I'd never considered the repercussions until they were laid out in front of me, until it became a direct threat to me—until everyone I loved was impacted by it. "So, you decided to stand in his way."

Dad nodded.

"But how did all that lead to my tracker becoming a vault of secrets? There had to have been another way."

His expression softened, silently apologizing for everything he'd put me through. "I never meant for that full burden to fall on you. We ran out of time. Scurry was starting to dig too deep into my work. I had to step down or he would discover the truth. The tracker, a single prototype to combat what Scurry had done, had to go into someone soon, someone I trusted and could prepare as I completed my work."

I took a deep breath and opened my mouth to express my frustration and anger at what he'd put me through, but he held up his hand, and I remained silent.

"I won't pretend that I understand the full ramifications of what I put you through. But you must know, had there been another way, I would have spared you from all of it. Every day you were gone, a pain exploded inside me. I feared for you, not knowing if you would be punished for my decisions. My mistake of not trusting you with this knowledge or preparing you for all of this ate away at me. I did my best to make sure you landed with the Ghosts, to make sure you were protected, that you had Jake and the others. But it still doesn't excuse the pain and confusion I put you through. For that, I am truly sorry."

I stared at the ground as his words sank in. That I had Jake. The words echoed in my mind and reverberated through the void inside my heart. I'd had him for such a short time. Dad was lucky I'd resonated so much with the Ghosts, or it all would have fallen apart after Jake's death. But even building trust with the Ghosts had taken time. It was a risk that may not have worked out. He had thrown a lot of faith into his relationships, a connection I never made until now.

"You have to know if there had been another way—"

I waited for him to finish the sentence, but he never did. I lifted my head to finally face him, to let him know that while it still hurt within my core, I finally understood. When my gaze met his, his glassy eyes were the only thing staring back at me.

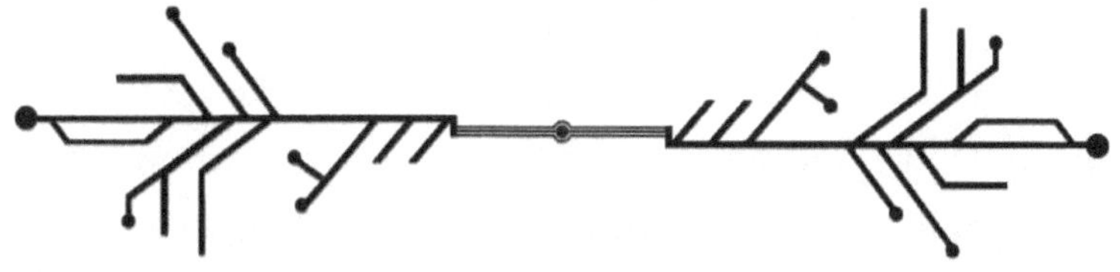

Twenty-Five

"Dad?" I asked, knowing he couldn't respond. "DAD!" I shook his shoulders. Despite his blank, glassy stare telling me everything I needed to know, my brain refused to believe who staring back at me.

Scurry.

He'd somehow managed to get through the Hive's defenses.

Dad's face twisted into an odd sneer. He was goading me, but the expression implied more than that. Through the person who first rebelled against the tracker network, Scurry was eying the one prize he couldn't have—me. He was proving he was a master manipulator. Always one step ahead. While I hadn't been naïve enough to think Scurry would never have the chance to do this again, I wondered how he'd gained access so quickly. But that wasn't the important question. It didn't matter what hole we threw Scurry in or how we incapacitated him, he would always come crawling out of it looking like a fresh coat of paint.

Across the room, Mr. Overland sat at a computer with the same glassy-eyed stare.

A strained laugh escaped my lips, but it was the furthest thing from funny. I pivoted and ran from the room in search of the one person I needed, hoping he hadn't met the same fate.

"BAILEN!" I screamed into the halls of the Hive, not caring who I disturbed.

I ran through the halls screaming his name until I crashed into rock hard abs. Harlow. Glassy eyed as well. I backed away slowly, as if any sudden movement might startle him into action.

Someone grabbed my arm. I yanked it away and spun to face them.

Bailen stood before me, his hands out defensively. "Kai, it's me." He called me that on occasion, like those closest to me. The rarely used nickname was exactly the thing I needed to hear to snap me back to reality.

I collapsed into his arms and cried, more out of frustration than sadness. "My Dad. Harlow. Your Dad." My chest heaved. He ran his fingers through my hair in silent understanding, then pulled me away from Harlow, who advanced toward us. I twisted out of his arms. Bailen reached for me again, but I moved my hand out of his reach. "Wait. I think I can get through to him."

Bailen nodded, and for the first time his face said he agreed. That I should try, and he was okay with it.

I inched toward Harlow. "I know you're in there. You're not alone."

Despite Harlow's blank stare, I continued. "We won't let him do this to you again." I reached out, offering Harlow a hand, not sure if he had any control to accept or if Scurry would exploit the situation by crushing my hand or tearing me away from Bailen. But I knew Harlow was in there. I wasn't going to abandon him.

"You're safe. We will protect you."

Harlow's arm shot out toward my hand, a sign he wasn't in control, but I didn't pull back. Before his hand wrapped around my wrist, he stopped with his arm extended outward, frozen. His fingers extended, shaking as he warred with an invisible force.

"That's it. Fight this, Harlow. I know you can. We're here to help." I closed my eyes and reached out with my mind, searching for whatever network was in play. I sent my support in a quick message. Things were silent.

Then a chat bubble appeared.

H.G.: I can't hold this much longer. You
need to run. Then stop hi...

The message truncated, but I knew what he meant. I turned from Harlow and said a silent goodbye, not knowing if I'd see him again. I had to end this once and for all. I grabbed Bailen's hand and dragged him down the hall.

"We don't have much time. He can't hold it much longer."

We ran, but Bailen looked at me. "You got through the mind-control?"

I nodded. "Tracker message."

"How?"

"I'm not sure. But it worked for a brief time, long enough for him to warn me he was losing control."

"Interesting." Bailen smirked, as if his mind was already churning out possibilities.

We ran into Jeremy in the computer room. He was tentatively watching my dad, who was still frozen in place.

"What's Scurry up to?" Jeremy asked. "I mean, I know, but

what's his *plan*?"

"I think the bigger question is, how is he doing this? He's in lockdown, supposedly sedated."

"I'll confirm he's still in custody," Jeremy said, pulling up a chair to the nearest computer.

"We don't have much time. If he's in the system, then his plan is already in motion. We need to stop him." I paused, looking at Bailen. "I don't think I can leave my dad."

"I know the feeling, but I don't think we have much of a choice. You said it yourself. Harlow warned you."

I nodded. He was right. This was going to be bad, but it didn't make it any easier to turn my back on them.

"I need to check some readings on these active trackers and try to understand how Scurry has access. I'll keep an eye on him while I'm here." Jeremy said with his usual strong confidence.

"I can't ask you to do that." I was done losing friends to this chaos. Done leaving people behind.

"You're not asking. I'm staying. I have a job to do. Besides, it could be a chance to see what his bigger plan is. I'll lay low and follow either of them if they leave, keep you posted via sat phone messages on any new developments."

"He has a point." Bailen shrugged.

I mouthed a silent thank you to Jeremy, knowing deep down that it could be a death sentence. I pushed the thought out of my mind, then led Bailen down the long hall toward the trap door.

Moments later, we were on our crotchrockets and airborne, headed for the Coderie. We needed everyone we could gather. Whoever was left. I hoped it wasn't just the two of us, but I had a renewed sense of confidence in our relationship. We'd done this before. We could do it again by ourselves if we had to, but it would be so much easier with a team.

As soon as I saw the roof of the Coderie, I tipped my bike downward to prepare for landing. My bike slammed to the ground in the alley behind the brick building. Bailen put his down a bit softer next to mine. By the time he landed, I was halfway up the concrete stairs to the door. I didn't stop to hold it open for him. I simply yelled down the hall, "PEYTON? AVA? LYDIA?"

I held my breath, waiting for a response and was met with silence. I screamed their names even louder, repeating myself over and over again. My heart pounded with each scream, fearing the worst, that they'd been lost too. Finally, Peyton emerged from the basement steps with Ava on her heels.

"Thank goodness." I threw my arms around Peyton and she froze in place.

"Pull yourself together." She puffed up her chest and expanded her arms, knocking me back with a pissed look on her face. It instantly changed when she saw Bailen behind me.

His face was serious—a mix of concern and relief. I grabbed Peyton's arm and dragged her down the hall to the main computer room. She yelled obscenities at me the whole way. When we reached the room, she finally yanked free and stepped back toward the door, where Ava leaned against the frame. Bailen pushed past the pair and joined me in the room.

"Enough dragging me around. Explain. You both look like the world is about to end." Peyton crossed her arms and scowled. Ava massaged Peyton's shoulders. The tension eased out of her ever so slightly.

"You're not far off," I spat. "He's got my dad. And yours. As well as Harlow again, too."

I didn't need to explain more than that. The expression on Peyton's face changed from anger to fear, a sentiment she normally wouldn't show. I sensed it was rooted in the thought that she or someone else close to her might be next. For Peyton, losing another person would be worse than Scurry taking over her own tracker. "Jeremy?" The single word was barely audible, as if she was afraid of the answer.

"He's fine… for now. But I don't know what Scurry's plan is for Dad." Bailen's gaze fell to the floor. He crossed the room and hugged Peyton so tightly. I thought she might push him away, but she collapsed into him and finally let her walls come crumbling down, more out of necessity than wanting to.

I didn't know how much longer any of us could take this. Before I could ask what came next, Ava was pointing over my shoulder at the news screen mounted on the far wall.

I whirled around to find images of glassy-eyed people all over the city with confused people shaking them or backing away. Others ran through the streets like they were being chased by zombies. The scenes moved to looting of storefronts and things being set ablaze in the streets. This wasn't just Harlow, Mr. Overland, or Dad. It went far beyond that.

I rushed across the room to turn up the volume, but I didn't need the newscaster to tell me it was the beginning of something much more elaborate. Jeremy didn't need to ask if Scurry was in custody. It didn't matter where they were holding Scurry, he was executing his plan and people were paying for it. There was no telling who was next.

As I got the volume turned up, the screen went black. At first, I thought I'd shut it off accidentally, but then white letters appeared across the screen one at a time. I backed away as if it had zapped me. My gaze locked on the sentence displayed.

THIS IS BECAUSE OF KAYA WEISS

Twenty-Six

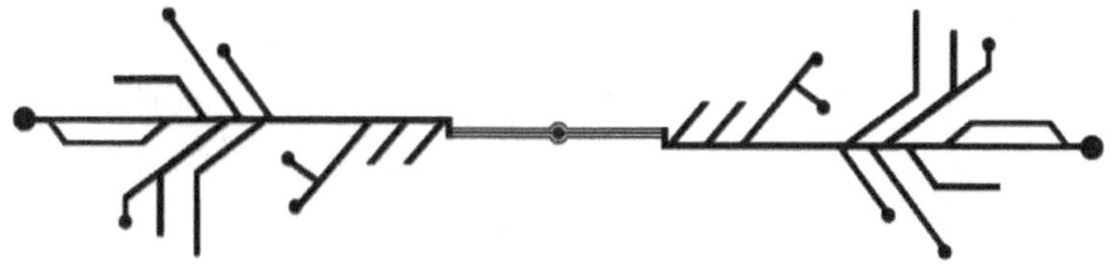

I couldn't take my eyes off the picture of me that appeared underneath the white text on the black background. My face stared back, mocking me. Asking what was next. What now? With a few words and a single picture, Scurry had turned the world against me.

I screamed. I don't know how long it lasted. When my mouth grew dry and no more sound came out, I collapsed to the floor in complete defeat. I couldn't fight this. There was no way out of this mess. I curled into a ball, never wanting to move again.

Bailen lowered next to me and pulled me into his comforting embrace. Ava and Peyton knelt on the other side, and they collapsed into one giant hug around me.

"What's going on?" Lydia's voice rang out from across the room.

I sat up and the others scooted back. I stared at Lydia across the room, the pain seeping out of every pore in my body. Her normally cheery disposition turned grim when she saw what was on the screen. She hadn't seen the newscast, but it was enough to tell her I was in serious trouble. Crossing the room, she enveloped me in a hug, Bailen and the others piled on again. We sat there unmoving until I stopped shaking.

Scurry was vindictive. He'd offered me up to the angry mob that was sure to ensue after folks lost those around them to this hack. No matter what my next move was, someone was bound to recognize me if I wasn't careful. It was all part of his master plan: put as much between him and me as possible. Slow me down and prevent me from stopping him.

"What do we do now?" It was a loaded question. There was only one thing to do, and that was to take him down once and for all. A small fire burned in my core. Even if I couldn't win, I had to go down trying.

"We need to figure out how he's doing this and end it once and for all," Bailen said.

"Maybe we should take a look at those files that flooded my tracker when Ava shot Scurry."

"And all your communications with him. It might provide some clues to his bigger plan and how we can stop him."

I nodded, unable to say anything else. The fear of my reality had set in.

"I won't let you face him alone." Bailen squeezed my shoulder.

"I'll get back on that USB drive. I was starting to make some progress." Ava pulled the stick out of her pocket and plugged it into her laptop.

"What USB drive?" Bailen eyed me with concern. "I thought we said no more secrets."

"Sorry, I tried to tell you, but…" I shrugged apologetically. My cheeks flushed as I remembered what happened after he stopped me from sharing the information. After losing myself for a minute, I looked at Peyton, silently asking for permission that I didn't need, but she nodded anyway. "I think it came from Jake, but after six months, I'm not sure how he arranged to have it delivered. It arrived at my house that Shabbat you came over. It has a ton of files on it, but they're all encrypted."

"Let me take a look." Bailen reached for a chair, but Peyton grabbed his arm before he got to it.

"The last time I saw that drive, Jake was acting strangely. Not himself, like he hadn't gotten much sleep. It was eating away at him. He was forgetting things. I thought he was just stressed about finding Kaya, and the whole Ghost agenda. But after everything that's happened, I think he was under Scurry's control. He was losing time and memories. I think Scurry made Jake do things…"

Bailen pulled Peyton into a hug and stroked her hair. Surprisingly, she let him do it. I watched the true power and comfort of their bond for the first time since I'd met them. Despite all their strained moments, they still knew they were there for each other, something I truly missed with Jake gone.

When Bailen released her, I asked, "Do you think Jake had something on Scurry, or do you think it was something Scurry made him do?"

Peyton shrugged. "I'm honestly not sure, but either could be helpful in theory. I'm willing to dig deeper if it means we nail this bastard to the wall once and for all."

"Well, let's find out." Bailen extended one hand to Peyton and grabbed a chair with the other. He led her to one side of Ava and then moved a third chair on the other side.

I motioned Lydia over. We both stood behind the group as Ava opened the files that had been unencrypted.

It was picture after picture of people with TRACKERU followed by unique numbers underneath them.

"I've seen these before," I said.

Bailen twisted in his chair. "Where?"

"You're not going to like this, but on the terminal in Scurry's server room." When Bailen and Ava returned confused faces, I added, "The one that blew up when the USB was removed."

"Sounds like he's covering his tracks," Peyton said without turning from the screen. "Which means there's something in these files he didn't want anyone to see. Jake must have risked everything to get this data out."

Ava clicked the next file, and Jake stared back at us with TRACKERU-70285 underneath. This image didn't say terminated like it had when I saw it in the server room. "Scurry really did this," I muttered under my breath. But there were so many meanings behind those few words.

Scurry murdered my brother and made it look like an accident. All because Jake was investigating and gathering evidence against him, fighting back until the very end. These files were evidence of the poor souls Scurry had tested his pilot program on. This was what he'd been plotting all along. This was his endgame. I wondered how many others had been killed since he'd started this. How many others had fought back? How many others had paid a price no person should ever have to?

My mind spun so quickly, trying to connect all the dots. There were so many paint splotches that, until now, looked like random drips. Now a picture was starting to form. Before I could finish putting it all together, the words tumbled out of my mouth.

"Jake was part of Scurry's demented test program. He was acting strange because he was losing time. I saw his poems about caves and darkness, the half-written notes to me trying to explain—"

Bailen rose from his chair and grabbed my shoulders. "Kaya, slow down."

"No, she's right. Jake was plagued by this. He was fighting back in the best way he knew how, with his words. I just wish I'd known how much he was carrying with him before I lost him." Peyton buried her head in her hands as though silently accepting that this was all her fault, even though it wasn't. Ava pulled her into a side hug and kissed the top of her head.

"But I think it goes far deeper than that," I said.

"You're right. The timing of the package can't be a coincidence," Lydia said. "Why now? Why six months after he died? Why not right away?"

"He knew this would happen," I blurted without thinking, but the words were true. "When I first opened that USB, the message was, 'beware the loophole.' He was warning us what was coming. Then the tracker messages…"

"The ones from the person who helped you in the tunnels?" Bailen looked at me with concern.

"Yes. I didn't think they were linked to this, but now I see it's all connected. It felt like Jake reaching out to me while I was on Scurry's demented scavenger hunt."

Peyton lifted her head, her eyes red and cheeks puffy. "But that's impossible. He's—"

She couldn't finish the word, but she didn't have to. I still struggled to say it too. I knew how she felt. She was just as confused as I was. "I still don't understand it myself, but when Scurry was messaging me, so was a J.W. with Jake's exact profile, down to each joke inside it. He was helping me every step of the way, almost like he knew what Scurry was up to. Even the responses had his sense of humor. If it wasn't him, it was someone who knew him well."

For the first time, I actually let myself hope for half a second that maybe he wasn't lost. I didn't know how that could be possible, but maybe Jake was still with us. Maybe that package had been sent to remind himself of what was coming.

"All right. I'm modifying the plan. Ava, when you're done reverse engineering the authority protocol on your tracker that kept Scurry from using the loophole, get on those files. Lydia and I will dig into Kaya's past tracker activity." Bailen grabbed my hand and led me toward the door, but I stopped dead in my tracks.

"There's one more thing you all should know before we do that." I bit my lip, afraid of the can of worms I was about to open. At this point, they needed every weapon and clue available to them.

"When you all were under Scurry's mind-control, I tried to brute force into his tracker to break the control he had on everyone."

"That's my girl!" Bailen raised his hand in the air, but I left it hanging there. His expression turned serious, and his arm fell to his side as he realized I wasn't gloating and there was more to it.

"I'm not sure it was successful. Ava did the hard work and took him down with an authority weapon."

A brief look of concern crossed Ava's face like she still wasn't sure she'd done the right thing. I gave her a reassuring nod. If she hadn't, we wouldn't be here now.

"That electric jolt to Scurry triggered something through the connection I'd established with the brute force code. My tracker was flooded with hundreds of files."

"Well, what are we waiting for?" Bailen looked like his favorite computer equipment had just gone on sale.

I swallowed hard, then made eye contact. "After the games

Scurry played with me, I have no idea what landmine I'm sitting on. I'm not sure if I came by these files by accident or if it's another one of his elaborate schemes."

Bailen exhaled deeply, less of a sigh and more of a resignation. "Sounds like we have a lot of work to do, then."

"Don't worry about us. I've got a jump on these files. When Peyton and I finish, we'll meet your downstairs to help with the rest of the data." Ava didn't look up from the computer screen. It was clear she had everything under control.

"How's your coding, Lydia?" Bailen asked with a glint of hope in his eyes.

"I'm better with the mechanical side of things, but I learned a few tricks from robotics that might help." She wiggled her eyebrows. "And you know I don't shy away from a challenge." She laughed.

Her laugh was infectious. I couldn't help myself. The others joined in. For a second, everything felt normal. When it died down, the room grew quiet and the weight of the disaster unfolding hung in the air. I followed Bailen toward the basement with Lydia on my heels. We were about to dump a whole lot of paint on the canvas, and it was going to take a lot of brushwork before the mysterious picture would take form.

Twenty-Seven

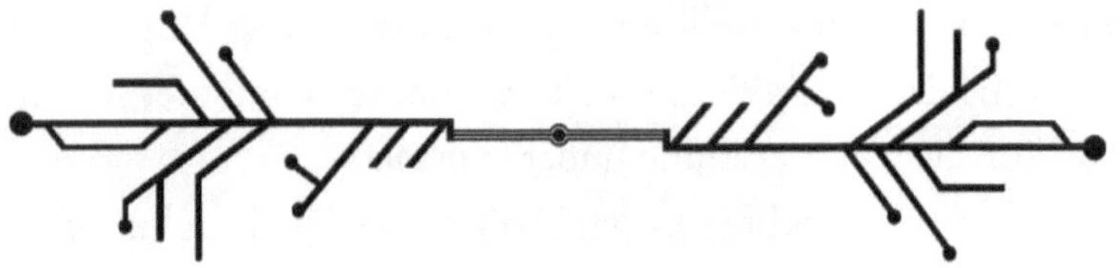

It didn't take long for me to settle into the chair with wires draped around me. Bailen was at his terminal with Lydia next to him. She had her own setup, complete with several giant monitors.

"This is going to be different from how we've done this in the past. I'm going to walk you through your tracker interactions over the last few days and monitor everything in real time. Once we learn everything we can, we will end with those files from Scurry. Sound good?"

I nodded, my mouth too dry to speak. I knew what was on the line. The faster we got this over with, the faster we could find Scurry and stop him.

"I'm going to do some diagnostics as you open files, chat messages, and profiles. I'll be looking at the data on the surface as well as digging into the source code for any hidden data packets or files you wouldn't have seen initially."

I nodded again, too overwhelmed to speak.

Bailen rubbed his hands together, then typed in some commands on his keyboard. "Let's see what we can uncover."

My temples buzzed as I wiped my sweaty hands on my pants. "This is going to take a while, isn't it?"

"It could, but I'll be here every step of the way. We can take breaks as often as you'd like." Bailen didn't have his usual excited-to-play-with-tech expression. It was the most serious I'd seen him, aside from our recent chat that put everything out in the open.

His lack of excitement left a pit in my stomach. It felt different from anything we'd done before. There were so many ways it could go wrong. Each one of them meant we could lose everything. I couldn't help but miss Jake. I could use some of his humor and reassurance to calm my frazzled nerves.

"Let's start with Scurry's messages. Can you open that chat thread?"

I closed my eyes and thought about the thread. It opened before my eyes. "Now what?"

"Just hold there for a minute. I'm going to scan each message for a location, see if he was on the move and search for hints that he might have masked his location when you were interacting. I'm not convinced he's been in prison this whole time." He turned to Lydia. "Can you capture the data and look for anomalies, changes in IPs, locations, or generally anything that doesn't seem to add up?"

Lydia nodded. Her fingers tapped on the keys as the data passed from my tracking chip to their terminals. The discs on my temples hummed louder. They didn't have the computing power to do a full download of all the data on my tracker, but they could study it for some answers. And the files they couldn't access or get information on, I'd draw like I had in the past. Whatever it took to find all the clues and put this puzzle together.

I closed my eyes and tried to let the soft buzzing lull me into a sense of calm, but my heart raced too fast for me to relax. I didn't know if I'd ever be able to fully calm down or feel safe again, especially with the world falling apart outside. How long did we have before an angry mob crashed through the front windows of the Coderie?

"Now open the J.W. messages."

I took a deep breath and allowed myself a brief moment to hope these messages might lead us back to Jake in some way. Then I blinked. The chat messages appeared before me. I read through the messages, reminding myself again how Jake-like they sounded. When I got to the final note, I noticed three dots at the bottom of the message like someone was actively having a conversation.

"Wait," I said loudly enough to get everyone's attention but staying as still as possible to not disturb any of my connections. "I think J.W. is reaching out."

"Now?" Bailen asked.

"Yeah."

"Change of plans. Lydia, keep an eye on this data that's compiling. Make sure nothing interrupts the connection." Bailen bolted across the room. He grabbed two small computer boxes and some wires, then circled back to his terminal and started plugging in the devices. "What's happening?" he asked as he untangled several cables.

"Nothing yet. Just looks like there's an incoming message." The three dots were still there, but nothing had appeared yet. I silently told J.W. to wait another minute so Bailen could set up whatever he needed.

Bailen's fingers flew over the keyboard with renewed purpose.

My heart raced as the seconds ticked on. Bailen's plan could crumble at any moment. Every lead we lost meant Scurry's chances of getting away with mind-controlling the world would multiply.

"What's going on?" Peyton called from across the room.

I peeled open my eyes and found her and Ava headed toward Bailen and Lydia.

"Perfect timing. I could use the extra hands." Bailen shoved some computer equipment at Ava and Peyton.

"No!" I shouted as the dots disappeared.

"Someone want to fill us in?" Peyton's sass had returned, almost as if she was someone else, not the vulnerable shell we'd left upstairs. She'd managed to rebuild her walls in such a short time.

"We were looking at the J.W. data," Bailen said without taking his eyes off the screen.

"And?" Peyton crossed her arms over her chest. Ava rubbed Peyton's back, but her shoulders didn't relax. Clearly the USB drive had taken its toll. Maybe her walls still had some cracks in them.

"While Bailen was pulling down data, J.W. was about to reach out. Until the dots went away."

"Say no more." Ava stepped up to a third terminal. "The authorities used to have a tracking protocol for incoming messages. Let me try something." The rhythmic clicking of the keys lulled me into a false sense of security.

"You can pull down an unsent message?" I asked, amazed at the lengths the authorities had gone to monitor trackers and control society.

"Not exactly, but we could often trace them." When Ava finished typing, she stepped back from the keyboard. "There." She pointed to something on her screen.

"Care to clue me in here…?" But my voice trailed off because I'd received a message from J.W. I blinked and let it fill my field of vision.

J.W.: Looking for someone?

"Guys… He's responding."

"What's he saying?" Peyton asked with both curiosity and a small hint of something that could only be interpreted as hope.

Everyone was starting to believe in J.W. It was infectious. I didn't know if I should get their hopes up or not, but at this point I had to be honest. "He asked if we were looking for him. Well, he said it in a more Jake-like way. Should I respond?"

"Yes!" Peyton said at the same time Ava and Bailen said, "No!"

The three of them looked at each other in a standoff. I knew how everyone felt. I'd give anything to have one more minute with Jake, but we couldn't jeopardize the only chance we might have to unravel what was happening with J.W.

Before I could respond, Ava, Bailen, and Peyton launched into a verbal tirade about the risks of proceeding or not. All I could do was watch in stunned silence, afraid to move and disconnect our only shot at this.

"Uh, guys." It was Lydia.

The others were still shouting what-if scenarios at each other. I met her gaze from across the room and nodded to encourage her to proceed. "GUYS!" I'd never heard Lydia get that loud.

The room fell silent and everyone turned to her. Her cheeks turned pink, embarrassed to interrupt their spirited discussion.

She glanced at me again, and I nodded once. "Go on."

I didn't know what she had to say, but I knew her *I found*

something important face, and this was it.

"I noticed a trend in the data." She swallowed and looked at me again for reassurance.

My insides went numb. I wouldn't like this.

"Spit it out!"

"Pey, let her talk." Bailen gave her a death stare, then focused on Lydia. "Whatever it is, just tell us. We can handle it."

"I was collating the data side by side in a spreadsheet and that's when I saw it." Lydia pointed at the screen. It took everything in my power not to rip the leads off my temples and rush around to see what was on that screen.

"Oh, for fuck's sake, just say it!" Peyton was about three seconds from self-combusting.

A small part of me was thankful for her bluntness because it meant they'd clue me in as well.

"The location data is exactly the same."

"Are you sure?" Bailen asked.

Lydia nodded. "I checked three times because I didn't believe it myself at first. It's identical."

"Then that means Scurry and J.W. have always been in the same place. Meaning they are likely the same person," Ava said with a question in her tone.

"That's impossible," I blurted. "It doesn't make sense." But it did make sense. It meant Scurry was even more manipulative than I'd thought.

"That's not all though." Lydia pointed at her screen. "This most recent input, it's different."

"So, it's not Scurry then?" I scrambled to hold on to the last bit of hope that a piece of Jake might still be out there.

"Maybe," Lydia said. "But that's not the strange part."

"Don't make me beat this out of you." Peyton stepped next to Lydia, but Ava grabbed Peyton's hand and squeezed it.

Lydia stood her ground. "Look at the map of those coordinates."

"Someone want to clue me in?" I was growing increasingly frustrated about my lack of mobility.

"The signal of the most recent message is coming from The Coderie."

"Here?" I asked, shocked. Before I could ask anything else, another J.W. chat bubble appeared in my vision.

I blinked twice and opened the chat message.

J.W.: Congrats! You found me.

Twenty-Eight

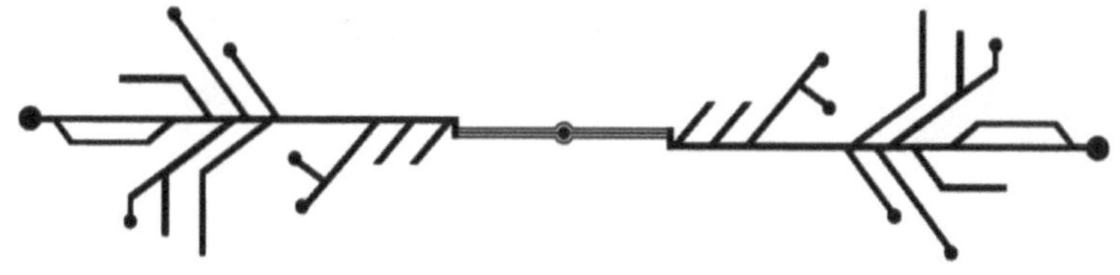

"He's here. How is that even possible?" I asked, hoping they had more answers than I did. But everyone was so engrossed in the data they didn't hear my question.

Before I lost my nerve, I did something brave and stupid. I thought of a reply and sent it.

K.W.: Who are you?

J.W.: The better question is WHAT am I?

What kind of cryptic answer was that? For the first time, whoever this was didn't sound like Jake. As a million possible explanations flooded my mind, my body filled with sadness. I'd let myself dare to dream something I should have told myself was impossible. The more I thought about it, the angrier with myself I became.

"His location just changed!" Ava said with a hint of shock.

"Is he masking it?" Bailen stepped up to her terminal.

"No, I ran some checks. And he just bounced locations a third time."

"How is that possible?" I asked, the anger and confusion swelling further inside me.

I was done playing games, with Scurry, with J.W., with everyone. This was over now. I closed my eyes and sent a message to J.W.

**K.W.: Enough games. Where are you?
Let's talk about this face to face.**

The three dots instantly disappeared. Maybe I scared him, or maybe he was plotting his next move. Had I tipped the balance a little bit? Then the message response appeared.

**J.W.: I'm everywhere and nowhere all at
once.**

What the heck did that mean? This was even worse than Scurry's taunting messages.

"He's jumping faster and faster. He's been here three times and halfway across the world right after. It doesn't make sense," Ava's rhythmic clicking had stopped, unsure how to proceed.

"Maybe we're thinking about this all wrong." Bailen said. "Maybe this isn't a person."

The pieces started falling into place. "I think you're right. I asked who J.W. was and his reply was, 'The better question is WHAT am I?'" J.W. wasn't a person at all, but that didn't explain what it was, how it could mimic Jake, or where it came from.

Bailen crossed the room and grew very quiet as he typed more commands into his terminal. "What if this is some sort of advanced machine learning or artificial intelligence?"

"It's a good theory. Let me check some things." Ava was back to typing commands; Bailen's suggestion must have given her a renewed sense of purpose.

"How is that possible?" Peyton's face was a swirl of confusion and sadness. The final ounce of hope had left her.

"And where did it come from? Who is monitoring it?" I had so many more questions, but I stopped when Bailen held up his arm.

He didn't speak though. The normally calming clicks of multiple people typing became noise in my head that reverberated from the inside out one stroke at a time.

Lydia was the first to break the insane clicking. "I think I found something." She paused as she considered her words.

"Don't make me—"

"Pey, seriously, I know this isn't easy for you, or any of us really, but let her talk. Lydia has a knack for patterns." Bailen's expression was a mixture of concern and frustration.

Lydia nodded. "It's not so much a pattern as a message. The pinging locations, they match the shapes of letters."

"AND?" Peyton was seconds from either exploding or collapsing inward. Both seemed just as likely.

"It spells, beware the loophole."

"That's the exact same message on the USB drive before Ava decrypted it." My mind was spinning. Why would J.W. mimic the warning Jake embedded on that drive? It had to be connected, but I was missing the one color in the painting that would help the picture come alive.

"Let's go back to what we know." Bailen typed in a bunch of commands, and data started populating on the big screens along the wall. Assumptions and data he'd collected appeared one line after the next. He typed furiously, as if his hands couldn't keep up with his brain. I watched as all the elements piled up. I craned over my shoulder to check that everything I knew was included, but I couldn't sit in this uncomfortable position forever.

When Bailen finished, he pushed the keyboard over to Ava, who added a couple more lines of information she'd gleaned from the USB drive. When she finished, she backed away, and a complicated web of clues was laid out before us.

"Can someone unhook me?"

"What if J.W. contacts you again? I think we need to keep an eye on the data," Bailen said with a hint of apology in his tone.

"Well, if you can't see the board, then we'll bring the board to you." Lydia grabbed the side of the lounger with one hand and the tangle of cables with the other. She turned me so I could face the screen and see everything all in one place. Ava and Peyton stood on my left side while Bailen made his way to my right side.

We all stared at the information in silence, expecting the answer to magically pop out at us. At this point, I wished for one easy win, for something we didn't have to work so hard for.

"If J.W. is a what and not a who, then we can't think three dimensionally," Bailen said finally, breaking many minutes of long silence.

"How is he moving around?" I asked, more confused than ever.

Ava pointed at the location data. "He's moving inside whatever network is being used to control people. The same network Scurry is using to reach you, Kaya."

"Yeah, but how did it get there in the first place? And is he moving on his own or is someone else doing it?" I asked. Something still didn't make sense. "Better question, why does all the data until recently line up with Scurry? And how do we know this isn't Scurry messing with me again?"

Now that I'd said the words, they felt more and more like a possibility. Somehow, I'd been manipulated even more than I'd originally thought. I didn't know how tangled the web was. The guilt inside me swelled like a festering wound. This was all my fault. Although I hadn't had much of a choice but to play along, it wasn't clear until now how deadly this game had become. I couldn't help but wonder, if I'd taken the risk sooner and told everyone what was happening, could we have stopped Scurry sooner? Or was I just doomed to fail no matter what?

Everyone let my questions hang in the air unanswered, and my stomach churned with each silent moment that passed. The guilt slowly ate away at me from the inside out. I wanted to puke. Bailen stared at the data, looking for some kind of code he needed to crack. Ava seemed equally perplexed. Lydia's eyes darted from line to line, searching for a pattern she might have missed. Peyton stared at the floor. I couldn't tell if it was helping her concentrate or if she was hoping the floor would swallow her whole so she wouldn't have to learn the truth about J.W.—that it wasn't really Jake.

I looked at the location data on the board. The list seemed short. I opened my chat with Scurry, then counted the number of chat instances we'd had. Sure enough, there was more on my tracker than there were locations on the board. Maybe some of the locations were duplicated? "Is that all the location data you downloaded?"

"Yeah, why?" Bailen asked.

"Because there's more chat instances in my thread than there are on the board."

Lydia circled back to the computers with Bailen on her heels. They both grew very quiet as they typed in commands and scrolled through data on the screen. Lydia pointed to something on the screen and Bailen nodded, but neither of them said anything.

My heart pounded in my chest. I opened my mouth to speak, then quietly closed it, afraid to break their concentration. The leads on my temples buzzed softly.

"What's the timestamp on the first message from Scurry?" Bailen asked.

"Nine forty-six AM."

Bailen typed in some additional commands.

"WHOA!" Lydia exclaimed.

"What?" I watched them both for some hint of what they might be seeing.

"There's a lot more location data here for Scurry, and it's unique compared to J.W.'s first connection." Lydia said with wide eyes.

"It's almost like J.W. joined Scurry here." Bailen pointed to the screen as if any of the rest of us could see what he was looking at.

"Where were you three nights ago?" Lydia asked.

I closed my eyes to try and retrace my steps, but it was Peyton who broke the silence. "The bomb." The words were quiet but firm, like she couldn't have forgotten that moment if she tried.

My mind scrambled to recall the events that night. I'd set off to confront S.I.R.E., who turned out to be Scurry mind-controlling Harlow. But it wasn't about Scurry or Harlow, or even the bomb, at least not directly. "I think I know where J.W. came from."

"Where?" Ava asked.

Peyton lifted her gaze and shot me a pleading expression.

"That was the night we stopped Scurry from mind-controlling Harlow. But it was also when we pulled that USB from the terminal with all the tracker upgrade victims."

Bailen's focus shot up from the computer screen. "You think whatever this is came from that terminal?"

I nodded. "If the terminal was set to self-destruct, and whatever this is has some conscious awareness, maybe it went into self-preservation mode and jumped into the first thing it could find on the network. Which would have been Harlow. If J.W. followed that connection, it would have led right to the source."

"Scurry," Bailen said with a scowl.

"It's not a bad theory," Ava said. "But how was J.W. able to hide from Scurry?"

"And where is it now if it's bouncing all over the world, sending us messages?" Bailen asked.

I shook my head. I only had loose theories at this point. "Whatever this is, it seems to live in the network and have a way to move around in there."

Before I could think about it further, another message popped up from J.W. I opened it.

**J.W.: Secure your network. I have
something to show you.**

"Bailen…"

"I see it. He's here. Whatever that means." Bailen's fingers sped over the keys like he was trying to catch up to a motorbike on a skyway.

"I'm not sure, but I think he's going to show us. He asked that we secure the network. I don't know what that means." My body tensed at the thought of letting whatever this was gain access to our network, especially if it was Scurry playing an awful trick.

"I know what he means." Ava rounded to the computer bank. "The authorities had a security monitoring protocol for upgrades so people couldn't leverage the downtime to access our servers."

Bailen sighed, then looked at me as if he was sad all over again that his previous attempt to leverage an authority upgrade had failed by mere seconds. It made sense the authorities had a protocol for everything, but it didn't make it any easier to stomach that, if we'd had Ava that day, we might not be in over our heads today. Despite the past, we still had to work within our current mess. Either way, we'd be dead if it wasn't for Ava now.

"There. I've set up a secure area and walled it off so J.W. can't get into any of our other systems. Just in case." Ava looked proud of herself.

Bailen gave her a slight nod of respect.

I thought of my response to J.W., but before I could send it, I had another note from him.

J.W.: I'm here, but there's darkness within.

My body froze, unsure how to respond. I recognized those words. I inhaled deeply, then allowed myself a moment to calm my frazzled nerves. "He says he's here, and he's quoting Jake's poetry."

Peyton's gaze lifted from the floor as a portion of the main screen in the room went black.

"I see him in the system, but I'm not sure what I'm looking

at." Bailen's brow furrowed as he studied the screen.

"I've never seen anything like this," Ava added, equally confused. "This is some extremely complex code."

Four white letters appeared on the black screen: FFOB. I sat up straighter in the chair. Whoever or whatever this was had my full attention. Peyton let out a soft sob next to me. I reached my hand out, and she surprisingly took it. I gave her a quick squeeze as more text appeared on the screen.

J.W.: I found family.

"What does that mean?" I asked before I could formulate coherent thoughts.

"Can we communicate with it?" Lydia asked.

"I think so, but what do we say to that?" Bailen ran his fingers through his shaggy hair, something he only did when he was unsure.

"Maybe bluntness is the best tactic?" Ava asked.

It was definitely her style, but I wasn't sure that was the best way to approach this. If J.W. was connected to Jake in any way, we needed something different… Humor.

"No, I don't think blunt is the way to go. Try something like, 'We're awfully funny looking for family.'" It was something that might have made Jake laugh.

"Are you sure?" Bailen asked.

"She's right." Peyton's voice was so quiet I almost missed what she said. "Whether J.W. is Jake or not, there's a link between them. We have to assume that's not a coincidence."

Bailen typed in the response and it appeared on the screen. The three dots appeared, followed by words.

J.W.: I must be funny looking, too.

Peyton squeezed my hand hard. I knew exactly how she felt. It was eerily similar to Jake.

"Now that we have his attention, try a question." I knew in my gut that was the best way to get our answers.

"Any suggestions?" Bailen looked like a crotchrocket was about to run him over. He may have worked with my brother for some time before I'd shown up at the Hive, but this was certainly uncharted territory for him.

I didn't have all the answers either, but enough of us in the room had plenty of past interactions with Jake to piece something together. With Jake, it was almost never straight forward, so I couldn't straight out ask who J.W. was.

"I think we need to ask how J.W. knows Jake." I squeezed Peyton's hand again and she squeezed back. AI or not, they were connected, and I needed to know how.

"Try, 'Did you work with Jake?'" Her voice shook as she said his name.

Bailen typed in the question, then focused on the screen. We all held our breath, waiting for what came next.

J.W.: Something like that.

"That's it?" Peyton dropped my hand and sank to the floor.

I wanted to hug her, but Ava rounded the computer bank and pulled Peyton into an embrace.

The three dots appeared again.

"There's more coming." I pointed at the screen.

Peyton's glistening eyes looked up at the screen, silently pleading for some answers.

I hoped this wasn't some awful trick. But despite the chaos churning inside me, I knew in my core J.W. had the answers we'd been looking for.

J.W.: He's my boss.

"Boss? That doesn't make any sense. Jake didn't have any employees, did he?" The uncertainty inside me swirled a little faster.

Everyone shook their heads but Lydia. "What if he means creator, instead of boss?" she asked.

"Lydia, you're a genius!" If I hadn't been tied to the chair with the wires attached to me, I'd have leapt from it and tackle-hugged her. I didn't need to ask. That was the answer; it was the only thing that made sense. Whatever this was, Jake had created it. It explained why it sounded so much like him. The program must have inherited his sense of humor as it grew and developed. But it didn't explain why it existed. "Ask what it was made for."

Bailen didn't wait for confirmation from the room. He typed in the question.

The three dots were brief this time before the reply appeared.

J.W.: The loophole.

That seemed simple and obvious, but I knew there was more to it than that. But J.W. must have read my thoughts because another response came just as fast.

J.W.: to track progress

J.W.: to remember

J.W.: to share data

J.W.: to destroy

J.W.: eventually

"That's a whole lot of purpose but not a lot of clarity," Ava said. She watched, perplexed, as Peyton stood, moved closer to the screen, and stared at it without a word, as if the phrases on the screen somehow helped her get closer to Jake.

"This is what he was doing. All those lines of code he wouldn't tell me about." The words were spilling out of Peyton faster and faster, the dots all connecting simultaneously. "He kept telling me he was working a special assignment for a future upgrade. It didn't make sense because I didn't know of any future upgrades. He brushed me off and said it was a secret. I believed him, didn't push it. But seeing this, it all makes sense now. He was trying to piece together his fragmented memories of what had happened to use against Scurry and stop the loophole. That drive, this program, he was trying to tell us what was happening because we weren't listening to him. He was trying to fight a war with a one-person army. All this was his backup plan if he failed." Peyton let out a long wail. "I wish I had heard him then. Maybe I could have helped him."

Ava opened her arms, and Peyton collapsed into them and sobbed. "But you hear him now. It's not in vain."

My mouth dropped open in surprise. A fresh wound ripped open inside me. We'd failed him. I'd failed him. I should have known this wasn't all just about me. I should have seen he was struggling. I didn't know how I'd missed it.

But I always knew Jake was not one to let things go. Despite everything he'd been going through, he managed to be there for me and everyone he cared about. From beyond the grave, he still got us the information we needed to piece this mess together. He'd given us J.W. and the USB drive.

"Okay, new plan…" Bailen's voice trailed off as a new message box popped up on the screen, this time from Jeremy.

J.J.: Harlow, Mr. Overland, and Mr. Weiss are on the move. All headed in different directions.

I closed my eyes and let the darkness envelop me. It was starting.

Twenty-Nine

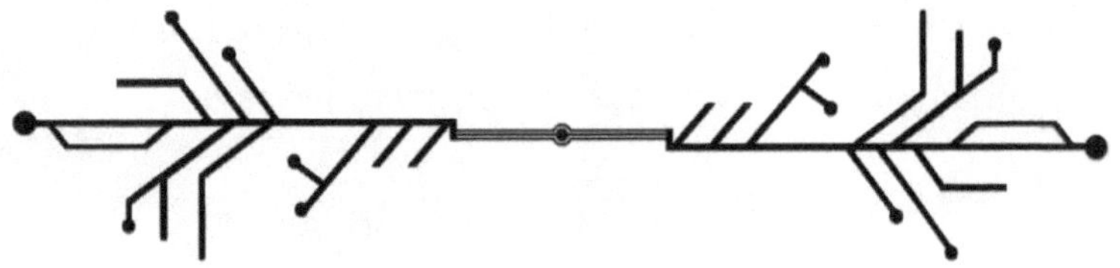

If I wasn't already sitting down, I might have collapsed. My breathing grew ragged. "Get me out of this chair." I pulled at the leads on my temples but didn't have the strength to yank them off. "We need to follow them. See what he's up to." And I needed to let Mom know what was going on, and check on Emily. There was so much to do. My mind raced a thousand miles an hour.

When I opened my eyes again, Bailen was beside me, unhooking the leads. "Take a deep breath."

I did.

"And another."

I didn't fight him on it.

"Better?"

I nodded. "A little. But—"

"We'll figure this out. I think the best plan is splitting up, though, to cover as much ground as possible."

I nodded, though I also sensed he was pulling me from the fight again.

"Find out who Jeremy is following," I said, secretly hoping it was my dad. We may not have figured everything out yet, but I couldn't lose him too. Not like this.

Lydia typed in the message and Jeremy's reply came quickly.

J.J.: Mr. Weiss.

I let out a long sigh of relief, but noticed Bailen's shoulders tighten. I squeezed his arm. The tension didn't ease. While I cared about Harlow and Mr. Overland too, my gut told me they were just pawns to Scurry. This was personal. He had a connection to Dad. "What about Harlow and your dad? Do we just let them go off on their own?"

"We'll follow them." Ava indicated herself and Peyton.

"I'll meet Jeremy. He might need help." Lydia was already packing some supplies in her backpack.

"Perfect. I'll stay here with Kaya and work on this data. I still need to look at Scurry's box and those files you downloaded."

I nodded, afraid my words would betray my disappointment. He was right. We were drowning in data that had the potential to bring all the pieces of the picture together.

The room was a flurry of activity and then, just as quickly, it went silent. Only Bailen and I remained. Bailen grabbed the box and started unfastening the casing. I peered inside as he lifted the cover. I didn't recognize most of what I was looking at, but I knew enough to realize it was badly damaged.

"What a mess," I mumbled.

"You did this?" he asked with a mixture of pain and admiration in his voice.

"Yeah, it was J.W.'s suggestion. I knew if Scurry wanted the box, I couldn't give it to him in working condition, regardless of what he might do to me as punishment." I gave an apologetic shrug, knowing it was the right move, but that damaging the box might now make Bailen's job examining it more difficult.

A smile erupted on his face. "Atta girl." He high fived me, then leaned over and kissed me, a quick peck but full of so much meaning and thanks. "That is one clever AI." He shook his head. "Maybe next time don't be so… thorough. This might take a while to pick through all the components."

My cheeks pinked a bit. "What can I do to help?" I felt a little less guilty about the damage to the box but became painfully aware I wouldn't be much help deciphering what was inside it.

"Want to help with those files?" He pointed to the corner of the room where several large rolls of paper sat.

I grinned. He wanted me to draw the mysterious files on my tracker, just like I had with the two-hundred and twenty schematic files Dad had hidden on my tracker. I rounded to my desk and opened the center drawer where I kept all my drawing supplies. Grabbing the box of pencils, I looked for a good-sized spool of paper. I unrolled it on the floor beneath the large screens still displaying Jeremy's and J.W.'s messages.

I accessed the first file, not sure what to expect. It wasn't a schematic; it looked like a map. I closed it and opened the next file, another map. I opened the third and found the same. Were these all maps? I skipped to the final file, expecting a map, but instead found the schematics I was looking for. After a quick search of the hundred or so files, I saw the majority were plans for various pieces of technology. The rest were maps. I scanned the files, searching for something familiar until I found what I was looking for.

"Bailen, I think there's a schematic for that box. Want to download that file?" It would be faster than me drawing the whole thing out.

His face lit up, but there was worry behind his eyes. "I think those files better stay on your tracker just in case there's something nasty hiding in them."

I nodded. "Drawing it is." I smiled, secretly excited to not only draw but also to have found my purpose in all this again.

As I examined the image, searching for where to start my drawing, I grabbed a couple of pencils, finding a tip that wasn't too sharp or dull. My hand floated over the page. The pencil scratched across the paper in a familiar rhythm as muscle memory took over.

Before I knew it, I had a complete drawing in front of me.

"Want to take a look?" I noticed for the first time all the components Bailen had removed from the box scattered across the table. There were so many. I wondered if he'd left anything in it.

"Yeah, I'm hoping it will shed some light on what I'm looking at." He rounded the table and knelt on the floor next to me. His gaze moved across the page like he was solving a complicated math problem in his head.

After a long silence, he pointed to an area toward the top of the schematic. "Is there any more detail about this component?" He pulled a particularly mangled piece of equipment from his pocket. "I think that's this part, but it's too badly damaged to tell exactly what it is."

"I'm not sure. There's lots more schematics in this data." I closed my eyes and opened another file, inspecting it closely. Then I opened my eyes and looked at my drawing. As I scanned the page, I found a component in the bottom right corner that matched the dimensions.

I opened a second file to test my theory and quickly located the matching component on my drawing. "These other files are the schematics for the individual components. Let me see if I can find that one and draw it next."

"Sounds like a plan. I'll keep working on the box while this program continues to run analysis on the other data we downloaded from your tracker. Let me know when you get this one drawn out."

"You got it." I grabbed a new pencil and unrolled more paper, then set to work opening files until I found the schematic for the component in question.

Partway through, I noticed a tracker message from J.W.

J.W.: Anything I can help with?

K.W.: Not unless you can move this
data onto Bailen's computer without
compromising our network.

J.W.: No.

I sighed, knowing the request was too good to be true. Then the three dots appeared again.

J.W.: But I can tell you about the box
and the different components inside.

K.W.: What about this one?

I shared an image of the component in our chat.

J.W.: It's a sequencer.

K.W.: What's that?

**J.W.: It allows for one person to process
a lot of data quickly.**

"Bailen!"

"What?" When he looked up from the box, his expression changed to concern.

"You were right to focus on that component. I think it's the key to everything Scurry was trying to do. Or at least that's what J.W. is telling me."

He glanced at the big screen, but it hadn't changed from the prior messages. He looked back at me. I nodded once, confirming his suspicions. "It's like you two have a secret bond or something."

My cheeks grew warm, but not out of guilt. More because of the unspoken bond I felt with this computer program or whatever it was. It may not be Jake, but there was definitely an unexplainable connection there. "Something like that. Maybe he's looking out for me." The minute the words came out, I knew it had more than one meaning. It was like Jake was watching over me from beyond.

"That's one strange guardian angel. But I'm glad you have extra protection. I don't know what I'd do if I lost you." Bailen smiled, but it wasn't full-on. He understood the pain Peyton had been through, but also knew how lucky he was not to have experienced it to the same level. "Tell me more about this component."

"J.W. told me it's a sequencer."

"That explains a lot."

"You know what that is?" Of course he did. The guy had

devoted his life to tech, especially the obsolete kind.

He nodded as if it was a simple piece of code he'd committed to memory. "This is the reason why Scurry can control more than one person at once. I don't know how I didn't think of this before." He stared off into a void, looking for answers. "If this one is damaged, that means he has at least one more. I don't know the exact computing power of this box, but the more of these he has, the more people he can control at once."

"If we find the others, we cut Scurry off at the knees?"

"Yep. But we also need to figure out how he's running this backup network. The only question is, where is he hiding all this?"

I shrugged. But despite the mystery, it all made a bit more sense now. Then an idea struck me.

"We have a lot of location data on Scurry. Maybe we start there." I looked up at the screen with all the chat conversations and data from my tracker.

"Process of elimination. I like it." Bailen pulled a chair up to his terminal. The large screens went blank, and then the chat logs appeared on them. "Let's setup a timeline."

I closed my eyes and retraced the last few days of events. "The most recent conversation is from the current facility we put him in after capture. Prior to that, he was in the run-down SuperMax. Did he ever leave?"

"I'll bring up the spreadsheet Lydia created. She was cross-referencing location data." Bailen leaned closer to his screen and used the scroll wheel on the mouse to read through the data. "Looks like he left the prison twice and went to the same coordinates." Bailen grew silent. The quiet clicking of the keyboard filled the void. "Why go back to prison if he could leave?"

I revisited the in-person conversation I'd had with Scurry. "He said staying in SuperMax was the perfect cover. No one would suspect him if he stayed. But he left twice, which means wherever he went and whatever he had to do there was important enough to risk blowing his cover."

"I'm trying to pull up the coordinates from the IP address on the map." When Bailen stopped typing, a giant map appeared on the overhead screens. A red circle indicated the spot. As he zoomed in on the area, I looked at the few surrounding roads and cities, but it didn't look familiar.

"Can you switch it to satellite mode?" I asked, hoping the sight of trees and buildings might help spur my memory.

The image morphed into a wooded area with a large clearing and a barn next to a farmhouse. A second smaller house sat off in the distance.

"You've got to me kidding me." My body filled with rage. Scurry had run me around secret passageways at that stupid farmhouse and threatened me. The whole time, he was hiding more secrets there, barely outside my grasp.

"What?" Bailen asked, but when he met my gaze, his expression softened. "You know this place?"

"You should, too. It was part of Scurry's demented scavenger hunt. He ran me through secret passageways and locked rooms before confronting me via video feed." I cursed under my breath. I knew he'd been toying with me this whole time, but I shouldn't have been surprised that the layers to his misdirection knew no bounds.

"We went there but never found any passageways. Think you can draw me a map of them?" A glint of excitement lit up within Bailen's eyes.

"Maybe, but I'm not sure it would do much good. It was all

underground and had revolving rooms. I doubt any of it would make sense, but I'm happy to share what I remember."

As soon as I finished talking, a notification from J.W. appeared in the corner of my vision. I blinked and opened it.

J.W.: You don't need to remember.

K.W.: What do you mean?

J.W.: You have everything you need already.

I had everything I needed? I wasn't sure what that meant.

J.W.: I'll show you.

A dozen files from Scurry's data opened in my field of vision. The images rotated and rearranged themselves like J.W. was putting a puzzle together before my eyes. When he finished, there was a gigantic map with multiple levels, floor plans for the three buildings on the property as well as numerous secret passageways that ran underground. It was a maze of tunnels. The few I'd traversed were a small fraction of what this map showed.

"Bailen, you're not going to believe this. Those files I got from Scurry are not only schematics but also maps to the farmhouse and all its underground passageways. J.W. put them together for me. We have a comprehensive map of the entire property."

I paused. It all seemed too easy. We finally had an advantage. But every time I thought we had one, it crumbled before me. I thought back to when we'd fought Scurry, how I'd brute forced his tracker and the connection to everyone in the room. I had overloaded his tracker the same way I had my own tracker and the network in the past. Similar to when I'd unlocked the files hidden on my tracker from Dad, I accessed files from my connection to Scurry. There didn't appear to be any trap to spring, just large amounts of data Scurry never imagined I'd gain access to. Maybe we actually had some fortune on our side this time.

"Finally, a breakthrough." Bailen gave me an inquisitive look.

"I'm on it. We can send copies to the others." I paused, the convenience of the situation still eating away at me.

Bailen closed the gap between us and pulled me into a tight hug. "What is it?"

"Doesn't this all feel just a little too easy? I know we're due some good luck, but something doesn't feel right about this."

"I think awareness is the first step. As long as we know it's too good to be true, we can keep an eye out for surprises."

"I think it's more than surprises. He wants us to find him. I'm not sure why, though."

Bailen leaned in and kissed me long and slow enough to drive the worry out of my mind for a small fraction of time. "Regardless of what he's up to, we'll do this together."

"Together," I repeated before heading to the floor to roll out more paper.

As I grabbed my pencil, a message from Jeremy popped up on the big screen.

J.J.: Mr. Weiss made a brief stop at
Global Tracking Systems before heading to
a remote farmhouse. I'll send coordinates.

"What are the odds we're talking about the same place?" I asked, knowing the answer already.

"One hundred percent. Jeremy just sent the coordinates and said Lydia's with him. I'm telling them to keep their distance and only move in if necessary."

J.J.: Looks like Peyton and Ava are
already here.
And we're outnumbered.

Thirty

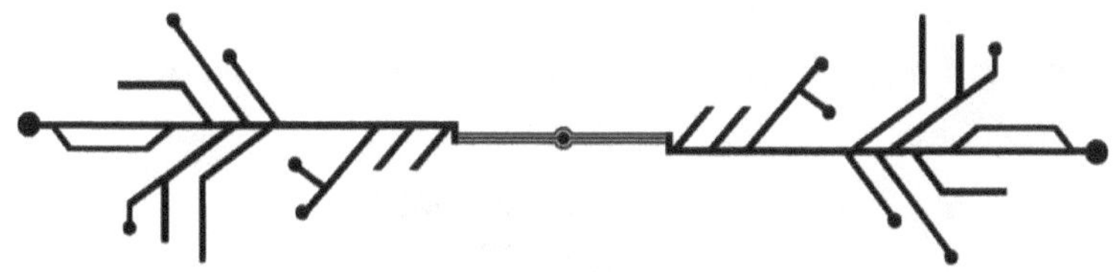

My blood ran cold.

"We aren't all going to survive this," I muttered under my breath.

The sheer terror on Bailen's face told me he heard what I said. He opened his mouth, but I waved my hand to say I didn't want to hear his confirmation.

I glanced up at the screen where Bailen had left Jeremy and the others a note to stay out of sight, that we would get there as soon as we could.

"I don't think I can draw this map in time." I shook my head, feeling like I'd failed everyone.

"And I don't have enough time to reverse engineer a solution to this sequencer. I'm sure Scurry was counting on that."

"He's a master chess player for sure." Dread swirled inside me. Our slight advantage was crumbling before us.

But a flashing message in the corner of my sight drew me out of my funk.

K.W.: Got any tricks up your sleeve that
will get this map to the team?

J.W.: One or two.
Allow me.

Within seconds, J.W. had sent the map to half a dozen people.

K.W.: Are you sure we won't get
caught?

J.W.: No.
But we don't have time to waste on
protocol and safety.

That was the most Jake-like thing I'd ever heard. He was right. It didn't matter if we got caught now; we couldn't be trapped holding information that might save us.

It was exactly the kind of thing Jake would have done, look a no-win scenario in the face and find a way to give it the middle finger. We had nothing to lose at this point. If we were going to survive this, I needed to start thinking like Jake. I had J.W. to thank for the reminder.

"Kaya, what did you do?" Bailen stared at me with a mixture of confusion and fear.

"It was J.W. He said we didn't have time to waste. Safe or not, we need to use every weapon we have." I smiled, hoping Bailen would agree. We could all use a little more Jake right about now.

Bailen nodded, grabbed some small computer equipment, and shoved it into his go kit.

Less than ten minutes later, we were up the back stairs and in the front room of the Coderie. Almost all the windows were smashed in and some of the computer terminals had been knocked over, but otherwise, amid the broken glass, everything else was untouched. We didn't have much time before the mind-controlled zombies destroyed everything at Scurry's command.

I peered across the street. The other businesses hadn't fared well either—shattered glass, small fires, flying cars overturned on the street, crotchrockets hanging from awnings and second-story balconies. The violent crowd must have moved on, but small fires still crackled in trash cans and burned-out cars. A few people walked the street with dazed expressions, but the usually bustling street was eerily quiet, considering. Some of the shop owners, covered in dirt with tattered clothes, had already started to clean up the mess as tears streamed down their faces.

A scream pierced through the scraping of glass and rubble being swept up. I glanced at Bailen, who returned a concerned expression. He was weighing the same question as me—pause to help or abandon them for the endgame? Sirens blared in the distance, but none seemed to be headed this way, which weighed heavy on my heart. There weren't enough resources to help everyone.

Bailen grabbed my hand and led me around to the back alley. "We have to go before someone spots us. Before he…"

I nodded, afraid to speak. We rounded the corner where we'd stashed our crotchrockets under the back stairs. I hoped no one had found our hiding spot. When I saw them untouched, I breathed a sigh of relief. We kick-started the bikes and secured the gear. Moments later, we were airborne and headed toward the farmhouse.

We landed about a quarter mile away from the open field and stashed our bikes in some underbrush. Bailen grabbed his gear. I took one of the backpacks with our supplies.

Bailen held his hand out to me and I accepted it. We walked to the rhythm of the crunching underbrush and snapping twigs but said nothing. When the moonlight from the clearing finally peeked through the trees, he pulled me behind some bushes and dropped his gear with a soft thud.

His gaze met mine. My breath caught in my throat as I lost myself in his piercing green eyes. I ran my fingers through his shaggy hair and squeezed the back of his neck. Wrapping his arm around my waist, he nudged me closer to him. His warm breath beat against my lips as the gap between us disappeared. His lips met mine slowly and softly at first, but the urgency increased as we realized time was ticking away. Whatever happened, we'd have this memory and every one that came before it.

Far too soon, he drew away. "No matter what happens, we're family. And family fights for one another."

I knew exactly what he meant. Together or not, we were bonded for life. I didn't need to wonder why he needed a reminder. He needed to hear it out loud, needed to hear me say that if he lost control again, I'd fight for him. And if it came to it, I'd die fighting for him, even if he'd have to go on without me.

It was an easy choice, but I told him anyway. "I'm not going to let anything happen to you. He won't win." But my mind betrayed me, wondering what would happen if Scurry did win. That was not a world I wanted to live in.

My words weren't as confident as I wanted, but I leaned in and sealed the promise with a passionate kiss.

When the moment passed, we both peered into the clearing. A

single figure stood unmoving, watching the woods. "Who do you think that is?" I whispered, pushing the worst fears from my mind. The petite form seemed familiar.

Bailen shook his head. "We're about to find out."

He squeezed my hand and pulled me from the security of the trees. As we approached the statuesque figure, I gasped. I'd know her leggings, stylish sweater, and cute boots anywhere.

Lydia.

I didn't say her name out loud because I knew she wouldn't respond. As we got within a few feet, her glassy-eyed stare confirmed my suspicions. My insides froze. This was my new reality. Staring into the glassy eyes of the people I cared about most and, if Scurry made me, facing them in a fight. I had to find a way to win without hurting my family.

"Took you long enough."

I whirled around. Ava emerged from her hiding spot amongst the underbrush. Her expression was neutral, but it was obvious she was hiding something. My shoulders sank as I realized no one was following behind her like I expected.

"How long?" I asked, several questions stemming from one seemingly so simple.

"She was like that when we arrived."

"And…" Bailen's unspoken question was obvious to Ava as her expression turned to a mixture of sadness and anger.

"Peyton went that way about ten minutes ago. You have no idea how hard it was for me to let her walk off and not follow." She choked out her final words. "But I did manage to gain access to her signal and started tracking it on my watch before she left."

Ava shrugged like it was no big deal, but the tension in Bailen's shoulders eased only slightly. It seemed silly to track Peyton, knowing she'd be forced to protect Scurry, but I couldn't ignore the small amount of relief washing over me either.

I stepped toward Ava and squeezed her shoulder, a silent thank you for waiting to fill us in instead of following her heart. Her body shook under my touch. She was likely hurting way more than she wanted anyone to know. I pulled her into a giant hug and held her until she stopped shaking. I watched Bailen over her shoulder to make sure he wasn't going to go postal, but where I expected him to go into warrior mode, he had a stone-cold glare.

"Bailen?" My breath caught in my throat as I released Ava and waited for a response.

"Yeah?"

My heart sped faster, relieved I hadn't lost him yet. But the clock was ticking. The question was, how much time was left on it?

"What's the plan?" Ava asked in a quiet voice.

"You got the maps?" I asked.

"Yeah. What a colossally stupid move, I might add."

My cheeks burned. Even though it wasn't me, I wanted to defend the choice. "I—"

Ava raised her arm and a smirk appeared on her face. "And exactly the thing Scurry will be least expecting."

I released a long breath, allowing my brain time to catch up. "While I'd love to take credit for a piece of epic stupidity, all that recognition goes to J.W. It was his idea."

"That little AI is more intelligent than we gave it credit for."

"You have no idea."

"It's a little scary if you ask me," Bailen said.

"You think it's a bad idea to let J.W. help us?" I couldn't tell if his comment was jealousy or genuine fear, or maybe a little of both.

"I didn't say that." He swallowed slowly, like he was buying time to come up with a good explanation for his skepticism of the tech. "It's just… something feels off, and I don't know if it's J.W., Lydia's glassy eyes staring back at me, or something else…"

I knew with certainty the "something else" was the idea that Scurry had Peyton under his thumb and with one twitch could end her, or any of us really.

"One step at a time." Ava broke the tense silence. "We have a map. Let's start with that."

"Right. Where's the most likely place he could be hiding?" Bailen's expression softened as he found a renewed sense of purpose.

I thought about the full map J.W. had pulled together and blinked twice to bring it into view. "The passageways from the barn and the shelter on the far side of the property didn't have a lot of places for him to hide." I inspected the other tunnels. Most of them had single exit and entry points. He'd want a backup plan, so I zoomed in on several passageways that had multiple escape routes. "There's a few that seem likely, two off the main farmhouse. I didn't have time to explore that area the last time I was here."

"And another one from the barn." Bailen must have been studying the maps as well.

There was a second system of tunnels starting with a trap door in the tack room off the barn. I cursed myself for not being more diligent in searching every nook and cranny before letting Scurry manipulate me. But scolding myself was pointless. There was no way Scurry would have allowed it before, and he'd send us exactly where he wanted as soon as he figured out what we were up to.

"Do we split up or stick together?" Ava gave no indication of which one was better.

"Split up." Bailen didn't hesitate. "You two go to the farmhouse and I'll take the barn."

"What, cause we're girls?" Ava's face contorted into an offended look.

Bailen wasn't fazed by the accusation. "No, because you've both alluded Scurry's mind-control, and there's more ground to cover in the farmhouse. The odds are better he's there. I'll search as fast as I can. If I don't find anything, I'll join you."

I opened my mouth to argue, but he pushed a finger to my lips.

"You know I'm right," he whispered against my ear.

"But—"

His gaze locked on mine, and I forgot any argument I'd compiled in my head. He was right. This was as much for my protection as his. Scurry would grab hold of him the first chance he had. I needed to be as far away as possible when that happened. I hated that he was right. The pain of not knowing what would happen grabbed hold of my insides and slowly ate away at me.

He removed a small device from his pocket. "So you can keep an eye on me."

"What is it?"

"GPS tracking device. It's obsolete tech but should interface with your tracker and let you know where I am." He winked, then placed the device back in his jeans pocket.

I located the signal with my tracker, then nodded. He kissed me again. When I withdrew, I turned around and didn't look back. If I did, I might not be able to leave him.

"Let's go, Ava."

Ava said nothing, but the soft padding of her feet told me she was close behind.

Thirty-One

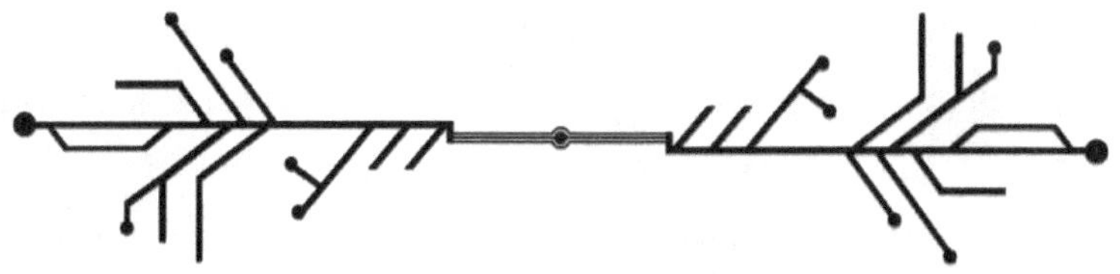

The echo of our boots on the farmhouse's wooden porch broke our silent trek. I reached for the screen door and Ava nodded. It creaked a warning as I pulled it open and pushed the front door of the farmhouse inward.

Shadows loomed across the dark interior littered with broken furniture and couches covered in dusty sheets. The air hung thick with a stench of mildew. Knick knacks were strewn across the floor, the more fragile ones shattered and left to collect dust. Curtains hung in tatters from the rods, and wallpaper peeled at the seams as if someone had tried to claw it from the walls.

We crept toward the back of the house, where we found a kitchen. I jumped as a large pot clanged against the far wall. A small black cat peered from behind the mess and hissed a warning before darting from the room. Remnants of shattered dishes littered the floor. The metal door of the refrigerator had been crushed in. Something terrible had happened here.

But none of the destruction explained where Scurry was now,

or why he'd returned to a place that must hold such awful memories and signs of struggles. Why this house?

Ava nodded me toward the stairs that led to the basement, where the map indicated we'd find one of two passageways that ended in multiple exit points, both in the field and within the shelter on the edge of the property.

The other passageway was located on the second floor. It was an odd place for a passageway, but the one Scurry had forced me to the last time I'd been here was located off the loft in the barn. Practicality didn't seem to be on the designer's mind. Maybe it was more about misdirection.

"What did you explore before?" I whispered to Ava.

"Not much. We checked the woods on the edge of the grounds, then ran into Lydia, who was already on guard. Before we could try to snap her out of it, Peyton was under his control too." Ava's shoulders slumped and she let out a long, ragged breath.

I didn't need her to finish to know what came next. "And Jeremy?"

"I kept an eye out but never caught sight of him."

I nodded, unsure what else to say. Ava took the steps slowly, each stair creaking as she put weight on it.

As my foot hit the first step, a message from Scurry appeared in my line of sight.

I closed my eyes, sucked in a deep breath, then allowed the message to fill my mind.

R.S.: Second floor.
Come alone.

I didn't dignify it with a response, but knew I'd better comply.

"I think *we* should search upstairs." The word *we* was in direct defiance of Scurry's request, but I didn't care. He had his plan, and now I had the start of mine.

Ava twisted on the stairs and looked up at me with a question on her face. "Are you sure?"

I nodded but held up two fingers up, letting her know to give me a couple minutes before she should follow. "He's watching." I gave her my best "make it convincing" look.

She returned a knowing expression, then proceeded down the stairs alone.

I circled back to the front door with a renewed sense of confidence. Ava wouldn't be far behind me. I found the stairs to the second floor. I winced as the floorboards popped with each step, a loud warning not to continue on. I ignored the sounds even as they grew louder and echoed inside my head.

On the second floor, I found three bedrooms and a bathroom. Another message appeared on my tracker.

R.S.: The room at the end of the hall.

I opened the map to check it out, then stepped toward the room at the end of the hall. The bedroom was a stark contrast to the rest of the house. The bed was made, and among the dust, it appeared the room hadn't been touched in years.

R.S.: In the closet.

I didn't need him to tell me, I'd figured it out from the map already. The closet door didn't open easily. I tugged at it and the dried paint cracked in protest—another warning to turn back that

I wanted to obey. But I had to keep going, to stop Scurry once and for all.

The closet contained a few pairs of pants and some sweatshirts but wasn't full. Boxes rested on the top shelf, collecting dust as well. I wondered whose room this was, but there wasn't enough detail to determine who the owner could have been.

At first glance, there didn't appear to be anything out of the ordinary in the closet, but I checked the map again and it indicated a passageway in the floor.

I tapped the wooden floorboards with my boots. Several shifted as I moved my foot around. I pulled them back and saw a dark hole with a metal ladder. Taking the bag off my back, I dug through it until I found a flashlight. I twisted it on. It wasn't bright enough to see the bottom of the hole.

I sucked in a breath. "Here goes nothing," I said to break the unnerving silence. I climbed onto the ladder, which seemed sturdy enough. The cold metal of the bars chilled me to my core.

My breath echoed in my ears as I descended rung by rung. Part way down, I stopped to shine the flashlight again, but the bottom still wasn't visible. After what felt like several stories down, my foot finally hit solid concrete.

I waved my flashlight around to get a better view, but as I moved, a series of lights illuminated a concrete tunnel ahead. I followed it. Around two turns, I stopped in an open area that branched off in three additional directions. None were lit, so it wasn't obvious which path to follow.

I stood unmoving as I collected my thoughts, trying to anticipate what was coming. I half expected another tracker message, but a figure slowly emerged on my right. As the individual approached, I recognized the large form.

Troy.

I didn't need to make eye contact to know he wasn't in control. His unnatural gait told me everything I needed to know.

I stepped up to the soccer player, unintimidated by his hulking form. He didn't move. I tried to squeeze around him, but his arm flew up and blocked my path. I moved to go around the other side, but he stepped to block me again.

So that's how this was going to be? I moved to the next passage, but another dark figure appeared, one I didn't recognize at first. The thin form slowly stepped into the light, his dirty blond hair illuminated. I hadn't seen him since the day in the Coderie when this all started with Harlow's attack.

"Wes?" I don't know why I said his name out loud; I knew he wouldn't respond. When I stepped toward him, he matched my single step. I took another step. He countered again.

I turned to the only other available passageway. Before continuing, I removed my backpack and pulled out a small box of circuit board components. I dropped a couple on the ground for Ava to find and hoped she wasn't far behind me. Throwing the bag back over my shoulder, I traversed the passageway. The tunnel illuminated every twenty feet or so until I hit another split, which again branched in three directions. This time a figure appeared from the left path.

Harlow.

I didn't need to see his face in the light to know he had the same glassy stare as the others. I didn't try to go around him. But when he emerged into the light, I made eye contact with his glassy stare. "Keep fighting, Harlow. I'll keep fighting, too."

I stepped to the tunnel straight ahead, but another figure emerged, dark-skinned and muscular.

Jeremy.

So, this is what happened to you.

I didn't try to make contact. It was becoming painfully obvious what Scurry was doing. A final display of the power he had over me. His attempt to intimidate me. Knowing his game only made it slightly easier to overcome. Before this was over, I'd have to face everyone I cared about. I tried to push the thought from my mind, but it kept creeping up, refusing to let me forget.

I dropped more circuit components in defiance, then followed the only remaining path to the right. Inching along, I allowed myself a few moments to slow my breathing and think. With my plan still coming together, I wasn't sure if it would be enough to stop him. My only hope was that Ava hadn't run into any trouble with Scurry's mind-controlled pawns.

When I was ready, I picked up my pace until I met a third decision point, this time with four passageways. Before I chose a direction, a larger shadow emerged from the passageway on my right. Peyton and Bailen's dad, Mr. Overland, blocked the way, glassy-eyed and unmoving. While I was glad to see him unharmed, I knew that might only be temporary.

I didn't try to go around him. Message received. Instead, I waited for the next person to make an appearance. My body shook as the figure stepped into the light.

Dad.

I swallowed down a quiet sob as two more figures appeared, one much shorter than the other.

"No," I gasped. Anything but this.

I didn't need the small shadow to step into the light to know it was Emily. The second figure stood just behind with a hand on her shoulder.

Mom.

The sight knocked the wind out of me. It was like staring at a photograph of the past, but one that sent icy terror through my veins. It should be me under Scurry's mind-control, not anyone else. Especially not Emily.

I rushed toward them and threw my arms around the girl who had become my sister. She didn't reciprocate, but neither of them moved to stop me, either. I whispered into her ear, "I promise not to fail you. I will be the one person in your life who keeps her promises."

I stepped back and, for the first time, saw the deep scratches on her tiny face and long cuts up and down her arms. This is what Scurry had done to her using Harlow as his pawn. I squeezed my eyes shut, but the tears streamed out. My stomach churned. I wheezed as I tried to catch my breath, and my chest ached. I couldn't lose another sibling, especially not at the hands of someone I loved. I would make Scurry pay. I balled my hands and ground my teeth, determined to win this fight.

My anger simmered. I opened my eyes. There was a tracker message from R.S. waiting for me. I didn't want to open it—he had nothing productive to offer me—but the consequences of ignoring it would be worse. My mind warred, but I finally blinked and opened the message.

**R.S.: Betrayal is a funny thing.
But I'll have my revenge.**

He was right. There had been so much betrayal. Dad betraying Scurry, and me betraying Scurry both by taking down the network and continuing to defy him now. But he was the worst betrayer of us all, taking away people's personal freedoms, privacy, and the right to ultimately make their own choices. For that, I'd have my revenge first.

I tossed more circuit parts to the floor, then darted down the only other path, clearly the direction Scurry wanted me to go. He wanted me vulnerable so I'd slip up, but the only thing the message accomplished was fueling the anger that now boiled inside me—anger about what he'd been allowed to get away with, what he'd done to Jake, and above all, anger that I'd let him get under my skin. I'd use all of it.

When I reached the next set of passageways, I hunched over and rested my hands on my knees, trying to catch my breath.

I looked up to find Peyton standing over me. I tripped backward, putting some space between me and her glassy stare. I'd have given anything for a smart-ass comment from her right now, something that told me she was back to her old self. Instead, I had a shell of a person in front of me.

Before I could attempt to reach out to her, another figure appeared in the tunnel on the left. I froze, overcome by pain and sadness.

I'd known this was coming. The glassy, unresponsive form staring back at me tore me apart from the inside out. As much as I didn't want to let this torture tactic work, it attacked my heart and soul and made me painfully aware of how alone I was.

I collapsed to my knees and let out a primal scream. Seeing Bailen alive and unharmed might have helped under normal circumstances, but the figure in front of me wasn't the guy I knew. This shell lacked his expression, his personality. All the things that made him who he was. All the things I cherished about him.

"Bailen." My voice shook, full of uncertainty. "I'm here. Pey's here, too.

"You're not alone.

"You fight this with everything you have.

"I know you can. I've seen the fight in you.

"I'll be here, right by your side. Fighting right along with you. For you.

"I won't quit fighting."

The words spilled out. I could only hope a small portion of them were making it through to him, fueling his fire.

His pinky twitched. I reached for his hand, wishing he would reciprocate, but he stood unmoving. When I squeezed his hand, it was lifeless within mine. I choked back a sob. I hadn't even faced Scurry yet, and he'd found a way to weaken me to my core. To break me into a million unrepairable pieces.

I took in several deep breaths to calm my emotions so I could focus on my revenge. I'd make him pay for every single bad thing he'd done. I'd make him pay, even if it was how I had to spend my dying breath. I owed it to myself and everyone I cared about. I couldn't lose anyone else, or life wouldn't be worth living anymore.

I forced my gaze to meet Bailen's glassy, dead eyes. "Bailen, I love you." I kissed him on the cheek. His fingers twitched in my grasp, then his hand squeezed mine. It wasn't tight, but I felt it. I felt every part of the emotion behind it, all the fight within it. I dropped his hand and ran down the only open tunnel, scattering the remaining components as I went.

I was ready to face whatever Scurry had for me.

Thirty-Two

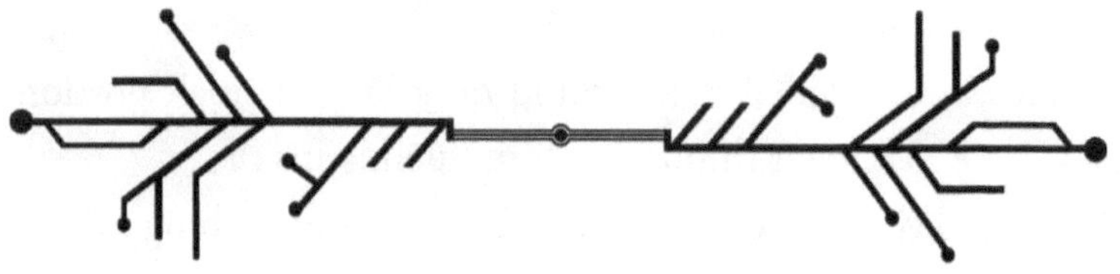

I lost track of how long I ran. At times I ran so fast the lights had trouble keeping up, illuminating after I'd crossed their dark threshold. A pain in my chest erupted, but I didn't stop. The pain propelled me forward. I would finish this. One way or another.

When I thought my body couldn't push forward anymore, I reached a metal door. I stopped to suck in air, my throat so dry it hurt to swallow. Yanking the metal water bottle from the side of the backpack, I took a long, slow drink, then saw a tracker message from R.S. I took another swig, then dropped the bottle on the ground with a clang.

R.S.: This ends now.

K.W.: I couldn't have said it better myself.

The door swung open silently. I stepped into a dark room. A single overhead light illuminated Scurry sitting in the center of the room. He wore a business suit and tie, a little too formal for the occasion but a good look for his upcoming funeral. Behind him, several rows of computer servers hummed softly. The lights blinked like a mini city, casting dark shadows over the back half of the room.

A triumphant smile appeared on his face, but he said nothing.

I returned a similar smile, then dropped my backpack on the floor. I walked slowly toward him and stopped about ten feet away.

"What could you possibly want now?" The question was stern but unwavering.

"That should be obvious."

"You're going to have to kill me."

"Patience." His smile turned wicked. "Your wish will be here before you know it." He closed his eyes as if he was picturing what killing me would look like.

Anticipating an attack, I stepped to the edge of the room so my back was against a wall. I closed my eyes and reached out to the tracker network to see what I was dealing with. At first glance, I could see his tracker and some standard programs. I knew there was much more below the surface. As I concentrated harder, the complicated threads of the network untangled before my eyes, revealing thousands of lines of encryption. The source code. It had to be a trap.

My eyes flew open at the sound of his deep laughter. Troy, Wes, and Harlow stood before me, all with glassy-eyed stares. "Looks like the team is back together."

"Three against one. This is hardly a fair fight." The obvious words were only meant to buy me some time. I had to keep him talking while I tried to push against his tracker connection and uncover his hidden connection to everyone.

"How about three against two?" Ava stood in the doorway, arms crossed, standard issue authority weapons strapped to her belt and legs.

I sighed in relief, never so happy to see her. I'd been afraid I would have to do this alone.

She drew a gun from her belt and it whined as it charged up. She pointed it directly at Scurry's head. "Give me one good reason not to end this right now. I won't hesitate this time."

"How about a distraction first?" I jerked my chin toward the boys, now Scurry's puppets. Her eyes met mine, and she nodded ever so slightly. My breathing slowed a bit. As I closed my eyes, Troy lunged for Ava. She tucked the weapon in the back of her pants and engaged. Squeezing my eyes tighter, I focused on the network. I accessed a search protocol to help me find the program I was looking for and manually ran some code to uncover what secrets Scurry was hiding.

Then I opened a chat window.

K.W.: Where should I be looking?

J.W.: Where you least expect.

It was just like J.W. to be cryptic, but he confirmed my suspicions about the source code that had revealed itself. I opened my eyes to check on Ava. Troy was out cold on the floor, but Wes and Harlow were putting up quite a fight.

I crossed the room to help, but Jeremy, Mr. Overland, and Dad emerged through the door. I skidded to a stop as I tried to regroup.

Scurry laughed again. I spun and ran at him, intent on knocking that smile from his face. As I braced myself for a collision, I passed through his image entirely. A freaking hologram? The laughter rang out like surround sound.

I cursed as the hologram disappeared. He had to be close. Otherwise, I wouldn't have seen his tracker on the network—unless that was a trick too.

"Tsk tsk. I thought you were smarter than that." The pleasure dripped from his voice as it echoed all around us.

Ignoring the taunt, I opened a command window on my tracker. I searched the connections, reaching out for Scurry's tracker again.

"A little help here?" Ava called, now surrounded by five people.

I darted across the room and kicked Wes in the thigh. He turned to face me, but no pain registered on his face. Harlow followed him, but that left Jeremy, Mr. Overland, and Dad on Ava.

"You up for a game of dodgeball?" I asked.

"Anything to keep from seriously hurting them."

I nodded. "Let's keep them moving. I'll try to disable them on the network one by one."

"I don't think we have that kind of time." Ava dodged Jeremy's fist and spun around to keep from colliding with Mr. Overland.

"You're right, but I don't have another plan yet. Unless you have any better ideas?"

She shrugged and tapped her watch. "Here, take over for a minute."

I dodged Harlow, moving toward Ava and the group she was fighting off. Wes dove into the fray. Harlow wasn't far behind. I went into defensive mode, bobbing around kicks and punches.

"Whatever you're doing, hurry. It's only a matter of time

before he sends more people after us." I paused to look for the best place to go. I could lead them around the tunnels, but without knowing where I was going, it could be a mistake.

Harlow punched in my direction. I spun and put myself between him and Wes, then ducked as Harlow swung again. This time, his fist connected with Wes's face. I slipped around Wes, who wasn't all that fazed by the attack.

"New plan!" I shouted to Ava. She dove back into the mix and peeled three people off from the group. She positioned herself so Jeremy was on one side and the dads on the other. Jeremy was fast. She dodged his kicks and punches with ease and even managed to direct some of them at the dads. I winced as Mr. Overland took a punch aimed for Ava right in the gut.

"Follow me." I bolted for the servers. Harlow and Wes followed like hounds on a hunt.

Ava whirled around to elude an additional attack, then ducked low around Dad. She bolted to meet me at the edge of the servers.

I nodded behind me.

A smirk erupted on her face. "Smart thinking."

Scurry would have to be careful with his pawns around the equipment, but neither Ava nor I cared about the collateral damage. In fact, a little damage to the servers might help our cause.

Once I oriented myself to take on more fighting, I thought through J.W.'s response. Scurry was hiding where I'd least expect, which meant it was something obvious that I'd easily overlook. I searched the open connections again and noticed Ava had launched some code that revealed everyone's trackers. I could see Wes's and Harlow's.

With the number of people Scurry had attacking us, I wouldn't be able to pick them off one by one. There was too much going on to access the network while evading those around me. But without the box and the additional sequencer, Scurry would be struggling for the amount of power he needed to control everyone. Even once he did have a sequencer, he'd likely need some sort of code to bring it online. There had to be a way I could use that to my advantage.

I had to figure out where he'd try to get the power from and keep him from accessing it. While I didn't immediately know where that was, I did know where he could get a coding boost from.

"You think you can handle them? I've got an idea." I felt awful putting the physical fight on Ava while she was arguably a better coder, but I wouldn't be able to fight alone like she could.

"No, but do what you need to do. I'll manage." Ava's response time had slowed significantly as her breathing grew heavy with exhaustion. We wouldn't last much longer.

I darted down the center path, pausing to glance up each row. I checked on Ava behind me. Harlow was slowly padding up the row like a lion stalking its prey. He seemed slower than usual. He must've been giving Scurry one hell of a fight.

I picked up my pace, searching each aisle until I skidded to a stop a few rows from the end. Peyton, Mom, Emily, and Lydia stood partway down the aisle like statues. Behind them, Bailen sat at a terminal typing, but not with his usual rhythm.

"Bailen!"

His hands slowed at my voice, but the keys still clicked. His fingers strained against a seemingly invisible rubber band, holding them back from the keys Scurry willed his brain to push. I watched the others for some kind of response. Nothing. I stepped toward them to test a theory. Emily stepped toward me. I stepped away and she remained in place. I took three steps forward and all four of them countered. When I stepped away, they didn't move.

The closer I got, the bigger the fight. But as long as I stayed out of range, they would too. I glanced behind me to check Harlow's progress. He was half a dozen rows back. He still headed my way, but it looked like he was walking through tar.

I closed my eyes. *Think, Kaya.* Bailen was working on something. Why wasn't I seeing it on the network? I reached out to his tracker profile, now viewable thanks to Ava. I searched it for clues. Maybe he'd left breadcrumbs. But nothing in his immediate profile set off any red flags. I dug deeper into his background info.

Student.

Family:

Dad: Myles Overland.

Mom: Deceased.

Sister: Peyton Overland (twin)

And then there was one more line.

Under additional family it read: Kaya Weiss.

I opened the item and a couple dozen coding files exploded across my field of vision.

This was going to take me forever. I'd have to take it one file at a time. I started with the first one. Before I got too far in, I had a tracker message from J.W.

J.W.: Allow me.

Notes began to pop up next to each file, giving more information about what the program did. I quickly read through each, trying to put the pieces together, but I couldn't make much sense of it.

"Ava! I need your coding prowess." I yelled down the aisle.

There was no response. I stepped closer to Harlow, then yelled louder. "AVA! Are you okay? I need some—"

I stopped as Harlow stepped aside. Behind him stood Ava, glassy eyed with Dad, Mr. Overland, Wes, and Jeremy flanking her.

"Not you too!" I muttered to myself. "How is this possible?" The question evaporated, unanswered. Scurry had managed to circumvent the Global Tracking Systems protocol on Ava's tracker. No one was off limits to him. Except me.

But if I failed, this was how it ended. The lone warrior fighting for everyone she cared about.

Thirty-Three

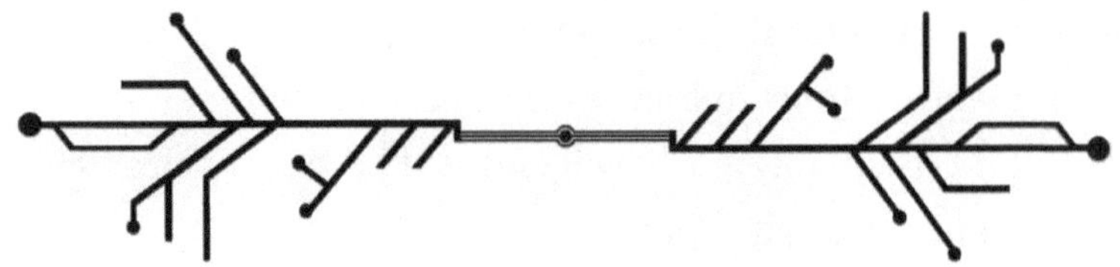

Scurry's laughter rang out around me. "You're next."

"You'll have to catch me first." I bolted down an empty aisle between rows of servers, but the speakers boomed with Scurry's voice all around me.

"I won't need to."

I circled back toward the metal door to the room.

"I've nearly hacked your tracker."

Racing back into the tunnels, I ran down random passageways, not caring which direction I took.

"I'll make you watch them kill each other," Scurry's voice echoed all around me.

I darted down a passage to the right, telling myself his taunts were just words but knowing deep down he was serious.

"And when you have nothing left, I'll make you beg me to take your life." He laughed so deep and thundering that it reverberated in my chest.

I froze. My body quaked as the words sank in, tearing me apart from the inside out. I slid to the floor and opened up the code files again, frantically reading through J.W.'s notes to find a clear path forward. A way to stop Scurry before he made good on his promises.

Unfortunately, the notes were as good as gibberish. I understood enough code to do simple tasks, not take down a mind-controlling egomaniac. My heart pounded in my chest as I gasped for air. I tried to calm my breathing but couldn't. There was too much running through my mind. It exploded with pain as I worked myself into a frenzy. I wasn't good enough to do this. I wasn't smart enough. I needed Dad or Bailen or Ava. Anyone.

Tears streamed down my face. Now that I'd finally admitted I wouldn't play Scurry's game, and I needed to let those around me in, none of them could help. But the alternative to fighting alone was a fate worse than death. If I failed, I'd have to accept the inevitable. It was a matter of time before Scurry would find me. Then he'd have everything he ever wanted.

I wasn't meant to do this alone. I needed my family. The reason the Ghosts worked well together was because they played off each other's strengths. That was something each Ghost knew, Bailen most of all.

I searched back through the notes J.W. had provided. I read each one carefully, taking time to make sure I understood it. The more I read, the more the pieces fell into place. I knew exactly how to take this muddy mess and turn it into a beautiful masterpiece. How to make all the colors work together.

Bailen had given me everything I needed—not that I'd ever doubted him. I'd have to work quickly to attack the sequencer and release everyone Scurry was using against me. I just needed a small piece of code to tie it all together, one Bailen had been teaching me all along. One that an AI wouldn't understand the subtle nuances of or be able to draw the necessary connections between the pieces. I opened a command prompt in my mind and wrote a couple dozen lines, tying together each item Bailen had left hidden for me.

As I completed the program, I had a message from J.W.

J.W.: Beautiful work. I knew you had it in you.

K.W.: Thanks. Mind checking it for bugs?

J.W.: 90% accuracy only cuts it with humor and hand grenades.
I took the liberty of cleaning up the errors for you.

K.W.: That's what I keep you around for.

J.W.: I found a nice hiding spot behind your glitch. You're stuck with me.

I should have been more freaked out that J.W. was camping out in my tracker, but without J.W., we were all dead.

It was nice to have a reminder of Jake's presence around. It propped me up when I needed it most. He was part of the team now.

And right now, my only ally.

There was one problem. When I ran this code, it would temporarily disconnect everyone, but there was nothing to stop Scurry from reinitiating the loophole. I needed time to attack

Scurry's loophole and prevent his reconnection while the others safeguarded the network.

K.W.: I need one more favor.

J.W.: Anything for you.

K.W.: How long can you keep Scurry
busy while I kick in the back door and
disrupt the loophole?

J.W.: A few minutes. Maybe more.
Depends on if he finds me or figures out
what you're doing.

K.W.: Then that will have to be enough.
I'll let you know when.

I opened the command prompt and set up everything so I only had to execute the program. Then I opened the maps and oriented myself to find my way back to the server room.

As I took slow steps back down the tunnels, I opened messages to each person I cared about and wrote out quick instructions but left them unsent. After kicking in the back door of Scurry's secondary network, I'd send each person explicit instructions right before I took the loophole offline. Our success depended on everyone doing their part. One break in the link, one tip off to Scurry that I'd used his connection against him, and this all fell apart. Scurry would win.

But I trusted each of them with my life, just as they trusted me with theirs.

When I reached the metal door, I stood outside. If everything went right when I entered the room, they'd all have control again, and would know the plan. I'd have my family back. I took a deep breath and closed my eyes.

K.W.: Ready?

J.W.: As I'll ever be.

A genuine laugh erupted from me as I executed the program. I yanked the door open and stepped inside, finding the room empty. My breath caught in my throat and my limbs froze, refusing to move. Where were they?

Scurry's control over them should have been broken near instantaneously. They should have received my messages: the plan to shut down the backup network and end the loophole once and for all.

I needed them. My insides grew cold as the reality set in. I ran down the rows of servers but only found blinking lights. Had Scurry figured it out? I opened the local tracker connections and found Scurry's unprotected tracker, revealing the sequencer he needed to keep everyone under his control.

I pushed my worries for the others out of my mind and focused on the sequencer. Of course, it was password protected. I launched a decryption program but didn't stop there. I accessed multiple streams of consciousness programs and sent them to Scurry's tracker, hoping it would distract him in addition to whatever J.W. threw at him. Then I began searching for another way around the password and into the core of the loophole.

After accessing the first program, I had a message from R.S.

R.S.: Clever girl.
But you won't win this.

I closed the chat window. Multiple more messages popped up, but they were mere distractions. I got to work isolating the parts of the loophole program Scurry was using. I developed small pieces of code on the fly to go after different parts of his control. If I threw enough stuff at it, eventually it would fail. But the more I pushed against his programs, the more I felt him stripping away my connection to his network. The connection slowed as his attack bogged down my programs.

K.W.: A little help with the speed?

J.W.: I'll give you every part of my
computing power I can spare.

My code began to run faster, then slowed again. It wasn't much, but it was enough to chip away at Scurry's hold on the network. I launched more code at him until finally it broke free.

A couple dozen programs flooded the network list, including the sequencer and the loophole protocols. I searched for key components that would cripple the whole system. I wanted to sever Scurry's connection to the tracker network and release his hold on everyone. It wouldn't stop someone from breaking into the protocols in the future, but it would eliminate the immediate threat.

I reached out with my mind to the connection. I updated my code with the proper location. Just as I was about to hit submit, a chat bomb from R.S. exploded in my line of sight, blocking my code.

> R.S.: Sever the link and I will fry their
> trackers and boil their brains.

I paused. My heart raced in my chest. Was it true or was he bluffing?

> R.S.: There's nothing you or your little AI
> can do about it.

But another message popped up, blocking out Scurry's threat.

> J.W.: There's one thing I can do to stop
> him, but it will be catastrophic.

> K.W.: To who?

> J.W.: Me.

> K.W.: You can't.

> J.W.: Then we all die.

I choked on a sob. I knew J.W. wasn't Jake, but he had given me a piece of my brother back, reminded me of things I never thought I'd have again. J.W. had a connection to Jake, in a way none of us had. He could tell us more about what Jake had gone through in his final days. I wasn't sure I could give that up. But he must have sensed my hesitation because he sent another message.

J.W.: Trust your heart.

"NOOOOOO!" I screamed, but it was too late. J.W. had gone silent. His profile disappeared from my chat log. He'd taken the choice out of my hands and pulled away from me, just like Jake.

The tears welled, but I refused to give in to them. I wouldn't let J.W.'s sacrifice be in vain. I executed the remaining piece of my code that knit together the final bits of Bailen's programs. One by one, Scurry's connections disappeared from the network list. I squeezed my eyes shut in a silent thank you to J.W.

When I opened my eyes, my tracker was the only thing remaining on the network. The servers around me were dark. No blinking lights. No fans. No quiet humming or whirring. Silence.

The sound of blood pulsing through my ears was the only thing that pierced the stillness. The glitch was now the system. Tears streaked down my face. I let out a loud sob as relief washed over me, even though this was far from over. At least we'd interrupted the loophole.

"Kai?" Dad appeared from behind one of the server aisles. He blinked as though trying to clear away the confusion of where he was and what had happened.

I ran to him and collapsed into his arms.

"Oh please, don't go all gooey on us now."

I choked back a laugh as I saw Peyton over his shoulder, thankful for her sarcasm. Ava stood next to her and gave me a silent nod.

Pulling back from Dad, I saw Wes, Harlow, Lydia, Mr. Overland, and Jeremy all trying to get their bearings. Even Mom appeared, guiding Emily into the aisle. She ran and gave me a huge hug, which I gladly returned.

But one person was missing.

"Where is he?" My heart pounded. Had Scurry gotten to him before I could end the loophole?

"Still trying to catch up to me." Ava laughed as Bailen appeared from the aisle on her left.

"You wish. She gave me the hardest part of the plan."

"I could have done it with one hand tied behind my back." Ava playfully punched his shoulder. Peyton laughed in approval next to her.

I sighed in relief and ran to Bailen, nearly knocking him over. He wrapped his arms around me. New tears streamed down my face as I pressed my forehead to his, relieved to see his brilliant green eyes inches from mine. Anything but the glassy version that haunted me.

"I knew you could handle it," I mumbled against his lips.

He laughed, then pressed his lips to mine. I lost myself in the kiss, not caring who was watching or for how long.

When he finally pulled away, I glanced at everyone around me. "Looks like you all got my message."

"Of course we did," Ava said.

"We might have had a little help from J.W.," Lydia added.

"It's over?" I asked, afraid of the answer.

"Not quite." Bailen wiped the tears from my cheeks.

"We figured you'd want to do the honors." Jeremy stepped next to me, holding a small box that looked similar to the one Scurry had me retrieve.

I gave Bailen a questioning look.

"Destroy the final sequencer and we destroy his last connection to the loophole." He grabbed the box from Jeremy and held it out to me. "You know, since you did such a bang-up job with the last one."

I choked down a laugh but hesitated, not because it wasn't the right thing to do, but because it shouldn't be me.

I turned to Dad. "You started this. I think you should be the one to finish it."

Bailen held the sequencer out to my dad. He reached for it. But as Bailen let go, Dad moved his hand and the box crashed to the floor.

"I've been waiting a long time to do that." He kicked it toward Mr. Overland, who kicked it over to Peyton.

We kicked the box around for a while. Sometimes we stomped on it. We laughed until it was thoroughly dented, the parts inside rattling a calming melody.

Finally, Dad picked up the sequencer and tucked it under his arm. "I'll make sure it's properly disposed of."

"What about Scurry?" I asked, unsure about all the loose ends.

"I've located Scurry's last known position. He won't get far without many resources." Jeremy said, checking one of the terminals. "I've also sent a request to local law enforcement to keep an eye out and secure him by any means necessary. But we're still going to need to disable him."

"I'd love a piece of that." Harlow paused, suddenly aware of everyone focusing on him. "If you'll have me." He hunched his shoulders, making him seem smaller.

I looked at Bailen, who nodded at Jeremy.

"Sure. We can use all the help we can get," Jeremy said, waving Harlow over.

"I'm not sure what I'm volunteering for, but I'm coming too." Wes clutched his head as if still trying to make sense of what had happened to him. "I'll see if I can wake Troy."

"I didn't mean to hit him that hard, but he came at me like a bull." Ava shrugged unapologetically.

"I would have hit him hard too, given the chance." I winced, the words a direct reminder of when he ripped my bike out of midair.

Harlow shot me a questioning look, but I shook my head, telling him to drop it.

"Let's get a move on." Jeremy waved toward the exit.

Wes and Harlow followed Jeremy toward the metal door.

"What about the network?" I was almost afraid to ask. It should have always been a choice, but somehow it had become a weapon. No one deserved that.

"We disrupted the network per your instructions," Ava said.

"But we still have some additional work to do in order to lock it down when we get back to the Coderie," Bailen added.

"But what do we do with it?" Lydia asked with a hint of concern in her voice.

I let out a long, relieved breath. They had gotten all my messages. I'd carefully constructed instructions to disable the network and lock it down but not destroy it.

"It's up to the world to decide what we allow to continue." I swallowed hard. It was difficult to admit, but there wasn't one right answer.

"Are you sure?" Dad asked.

I nodded. I'd made the choice for everyone before. For some it had been the right one, for others it hadn't. "Regardless of how I feel, it's not up to me. It never should have been."

"Is that the decision you think I put on you?"

I met Dad's gaze but said nothing. He pulled me into another hug. "I never meant for you to shoulder the weight of the world."

"I know. But it didn't change what had to be done at the time. Now we have an opportunity to do better." I stepped back from Dad. "But I don't think it's up to any one person what better looks like."

"She's right." Bailen squeezed my hand. "Not everything about trackers was bad. We need balance."

I squeezed his hand in return. "We have to find the good in all this and focus on that."

"Sounds like we have a lot of work to do," Mr. Overland said.

"I can't think of a better team." Dad extended his hand to Mr. Overland, and he shook it.

As the others made their way to the exit, I stayed behind with Bailen. I stared into the dark servers, paying extra close attention to ensure they really were off. Nothing illuminated. I found comfort in the darkness.

I closed my eyes and, with a single thought, shut off my tracker.

Thirty-Four

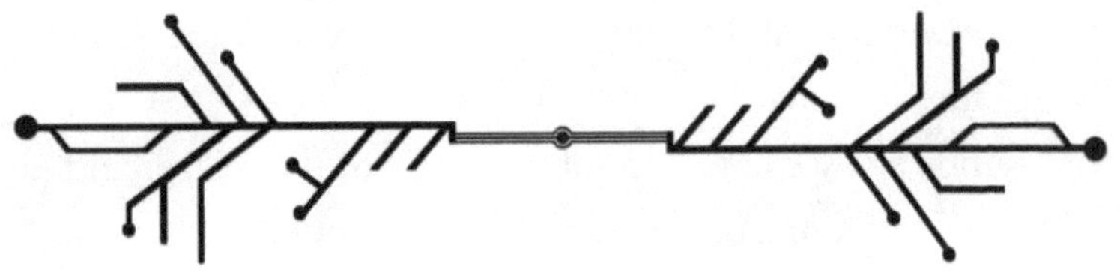

Two weeks later, we sat in the Coderie discussing ideas. People were unsure what to do with the tracker network, and the government had asked for a proposal. The Ghosts took it upon themselves to start work on one. We'd invited whoever wanted to weigh in, to join or provide feedback. It was the largest open-source endeavor ever, the way it probably should have been all along.

Several large screens projected around us with lists of ideas. Everything was broken down into categories: definites, maybes, definitely nots, and things that might cause problems. At the top of the "definites" list sat health monitoring, while in the "definitely nots," someone had written MIND-CONTROL in big letters and underlined it—as if we all needed to be reminded.

I sat with Lydia and Jeremy, mulling over some code that would further lock down the remnants of the network. We needed to prevent anyone else from accessing it until the next iteration was ready for release. But my mind wandered. Lydia laughed at something Jeremy said, and it drew me from my haze.

Across the room, Dad and Mr. Overland were bent over a monitor as they worked on some of the more complex tracker protocol scenarios people had thrown at us. Mom stopped by to pull them away from the screen for a coffee and snack break.

Harlow enlisted the soccer team to help. They sat around a large table, mostly goofing off, but Wes, Troy, and Harlow were engaged in a heated discussion about who got to choose who had control over what, and what level of monitoring there should be for public safety. When Harlow saw me watching their discussion, his cheeks flushed. Once he composed himself, he waved. I smiled and returned the gesture. It was good to see him somewhat back to his old self, even if he was different. His experience had changed him. I was pretty sure it was for the better.

I grabbed my notebook and headed to one of the back offices. Bailen was hunched over a laptop, deep in thought.

I leaned against the door and watched him type for a couple minutes before I broke his rhythmic clicking. "Working hard or hardly working?"

"Hah! You know me. Always looking for a good challenge."

"I think I've had enough challenges for a while." I laughed. "Aside from you, of course."

"Oh, you think that's funny?" He crossed the room and wrapped his arms around my waist.

"You're one challenge I never want to stop trying to figure out."

"I couldn't agree more."

He leaned in and kissed me, then reached for my hand, lacing his fingers between mine. Bailen led me over to the couch along the far wall. He flopped down. I sat next to him and rested my head on his shoulder.

"There's one puzzle that's still a mystery to me."

"What's that?" I wondered, curious what piece of this whole tracker mess he was going to ask about.

"Why you waited to drop the L-bomb until Scurry was mind-controlling me." He squeezed my hand.

My cheeks warmed. I stared straight ahead, hoping he wouldn't notice the growing heat on my face. "You heard that?"

He nodded, then twisted to face me. He lifted my chin so we were staring into each other's eyes. "I heard everything you said, even if I couldn't answer."

I opened my mouth to speak, but he pushed his fingers to my lips.

"Those words helped me fight the control."

"Good, 'cause I meant them." Regardless of what had happened, I needed him to know how I felt and that our experience hadn't changed my feelings. In fact, it made them stronger.

"Then I want you to know I love you, too. And nothing could change that." His gaze searched mine as a huge grin erupted on his face.

I smiled back, and we kissed. For the first time, there was no urgency. Kissing just because we could.

When we finally pulled apart, I laid my head on his chest and listened to his heartbeat. I lost myself in the sound of its quiet thumping.

"I just have one more question," I said playfully. "It's something that's been on my mind for a while."

"Sure, anything." He tickled my ribs and I let out a short burst of laughter.

"Why a four-leaf clover on your bike? You don't seem like the superstitious type."

He laughed. "After everything, that's what you want to know?"

"Yep." I thought about my conversation with J.W., about the green wire. It seemed like an homage to him.

"It was an inside joke between Jake and me. He called me his good luck charm because I was always getting him out of sticky situations. I'd told him I didn't need luck when I had amazing coding skills, but he'd painted it on my bike as a reminder that sometimes you need a little luck."

I smiled, glad I asked. It felt like I'd gotten another piece of Jake back. I only wished I could have seen them interact more. "I'm surprised you didn't have it stripped off."

"I wanted to, but despite never admitting it to him, he was right. I needed the reminder."

"Sometimes, when things are out of our control, a little luck is all you need."

He smiled, then leaned in. I met him halfway with a kiss, thankful that some luck had been on our side all along.

A quiet knock on the door frame drew my attention. Dad.

Bailen looked at me. I nodded. I sat up and Bailen left the room.

Crossing the room, Dad stopped at a nearby chair. I patted the couch next to me. He sank into the well-loved cushion.

"I've been thinking about how proud I am of you. After all this, you still are working to find the best solution."

Those weren't the words I expected from him, especially since this was his first day back at the Coderie after helping local law enforcement clean up the mess Scurry left behind. Despite everything, it was exactly what I needed to hear.

"Thanks. But I've had a lot of help."

"You should have had more." His gaze dropped to the floor.

"You showed up when it mattered. That's what family does." I threw my arms around him.

His gaze met mine, then he closed the hug. He kissed the top of my head. "I'll always be there for you, even when you don't want me to be."

I laughed. "Thanks."

We sat in silence for a minute, but there was a quiet understanding between us now. Where things had once been broken, now I knew we could put aside differences and be there for each other when we needed it. That was what mattered most.

I turned to him and paused, struggling to find the words for my next question. "And Scurry?"

"He was captured and taken to a secure facility where they performed an immediate tracker retraction. He's being kept sedated for the time being and will never be allowed near any tech again."

I nodded. I supposed that was good enough for now.

"He still has to be tried for his crimes. We may be called to testify."

I swallowed. That seemed easy compared to everything else I'd been through. It was something I could put out of my mind for now.

Bailen appeared in the doorway. "Sorry to interrupt, but I've got something to show you."

I met him at the door, leaving Dad on the couch. I smiled at him as a thank you, then turned to Bailen with my eyebrows raised in question.

His sly smile said this would be good. "You too, Mr. Weiss."

I nodded Dad over. We followed Bailen to the back corner of

the computer room, where Ava, Peyton, and the rest of the gang were bent over a few laptops.

"I've got a surprise for you." Excitement sparkled in Bailen's eyes, the kind he used to get when he was about to dive into some new piece of tech.

"I don't think I can handle any more surprises." But I grabbed a chair knowing he wouldn't let me off easily.

"Well, it's not just for you." Ava nudged her hip into Peyton, who cracked a small smile.

It was good to see her happy.

"Were you in on this too?" I asked, concerned I was the only one out of loop.

"Nope. I got here a minute before you. These two refused to let me in on the secret, despite my persuasion tactics." Peyton pulled Ava in for a kiss. When Ava backed away, Peyton pulled her close again and laughed.

"Oh yes, very persuasive." Ava laughed with her. "But I still wasn't going to tell you without Kaya here."

Peyton playfully punched her arm. Then turned to Bailen. "You're lucky she showed up. My persuasive tactics on you wouldn't have been nearly as nice."

"Love you too, Pey." Bailen kept his attention on his computer screen, refusing to dignify her with a reaction.

"As fun as this lovefest is, someone did say something about a surprise. You know how much I hate those." I crossed my arms in an attempt to appear impatient and hurry things along.

Bailen gave me a feigned hurt expression. "It's good, I promise."

"Better be." Peyton held up her fists in a mock threat.

Ava squeezed her shoulder. "All right Bailen, let it rip."

Bailen's hands flew over the keyboard and a chat window opened.

B.O.: Wake up, sleepyhead.

J.W.: Five more minutes, Mom!

"No way!" Peyton's eyes lit up with a sense of excitement I'd never seen.

"How?" It was the only word I could get out. I swallowed and collected my thoughts. "J.W. sacrificed himself."

"And left some breadcrumbs along the way," Ava said.

"We were able to follow the clues and pull-down remnants of his programming from when he visited our secure network."

"It'll take some time to fully rebuild and train him, but he's back." Bailen raised his hand in Ava's direction and she high fived him.

Peyton tackle-hugged Ava, yanking her away from Bailen. I turned from them to mouth *thank you* to him, but there was so much more behind that. The smile on his face told me he knew it.

"What do we do now?" I asked, for the first time not knowing what came next. Without a major crisis to address, the world seemed a lot bigger, with a million possibilities.

"Whatever we want." Dad squeezed my shoulder.

"Within reason, of course," Bailen added, warily watching Dad's reaction.

"Of course," Dad said.

We all laughed. As the laughter died down, J.W.'s words entered my mind.

I found family.

No truer words could have captured this moment. With the blood family I'd chosen to accept and the family I'd adopted along the way, I'd found my mishpuchah. With them, I had everything I needed.

The End

Acknowledgements

Words can't express how excited I am about this sequel. I loved getting to revisit this world. I'm so thankful for so many people who helped make this possible.

First, to the fans. I always knew there was more to Kaya's story, but I never would have had the courage to write it without you. To every one of you that reached out to tell me what you loved about the story, know that those words have fueled me.

Jennifer Stolzer, you've once again worked your magic on the cover as well as entertained my hairbrained idea to put Kaya's sketches into her journal entry. Thank you for humoring my insane babbling and turning it into a masterpiece. In addition, thank you for being the very first reader who helped shape the story into something so much stronger. I appreciated all the brainstorming sessions.

Michelle Mason, as always, you've provided me with invaluable feedback that helped this story shine. Thanks for not shying away from the tough comments and for all the cupcakes and lunch meetups.

Meredith Tate, thanks for all the writing sessions and the constant friendship. I know I can always talk writing or anything else with you.

Main Street Books in St. Charles, thank you Emily and your entire staff for selling the heck out of Tracker220. You are the best champion for this series. I couldn't ask for a better indie bookstore partnership!

K.J. Harrowick, thanks for being an indie SFF and Write Hive partner in crime. I appreciate our chats and sharing stories and advice.

Amanda Bonilla, you elevated this story to another level and I am so thankful for your incredible editing notes. Thanks for picking this story up midstream and continuing on with the journey.

Kelly Scriven, you are a consistency wizard. Thank you for helping me clean up the first book and for making sure this one shines just as brightly.

To the CSS, Sarah Johnson, Nicole Lanahan, Shawntelle Madison, Heather Reid, Emily Hall Schroen, Linda Stevens, and Cori Bair. I know I said this last time, but thanks for the laughs, the tears, the coffee (even though I don't drink it), and more importantly the wine. You're the best sounding board a girl could ever have. I'm honored to go on this journey with all of you.

To all of the Snowy Wings Publishing crew, you've been a fantastic network and continue to be a wealth of knowledge. We're all in this together. I couldn't do it without each and every one of you. You've been a light in a very dark tunnel. Thank you for all the guidance and support. You lifted a huge weight off my shoulders and made all this possible.

To the Write Pack/SLWG clan, Jessica Mathews, Jennifer Stolzer, Amy Zlatic, Brad Cook, Teresa Fendley, Kathy Brown, John Allen, LaShaunda Hoffman, Lyri Merrill, Debbie Manber Kupfer, Phyllis Wheeler, and Cherie Postill, thanks for continuing to be a great writing network. For sharing tables at cons and being my fellow panelists. I love getting to hang out with the local writing community.

To anyone else who supported Tracker220, thank you from the bottom of my heart.

And last but not least, thank you to my family. Thanks, Mom and Erin, for the continued interest and enthusiastic support of my books. Thank you, Andrew, for giving me the time and space to write and being a better salesman for my work than I am. To "little man," I've loved watching you grow, seeing your personality shine, and experiencing your love for books continue to blossom. Keep smiling and laughing. I love you all.

About the Author

Growing up with a fascination for space and things that fly, Jamie turned that love into a career as an Aerospace Engineer. Combining her natural enthusiasm for Science Fiction and her love of reading, she now spends a lot of her time writing Middle Grade and Young Adult Science Fiction and Fantasy.

Jamie lives in St. Louis, Missouri with her husband, Andrew, their son, and their dog, Rogue (named after the X-men not Star Wars, although she loves both). When she isn't being a Rocket Scientist by day and a writer by night, she can be found catching up on the latest sci fi TV, books, and movies as well as chatting on social media (maybe a little too much :-P). And no, the rocket science jokes never get old!

Through Snowy Wings Publishing, Jamie is the author of The Tracker Sequence which includes Tracker220 (October 2020) and the sequel Authority (August 2024). She also has two STEM short stories featuring young women with a knack for STEM, published in the Brave New Girls anthologies, and two engineering-centered nonfiction pieces that are published in Writer's Digest's Putting the Science in Fiction.

Social Media Links

Blog – http://jamiekrakover.blogspot.com/

Twitter – https://twitter.com/Rockets2Writing

Instagram – https://www.instagram.com/jamiekrakover/

Bluesky - https://bsky.app/profile/rockets2writing.bsky.social

Goodreads – https://www.goodreads.com/author/show/16483406.Jamie_Krakover